# A CONVENIENT RING TO CLAIM HER

## DANI COLLINS

# THE BOSS'S STOLEN BRIDE

## NATALIE ANDERSON

**MILLS & BOON**

First published in Great Britain 2023
by Mills & Boon, an imprint of HarperCollins*Publishers* Ltd,
1 London Bridge Street, London, SE1 9GF

www.harpercollins.co.uk

HarperCollins*Publishers*
Macken House, 39/40 Mayor Street Upper,
Dublin 1, D01 C9W8, Ireland

ISBN: 978-0-263-30666-8

02/23

This book is produced from independently certified FSC™ paper
to ensure responsible forest management.
For more information visit: www.harpercollins.co.uk/green.

Printed and Bound in Spain using 100% Renewable Electricity
at CPI Black Print, Barcelona

# A
# CONVENIENT RING
# TO CLAIM HER

DANI COLLINS

**MILLS & BOON**

To my husband, Doug,
whose shoulder trouble inspired poor Quinn's injury.

Thanks for doing such dedicated research for me
on this one, darling. I love you.

# PROLOGUE

HE WOULD NEVER forgive her for this.

That knowledge stabbed into Quinn Harper's belly like a blade as she announced, "Micah and I have been having an affair. It's been going on for years."

Birdsong ceased and the fragrance of the flowers that surrounded the gazebo turned sour. Quinn was aware of soft gasps of surprise next to her, but all she saw was Micah.

Micah Gould, a man she loved to hate and hated to l—*lust* after. That's definitely all it was, she stressed to herself. She was not a self-destructive person who set herself up for heartbreak. It was lust with a side of long-term friendly acquaintanceship. Best friend's brother with benefits.

Micah didn't move. He had arrived the way he always did, with the energy of a gathering thunderstorm, wearing one of his bespoke suits without a wrinkle or fleck of lint upon it.

He must have traveled with urgency to arrive in Gibraltar at this moment, but if he was tired or distressed, he didn't show it. He was superhuman that way, always impeccably turned out, clean-shaven and crisp. His short, dark brown hair was only notable because it was thick and absent of a single gray strand. His features were more rugged than handsome and rarely betrayed what he was thinking or feeling.

His expression didn't need to change for Quinn to know he was livid, though. His whole body condensed the way concrete solidified in the unrelenting sun. The way water compressed into a glacier. The way carbon crystalized under pressure to become the hardest substance in the world—a beautiful, icy diamond that could cut through anything.

"Why are you doing this? Now? Like this?" His voice was calm. Too calm. Deadly as a quiet pool that hid riptides and piranhas and bloodthirsty monsters.

"Like this" was in front of his half sister, Eden, who was Quinn's closest friend. And Eden's groom, Remy, Micah's longtime enemy. And Remy's sister, a very innocent Yasmine, still in shock.

The three stood in silence around Quinn, reeling at what she had just revealed.

Quinn was doing this for Micah, not that he knew it. Perhaps he would never fully understand why she was doing this. The layers of secrets were so thick around her, Quinn could hardly breathe beneath their suffocating weight, but deep in the heart of those secrets was a truth so painful, she had to stop Micah from forcing its exposure. He wasn't ready to hear it. It had the potential to destroy him.

If he was forced to realize that Remy's sister—half sister!—was also his own, that he shared a father with Yasmine… If he had to face that devastating reality as Eden married Remy, it might cause Micah to sever the few tenuous threads of family he had, leaving him even more isolated than he made himself.

Someday his father's darkest actions might come to light, but not today. Not when emotions were already fevered and knife-sharp. That ugliness would not besmirch Eden's wedding day. Her *real* wedding day. Quinn refused to let that happen to her very best friend.

Micah looked ready to cause mass destruction if Eden didn't walk away from her elopement with Remy, but the vows had been spoken. If Quinn didn't draw his ire, his feud with Remy would escalate to include Eden and become something that couldn't be repaired.

Quinn calculated all of that in the few seconds following his sudden appearance. She threw herself forward in sacrifice, drawing all the cold loathing Micah aimed at Remy onto herself.

"It was completely consensual," Quinn assured everyone. "I'm not accusing him of anything but appalling double standards. Your sister is allowed to marry whoever she wants." She directed that last statement at Micah. Eden had been pining for Remy for five years. Surely he could see what a lost cause it was to try to stop them?

Micah stared so hard at Quinn, she felt her soul being shredded by the force of it, as though his gaze blasted golf-ball-sized hailstones through her. She had to fight shrinking into herself under that hostile glare.

Then Micah dismissed her in a cold blink that was the cruelest thing he could have ever done to her.

"Are you coming with me or not?" he asked Eden.

"I can't. We're married. I love him."

"He's convinced you of that, has he?" Micah rocked on his heels. His contempt for that particular emotion was thick in his tone. "You can all go to hell, then." He pivoted and walked away.

Quinn watched him retreat, feeling as though her very life force was pulled from her body, trying to stay with him even as he cast her off like a sticky spiderweb that only disgusted him. She swayed where she stood, hollow as an empty shell.

# CHAPTER ONE

*One week ago, Niagara-on-the-Lake, Canada*

SOMEHOW, QUINN WASN'T surprised her maid-of-honor duties included delivering the message that the wedding was off and throwing a change of clothes into a shoulder bag for a fleeing bride. Eden had been very tepid on her groom, stubbornly pursuing marriage for business reasons despite the fact that she was obviously in love with someone else.

When Eden had announced she was marrying Hunter Waverly, Quinn had expressed her concerns, but Eden was her best friend. Ultimately, Quinn supported her. That's what best friends did.

If only Eden had been the one to come to her senses today and cancel of her own accord. No, the wedding march had started when a gray-haired grizzly of a man had charged across the lawn and accused the groom of making a baby with his daughter.

The baby in question had been in the arms of its mother right behind him. That poor woman had been mortified, but the kitten was very much out of the bag. The music was paused, conversations were conducted behind closed doors, and Eden had been thrown over.

Now she was gone.

Conspicuously, she had run away with the best man, Remy Sylvain, which didn't really surprise Quinn, either.

The part where Eden had inadvertently stolen Quinn's car keys was a nuisance, but Quinn wouldn't hold it against her. As rotten days went, Eden was winning first prize. Quinn would accept whatever collateral damage blew onto her.

She peeled off her bridesmaid dress and the shape-wear beneath, then yanked on a drop-waist sundress. She spared a few minutes to wash off her makeup, hating the feel of cover-up more than she disliked her freckles. She liberally applied moisturizer and sunscreen and left her red-gold hair in its updo, but grabbed a hairbrush so she could pull the pins and brush it out in the rideshare car.

As she picked up the notification on her phone that her driver was minutes away, she added an apple to her bag along with a bottle of water and a protein bar. Eden had her own purse and phone, but might want her silk sleep bonnet and that pricy moisturizer she liked so much. Quinn threw those into her bag, drained a warm mimosa, double-checked for her own wallet and phone, then kicked into her sandals.

Outside, the parking lot was busy as a colony of ants on a barrel of syrup. Between astonished vineyard staff, shocked wedding guests and the sleazy paparazzi who had trespassed onto the grounds, word was out that the much-anticipated Bellamy-Waverly wedding had collapsed. The groom had left with the mother of his infant daughter. The bride had fled with the best man—not that that was common knowledge yet. Quinn was hoping to forestall that by meeting Eden in Niagara Falls.

"Where are *you* going?" Micah asked behind her shoulder.

Quinn jolted, not so much startled by his catching her as reacting the way she always did to Eden's older half brother. It was an infuriating mixture of joy and apprehension. A flood of yearning and a reflexive tension and a need to self-protect. It was sexual desire and abject annoyance because Micah Gould was too much. Too tall, too confident, too masculine and too bossy and *so* superior. He was far too capable of tying her in knots without any effort. The sound of his *name* tightened her abdomen. His breath on her neck made her skin feel hot.

She spun around to look at him and that was too much, too. He had changed from his morning suit. He had been tagged to stand in as father of the bride, but now had that European flair that elevated a pair of raw linen trousers with a short-sleeved camel-colored shirt into something out of an Italian designer's summer catalog. His shirt was some kind of knit that hung lovingly off his muscled shoulders. How did he have the perfect number of fine dark hairs peeking from his unbuttoned collar?

"I'm ready for some peace and quiet," Quinn said. It wasn't untrue. The wedding planner would ensure the guests enjoyed dinner and dancing as scheduled, but Quinn was an introvert at the best of times. "I'll get a room up the road."

"I told you, if you pack her bag—" his voice was silky and lethal as he poked the overstuffed bag hanging off her shoulder "—*I'll* take it to Eden."

"No need. My rideshare is here." She could see a driver craning his neck and waved.

"So you are meeting her."

"Yes. Alone. Not because she was kidnapped—" Micah always assumed the worst where Remy Sylvain was concerned "—but because she doesn't want to deal with you and your elevated testosterone right now."

The car stopped. Quinn leaned down to the open window. "Dave?"

"Niagara Falls?" the driver asked.

"Yes, thanks." She started to open the door, but Micah wrapped his arm around her, pinning her to his side. His size and heat enveloped her as he kept her bent.

She hated how much she loved the feel of his strength as he overpowered her. She could have screamed and elbowed him and made a terrific scene, but he made her weak simply by touching her. She wanted to close her eyes and curl into him and turn her face into his neck. She wanted to kiss his throat and make him groan.

This hold he had on her, both physical and metaphorical, was maddening. It always had been.

"Did you say you're going to Niagara Falls?"

"Yes," the oblivious driver replied. "Are you joining—"

"No. Don't bill her for the trip." Micah dropped a pair of hundred-dollar bills through the window and straightened, pulling her back so the driver could inch his way out of the lot.

"You don't have the right to manhandle me simply because—"

"Are you coming with me?" He released her and walked toward a black BMW.

Quinn knew him too well to stand there and shout at his back. She hurried after him and threw herself into the passenger seat, letting out a huff of annoyance as she buckled.

"He left her at a hotel?" Micah neatly backed out of his spot.

"That's what he said he would do," Quinn said stiffly.

An hour ago, Quinn had realized Eden was no longer at the vineyard. She had called her and Eden had been in Remy's car when she picked up. Quinn and Micah had played tug-of-war over Quinn's phone, Micah performing his overprotective brother act, demanding Remy return Eden to the vineyard. Eden had hung up on them.

A short while ago, Quinn had picked up a text from Eden, telling her she would leave Quinn's keys with the concierge at a five-star hotel in Niagara Falls. Whether Eden was staying there, with or without Remy, was a mystery to be solved when Quinn arrived.

"Why didn't you tell me you were going to meet her?" Micah cut off an SUV and darted onto the main road. He accelerated hard enough she was pressed into her bucket seat.

"Because, in my perfect world, Eden and I will have a good old-fashioned slumber party complete with cheap wine and lots of complaining about men. She just got dumped at the altar, Micah. She doesn't need you showing up to offer I-told-you-sos."

"I won't voice any. I'm the one who gave Sylvain the benefit of the doubt, trusting he wouldn't sabotage his best friend's wedding. I should have insisted Hunter choose a different man to stand up for him."

"As much as I love hearing you admit you're wrong, you're giving yourself too much credit. Hunter has a baby with another woman. I don't see how Remy is at fault for that."

"He wasn't shocked when that woman turned up. He

must have had something to do with her crashing the wedding."

"Do you really—" He was so infuriating. "Remy recognized her because he brought Hunter here last summer for a golf weekend. I heard Hunter's sister, Vienna, tell Eden that."

"So Sylvain knew who she was."

"Sure, but are you seriously postulating that Remy arranged this entire thing? That would mean he consulted a psychic last year who predicted that Hunter would meet Eden and decide to propose to her. Then he preemptively took Hunter away weeks prior to that meeting, sabotaged his condoms and somehow forced Hunter to engage in relations with a waitress. You're right. Remy Sylvain *is* an evil genius."

Micah's look swung toward her with the weight of a broad sword.

"*Hunter* is the reason this wedding fell apart," Quinn stated firmly. "Look at the Waverly history. Turning a society wedding into a train wreck is a regular Saturday afternoon for them." Quinn felt a sting of remorse at besmirching Vienna with that brush. She liked her, but it didn't make the statement less true. "Eden doesn't feel it now, but she's *lucky* she's not married to Hunter right now."

"If you didn't like him, you should have told me," Micah said grittily. "Between us, we could have stopped her from taking it this far."

"I am never going to gang up on your sister with you." Eden was the most loyal friend Quinn had ever had. She would never betray her, not even for Micah.

Plus, Eden marrying Hunter would have worked for

Quinn in ways that were very selfish and not very honorable, but she kept that to herself.

"Hunter is not a bad person. I think he was going into this marriage in good faith. So was Eden, but she didn't love him." Eden was a romantic and had always wanted to marry for love. "Plus, I don't see the value in marriage. Well, I saw the literal value for her in this one. Obviously." Eden stood to lose her father's chain of stores, Bellamy Home and Garden, if she didn't get an influx of cash, fast.

Quinn hated bringing up marriage and money around Micah, though. She was always conscious of the fact that women threw themselves at him all the time, thinking he was their ticket to both. She'd seen at least two make a play for him at the rehearsal dinner alone.

Whereas she threw herself at him purely for sex and that complicated approximation of affection that he offered when they were between the sheets.

"Given all that Eden was up against, I saw why she thought marrying Hunter made sense. Once she made her decision, I had to support her. That's what friends do. Hunter is clearly a decent man since he put his child first the moment he learned he had one."

"That's where the bar is?" Micah drawled.

"*You* could have bailed her out."

"I *tried*. Our mother refuses to let Eden take my father's money for her father's business. If I could change that, I would. I can't." His hands gripped the wheel so tightly, his knuckles turned white.

He released his frustration by overtaking a couple of cars that were already speeding. The river glittered on one side of them while rows of grapes flashed by on the other.

"Has she been seeing him all this time?" he asked.

"Remy? *No*. When? He was at their engagement party for, like, a minute. He didn't show up at the vineyard until late last night. As far as I know, they've only spoken two or three times since—" She cut herself off, throat always going tight when she thought about that trip five years ago.

"Paris?"

"Yes."

*You're a child.*

That ancient declaration of his still made her feel so *small*.

"Then why did she leave with him today?"

"I don't know. Eden is my friend, not my preschool daughter. Why do you care who she kisses at a nightclub or catches a lift with?"

"It's not about what Eden does. I'm worried Sylvain is using her to take shots at me. That is what I refuse to tolerate."

Quinn had plenty of experience with people who had ulterior motives. She had learned long ago to spot the opportunists who took in foster children to line their own pockets. Her radar was always alert for shifty eyes and straying hands. She might not have the curviest figure, but from the time her breasts had begun to bud, she'd been subjected to unwanted male attention and the pawing palms that seemed to follow those leering looks.

As naturally suspicious as she was, she had never seen Remy as nefarious. When Eden had met him five years ago, he had casually suggested they join him at a nightclub where he was meeting friends. That was a very normal thing to do.

When they arrived, Remy had tried to include Quinn

when he asked Eden to dance, but Quinn had preferred to sulk over Micah dismissing her as a child. Then, after Micah turned up and confronted Remy, nearly coming to blows with him, Remy had kept his distance from Eden for five years. He had seemed prepared to let her marry his best friend even though Quinn had caught him looking at Eden in a way that was both anguished and covetous. Fatalistic and tortured.

It had hurt her to see it and it had mirrored something in Eden's expression when she had told Quinn that, much to her shock, Remy was Hunter's best man.

This was why she never wanted to fall in love! It looked very messy and painful.

But Eden deserved to be loved. She was kind and supportive and had given Quinn so many advantages and experiences she otherwise wouldn't have had. She would do anything for her, even try to get her grumpy brother's buy-in on their forbidden relationship.

"Tell me about this feud of yours with Remy." Quinn began to pick out her hairpins. "His father stole proprietary information from yours and you're still mad about it?"

"No."

"No that's not what happened? Or no, you won't tell me?"

"Both."

Typical. "Fine. Remember this obstructionism of yours the next time you want to know why I always side with Eden." Her friend gave her unconditional love and unvarnished truth. Micah gave her great orgasms and very little of himself.

"I know he's bad news. That's all you need to know."

*Because I'm a child?*

No matter how much she wanted to sneer that at him, she still cringed when she thought of it.

Still unwinding the twists and braids in her hair, she pretended great interest in the landscape, but she didn't see it. She was thinking about how she had even come to be sitting here, ever grateful for a tiny crumb of contact with this very exasperating man.

Micah loved his kid sister, distance and different fathers notwithstanding. From the time he had reached adulthood and could arrange it, he had brought Eden to visit him in Europe where he spoiled her mercilessly. Eventually, when his work commitments and her desire for shopping and other frivolous pursuits conflicted, he had begun suggesting she invite a friend.

Quinn secretly believed he had been vetting her friendships, culling the ones who hung on to Eden because of her modest celebrity and significant wealth. Bellamy Home and Garden was an iconic Canadian chain, and one of Eden's grandfathers was a radio personality.

Quinn had met Eden when they were fifteen, both attending a French immersion program in Montreal. Many of the students had booked into it as a chance to get away midsummer. Their parents had sent them for the same reason, but Quinn had been there on a scholarship for the disadvantaged. In the disorder of the registration hall, someone behind Quinn had overheard her being redirected to the desk for "those on financial assistance."

Quinn had earned a pithy look from the student as she turned.

He had given her an up-and-down scan to take in her out of fashion jeans and secondhand top. "They let anyone in, don't they?" he said to the girl next to him. "And *our* parents' taxes pay for it."

"I earned my place on merit," Quinn had shot back in solid French, used to having to stand up for herself. "That's more than you can say, isn't it?"

Eden, standing in the next queue over, had been the only one with enough French to catch the pun. She had burst out laughing.

"*Please* let me be your roommate. I don't want to get stuck with a dud who can't even make me laugh."

Quinn had been pushed around and moved around most of her life. She didn't form solid connections with anyone. She had roomed with Eden and they had some good laughs, but she expected it would be yet another nice but superficial and temporary friendship.

Eden wasn't like that. She checked in and reached out. She stuck.

It had taken years for Quinn to quit being surprised by that and accept that Eden expected them to be friends forever. Thus, she'd hadn't expected Eden's invitation the following summer to come with her to her brother's villa in Greece.

It was such a ridiculous idea, Quinn had immediately dismissed it. The bureaucracy alone was prohibitive. Quinn had still been a ward of the government. Eden was the patient, persistent, anything-is-possible type, though. She had downloaded forms and made calls and somehow all the hoops and barrels were jumped. Quinn had been allowed to go.

Meeting Micah at sixteen, Quinn had been both intimidated and infatuated. He was seven years older and already running a global enterprise that had its footings in robotics engineering. He was rich and handsome and radiated caged energy. His aloof, sarcastic demeanor would have scared the hell out of her if she hadn't seen his indulgent human side with his sister. Eden wasn't afraid to tease him and it made Quinn envious of her confidence in their relationship.

Quinn knew she was on trial as far as he was concerned. She was always on trial in a new house with new people, but she must have passed muster. She'd been invited to ski with them that winter in Saint Moritz. The following summer, Quinn declined Eden's invitation. She had a summer job and was saving for her postsecondary education. Eden visited her for a week in PEI, then took someone else to Micah's London penthouse.

He must not have cared for that friend because he insisted Eden bring Quinn when they met him in Rome the next year, when they graduated from high school. Quinn had only been able to steal ten days, needing to hurry back to the summer job she had lined up, but she dragged Eden through every cathedral and ruin she could find within a few hours' radius before joining Micah in the evenings.

"You genuinely enjoy relics and history, don't you?" Micah said with something like bemusement after she finished an animated description of their day trip to Pompeii.

"I like to learn," she agreed, self-conscious of her enthusiasm. "I find it both frustrating and reassuring that the more things change, the more they stay the same. Two thousand years later, it's still go to work, feed the kids. Visit a brothel." She rolled her eyes.

Micah snorted. "Someone says the world is ending. No one believes him."

"Exactly." When their amused gazes locked, she felt something inside her click.

"You should stay another week." He glanced to Eden,

breaking the brief spell. "I'm returning to Vienna, but you could come. There are some excellent museums there."

"You could take us to the opera." Eden smiled slyly.

"I could buy you tickets to the opera," Micah corrected, clearly not a fan. He glanced back at Quinn.

Longing had squeezed her, both for the culture and the time with Eden and the chance to see more of Micah.

"That sounds fun, but I have to get back and start my summer job. They're holding it for me."

"Do you need help paying for school? Let me arrange it," Micah urged. "You're clearly not someone planning to drink her way through freshman year."

"I'm not. You're right." Her chest had filled with the hive of bees that arrived when she was presented with charity. "But no, thanks. I have a scholarship and my dorm fee is included. The summer job is my mad money." If "mad money" included groceries and the cheapest phone plan she could find. "Also, my foster family is being really good to me. They don't have to support me anymore, now that I'm eighteen, but they said I could stay in my room rent-free until I leave in September. I'll go back and help in their garden and with the other kids."

She caught a look that flashed between Eden and Micah, one she feared was pity-related, but Eden said brightly, "Then we'll finally be together for good. We'll tear that campus *up*."

"Oh, yes. I expect our study parties to become legendary," Quinn drawled. "We might live on the edge and put raisins in our cookies."

Quinn had thought she wouldn't see Micah again, but he always visited Toronto when it was Eden's or their mother's birthday. They had begun including her on those occasions and Micah had personally asked her if she planned to come to Paris with Eden when they finished their first year of university.

"She can run up my credit card all she wants, but I refuse to hold her purse while she sends someone on the hunt for a shorter sleeve. You'll spare me that, I hope?"

"Spare *me*," Eden urged. "He's the worst to shop with. Also, you could finally see the Louvre," she coaxed.

"And the Catacombs?" It was Micah she really wanted to see. Quinn had yet to line up her summer job, but she was too tempted to be sensible. She had agreed to go.

The day they arrived in Paris five years ago, Micah had said to Quinn, "You turned nineteen, too. Put some things on my accounts for yourself."

Quinn had a very complicated relationship with accepting generosity. Coming away with Eden at Micah's expense bothered her, but if she hadn't accepted, Eden would have brought someone else, so Quinn managed to justify it to herself. Buying clothes on Micah's card felt wrong, but Eden would have added outfits for her anyway, so Quinn decided she should at least pick some she liked.

She stuck to simple coordinates that she could wear for school or a job interview, but the quality and tailoring made her feel very grown-up and sophisticated. Secretly, they made her feel as though she belonged in his world.

On their second-to-last night in Paris, Eden took to her room after dinner, fussing over how to do her hair for the nightclub. Quinn had preferred to use the hour to pre-read material for a summer class she was taking online.

She wasn't expecting Micah. He'd told them he had commitments that evening and they'd already eaten dinner alone, but he had suddenly appeared in the lounge where Quinn was curled on the sofa.

"We thought you were out tonight." She tried to pretend her heart hadn't leaped into her throat.

"I thought you two were going out. I'm only here to change into my tux." His attention flickered from her throat to her bare, pedicured toes and back.

Quinn might have made a different clothing choice if she had known he would see her. Her new silk pedal-pushers and striped sleeveless top were smart, but unremarkable. Certainly not sexy, but that glance of his caused a pleasant, squiggling sensation to invade her stomach. Her breath shortened with excitement. Her cheeks stung and she felt both vulnerable and powerful as she held his gaze.

Micah's dark brown eyes were always impossible to read, but she thought she detected heat there. Banked, because he always kept himself behind an invisible wall, but she suspected it would be a conflagration if he ever let it loose.

"Where is Eden?" His voice sounded deeper than usual.

"In her room. Why?" Quinn was riding a wave of sudden confidence in her femininity. "Are you afraid to be alone with me?"

"Of course not. You're a child." His response was whip-fast and stung like the devil.

Considering she had been raised in a series of foster homes without a childhood to speak of, it was a particularly harsh comment. Quinn had been earning money since she was old enough to babysit. Now that she'd turned nineteen, she supported herself, working around her heavy course load so she could eat. She had been adulting as long as she could remember.

His pithy dismissal cut so deep, however, she regressed into a juvenile retort.

"Good thing the *boys* we're meeting at the nightclub are more my age than yours, then." She rose and sent him a look of disinterest as she slipped into her heeled sandals.

"You're *meeting* someone? This morning, you made it sound as though it was a night out." *He* made it sound as though he'd caught her in a lie.

"I didn't say anything." Eden had told him they were going dancing. Quinn hadn't been compelled to fill in any blanks. She felt disloyal at what she had just revealed, but she was also still clapping back at his rebuff.

"Who are you meeting?" he demanded to know.

"No one you'll have to duel at dawn." She deliberately rolled her eyes at him. How did he like being treated like an annoying, interfering adult? "Eden met him at the Louvre the other day. Remy something. He asked us to join him at his friend's club. We meet up with guys at clubs in Toronto all the time." By that she meant virtually never. "I should change. Have a nice evening."

The penetrating way he had stared at her as she walked away had been deeply satisfying. Quinn had flattered herself he was jealous, but that wasn't what it had been at all.

Not. At. All.

"Which hotel?" Micah asked, abruptly slowing for traffic and yanking her mind back to this circus train wreck of a day.

They were entering Niagara Falls, a natural wonder surrounded by high-rise hotels and gaudy tourist traps.

"I don't recall." She pulled out her phone.

"You always recall."

She did have an excellent memory. She also needed to text Eden to warn her Micah was with her. She did that as she told him the name of the hotel.

It was easy to spot, being one of the best situated behemoths with a view of the falls.

Micah pulled into the entrance and handed his keys to the valet, telling him to keep it handy.

"Which room?" he asked Quinn.

"She's not responding." Quinn texted again.

Micah strode to the concierge and asked him to ring Eden Bellamy's room.

A few taps of the keys, then, "I'm sorry, sir. We don't seem to have—"

"Try Remy Sylvain."

"Of course. If you'd like to pick up the extension there…" He pointed at the nearby table.

Micah snatched up the receiver and, when the call was answered, said, "Give me Eden." A pause, then, "Why are you in his room?"

Ugh. What was it about this man and that one?

"He caught me catching the rideshare." Quinn stood close enough to Micah that Eden would hear her through the receiver. "Read your texts."

"You." Micah waved the concierge to approach them. "Tell him to let us up to your room," he told Eden, then handed the phone to the confused young man.

Seconds later, they were striding into an elevator. The young man leaning in to tap his card and push a button.

As the doors closed, Quinn was compelled to ask, "Do you ever stand outside yourself and see what a rampaging grizzly bear you are?"

"This is not a good moment to pick a fight with me, Quinn."

He wanted one, she realized. Maybe a real one.

A grave fear settled over her like a dark shadow.

"Micah, please don't be violent."

His cheek ticked. "I won't."

She honestly believed he had not meant to be violent the first time, that night at the club. He hadn't been, but it had been close. He had dragged Remy back from kissing Eden and whirled him around into a confrontation that had descended into shoving.

It was the only time Quinn had ever seen him lose his temper, let alone come close to blows. Thankfully, the bouncers had immobilized both men before anyone was assaulted, but it had still been very unsettling.

The silence in the car on the way back to Micah's home had been deafening.

The elevator doors opened on the top floor. Quinn hurried after him as he strode purposefully down the hall. The room door had been propped open by the inside lock-latch. He shoved in.

Quinn followed and was hit by the same thing that halted Micah.

Nothing.

Eden and Remy had flown the coop. Again.

# CHAPTER TWO

MICAH QUICKLY SEARCHED the suite of rooms. It was likely billed as a VIP residence since it was on a top floor and had accoutrements like a bar, a kitchenette and dining area, and a large jet tub placed to allow a view of the falls. He was more interested in the fact that the shower had been used and Eden's wedding gown was abandoned on the chair next to the king-size bed.

The bed appeared unrumpled and he didn't like to spend any time contemplating his sister's sex life, but Remy Sylvain had tried the route of coldly seducing Eden before.

Micah came back to the living room where he took note of the contents of various gift baskets strewn about. The wine in the bucket was open, as was the bottle of scotch on the bar. There was a rack of women's clothing that he assumed had provided whatever Eden was wearing.

He was not a man who gave up, but even as his haze of fury urged him to race back to the lobby to confront them, the thunderous rush filling his ears became deafening.

It was the falls. Quinn had opened the doors to the

balcony and stood outside to photograph them with her phone.

It was just like her to make the most of a moment in case she didn't have another opportunity. Over the years, he had learned small quirks like that about her.

Not everything, of course. She was a closed book. Or rather, a set of encyclopedias that appeared unobtrusive at first glance, but brimmed with more knowledge than a single brain ought to be able to contain.

She drove him a little mad for that reason. Most people were obvious in their motives, eager for attention, and were wrong more often than they were right. Quinn was focused, ambitious and understood human nature better than most.

*Please don't be violent.*

He hadn't planned to be, but that didn't stop a hot brand of shame from settling in the pit of his stomach. Paris had been the closest he'd ever come to behaving like his father. He had actually sought counselling for a time afterward. Eventually, he was reassured that he didn't have the same potential to lash out, but Remy Sylvain still got under his skin in a way no one else did.

Micah knew Quinn thought he was overreacting, but Quinn didn't understand all that Remy had cost him. Maybe Remy felt equally justified in coming after Micah. He, too, had had a taste of Kelvin Gould's temper, but that didn't mean Remy should involve Eden in their conflict. Eden was the most precious person in Micah's life, untouched by the belittling and manipulations that had permeated his own life and that of their mother. He would protect Eden at all costs.

And he had *tried* giving Remy the benefit of the

doubt. When he had learned Remy was Hunter's best man, he hadn't interfered, hadn't assumed the worst.

His complacency had come back to bite him, though, hadn't it? Remy kept persuading Eden to go with him.

*Why? What did he want with her?*

Outside, Quinn lowered her phone to read it. In the car, she'd pulled her hair loose from its complex wedding arrangement. The red-gold strands were frizzing in the humid breeze and the same wind ruffled the hem of her sundress, pressing it to her ass so he could discern the Y shape of her thong.

*Be mine, valentine.*

A knot of want twisted in his gut, messing with his ability to think.

He tried to tamp it down as she turned and came inside to waggle her phone at him.

"Eden says Remy is taking her to Toronto."

Micah swore tiredly and looked to the door. Did a car chase all the way to Toronto make any sense? No. Not when their mother was still at the vineyard, expecting Micah to drive her home in the morning.

He swore again, hating to lose on any level. This loss was particularly punishing.

"Relax. He's not a serial killer."

"You don't know that," he growled. "Did she leave your keys at least?"

"I put them in my bag."

"Good. Let's go." He moved to the door.

"You go. Eden told me to enjoy the room. I plan to do exactly that." She collected a clean glass from the bar and brought it to the coffee table, where she glugged a healthy pour from the open bottle of rosé.

"Your car is at the vineyard. How will you get back to it?"

"Hitchhike?" She sipped her wine as she moved to flick through the rack of clothing.

"I know you're saying that to wind me up."

"I don't understand why it works."

"Because I *care*, Quinn. You're my sister's best friend."

"Is that what I am?" She pressed the rim of her glass to her mouth, but her lashes lifted to send him a look that kicked him in the chest.

"Did you want to be something more than my sister's best friend?" he challenged.

Her gaze dropped to a blouse. "No."

"No," he repeated. The word tasted sour on his tongue. He wasn't sure why.

They had incredible chemistry in bed, but Quinn had made clear on many occasions that she didn't want anything more from him than sex. Micah was reminded often by his aunt that he should marry and "secure the Gould legacy," but he wasn't ready to tie himself down, either.

He often wondered how he had come to have a secretive sometimes-affair with Quinn at all. Initially, he'd been very suspicious of her.

Eden's wealth and pedigree as a Bellamy, coupled with her soft heart, had made her a target in her teens for users and vapid social climbers. Quinn had been different—a dry-witted orphan with eyes too big for her narrow face. Unlike the squealing girls who wanted to troll beaches for boys, Quinn had persuaded Eden to visit cultural sites and be home on time for dinner.

Cynic that he was, Micah assumed he was being

lulled toward a false sense of security. That's why, during their trip to Saint Moritz, when Quinn had behaved very shiftily, passing something to Eden, Micah had presumed it was drugs.

It had turned out to be a feminine necessity. Eden had been mortified.

*Why are you embarrassing me?*

He had apologized and Quinn had accepted it, but she'd been stoic after that. Micah had told himself he didn't care what she thought of him. Eden was his priority, but the glimpse of hurt and injured pride that Quinn quickly masked had sat on his conscience.

As time wore on, she became the friend Eden most often brought when she visited him—and the one he most preferred. She was pleasant, intelligent and savvy. She was a grounding influence on his sister, not caring for fashion or parties. Quinn was focused on her education, planning a career in social work, but not ruling out politics if that was the best way to make a difference.

Anyone else saying those things would have struck him as idealistic, or too full of themselves. He found himself respecting someone so driven at such an early age, though.

Then, one day, he had walked into his Paris mansion and found a composed young woman whose lithe figure lit such a bonfire of lust in him, he immediately rejected it. She was his sister's friend. A *child*.

She'd been nineteen and mature beyond her years, but still. It hadn't felt right to look at her the way a man looked at a woman.

She had thrown some remark in his face and things had deteriorated further that night, when he accosted Remy. He knew she'd been insulted by his patronizing dismissal of her because she didn't take any of the clothes she had put on his account. She had asked his housekeeper to have them returned instead.

As far as people who held grudges went, Quinn was his equal, which didn't exactly help them get along in the long term.

*So leave*, he told himself.

She was ignoring him, sipping her wine as she held different items of clothing against her front.

His plethora of responsibilities danced in his periphery, but Eden didn't want his help right now. She'd run away to prevent him from offering it. His mother wouldn't be missing him. Despite the drama of her daughter's wedding being called off, she was enjoying the chance to catch up with various relatives.

He turned to fix the latch that was propping the door open.

Behind him, he heard Quinn draw a breath as though she was about to say something.

He pressed the door closed and swung the latch into place, then turned to see Quinn rearranging whatever had been in her expression to something more blasé.

"You've decided to enjoy the room, too?" Her tone lilted with amused challenge.

"If you'd rather be alone, say so."

"And deny you the view of Canada's most famous natural wonder? I couldn't."

"I presume you're referring to yourself?" He glanced up from behind the bar where he found a clean glass.

Her cheekbones had gone bright red. Her reddish-blonde brows pulled into a flat line.

"Why do you always assume my compliments are mockery?" he asked with exasperation.

"Because it wasn't a compliment. You were being sarcastic."

And there was the clash. He had thought he was throwing out clever and sincere flattery, but she loved to take everything he said the wrong way.

He poured himself a scotch that he took to the sofa, sitting and propping his feet on the coffee table, far happier to watch her shop than stare at however many liters of water were falling off a cliff.

She continued to glare at him.

"What do you want me to say? That I *don't* find you attractive? I think you'd call that disingenuous."

"I'm pretty sure you find me convenient," she muttered.

Did she really think living with an ocean between them was convenient?

"If you really believe that's all I think of you, then you ought to tell me to take a leap over those falls. You're better than that and we both know it."

She rolled her eyes.

"Oh, am I giving you too much credit? Or is it that I'm *your* convenience?"

"You are many things. Convenient has never been one of them." She gave the clothes a final swish and turned away from the rack in disgust. "You're a distraction."

"*I* am," he scoffed. She filled his head at the most inopportune times. From the moment Eden's wedding had been announced, Micah had been wondering when he would see Quinn. How often. She was his quiet obsession and he would love it to stop.

"If I hadn't been so consumed with getting away from the vineyard without you catching me, I would have remembered to bring my laptop. I could be working right now."

"So I'll take you back to the vineyard and you can work. What are you working on?" he asked with confusion. "Did you get a job?"

"My proposal for my PhD. But I wouldn't get anything done there and you know it." She set aside her half-empty glass and casually stepped over his knee so she straddled his thighs. As she set her knee next to his hip, the hem of her dress rode up, almost exposing her underwear. The cushions sank on either side of him as her weight settled warmly across his legs. "Let's get this over with."

"I don't claim to be a romantic, but even I find that off-putting." It was a lie. His blood was already singing. The fragrance of sunscreen and sunshine and that subtler honey and nutmeg she naturally exuded began to numb his brain. He set aside his glass so his hands could settle on her waist and tug her an inch closer.

"We both know it's going to happen. At least once it's done, we can start behaving like adults again."

He snorted, doubtful, but she was right. This seemed to have become inevitable whenever they crossed paths. Without conscious thought, he was slouching lower and pulling her tighter into his lap. A rough noise rattled in his chest as her heat penetrated his fly and warmed his hardening flesh.

The way her ice-blue eyes melted and her golden lashes drooped was deeply satisfying. He watched her catch her bottom lip, all shiny and pink. He *needed* to suck it.

"Do I need a condom?" He had one. Three, actually.

He had anticipated he would be alone with her at some point and had wanted to be prepared.

"I haven't been with anyone else since last time."

"Me, either." He refused to contemplate what it meant that they seemed to say that every time. "C'mere." His voice was a rumble he barely recognized.

Her hands moved from his shoulders to his neck and she slanted her head as she pressed her mouth to his, their connection as effortless as always.

The taste and feel of him swept through Quinn's senses. Much as she'd tried to resist, contact with him had become so intensely necessary for her, it was painful. Why was he the only man to make her feel this way? Sometimes she feared that she had imprinted on him for life. His hands were the only ones she would ever let touch her. His lips the only ones she wanted against her own.

Granted, they were very clever hands and lips. He knew exactly how to pet her, using the right amount of pressure and lazy, precise urgency as he slid his touch down to her buttocks, seeming to savor the feel of her while infusing her with deep pleasure. She was kissing him, but he was the one who made it so compelling. His tongue brushed hers, inviting her to deepen their connection. She did and moaned as she sank into the sheer luxury of being with him like this.

Sometimes she thought a kiss would be enough. That she just needed a taste of him, but it was never enough. Even on a humid day like today, she couldn't get close enough. Couldn't be held hard enough. She wanted to be absorbed through his skin so she was inside him forever.

It was a neediness that brought a sting to her eyes, one that should have had her pushing away from him so she wouldn't succumb to it, but she sank into sensuality and the sense of belonging—not to him, but *with* him. It was only lust, she reminded herself, but there was no place for blunt reality right now. Not when she could wallow in the hungry pull of his lips and the wiry thickness of his hair between her fingers and the thick ridge of his erection right where she wanted to feel it.

Well, almost where she wanted it.

Cool air swept up her back as he gathered the skirt of her dress, sweeping it up her torso. She lifted her arms and he didn't stop until the soft cotton was floating toward the floor. His arms stayed up and he leaned forward. She raked at his shirt, dragging it up and off, throwing it after her dress.

She removed her bra herself while he slouched back and worked on his belt buckle. His thighs pressed hers apart another inch as he opened his fly. He shoved his hand into his boxer briefs, pushing his clothing out of the way to fully free himself.

Oh, she adored the way he was built. Every single bit of him from the whorl at the crown of his head to the soles of his feet. It was pure animalistic instinct to want the most powerful male in the pack, the one with lean muscles that radiated strength and endurance. She let her greedy hands take in all the skin he had exposed—his thick shoulders and meaty pecs, his flexing biceps and his washboard abs. His hot, ever-so-hard erection that pulsed in her grip as she squeezed him and made him groan.

She had an urge to slip to the floor and take him in her mouth, but he swept the backs of two fingers beneath the string of her thong. His knuckle petted and caressed down her center, grazing the sweetest spot, making her breath catch.

A satisfied growl left him. He was watching her through slitted eyes as he did it again, this time with more purpose.

She bit her lip, squeezing him while holding very still for his deliberate touch. When he pulled away, she gave a sob of loss, but he casually snapped the thong and dragged it free, tossing it away before he cupped her mound with his wide palm.

Her body instinctually rocked against his hand, seeking the delicious waves of pleasure and heat he incited. She dipped her head to kiss him again and for long minutes they caressed each other, both of them doing the delicate, knowing things that made it good for the other. She swept her thumb across his weeping tip. He slid a finger deep inside her and his free hand cupped her breast, teasing her nipple until she was quivering in acute arousal.

"You're almost there, aren't you? Take me inside you," he commanded in a voice that was raspy and filled with carnal hunger. "I want to feel it when you shatter."

She wanted to feel him inside her when she shattered. With a small, helpless noise, she shifted higher on her knees and guided him. As the wide dome of his crown pressed at her entrance, he curled his arm around her back and angled his head, capturing her nipple in the hot cavern of his mouth, trapping her high on her knees.

She was so close! He held her there, pulled taut between two points of need, between the draw of his mouth on her nipple and the thickness her yearning flesh craved. She curled her fists into his hair, each breath a ragged flame. Every pulsebeat was a throb of unanswered need.

"Micah!" She dragged his head up and he let her

weight press down. His hard flesh slid effortlessly into her, filling her with intense satisfaction as the pressure of his pubic bone took her over the edge.

She threw back her head and rolled her hips, instantly subsumed in orgasm, reveling in the shivering contractions and the way his hands kept her deep in his lap.

As the sharpest waves began to subside, she brought her head up and saw his nostrils were flared, his teeth bared in his effort to hold back his own climax. His fingers dug into her hips and his eyes were glazed with heat.

"See? A natural wonder." He gathered her up and flipped her onto her back on the cushions, the weight of his pelvis settling against hers in a way that brought all her nerve endings back to life. "Now, let me see that again from this angle."

## CHAPTER THREE

MICAH HADN'T SLEPT LONG, ten or fifteen minutes tops, but it had been deep and solid. He was naked on the sofa, unsurprised to find himself alone. Quinn always seemed to slip away before they had to look each other in the eye.

The door to the balcony was still open. Mist had condensed on his skin, leaving him damp and chilled. It was a little too depressing for his otherwise physical contentment, but he was too lazy to move.

Quinn was right. He was thinking like an adult again, wondering why the hell he kept doing this with her. It definitely wasn't a convenient affair. They lived on opposite sides of the Atlantic, crossing paths only a few times a year.

Nevertheless, it had become their habit to tear each other's clothes off, then act as if it hadn't happened. That was more her choice than his. He wasn't embarrassed by their affair, but he agreed that Eden would make more of it than it was.

It had started two years ago, when Eden had finished her business degree. Quinn's major was feminism and gender studies, a topic she was very passionate about—thus her insistence on independence and agency and his extensive education in respecting her choices.

Not that he minded. Much as his inner Neanderthal wanted to say, *Woman. My bed. Stay there*, he couldn't help appreciating how confident and self-sufficient she was.

That's why he'd insisted on including her when he invited Eden to his Greek villa. Quinn had put herself through school and graduated with honors. That deserved recognition.

Things had been unsettled between all of them after Paris, though. Micah had acknowledged and apologized for his poor behavior with Remy before they left, but Quinn hadn't come with Eden the next time she visited. She had been busy with an accelerated track at school, but Micah had still taken it personally.

Perhaps he should have told them that he had sought counseling after acting so irrationally in Paris, but his sessions had been deeply private, forcing him to dredge through some painful memories in his childhood. Today had tested the equilibrium he'd gained since then. He was still angry at Remy for absconding with Eden, but he accepted that she was a willing participant in her abduction. Surely that proved him fully evolved, he thought dourly.

Either way, he had blamed himself when Quinn initially hesitated at coming to Greece. It turned out she was prepping for her master's degree. Eden had persuaded her to take a week away and Micah had hoped they would get back to the relaxed dynamic where Eden teased him into lightening up and her chatter with her friend made his home less tomblike.

It wasn't like it had been, though. His sister had been an adult moving into a position of responsibility at her father's corporation. She'd been somber, beginning to feel the weight of it.

As for Quinn...

He blew out a constrained breath. Quinn had not been a child, either. She had had at least one boyfriend by then, or so he'd heard through Eden. The earnest biologist had had a manageable amount of debt and a passion for conservation, according to the dossier Micah had commissioned on him.

Much like the handful of men Eden had dated, Micah had shamelessly checked up on him. He didn't think the man was good enough for her, but without any serious red flags, he had had to let her find that out for herself.

Quinn must have come to that realization, because she had broken up with him by the time she touched down in Greece.

Micah had recently ended an affair himself and, given their respective singlehood, Eden had gotten the idea they should become a couple.

"Quinn would make the best sister-in-law you could give me." She had played it off as teasing, but Micah knew that, deep down, she really wanted it.

Quinn knew it, too, and addressed it head-on when they had a moment alone a few days later.

"Where's Eden?" he had asked when he found her reading on the terrace.

"Salon. Getting her vacation braids." She set down her book, expression serious. "Can I speak to you about something?"

"Problem?" He settled across from her, trying not to notice the way her freckles went down past the scooped neckline of her top where it exposed her upper chest, or the way her legs uncurled as she brought her feet to the paving stones, toes painted neon pink.

"I would do almost anything for Eden, you know that,

but I won't marry you," she had announced. "It's not personal. I doubt I'll ever marry anyone."

Micah was used to women presuming they had a shot with him, so he couldn't resist drawling, "You could wait until you're asked."

"That's why I find it so objectionable." Her mouth stretched into a humorless smile. "Why must a woman wait until she's asked? It's a patriarchal institution that only benefits men."

God, he enjoyed when she got all superior and pushed back on him like this. She was the tennis adversary who forced him to work for every point.

"You're making a vast overgeneralization." He deliberately dug into a contrary position. "I'm filthy rich. A woman would gain a very comfortable life, marrying me."

"Doing what?" Her tone was scathing. "My independence is priceless. Can your wealth and wedding band give me that? On the contrary, I bet you'd insist on a prenuptial agreement that would actually constrain your wife even if she left you. Don't pretend that marrying you would gain a woman anything when it starts out with concessions."

"A prenup is a sound precaution. That's a fact. Many would argue it's a chance for both parties to protect themselves."

"It's a contract. Don't call it marriage if it's a business deal. I am happy to consider a business partnership where I'll be treated as an equal, but I won't give up my freedom so I can fulfil an outdated domestic role that immediately gives you the advantage simply because I'm the woman and you're the man."

"Really, Ms. Gender Studies? People aren't locked

into such rigid roles anymore. What about same-sex marriage?"

"What about it? Even when there are two husbands, it's still the norm for one partner to become a caregiver while the other is the breadwinner. Marriage promotes inequality. Therefore, no thank you."

"You really believe that? You don't see it as two people bringing a broad array of resources to bear, providing their offspring the best chance at thriving?"

"If you think marriage is the only way babies are made, I have a picture book you'll find very enlightening. Look, if you want to get married and have children, go right ahead. I'm only saying I don't plan to do either."

"You don't want children?" That did surprise him.

"*Want* is the wrong word. I don't intend to *make* children. There are plenty in existence who need a parent. I'll choose fostering or adoption when I'm ready."

Ah. "Sometimes I wonder how someone so analytical and, dare I say, cynical, could be such good friends with a romantic like my sister. Then you say something like that."

"Call me a bleeding heart. I dare you." She narrowed her eyes.

"A soft heart," he amended. "Behind the thick wall of thorns."

"It's a thick wall of cast iron, Sir Kettle."

He snorted. This was also why she was friends with his sister. Even when she voiced strong opinions, she never took herself too seriously.

He enjoyed her company. He always had. In that moment, he couldn't help admiring her as an introspective, self-possessed adult who knew exactly what she wanted out of life.

For just a moment, he let himself wonder if her passion and playfulness extended to the bedroom. How would it feel to be the recipient of her intensity if it turned sensual? Hellishly good, he would bet.

When his gaze climbed from the open button at her throat, her blue eyes were waiting for him. The sexual awareness he had ignored since Paris was suddenly a glowing fire between them, impossible to hide or smother.

Her short lashes flared wide, then fluttered in the briefest moment of disconcertment. Just as quickly, she made up her mind and lifted her chin. One ribbon of red-gold hair sat against her freckled cheek. Her eyes were flickering between the hot center of a flame and the inviting hue of a tropical sea.

"Would you like to have sex?"

For a frozen second, he wondered if she was reading his thoughts.

His scrambled brain tried to find a reason why she was off-limits, but they were consenting adults with an empty house.

Nevertheless, he was compelled to clarify, "Are we still debating the pros and cons of marriage?"

"Are you still expecting me to wait until I'm asked?" Her tone was lightly mocking, but he noted the tension across her shoulders.

This had taken some courage on her part, given the fact that he had rebuffed her the last time she'd acknowledged the attraction between them.

He did not have the strength to do it again.

"You really want to have sex?" His voice had descended to the bottom of his chest. "Why?"

"I believe they're called orgasms," she said with a bland smile.

"I would have thought an independent spirit such as yourself wouldn't need a man for that."

"Too right." She rose. Her mouth was a tight line of indignation. "I'll see what I can manage on my own."

He was on his feet before he knew it, catching at her to draw her back in front of him. He hadn't expected the simple act of setting his hands on her to send hunger sweeping through him, numbing his brain to rational thought.

There was a flash of vulnerability behind her startled gaze, then her hands alighted on his chest like nervous, light-as-air hummingbirds.

"What about Eden?" he managed to ask.

"She won't be back for at least an hour."

Not long enough. That was his basest thought, but, "I mean she'll think—"

Quinn was already shaking her head. "I don't want to give her any wild ideas. This is only for today. We'll keep it between us."

That caused a small schism in his head, but he let it go because if he only had today, only a single hour, he wouldn't waste it talking. He suddenly had a lot of fantasies to explore.

He might have replayed every one of them while he lay here coated in mist off the falls, but an abrupt silence yanked him back to the hotel room.

The sound of running water hadn't all come from outside. Some had been flowing from a tap into a tub and now it had shut off.

*Quinn was still here.*

Being human was so wonderfully annoying.

There were the decadent man-made pleasures like

a deep tub of warm water, the luxury of a tall building overlooking a stunning view, and the cool tang of wine on her lips. Then there was the animalistic fascination that slithered through her when Micah appeared, naked and heavy-lidded, the latent smugness around his mouth reminding her that this languorous bliss in her veins was all thanks to him.

Quinn always felt very raw and defenseless after sex. Anytime she interacted with him, really, but especially after he dismantled her with her own needs and desires.

"Do the jets not work?" His hand went to the dial on the wall.

"I was trying not to wake you."

He twisted the knob and the jets rumbled to life. He entered the tub without invitation, but it was built for two, vaguely heart-shaped so his elbow brushed hers as they settled in their seats facing the view of the falls.

"You're always careful to give me my beauty sleep. Why is that?"

Why did she run away before he opened his eyes? So she could put herself back together before she had to face him again. Today, that would have entailed getting dressed and hiring a car. This tub had been too inviting to resist so here she was, trying to pull her defenses in place while naked next to him.

It wasn't working.

"You always fall asleep. What am I supposed to do? Lie there like a good girl, waiting for you to wake up and notice me again?"

"I notice you," he chided. "Always."

He was doing it now. She felt his gaze on the side of her face like winter sunshine, but only sipped her wine, refusing to look at him.

"Why does it bother you that I said that?"

"It doesn't."

He sighed to the ceiling and splayed his arms across the rim as he sank an inch lower in the water, fingertips close enough to her shoulder to make her skin tingle.

She knew that sigh, though. He thought she was being stroppy and she was.

"Being noticed isn't good," she blurted. "It means you're different. When you're singled out, you're vulnerable. It makes you the prey for hyenas that run you down and rip you apart."

She felt his surprise and the uncomfortable heat of his full attention again.

"Do you genuinely feel threatened when I say you look nice?"

"Do you realize you're looking at me like I'm some kind of weirdo for feeling that way? I wasn't a pretty kid. I was gangly and wore glasses and my clothes never fit. I was called 'matchstick' because of my hair and 'bucky' because of my overbite. Yes. I feel threatened when you comment on my appearance. I'd rather you didn't."

"I didn't know that." He didn't say anything else while, outside, thirty-one hundred tons of water pooled above the falls before plummeting into the mist.

Just as she started to think, *Oh, God, I never should have told him what a freak I am*, he spoke again.

"I don't ever want to make you feel threatened, Quinn." His voice was low, but she didn't think that disturbing rumble in his tone was from the jets rolling against his back. "I can't help being suspicious of Remy, but I won't resort to violence. Not toward him and never, ever toward you."

It was something she had already believed in her heart, but hearing it aloud brought emotive tears to her eyes. She wasn't sure why. Maybe because any promises he made her wouldn't be put to the test of time. They didn't have a future, not really. Not beyond a few more trysts like this one, and those would only come about if she was lucky.

She didn't tell him what she suspected, though—that Eden wasn't simply catching a lift with Remy. Quinn had a hunch Eden would be drawn further into Remy's life and would pull away from both of them. The sliver of space and time that Eden created, the one that allowed Quinn and Micah's worlds to overlap, would disappear. There had been something inevitable between Eden and Remy the first time they had laid eyes on each other. Quinn had sensed it and felt threatened by it. That's how she knew it was real.

"Will you help me understand why you hate him so much? Or at least explain why your mom won't let you help Eden?" This day of upheaval and disaster wouldn't have happened if Eden hadn't been so convinced that Hunter was her only means of saving her father's company.

Micah's expression twisted with distaste. He stole her wine and took a healthy gulp, keeping her glass.

"My father's family—*my* family—" his lip curled again "—were very hostile to my mother when she married him. I can't blame her for resenting them. My grandparents are gone, but I remember them as cold and disapproving. My aunt is very entrenched in the highest social circles and made it very difficult for my mother to make any connections. My father knew how to be charming when he wanted something, but he was a bully."

"Toward your mother?" Quinn asked, thinking of something Eden had told her earlier today. Eden didn't know whether Micah's father had been abusive, but she suspected he had been.

Micah held the glass near his mouth, profile hardening. "My mother has never said outright that he physically hurt her, but he certainly wasn't a kind man, especially after she left him."

It hurt to think of Lucille being treated so badly. Quinn had great fondness for her. As for Micah...

Her heart felt as though it were peeled raw as she asked, "Did he hurt you?"

"I caught a backhand now and again, but he didn't beat me, if that's what you're asking." His gaze went into the glass that he held tilted toward his tense mouth. "I mostly lived with my grandparents when I wasn't at boarding school so I honestly didn't see him that much. I only ever saw him resort to real violence once. Against Remy Sylvain and his father."

"What?" She sat up and twisted to face him. "When?"

Micah swallowed a gulp of wine. "I was twelve. I had finally talked my father into letting me live in Canada with my mother, or so I thought. I started school and joined the basketball team, since that's what all the cool kids did. Remy and I were on opposing teams in a tournament. We had an altercation, as boys do. My father attacked him in retaliation. His father waded in to stop it. They bloodied each other's lips and were kicked out. My father took me directly back to Europe. I resented the hell out of the Sylvains for causing me to be sent back to exile."

"That wasn't Remy's fault. It sounds as though it was your father's."

"Agreed. But why the hell would Remy target my sister if he wasn't still holding a grudge, years later?" He swung a piercing look at her.

"Because he's attracted to her! I know she's your sister, but she's very appealing, Micah. Men hit on her all the time. They always have."

He only drained the glass and set it aside. "You asked why my mother won't let me underwrite Bellamy Home and Garden. It's because of that. In a thousand ways, my father hurt her beyond her capacity to forgive. He married her when she became pregnant with me, but his parents thought she had done it intentionally to trap him. Their cruelty drove her back to Canada. He refused to grant her custody and gave her minimal access. When she finally had me in her house, he took me away again. She happily cooks for me and occasionally allows me to buy her dinner, but she absolutely will not allow me to pollute the life she made with Eden and Oscar with my father's money."

"That's hard," Quinn murmured. "You should tell Eden. She thinks your mother is being proud, but I get it. Lucille wants to keep ownership of the life she's built. If she lets you step in, it becomes someone else's accomplishment. His."

"BH&G is not hers, though. It's Eden's now. If she makes the decision to accept my help, that will be her own good sense that bails out the company. At least, that's what I've been trying to convince her to see."

Quinn's phone pinged on the shelf where she'd left it. She picked it up and read the text Eden had just sent.

"Don't shoot the messenger, but Eden isn't going to Toronto. They're in Remy's helicopter, on their way to Montreal." They were heading to Martinique from there, but she didn't get a chance to say so.

"They're *flying*? Damn him!" The water sloshed as Micah stood. Water sluiced off his powerful, naked form and splashed across the tiles as he left the tub.

As much as Quinn would have loved to pretend she was an A-list celebrity on vacation, she was practical enough—and tight-fisted enough—to dry off and go back to the vineyard with Micah.

She didn't linger, though. She packed the rest of Eden's things along with her own and drove to Eden's apartment in Toronto. Eden had offered it to Quinn for the next two weeks, since her plan had been to go on honeymoon with Hunter, then sell this apartment and move into a house with him.

Eden would need it for herself now, Quinn imagined, but at least she had a roof over her head while she searched for a place of her own. Until the semester ended, she'd been living on campus as a dorm adviser, which discounted her rent, making it possible to live on her anemic salary as a teaching assistant while she completed her master's. Most summers she went back to PEI to work and save up for the next year since housing was usually cheaper there, but with Eden's wedding taking up her focus, she had yet to make any decisions about where she would live or work.

To her surprise, Micah turned up the next morning, after dropping Lucille at her home in the suburbs.

"Eden told our mother she's taking 'me' time in the Caribbean."

"She texted me the same. I asked if she wanted company," Quinn joked, but Micah was back to oozing resentment.

"I'm sure she has company. Sylvain has homes in both Haiti and Martinique."

"What are you going to do, Raging Bull? Charge down there and tell two consenting adults they're not allowed to have sex?"

"Are they having sex?"

"I don't know! It's none of my business and it's not yours, either."

"Why can't you see my side of it?" he demanded.

"You are knee-deep in hypocrisy, Micah. Would you stop having sex with me if Eden told you to?"

His expression darkened with what she interpreted as dismay. Her heart lurched.

"I'm not going to tell her. Don't worry." She put up a halting palm. "All I'm saying is that sex happens and it's *just* sex. Let it happen so she can move on." She really ought to learn to take her own advice.

"Fine, but if she contacts you, I want to hear about it." He started toward the door.

"What, no goodbye kiss?" she asked facetiously.

He spun around and strode back toward her with such purpose, she stumbled backward and came up against the kitchen island.

Then she was inside the eye of the hurricane. His strong arms surrounded her, dragging her into the storm. His mouth devoured hers, wiping her thoughts clean as he laid claim to her entire being. To her body, with his firm hands running over her, thorough and hungry as he mapped each subtle dip and curve. To her soul, pulling it from her body so she felt empty when he abruptly ended the kiss and stared deeply into her eyes. Into her heart.

"One of these days, we need to make a decision."

He walked out while she stood there, dazed, fingertips pressed to her sizzling lips.

# CHAPTER FOUR

*Five weeks later*

HE *REALLY* WASN'T going to forgive her.

Quinn had expected their affair would be over after her announcement in Gibraltar a month ago. She had expected a cold shoulder from him in future. If she was lucky, he might offer a few heated words the next time Eden had a birthday or some other event they might both attend.

She had not expected him to deliberately undermine her ability to pursue her doctorate. Not when he had always been so supportive of her education. Not when he had sent her an anthology of feminist writings from the seventeenth century when she had been finishing up her master's degree.

But there it was in her email.

Herr Gould has declined to vouch for you. I'm afraid we can't share the letters with you at this time.

"I didn't *ask* him to vouch for me!" she cried, causing one of the other hostel guests to glance at her.

Quinn shook her head to indicate she was fine and

scowled again at her laptop, wondering how Micah had gotten involved at all. Yes, she had mentioned him when she was chatting up the volunteer on the help desk, saying Micah had once recommended she visit this particular museum in Vienna. But *she* was the one who had learned they had a collection of letters from the wife of a chancellor to her husband, imploring him to improve the conditions for women and their children in the 1800s. All she had asked was whether she could obtain scans of the originals. Her German was rudimentary and they were apparently written in a Bavarian dialect, but the chance to study a primary source was too exciting to overlook.

The volunteer had said, "Let me check with the curator and get back to you. We've done it before for academics. Your credentials are excellent so I don't anticipate a problem."

Her credentials *were* excellent. Since she hadn't yet found a place to live in Canada, and Eden had flown her to Gibraltar for her wedding, Quinn had decided to seize the opportunity to expand her dissertation research. She dented her modest savings with the cost of a train pass and was buffering the cost of her room and board with whatever field picking or serving shifts she could pick up here and there.

She was really excited about the broader view her research would allow on her topic and, so far, all the historians in Spain and France had offered her an open-armed welcome.

This museum curator had felt compelled to check with Micah, though. And Micah had put her on some sort of blacklist. What a jerk.

Quinn checked the time, then impulsively placed a

call to Lucille. She could have tried Eden, but had a feeling Micah was still ignoring her calls, too.

"Quinn!" Lucille's warm greeting made her smile—and breathe a small sigh of relief. Apparently, no one had told Lucille about Quinn's bombshell revelation in Gibraltar.

"Hi, Lucille. Have I caught you at a bad time?"

"Not at all. I was taking a break from my garden until it's in the shade again. Where are you?"

"Vienna. That's why I'm calling, actually. I wondered if you knew where Micah is right now? I'd love to catch him in person if I can."

"Oh, I can never keep track of where that man will be next," Lucille said. "He's usually on his yacht for the summer, but he mentioned something about his aunt planning a dinner. She'll host that at her villa on Lake Como so if I had to guess, I would imagine he's heading to his villa in Bellagio if he isn't already there. Let me give you his assistant's number. He'll put you in Micah's calendar so you're sure to see him."

*Not if he sees me first.*

Quinn patiently pretended she needed the contact details Lucille gave her even as she checked the train schedule to Italy.

"Quinn?" Lucille's shift to something more tentative made Quinn's stomach curdle. Maybe she did know about her affair with Micah. Maybe she disapproved.

"Yes?" She tightened her hand on her phone.

"Will you *please* ask him to call Eden? She's upset that he's still refusing her calls."

"Is he?" At least he wasn't actively sabotaging his sister's future. "I'll bring it up, yes. How are you doing with Eden's surprise marriage to Remy?"

"Still shocked, obviously. It all happened very fast. I already miss having her close by, but I've been to Montreal to see them. They're settling in and seem deeply in love."

"They do, don't they?" Quinn said wistfully. She was tremendously happy for her friend, but felt bereft at how quickly Eden had thrown herself into her new life. This painfully familiar sense of abandonment was another reason Quinn was burying herself in research. She didn't *want* to go back to Canada where her best friend would have so many other priorities ahead of her.

"It was good for the business, too. Remy has been very generous in helping her there," Lucille continued. Her relief that her husband's company was secure again rang strong in her voice. "Eden has her hands full, obviously, bringing things back on course, otherwise I'm sure she'd be on a plane to see Micah herself. He can be so stubborn sometimes."

"Only sometimes?" Quinn asked sweetly.

"You do know him well, don't you?" Lucille chortled.

A sharper twist of yearning went through her. Quinn knew Micah the way she knew most people—by observation. She often wished she knew his deeper thoughts and feelings, but that's not who they were.

"Oh, here comes my neighbor looking for the Bundt pan I offered her. I'll have to go."

"That's fine. Thanks again." Quinn signed off, then pondered her line of attack.

When a knock at the door to his private lounge sounded, Micah muted the headlines he was watching and called, "Come."

"Sorry to disturb you, signore." His housekeeper

slipped in and mostly closed the door, then lowered her voice as she continued in Italian. "There's a young woman in the foyer. She claims to be a friend of your sister. She said you might remember her. Quinn Harper? She asks if you have five minutes."

*You might remember her.* He gritted his teeth at how easily she got a dig in without even being in the room. She had to know it, too.

After the call he'd taken yesterday, Micah had half expected she would make an effort to get in touch. He hadn't anticipated she would show up at his lakeside villa in Bellagio, or that knowing she was in his home would cause his hackles to rise while pouring hot anticipation into his groin.

He did have five minutes, but they'd been earmarked for exactly what he was doing, nursing a shot of scotch while he caught up on current events before he changed and attended a dinner for which he had no appetite.

*Send her away.* That's what he should have said. He was coldly furious at the way she'd treated him in Gibraltar. It still didn't make sense to him, but he would be damned if he would beg her to tell him why she had revealed their relationship with such blithe indifference. She always took Eden's side against him, he was used to that, but that's not what she had been doing. She had been defending Remy. Micah couldn't stomach that level of turncoat betrayal, he really couldn't.

The whole episode was so infuriating, he could hardly bear to think of it so he really ought to *send her away*.

"Have her wait in the study." He shot back his drink, savoring the harsh burn down his throat before he took his time rising, then showering and shaving. He dressed in his dinner suit, leaving his white jacket off, too hot under the collar to wear it. He blamed the July heat, even though his stone villa was comfortably cool.

When he strolled into his study, Quinn replaced a book on the shelf.

She squared herself to face him, brushing whatever dust was on her fingertips against her crinkled blue skirt. Her sleeveless cotton top was ribbed so it hugged her subtle curves. Her sandals were practical walking shoes. A straw bag sat on the floor near the sofa.

She looked the way she always looked to him—like a ballerina poised to flit and twirl and race off stage left. Her hair was rolled into a knot on the top of her head; her aloof expression was clean of makeup. She always seemed very cool and disinterested, but he knew how sensuous she was and that always heated his gut. The way her lips betrayed her mood, pursed now in preparation for making some sharp remark, fascinated him no end.

Her direct blue gaze landed like a punch in the chest.

"Yes?" he prompted when she didn't speak. He steeled himself against whatever apology she might try to make.

"Why did you tell the museum in Vienna to withhold those letters from me?"

He snorted. So no apology, then.

"An acquaintance called to say you were using my name to gain access to their archives. I said you were overstepping our relationship and that I couldn't vouch for your character."

"Really." The tendons in her neck flexed. "You said those words with a straight face?"

"How are you keeping a straight face now?" he shot back. "After all your lectures on personal choice and agency, you failed to ask my permission before you publicly shared something that you and I agreed we would keep between us. I can't vouch for your character when you no longer have my trust or respect."

She flinched as if he'd slapped her.

He had come out swinging, determined to strike back for the sting of exposure she'd caused him, but he hadn't expected she would go white like that, and grasp at the edge of the bookshelf as though she needed the support.

Alarmed, he took a step forward, but she recovered just as quickly.

Her hand dropped to her side and closed into a fist. She firmed her footing as though bracing for a physical fight. Her mouth became a flat line and her glare, sharp as a laser, sliced him into fillets.

"You're right. I did that. I knew you would hate me for it, but I did it to protect your sister. It's clear you have never really trusted me or you would have known that. So fine. Make my life harder. I don't care what you think of me."

"Obviously," he couldn't resist pointing out, but his conscience twisted. He did know she would do anything for Eden. Quinn was Eden's best friend in the most literal sense.

She might have flinched again, but she had moved to snatch up her straw bag so he missed seeing her expression. She looped the long handles over her shoulder as she straightened.

"I have never tried to trade on my relationship with you. You know that," she said with dignity. "It wasn't even a relationship and this is why. I knew it would end and I knew that when it did, you would be ruthless about severing all ties. I don't care how you treat me. Do you understand that? *I don't care.*"

"Have you ever heard the expression about the lady protesting too much?" He had wanted to hurt her and he had. He could hear it in the strain of her voice and saw it in the brightness of her eyes, but there was absolutely no satisfaction in it. He felt sick with himself.

"Okay, you're right about that, too. Does that feel good?" Her cheeks wore bright spots of red. Her mouth quivered, but her chin was up, her shoulders squared for conflict. "I wanted to believe we could remain friendly once our affair ended. It galls me to hear I've lost your trust and respect, but guess what? *You've lost mine.*"

He snapped his head back, shocked to discover what a heart-punch that was. He was deeply insulted by her icy declaration. "Because I told the truth to a museum curator?"

"Because you throw people away. Go ahead and toss me." She touched her breastbone. "I get that. I never meant anything to you in the first place, but Eden is your *sister.* Do you know what I would do to have one of those?"

The break in her voice cracked against his eardrum. She was blinking fast, chest rising and falling as though she had run all the way from Vienna to confront him here.

"I guess you're so rich, you can afford to throw away one and get another when it suits you." The profound contempt in her bitter words left a pall in the back of his throat.

"Don't make this about Eden," he scoffed as she started to turn away. "You betrayed my confidence. Own it."

"You—!" She spun around and pierced holes through

him with her icicle gaze. Her whole body was visibly shaking.

For a split second, he had the sense she was going to say something that... Hell, he didn't know what was about to happen, but he was facing a deadly creature right now, the kind that would strike with poisonous venom or charge and run him through.

He held his breath, tense and waiting, but her voice was eerily calm when she spoke.

"You want to make this about us? Fine. I knew you would find it hard to forgive me. It was a test and you *failed*. More than that, the way you're treating Eden tells me I was right to never envision a future with you. If you can cut your own sister out of your life so heartlessly, what chance would I have had? I did us both a favor, Micah. Say 'thank you.'"

A strangled laugh hit his throat even as she flung open the study door and slammed it behind her.

In two steps, he had his hand on the door latch, but he could already hear the front door opening and closing.

He swore and let his hand fall to his side, not bothering to chase her. What was the point? To insist she was wrong? That he hadn't cut Eden out of his life? He hadn't.

But he was being a stubborn ass toward his sister, avoiding her calls.

What was his alternative, though? Let her try to convince him she'd made the right decision in marrying a man he hated? Invite them into his home and start going on family vacations with them?

He wanted to believe he was taking time to cool down, but he wasn't coming around to the idea. On the contrary, he was clinging to his anger, returning again and again to betrayal and blame because it felt familiar if not good.

*It was a test and you failed.*

Why the hell did Quinn have to be right? God, she infuriated him when she called him out on his own intransigence.

He pinched the bridge of his nose, starting to see the gauntlet he'd thrown down when he had told the curator that he couldn't vouch for her. He had wanted this confrontation, but Quinn had picked up his tin glove and slapped him across the face with it.

*If you can cut her out of your life so heartlessly, what chance would I have had?*

Did she *want* a chance? If she did, that was news to him because she'd always been very adamant that she had other places to be that were anywhere except with him.

"Signore?" His housekeeper tentatively tapped on the door, breaking into his brooding. "The chauffeur has pulled the car around. He's ready when you are."

The dinner party. Micah bit back a weary curse. His aunt worked the levers of society with cold-blooded alacrity, always looking after her own interests, but those included ensuring the Gould side of his family thrived, so she was occasionally useful.

Micah had agreed to meet her grandson-in-law, whom she wanted him to hire into an executive position despite the young man still being wet behind the ears. Micah suspected she would thrust a potential wife under his nose again, the niece or daughter of someone whose favor she wanted to curry. There would be the usual shop talk about a property or project she thought he should consider and she would have opinions on Eden's recent marriage, not that he had any desire to hear them.

It would all be addressed in the space of two hours and served up with a pleasing menu and a carefully chosen flight of wines. She was an efficient and attentive hostess, but those were the nicest things he could say about her.

He shrugged on his jacket and walked outside to his car. The late-day sun was sinking, throwing long shadows. The soft breeze carried the sounds and smells of summer—dry grass and motors on the lake and the distant wail of an ambulance siren.

It all vanished as his driver sealed him into the capsule of the car. Moments later, they crept up the lane and joined the traffic jam on the main road.

The congestion was normal at this time of evening. Micah took out his phone, half thinking to call Eden, but he wanted more time and privacy when he did.

He rolled the edge of his phone against his thigh, corner to corner to corner, pondering how they could get past something that might not be unforgivable, but it was incomprehensible. To him, at least.

Damn Quinn for making him feel so guilty about this!

"I think there was an accident, sir," his driver said. "I see the ambulance is there. Shouldn't be long now."

Micah had a flash of premonition, but reflexively dismissed it. He wasn't the type to make up things to worry about or latch onto them when he did. Besides, he would know if something had ever happened to Quinn.

*That* was a ridiculous thought. He wasn't psychic and was highly skeptical of anyone who claimed to be.

But his gut was filling with cement. He hadn't heard a car when Quinn left. She must have been on foot or catching a rideshare at the top of the drive? Maybe a bus. He'd never noticed where the closest bus stop was to his home. He had no way of knowing which direction she'd taken as she left, either, but he did know she had been fueled with anger.

Walking fast, she could have reached the intersection up ahead and *why the hell* was he putting himself through this ridiculous exercise?

She was fine. Quinn was always fine. She said so anytime he asked.

"There goes the ambulance. We'll start moving now." His driver crawled forward.

Micah's heart began to crash in his chest for absolutely no logical reason at all.

As they came toward the corner, a policeman seemed to be taking a statement from a woman. The woman offered the policeman something red and white.

"Stop!" Micah shouted.

He was briefly thrown forward as his driver stood on the brake. Micah leaped from the car before his chauffeur could find a place to pull over.

"Let me see that," Micah barked as he charged up to the cop and the woman.

"Signore!" The policeman tensed as though confronting a madman while the woman fearfully offered the phone.

It was exactly what Micah had feared. The screen was smashed to a broken web. The back of the case wore tire tracks across the *I Heart PEI* lettering.

Micah wanted to throw up. His vision tunneled and he thought his knees might unhinge.

"Do you know who it belongs to, signore?" the policeman asked from a thousand miles away.

"I do."

# CHAPTER FIVE

QUINN WAS WAITING for the painkiller to kick in, aware that even when it did, it wouldn't fully relieve her agony because not all of it was physical. None of it was particularly new, either, which made it extra excruciating.

Her shoulder was dislocated again. The misalignment in her joint hurt so much she could hardly breathe, but at least she was no longer jostling through the narrow streets of Bellagio in the back of an ambulance. She was in a hospital bed in the emergency room, trying to comprehend the Italian spoken beyond the curtain... *benefici medici* must be something to do with her medical benefits.

She'd given a young woman her wallet. They must have found the card, but it was a low-premium travel plan for students. She doubted it offered much coverage.

The headache of dealing with bureaucracy was already upon her, coupling up with the sting of a shallow pocketbook that had dogged her all her life.

Atop that was the depression of having lost Eden, the one person she might have called in a case like this, but now didn't feel right. Plus, even though she'd thrown a metric ton of superiority at Micah because he wasn't speaking to his sister, Quinn had been dodging meaningful conversations with Eden herself, pretending she was hideously busy so Eden wouldn't guess she was steeped in possessiveness and loss simply because Eden was in love and married and living her best life.

Then there was Micah.

She might have thrown her arm over her eyes in chagrin, but the second she so much as thought about it, a knifing sensation cut across her chest. Hot tears pressed behind her eyes and her throat closed over a cry of pain.

Damn him for cutting her loose the minute she had acknowledged they were together. Damn him, damn him, damn him.

"Signorina Harper?" The curtain around her fluttered. The nurse gave her a compassionate smile. "You have a visitor."

Ugh. His blinding good looks seared into the backs of her eyeballs. He'd put on a white jacket so he was even more crisp and formal and secret-agent sexy than ever.

She closed her eyes against him, the only defense she had right now. *No.* Just *no.*

"You were hit by a *bicycle*?" His tone of outrage was thick with blame, as if she was at fault.

"Apparently, I really am skinny as a lamppost. He didn't see me until I stepped out from behind it."

"And stepped in front of him. Why would you do that?"

"I didn't do it on purpose! I had the signal to walk. The cars were stopped. I thought it was fine." The cyclist had been riding into the sun. He hadn't slowed, believing he could make the turn ahead of the oncoming cars.

He'd been very apologetic when he had stood over her, blood pouring from his chin and knee. He was probably in an adjacent bed, getting bandages hastily slapped over his scrapes, same as they'd given her.

"You're conscious, at least." Micah sounded…

Oh, she didn't want to imagine he sounded relieved or worried or as though he cared one wit.

*You no longer have my trust or respect.*

Funny how learning she didn't even have that had made her realize she had always yearned for even more.

"Do you have any sense of the severity of your injuries? The nurse said your shoulder appears to be dislocated. Did you hit your head? Anything broken?"

"No. Just my shoulder." And, "appear"? She'd felt it dislocate as the two-hundred-pound man had slammed into her. The impact had knocked her off her feet and the screaming pain had kept her from softening her tumble across the pavement. That had added various scrapes that the nurse had already sprayed with antiseptic and covered. By tomorrow, she would have more bruises than freckles, but she hadn't hit her head or fractured anything that she knew of, so that was something.

"I don't suppose you've called Eden." He set her shattered phone on the table beside her, then took his own phone from his pristine jacket.

"Don't," she said flatly. "I'll call her later."

He scowled. "She'll want to know you're in hospital, Quinn."

"She'll think she has to drop everything and come, but she's busy trying to put her company back on the rails while starting her marriage in a new city. There's nothing she can do anyway. They'll take an X-ray, treat me like a heretic at an Inquisition while they put it back, then wrap it and tell me to be more careful next time."

"This has happened before?" His restless gaze flickered from her cheekbone to the ice pack on the front of her shoulder, down to her limp hand resting on the blanket across her stomach, and ended at the tent of her feet.

"Why are you here?" she asked with annoyance that was a mask for the pain of knowing he hated her.

"To see how badly you're hurt. Obviously."

"I'll live. You can go."

His gaze clashed into hers with the force of a full-on electric storm, making her breath hitch, but the nurse came back with a rake of the curtain.

"I'll take you for your X-ray now." She set a wheelchair by the bed and lowered the rail.

This was going to be a nightmare, one she would rather Micah didn't witness, but she didn't have the breath to say so. With the nurse's help, Quinn very gingerly sat up, blinking as the pain intensified.

Micah stepped forward, reaching out, but she warned him with one raised finger not to touch her. Her eyes were watering and her whole body was shaking by the time she eased herself into the wheelchair.

"I'll wait here," he said grimly as the nurse turned her chair.

"Don't bother." She meant it. She couldn't take him right now, acting like he cared when he didn't. Thank God she had this horrific injury to explain the way her lip was quivering.

By the time she returned to her bed, the drugs were doing their job. She was indifferent to the physical agony and emotional angst of existence. She wasn't indifferent to him, though. To her shame, she was relieved he was still here, even though he radiated the energy of a caged tiger.

"You're shaking," he noted as the nurse got her on the bed and under the sheet.

"I'm cold." They'd helped her change into a hospital gown before the X-ray. None of it had been fun.

"It's shock. I'll fetch a warmed blanket," the nurse murmured.

Micah removed his jacket and draped it over her. Now the smell of his aftershave was filling her nostrils. She closed her eyes against all the memories his scent evoked—like losing her virginity to him.

She pushed at the jacket. "Don't you have to put this on and be somewhere?" She was seconds away from a full breakdown, she really was.

"I told my aunt that something came up. And I texted Eden that you were here and I would keep her updated. I haven't heard back, but when she sees it, she'll want to know how you're doing."

She was terrible, both dreading and urgent for the treatment. She knew the worst of the pain would subside to a dull ache afterward, but the transition would be insufferable.

The nurse came back, thankfully giving her an excuse not to answer. The woman tucked a blanket around Quinn that was so deliciously warm, she could have wept with gratitude and nearly did.

"The doctor will be along shortly. He's reviewing your X-ray now."

Quinn closed her eyes again, concentrating on her breathing and trying to relax muscles that were filled with flight chemicals, wanting to run to somewhere safe, away from this pain.

It felt like a hundred years, probably because she

could feel impatience wafting off Micah every time footsteps passed beyond her curtain without coming in.

Finally, the doctor slipped in, apologizing for the delay.

"I've asked our orthopedic surgeon to consult. She should be here any moment." He brought up an X-ray on a monitor that he pulled around so it was in Quinn's line of sight. "There's a lot of damage here, not all of it from today." He pointed at the image. "There's scar tissue here and this tendon has completely torn away. This has happened before?"

Quinn wanted to lie, she really did. Dredging through the past was her absolutely least favorite thing to do, especially with Micah standing there listening.

"Once when I was nine, once when I was fifteen," she admitted. "But I do all my exercises very faithfully. It hasn't given me any trouble until this happened." *Just put it back and let me go home.*

Or rather, back to her hostel. Ugh. It was going to be a long, uncomfortable night and a hellish flight home that would probably cost the earth once she booked it. She already dreaded however many buses and trains and transfers it would take.

"Were those falls? Or sports…?" the doctor prodded with a concerned frown.

Why was he forcing this?

"The first one happened when I didn't hear my foster father tell me it was time to get out of the pool. He caught my arm and pulled me out." She'd been so unprepared, she hadn't braced herself for the yank on her arm.

There was a choked sound off to her right that Quinn distantly realized was Micah, but she quickly got out the rest.

"The second time was in high school, when my PE teacher didn't believe me when I said I was afraid I would pop my shoulder if I fell during the tumbling she insisted I try." The teacher had given Quinn some potted daffodils the following week, when Quinn had sat on the bench doing her algebra homework with her wrong hand.

The doctor made a noise of dismay as he looked back at the X-ray. "This tendon needs to be reattached or this will continue to happen."

"I'll keep getting hit by bicycles?"

The doctor only blinked at her. She couldn't even get a laugh right now? That put the cherry on her sundae of misery.

"I can't get an operation right now. I have to go back to Canada," Quinn told him.

"How do you plan to do that?" Micah asked tightly.

"I believe it's called an airplane."

"You can't lift your arm, Quinn, let alone luggage. She'll stay with me while she has the surgery and recovers."

"Fun as *that* sounds, no thank you." She looked to the doctor. "Would you *please* put my bone back where it belongs and wrap me up? I promise I'll see my doctor as soon as I get home."

"Ah. Here's Dr. Fabrizio," he said as the curtain hooks rattled.

A petite woman appeared. She had her hair up and diamonds dangling from her ears. She wore a white coat over what looked like an evening gown.

After a brief introduction, she and the emergency physician consulted in Italian for several minutes, pointing and circling things on the image.

Micah listened intently while Quinn was totally lost.

She blamed the drugs, but it bothered her that they were all so serious. When Micah asked a question, their answer made him nod grimly. Her anxiety skyrocketed.

"I agree this can't wait." The surgeon finally spoke directly to Quinn in heavily accented English. "This joint needs to be stabilized and you look to have some nerve impingement from one of your previous injuries. Are you numb on the back of your arm?"

"Sometimes," she admitted reluctantly, not revealing that she couldn't put anything heavier than a hat into an overhead bin on an airplane.

"I have a full roster tomorrow so I'll do it tonight." The surgeon nodded at the hovering nurse, who promptly hurried away. "It might take a little time to get you in, but we will."

"Wait. What? Tonight? That can't happen." Genuine panic began to take over Quinn's system. She looked to Micah, desperate for him to step in and save her.

"You need the operation, Quinn," he said, quiet and firm.

"No, I just need to keep it still for a few weeks, then do my exercises. I've done this. I know what to do."

"Dr. Fabrizio treats some of our nation's top athletes," the original doctor assured her. "You won't find better care anywhere."

This was just like all those times when grown-ups had made decisions for her without listening, only this time the bill would come to her instead of the government.

"I can't pay for this. Have you checked my insurance? They won't cover it."

"I spoke to the admissions desk while you were getting your X-ray." Micah brushed away her argument with a brisk. "It's all taken care of."

Which was probably why the exalted surgeon had rushed from whatever gala she'd been enjoying to attend to Quinn, but the only thing worse than having to pay for emergency surgery in a foreign country was owing the cost of it to Micah Gould.

"We'll realign the socket, then do the surgery arthroscopically. It's low invasion so it won't affect your healing time too much," the surgeon said cheerfully.

"This way you will only have to go through the healing process once," Micah added before she could protest again. "This has to be done, Quinn." He was using his most implacable voice. "Do it now so it's over with."

It was harsh logic, but she saw the sense in it. Short of refusing treatment out of belligerence, she didn't really have a choice. That made her chin crinkle in helplessness, though. She didn't want surgery!

She fought tears as she gave a mute nod of agreement.

Micah was not squeamish, but standing by while Quinn had her shoulder set was the worst thing he'd ever witnessed. Whether the pain drugs had helped was up for debate. She didn't scream or cry, but the yelp that escaped her at one point would ring in his ears forever.

So would the knowledge that a man had grabbed her in anger when she'd been *nine*, causing her to suffer to this day.

He had imagined nothing could make him feel so helpless as he had on the way here, not knowing the extent of her injuries. *I'll have to tell Eden*, had been his single grim thought, but he hadn't known how he would do it if the news was truly bad. He'd been unable to breathe until he'd seen that Quinn was conscious.

Then he'd had to listen to the doctors point out issues

that should have been dealt with properly in the past. The impotency of his rage on that front was something he had to push aside while he took a fraction of her pain in the form of her nails digging into his hand.

When she released him, he snatched up a tissue and mopped her temples. Tears were streaming from the corners of her closed eyes and she was shaking again.

"It's over now," he tried to soothe.

"No, it's not," she croaked, turning her face away from his attempts to dry her eyes.

She was blaming him for insisting she needed the surgery. She didn't want it and who would? The best he could do for her was ensure she was given the highest level of care, so that's what he was doing. It was a helluva lot better than people had done for her in the past. What sort of teacher bullied a girl into reinjuring herself?

"Was he charged?" Micah asked grimly as they were briefly left alone.

"The cyclist?" She frowned through her haze of drugs and pain. "It was an accident."

"The first man who dislocated your shoulder."

"No. That was an accident, too." That had to be sarcasm, but she closed her eyes again, voice drifting with disinterest so it disguised her real thoughts. "I was moved to another home, though."

As if that was any compensation?

The nurse returned with an IV bag and a tray of instruments. "I have to prepare her for surgery and finish her paperwork now."

He nodded, but didn't move. He'd never seen Quinn look so utterly outdone. The fierce light that usually beamed out of her was firmly doused and it made his veins feel full of grit.

"Is there anyone I can call besides Eden?" It was disgraceful that he didn't know. At the same time, he braced against hearing she'd met someone in recent weeks.

"The youth hostel on Via Patrice," she said with a wince of discomfort. "They were adamant that they kick you out if you tie up a bed and don't use it. Tell them they can put my things in storage. I'll pick it up as soon as I can."

No one else? Her lack of an emergency contact was actually worse than hearing she had a secret lover he didn't know about.

"Signor Gould?" An assistant with a clipboard caught his eye and motioned that he had paperwork of his own to sign.

He stepped away and the curtain was pulled firmly closed behind him.

# CHAPTER SIX

HE DIDN'T SEE her again for hours. The nurse told him there was a delay as they assembled the team and prepared the theater, that Quinn was lightly sedated and resting comfortably, but it annoyed him that she was abandoned like luggage in some prep ward where he couldn't be with her.

He made a number of calls and answered a few emails, then he was stuck pacing the private room Quinn had been given.

The suite more closely resembled a five-star hotel than a hospital room. The bed had a wooden head and footboard and was made up with cheerful yellow bedding and a colorful throw. Mahogany panels hid equipment inside the walls while spring-green drapes covered a window that ran the length of the room.

It was dark, so he left them closed.

Along with two armchairs, there were two dining chairs, a small table, and a kitchenette with a kettle, a microwave and a selection of light snacks in the small refrigerator.

No booze, which was a pity, but he made coffee, feeling as though he'd lived a lifetime since Quinn had shown up in his foyer four hours ago. He kept thinking about that moment when he'd almost gone after her, then let her go. If he'd delayed her by seconds, this accident wouldn't have happened.

*It was a test and you failed.*

Those words were barbed thorns that dug deeper under his skin each time he tried to pick them out. He wanted to reject them. He was no expert on relationships, but he knew they weren't supposed to be like that, where you set someone up and cut them off when they disappointed you. He was trained to hate failure of any kind. To feel it as deep shame. His perfectionist tendencies were the result of drills, not a true compulsion to be flawless.

If she had told him what the test was, he would have passed, damn it.

Maybe.

*It wasn't even a relationship and this is why. I knew it would end and I knew that when it did, you would be ruthless about severing all ties.*

He had never expected their affair to go on as long as it did. Their first time was supposed to be their only time. It had been her first time ever, which had shocked him when he had realized. He'd been past the point of no return, buried to his root inside her, nearly mindless with carnal need, but it had penetrated that her tension was more than nervous shyness. It was discomfort, despite her enthusiastic encouragement and the powerful orgasm he'd just delivered with his mouth.

"Why me?" He'd been floored. Humbled.

"I trust you'll never hurt me."

"I just did." He'd never been so overcome with tenderness and chagrin.

"Not that bad." She turned her mouth into his neck.

He'd taken such care with her after that, determined

to make it good for her. It had been amazing. Giving her orgasms had been a drug he couldn't quit. Their "only today" had turned into three more stolen opportunities before she left.

Maybe there'd been a part of him that had tested *her* after that. She'd claimed it would be a one-off and he had deliberately not reached out afterward, convinced she would text or call first. He was a wanted man—a bachelor with a fortune—but that had never seemed to impress her.

The complete radio silence from her had dented his ego, if he was honest. Then he'd turned up for Eden's birthday and during a lively round of singing over a cake full of candles, Quinn had leaned over to him.

"Do you want me to come to your room later?"

"Yes." He'd spent the rest of that dinner drowning in anticipation.

His mother's birthday had been the next time, then a New Year's Eve party, another birthday—he couldn't remember whose. They'd even hooked up after Eden's father's funeral. That had felt wrong, but also incredibly right. They were getting good at sex by then, stripping without ceremony and testing the load-bearing weight of various pieces of furniture.

Micah had come to Toronto to meet Hunter when Eden was contemplating becoming engaged to him and it had felt strange to have a family dinner without Quinn at the table. She'd been tied up with her thesis, according to Eden.

Quinn had texted him later that night, though.

You up for a nightcap? I need a break from the books.

She'd only been in his hotel room an hour, but what an hour. They'd barely spoken, consuming each other like animals. She'd been gone when he woke, almost leaving him with the sense it had been a particularly vivid wet dream.

He'd missed Eden's engagement party, which had meant he missed an opportunity to see Quinn. He'd felt it, much to his disgruntlement. By the time Eden's wedding had rolled around, he'd been champing at the bit to see Quinn. There'd been too many social demands at the rehearsal dinner to steal away with her and Quinn had been glued to Eden's side all night.

Micah had stood by, watching a couple of grooms-men and even a winery employee take a shot at her. He'd wanted to shove every single one of those men to the floor, but she hadn't given any of them more than a vague moment of her attention.

She had been waiting for him. He didn't know how he'd known that, but he had.

They hadn't found their chance until they were in that hotel room in Niagara Falls. It had been spectacular, as usual, but he'd been distracted by his sister running away with Remy.

The next time he'd seen her, she'd blurted out their affair like it was nothing worth protecting. He'd walked away from it and her. Furious.

Hurt.

"Signore?" The nurse broke into his brooding. "The doctor said to tell you everything went well and she's in recovery. She'll be brought up in an hour or so."

"Grazie." He pulled out his phone and texted yet another update to Eden, noting it was dinner hour, there. It wasn't like her to be out of touch like this. Had she blocked him?

He started to call their mother, but his phone rang with a video call.

Eden.

His first unsettling reaction was a reflexive desire to hit Ignore. He was still unable to wrap his head around how his half sister could have married a Sylvain. How could she believe herself in love with Remy? As far as Micah knew, until Eden's wedding to Hunter fell apart, Eden had only spoken to Remy a handful of times.

The other reason he'd been avoiding Eden, however, was one he hadn't even acknowledged to himself.

*Would you stop having sex with me if Eden told you to?*

His sister knew that he'd been sleeping with her best friend. He wasn't prepared for her to tell him how to behave toward Quinn—or for any questions on how he'd already behaved toward her.

That's not what this was, though. She was worried about her friend.

He accepted the call.

Eden was in a robe, her hair hidden beneath a towel, her eyes wide with anxious alarm. She sat up against the headboard of an unfamiliar bed.

"We had his and hers massages and, um, a nap. I just woke up and saw all your texts. What *happened*?"

Honeymooners. He tried not to dwell on it.

"Exactly what I said." He'd sent a few updates as things had developed. "They should bring her up soon, but I imagine she'll be asleep."

"Who?" a male voice rumbled off-screen. Remy.

"Quinn was hit by a cyclist."

"Is she all right?"

"Not really. She just came out of surgery," Eden replied.

"I'll make coffee." There was a rustle as Remy rose and left.

"Thank God you're with her and she's not going through that alone." Eden touched her brow. "Are you two—"

"No."

*It wasn't even a relationship and this is why.*

"She came to see me here in Italy. We had an argument, she walked out and…" *I should have stopped her.* "I guess she stepped off the sidewalk as the cyclist came up to the intersection. No concussion or broken bones." Thank God. "She's banged up, though." He'd seen the blood on her clothes and that, too, had given him chills at how much worse it could have been. "As soon as I learned she was in hospital, I came to make sure she got the treatment she needs."

"Thank you," Eden said solemnly.

*It wasn't for you*, he wanted to say. But he also didn't want to say it.

He sipped his coffee, finding it had gone bitter and cold.

"When she wakes up, tell her to call me. I can come if she needs me to, but you could get her to an airport if Remy arranges a flight, couldn't you? She can stay with us while she recovers."

Micah's heart flared with something like possessiveness. Remy already had his sister. He wasn't getting Quinn, too.

"She'll need follow-ups. I'll keep her with me and bring her when I come for Mom's birthday. Did you know Quinn's had her shoulder dislocated twice before?"

She nodded, quiet and grave. "I did. Yes."

For some reason, that made his chest feel scooped out. He knew that the two had their secrets, but he had always thought they were girlish ones. Crushes and padded bras and which pain reliever worked best on menstrual cramps.

It struck him that Eden knew deeply personal and painful things about Quinn that he had never been privy to. He felt cheated. Or rather, he was bothered that Eden knew how bad Quinn's childhood had been, but he was even more perturbed by the fact that it had been bad. That Quinn had never shared that with him, beyond telling him once that she trusted he would never hurt her. Not that she trusted him, but that she had trusted him not to hurt her. Physically, he realized.

*It was a test and you failed.*

"Today might have brought up some stuff for her. She doesn't like people making decisions for her. How is she doing? Emotionally?" she asked with concern.

She'd been so fragile, he couldn't stand to think of it.

He swore as he recollected, "Do you know what she said?" He threw himself into an armchair, able to see the humor now. "The doctor said she needed the surgery or this would keep happening and she said, 'I'll keep getting hit by bicycles?'"

Eden released a burst of surprised laughter. "That's on-brand, isn't it?"

He shook his head, exasperated all over again, but his heavy veil of concern lifted marginally. There was something heartening in this—sharing his amusement with his sister over Quinn's cheeky remark. How many times over the years had she been the one to repeat some witty crack Quinn had thrown out? He'd always liked those snippets, unconsciously waiting for them when he talked to Eden because they always gave him a kick.

*The way you're treating Eden tells me I was right to never envision a future with you. If you can cut your own sister out of your life so heartlessly, what chance would I have had?*

He mentally swore at himself that it had come to Quinn being in hospital for him to reach out to Eden. What if he hadn't left the house right after and seen the aftermath of the accident? What if he hadn't known she was here? He would still be giving Eden the silent treatment and Quinn would be wearing a sling in some dumpy hostel, shoulder causing nerve damage while she tried to book a flight home.

"Listen, I know I've been dodging your calls—" He was ready to own up to his intransigence.

"Hmm?" Eden wasn't listening. She was looking off-screen. "Now? Are you sure?"

"Yes." Remy's deep voice was distant enough from the screen it was hard to hear. "I told her the other day that he still wasn't taking your calls. She said to tell him if it would help."

Tell who what?

"And you want me…? No, I think it will be better from me, but okay…um…" Eden gathered herself with a deep breath. Her body shifted as Remy sat next to her on the bed, but he stayed off camera.

Micah instinctively braced himself, already knowing he didn't want to hear whatever she was about to say.

"I know you're still upset with me for getting married without telling you—" Eden began.

"Live your life," he cut in. "Marry who you want. Do what you want with BH&G. I'm here if you need anything. We don't need a postmortem." That's all he'd wanted to say a minute ago. He would always be her brother, no matter what.

"We *do* need a forensic audit," she said pointedly. "Because I hate that you're angry with me for falling in love, but that's not what I need to tell you. Has Quinn said anything about why she revealed your affair that day in Gibraltar?"

"No," he said flatly, and shot the dregs of his coffee. "We don't need a postgame on that, either. It's late here. I want to get some sleep." He looked to the door, hoping an orderly would arrive with Quinn.

"Don't hang up. This is important," Eden insisted.

Micah bit back a sigh. "Look, Quinn said she was protecting you. I believe her. Okay? She knew I was on the verge of saying something unforgivable. It was your wedding day so she put me in check. I'm not thrilled with the choices you've made, but you and I are fine, Eden. We'll work it out over time. It doesn't have to happen right now." With her asshat of a husband listening nearby.

"We absolutely have to circle back to everything that has been going on between you and Quinn, but… She really said she was trying to protect *me*?" She looked to her husband, who remained beside her off-screen. "Or did she say 'your sister'?"

"I honestly can't remember, Eden. Today was the first time we've spoken since Gibraltar. A lot has happened."

"You haven't talked to Quinn at *all* since then? You were having an affair with her for *years*, Micah. In all the time you've known her, have you come to understand her at *all*?"

*She makes her own choices*, he wanted to say, but his

sister's mouth clamped shut with such disapproval he locked his own teeth together.

"What's between Quinn and me is between Quinn and me."

"Go ahead and believe that, but we *will* come back to it," Eden said sternly. "What you need to know right now is that she wasn't protecting *me*, Micah. She was protecting…" She swallowed and glanced at Remy again before her expression became entreating. When she continued, her voice was very gentle. "She was protecting your other sister, Micah."

"I don't have—" Micah cut himself off as the pennies dropped. Hundreds of millions of them. They landed on him with hard, peppering weight until it was the volume of a mountainside avalanche.

Quinn's shoulder was throbbing, pulling her from slumber. She released a discontented sob of frustration and was yanked fully awake by Micah's rasped voice.

"Pain? I'll get the nurse."

His footsteps walked away while she blinked at the palatial room dimly lit by a single golden lamp and pale dawn light coming through the crack in the drapes.

Damn that man. She couldn't afford this.

She looked down at the sling she wore. It wasn't the simple kind she'd worn in the past, but a number of straps that tied a padded pillow to her hip. Her forearm rested upon it while her upper arm was snug against her rib cage. Wonderful. This was going to make life easy.

A night nurse came in to say, "The anesthetic from the surgery has worn off. I'll adjust the drip with your pain medication."

She checked Quinn's pulse and temperature. Quinn

was already arranged in a half-sitting position. She offered her a few sips of water before she helped her use the bathroom.

Micah was still there when she came out. He still wore his suit, minus the tie and jacket. His sleeves were pushed up his arms, but otherwise he was his commanding self.

She quickly averted her gaze, feeling weak and pitiful, shuffling around so shakily.

"What time is it?" Quinn asked as she carefully settled back on the bed.

"Four thirty-seven." The nurse tucked the blankets around her. "You have lots of time to rest before the doctor does her rounds." She nodded at Micah and left.

Micah continued to loom on the other side of the room. It didn't make sense that he was here. It made her want to see significance in it when she already knew there wouldn't be.

"Have you been here the whole time? Oh, God, did I say something stupid when they brought me in here?" She had no recollection of it, but did have a sudden flash of those emotional videos online of people coming out of anesthetic, crying and swearing and saying revealing things.

"You only woke up enough to help shift yourself onto that bed, then went right back to sleep. Eden was disappointed. She was hoping to talk to you."

Eden. That was it. Despite what Quinn had said about how he was treating Eden, he loved his sister and, for her, would stay with her friend, even if he no longer liked said friend.

Quinn didn't want to think about their argument or what she would owe him after this. Sometimes you had to accept help from people who held you in contempt.

She had survived it before and would again. She would get through all if this and live to fight another day.

Maybe. Now that she was awake enough to assess it, she was dangerously close to crying over the mess she'd landed in. She was tired and hurting, broke, and a very long way from home. She didn't have Micah as a lover anymore, or even as a friend. Her education, the one thing she had always told herself no one could take away from her, had been undermined, not just by him, but also by her own clumsiness in not looking properly before she had stepped off the curb. How was she supposed to continue her dissertation now?

She really didn't need him watching her have an emotional breakdown on top of the rest of what he'd witnessed today. She opened her mouth to tell him to go home, but noticed how haggard he looked.

Maybe it was the pale light that made his expression seem so devastated, but his eyes seemed sunken into dark bruises. The lines bracketing his mouth were deeper than she'd ever seen them. Stubble shadowed his jaw and his hair was not the smooth cap he usually wore.

"Have you slept at all?" she asked, flickering a glance at the way he'd angled an armchair to use one of the other chairs as a footstool.

"No."

"Why not?" *Was* he worried about her? Her heart lurched.

"What—" He cut himself off and ran his hand over his face, then gave his hair a disgruntled scrub. "What did she say to you? In Gibraltar. Yasmine," he clarified.

"What?" Quinn's heart lurched again.

His distress wasn't about her, then. It was never about her. She should have realized that.

She ignored the squeeze that compressed her lungs and used the excuse of adjusting the sheet to avoid looking at him.

"I'm not sure what you mean," she prevaricated. Her heart quivered with apprehension.

"Eden told me she's my half sister, Quinn. She said that Yasmine found out the day she joined the three of you in Gibraltar. She said Yasmine was still in shock and went across to your room when Eden and Remy had gone to theirs. She told you everything, yes? That's why you threw our relationship under the bus, to keep me from finding out she was my sister before she was ready for me to hear it. What did you think I was going to do to her? Blame her? *Hurt* her? I'm not like him!" He swore and pushed his finger and thumb into the corners of his eyes, muttering, "I work so damned hard not to be like him."

"Oh, God, Micah," she breathed, instantly aching for him. For Yasmine, too, and for Remy who had carried the secret of his sister's conception for years.

"You weren't in a fit state to hear it," she said gently. "You know you weren't. With Remy right there? You thought he was conning Eden out of her company by marrying her. You weren't ready to learn this entire war started because your father did something heinous to his mother. So yes, I changed the conversation. I admitted you and I had sex. Big deal."

"I'm the only man you've ever had sex with. It is a big deal." He was practically shouting and pointed at the floor.

She rolled her lips inward, surprised he'd put that together and more than a little chagrined that it was true.

"Look. I won't betray Yasmine's confidence, but the

things she said were just processing. Everything she had thought she knew about herself took a sharp turn so she had a lot to work through. She was curious about you, though. That's why she talked to me. She wanted my take on what kind of person you were."

"What did you say?" His hands went into the pockets on his trousers. His posture seemed tense.

"Nothing personal. I told her that even though I've known you a long time, I don't know you that well—"

"Really," he scoffed.

"It's true," she insisted even as her throat grew dry. "We don't exactly share secrets."

"You knew this secret about *me* before *I* did." His finger pointed about, assigning blame to invisible people for that. "Why the hell wouldn't you tell me yourself?"

The crack in his voice fractured her heart.

"When?" she asked helplessly. "You weren't in a mood for explosive revelations when you arrived in Gibraltar. I've texted you three times since then, asking if you wanted to talk."

"You almost told me today. Didn't you?" he challenged.

She had. It made her cringe with shame.

"I was tempted, but I was angry. This news isn't a weapon. I know it hurts to hear it, Micah. That's why I took one for the team at Eden's wedding."

"Whose team?" he muttered, and rearranged his features with his hand again, still spitting out curses under his breath. "Remy told Yasmine I wasn't speaking to Eden so she told them to tell me. What am I supposed to do with this information? My father assaulted their mother. No wonder their whole family has been out to get me all these years. What if there are more children

out there?" His hands went up as if that had just occurred to him.

"It's a lot," she murmured. "But you can't make sense
of it if you're exhausted. You need to sleep."

"I can't." He paced a few steps, scrubbing his hair
again. "I'm too keyed up."

"Well, I can't sleep with you hovering like the grim
reaper. Go home." She wasn't supposed to sleep flat yet,
but she was a side sleeper so lowered the head of the
bed a little and shuffled, trying to get her good shoulder under her a little.

Micah came to stand over her, hands on his hips,
shoulders sloped with defeat.

"What? You paid for the bed so you want to share it?"

"No. I want you to stay up and fight," he admitted
without heat. "I'm still really angry with you for hiding
the truth and saying what you did without asking me
first. But you need your sleep so yes. If you're sleeping
like that, there's room on this side."

"You're unbelievable. You know that?"

"I know what you're like, Quinn. If I go home, I'll
come back to an empty room and I won't see you until
Eden's baby shower." His voice was gruff, but he was
infinitely careful as he dropped his shoes and settled in
behind her.

She didn't deny that she would absolutely leave if she
could. Or admit that having him behind her like that created a nice, warm brace for her to lie back against. He
curled his arm under her pillow and she snuggled deeper
into the crevice he created.

She had always wanted to sleep with him, but had
invariably claimed she didn't want to get caught in his
room. In reality, sleeping together was too intimate. It

was the ultimate vulnerability. The ultimate bonding exercise. Lying close with him like this was comforting and made her feel like he would keep her safe forever.

Which was an illusion.

"Why did they let you stay all night here?" she asked truculently.

"Because I told them to."

No doubt.

"Comfortable?" he murmured.

"Mm-hmm." She was fighting inexplicable tears. Why would he insist on staying with her? Really just to fight? Or softer reasons?

She didn't want to think he felt more than an obligation toward a woman he sometimes slept with, though. She didn't want to imagine and hope and believe in things that would never be true.

"Good night, then," he said.

She closed her eyes and matched her breathing to his, mind soon blanking into sleep.

## CHAPTER SEVEN

"OH!" THE NURSE'S gasp woke Quinn.

Micah, too, judging by the small jolt that went through him and the way his arm twitched, then eased from beneath her pillow.

"How are you feeling?" the nurse asked cheerfully as she yanked open the drapes and allowed light to pour in.

"Like I've been hit by a bicycle, missed two meals, and I'm not allowed to shower."

She'd been feeling really nice all snuggled into Micah, but he was already pulling away, rising and rolling his shoulders.

"Breakfast will be here shortly. Then the doctor will come by to discuss follow-up and when you're likely to be discharged. Let me remove your IV, then I can help you in the bathroom, if you like."

"I can manage. I've done this before." There was still a lot of pain, but it was the pain of fresh stitches and healing. It would kill her to admit it, but she was glad she had the surgery behind her rather than in front of her.

"Your things are here," Micah said in a gravelly morning voice. He set her bag from the hostel on the bed.

"How did you get that?"

"My driver picked it up on his way to fetching my

own bag." He collected a small duffel and disappeared down the hall.

At least she had her own toothbrush and would have some of her own clothes to change into when she was discharged. Her laptop was here and everything.

Feeling almost cheerful, she gave her face and teeth a clumsy scrub, then ran a brush through her hair. She would have to buy a couple of hairbands to keep it off her face. That always made her look more like Anne of Green Gables than usual.

She came back into her room with one arm through the robe and discovered Micah had shaved. What a monster. He had a clean shirt and smooth hair and was removing the covers from two plates on the small round dining table.

"That's just mean," she said as she sat down across from him. "I had to brush my teeth with my wrong hand. I couldn't even put my hair up."

"I like it down. Don't bother," he forestalled, holding up a hand as she opened her mouth. "I know you don't exist to please the male gaze. Sue me for thinking your hair is pretty when it catches the sun."

Like now? The sun was streaming through the massive window, warming her through the robe she was half wearing, but he couldn't possibly think she looked like anything but washed-up seaweed in this state.

She kept her gaze on the fresh fruit and muesli, pastries and cheeses that had been revealed. "I have never seen hospital food like this."

"I ordered it last night. My driver brought it up as soon as I texted."

Of course he did.

"I appreciate it. Thank you." She filled her plate with

the easiest items to eat one-handed, too hungry to be proud. "And I will pay you back for all of this."

"That's not necessary." He poured two cups of coffee and set one in her reach. "You wouldn't have taken this side trip and wound up injured if I hadn't interfered in your research."

"I made the choice to come here, Micah. This is not on you."

"You were upset when you left yesterday."

"I was upset when I arrived."

"We both know I was a bastard to you. Let me apologize," he insisted. "I did believe you were protecting Eden in Gibraltar when you revealed our affair. I have always appreciated your loyalty to her, but she was with Remy. *With* him. He has always been a sore point for me. When you did that, I felt pushed out. Ganged up on. That's no excuse for my interference between you and the museum, though. That was beneath me."

"I should have taken more care to protect your privacy. You have every right to be angry with me. I won't do anything like it again," she promised with a pang in her throat, keeping her eyes on the strawberry she was stabbing.

In the thick silence, she swore she could hear him wondering exactly what she wouldn't repeat, *The affair? Or the exposure of it?*

"I'll talk to the museum, ensure you have full access going forward," he said.

As an olive branch, it was kind but… "I won't need it. This is going to slow me down so I'll go back to my original proposal for my dissertation and go home." She nodded at her bound shoulder. "It's not as ambitious, but Cs get degrees." She had never been graded less than a

B-plus and those were an F as far as she was concerned, but as the song went, she couldn't always get what she wanted.

"You would never be able to live with half-assed effort," he scoffed, giving her a funny feeling in her chest at how well he knew her.

"True, but I can't be a student forever. I thought I could push myself through a few more years of full-time school to get my doctorate, but it wouldn't be the end of the world if I worked for a few years and picked away at the degree. The downside is, I wanted a fighting chance at making policy changes once I got into social work, rather than being one of those people who can see what's wrong, can see how to fix it, but doesn't have the power or credentials to push for change."

"That's your end game? Fix the system?"

"Nuts, right?" She knew how pie-in-the-sky that was. "But what's the alternative? Not even bother to try?"

He studied her the way he did sometimes, like he was seeing her. Seeing *into* her.

She swallowed, remembering that they actually hated each other. She'd forgotten that, briefly, and had talked the way she used to, when he asked about school and her plans for her future. When she felt as though they were equals in some ways. Never in all ways, but intellectually, at least.

"I'm not important so I want to do something important," she said with pithy self-deprecation.

His frown deepened, but thankfully, the surgeon entered, putting an end to his intense scrutiny. Or rather, now it became focused on him listening to the details of her reconstruction, asking pointed questions about her follow-up appointments and the physiotherapy she would need.

"I'll do all that at home," Quinn insisted. "I'm clear to fly, right?"

"I'd prefer to do the follow-up myself," the surgeon said, flickering her thickly lashed brown eyes at Micah.

Quinn bet she would, especially as Quinn's desire to rush back to Canada made it clear she wasn't involved with Micah.

"Where are you going to stay when you get back to Canada?" Micah asked with impatience, as though she was being unreasonable. "With the newlyweds? You can't live alone. Not when you can't cook or even get groceries. You can't work. You might as well stay and continue with your proposal for your dissertation. My place in Vienna is walking distance to the museum."

"I can't type." She could actually, and she could also write decently wrong-handed. She'd had enough practice, but she didn't want to owe him more than she already did.

"Use dictation equipment. I have some if you don't want to buy your own." His frown told her to find an argument with legs. "Let Dr. Fabrizio continue your care. I'll take you home when I fly to see my mother for her birthday. What day would you like to see her again?" he asked the surgeon.

Quinn only went along with the arrangements because it meant she was allowed to put on clothes and leave. Of course, she couldn't carry both her straw day bag and the small backpack she was using for travel. Micah had to carry the bigger bag down to the car for her. He handed it with his own to the driver of a BMW, then helped her into the back seat.

"You can drop me at the youth hostel," she said as Micah came in beside her.

"Give us a minute," he said as the driver started to take his position behind the wheel.

The man murmured something in Italian and closed the door, then moved to stand a short distance away.

"You and I said some cruel things to each other yesterday. Maybe we even thought we meant them. At the time." Micah turned his head and his mahogany eyes held indecipherable swirls and shadows. "But we have a lot of history. I can't cut you out of my life. It simply isn't possible."

The bottom of her stomach wobbled, unsure how to interpret that.

"No matter how big a snit you and I get into, you have my promise that you can always come to me for any reason. Put me in your phone as an emergency contact," he ordered, then seemed to recollect, "The phone I will get you because yours was run over. Call me if you need money. A dry bed. Anything."

She was so moved, she thought her throat would close up completely, so she did what she always did when emotions got too much for her. She cracked a joke.

"What about hiding a body? Because I can't manage a shovel right now and the man who ran me down has really ticked me off."

He stared at her for one, two, three heartbeats. Then the corner of his mouth twitched.

"He's already in the bottom of the lake." He looked forward and knocked on his side window to get his chauffeur's attention. "I missed dinner with my aunt and now I have to reschedule."

Quinn bit her smile as she looked out her own side window.

# CHAPTER EIGHT

EDEN TEXTED HIM *AGAIN*, so Micah walked into the lounge where Quinn had sat down to catch her breath when they'd arrived back at his villa.

She might sound chipper, but she was still drugged up and sore all over. In the time it had taken him to explain to his housekeeper that a room should be prepared, Quinn had tucked herself into the corner of a wingback chair and had fallen fast asleep.

He'd thought about carrying her up to a bedroom, but aside from worrying he would put too much pressure on her shoulder, he liked that he was able to walk in here and check that she was breathing and comfortable.

It had been nearly two hours, though. He brushed his knuckle against her soft cheek and watched her eyelids flutter in confusion.

"If you sleep much longer, you won't sleep tonight."

"I beg to differ." She straightened and winced, yawned. Her hair fell in her face and she brushed it away, but it wasn't in a mood to behave. "Those pain-killers could drop a bull elephant."

She wore one rolled-back sleeve of his shirt, since it had been the easiest item for her to put on around the contraption she wore. Her bottoms were her own boxer-style pajama shorts in pink and green. She should have looked ridiculous, but he had to tear his eyes off her bare legs and the freckles peeking from the open collar of his shirt.

"Eden is desperate for proof of life." He didn't have Quinn's credentials or he would have set up the new phone that had arrived. He offered his own. Eden's number was at the top of his recent calls so she only had to touch the button to place the call. "I'll let the housekeeper know you're up and need lunch."

"Thanks." She took the phone and it connected as he reached the door.

"Is she— Oh, it's you!"

"It's me," Quinn said sheepishly. "I'm fine. I look like twenty miles of dirt road, but I was only knocked, like, ten feet."

"Don't make jokes. You *scared* me. I'm so glad Micah was there. What if you'd been stuck in a hospital and I didn't even know?"

That question had been repeating in Micah's head all this time, along with a thousand other thoughts and reactions to news about his other sister. He'd been agitated last night after that news. Freshly furious with his father—he'd been angry with that man his whole life—and deeply chagrined at the hostility he'd shown toward Remy. Eden had explained that Remy's family had been worried Micah's father would try to claim Yasmine if he knew about her. They'd hidden the truth of her DNA even from her, but all that meant was that his father had yet again dodged taking responsibility for his actions. It fell to Micah to do it.

And there was Quinn, knowing that intensely private information about him, holding it in and navigating his anger while she protected his sister. He hadn't known how to make sense of that, of the fact that he was grateful she hadn't let him do anything stupid, but also furious that she hadn't told him. Why was she always on someone else's side, never his?

Which was a childish reaction, he knew, but in the fraught midnight hours, he'd wallowed in that sense of betrayal, drawing deeply on the pain of it because in some ways, that was the way he understood close relationships were meant to be—painful. As a child, he had loved his mother and sister, but wasn't allowed to be with them. The family he was allowed to see were critical and cold.

When Quinn had told him to go home, he'd been hurt by it and tempted to go. He'd been exhausted and wanted to lick his wounds, but he simply couldn't leave her there. Couldn't risk coming back to her having disappeared.

There was irony in the fact that Quinn always said they could think better after they'd slept together because he'd woken far more clearheaded once he'd slept with her head numbing his biceps and her ass against his hip for a few hours. They had a lot to talk through, but he had the patience now to take it one thing at a time.

Then she'd started talking about going home and compromising her goals and that had been a hard no for him.

In fact, she was probably conspiring right now with his sister to get on a plane, he realized.

He left his instructions with the housekeeper and arrived outside the lounge in time to hear Quinn saying, "Micah has offered to let me stay at his place in Vienna, but I haven't decided."

Maybe *she* hadn't, but he had.

"Are you two…"

"No." Quinn sighed. "This is why we kept it off your radar. We didn't want you to think this was anything serious. It was just…something that happened sometimes. It never meant anything."

"I know you better than that," Eden admonished. "Listen, if you're letting my brother treat you as if you don't mean anything, then I need to have a talk with him. You should expect more from him."

"He's giving me exactly what I want," Quinn insisted. "I don't want to get married and have babies. That's fine for you," she hurried to say. "But I don't want those obligations and responsibilities. I want an education and a career and sometimes I want to sleep with someone. Micah gives me that without trying to take over my life. Why is that wrong?"

"Because you deserve to be loved, Quinn."

"You love me. Don't you? Or are you mad about—?"

"I'm not mad at you for sleeping with my brother. I'm mad at him for taking advantage of you."

Micah's throat tightened with affront.

"I am not that vulnerable," Quinn grumbled.

"From where I'm sitting, you damned well are," Eden shot back.

Micah saw it now, too. He'd always let himself be blinded by Quinn's confidence and saucy comebacks. She was so ferociously independent he'd been fooled into believing she had her entire life under control.

She had very few resources, though. She had health, which had been compromised with this injury, and her education, which he had also impacted.

"Would you *please* stay out of it?" Quinn pleaded.

"Fine." Eden wouldn't. He could already hear the lecture she was planning on giving him. "But Remy is sending you a voucher that will basically get you on any available flight to Montreal. You can stay with us as long as you need. Or use my place in Toronto. I haven't sold it yet."

"I'll bring her home when I come for Mom's birthday," Micah said, striding into the room.

Quinn's gaze whirled up to his, surprise and self-consciousness in the blue depths.

*Yes*, he transmitted with his steady stare. *I was listening.*

"Quinn wants to do some research in Vienna," Micah stated. "Don't you?"

Her face twisted with indecision.

"You're not a quitter, Quinn. Finish what you started," he pressed.

Another flash of startlement struck her expression. Something that dipped her chin as she tried to read what he meant by that. He wasn't sure what to make of his double entendre, either.

"We have to say goodbye, Eden," he said. "Lunch is ready on the terrace."

Quinn had stayed with Micah in the past. She knew how he lived, so she shouldn't have been surprised at the fine cuisine that was placed before her: handmade tortellini stuffed with crab coated in a saffron sauce. It was accented with olives, bocconcini balls and roasted cherry tomatoes in three colors. The final touch was a sprig of fragrant basil.

Maybe what surprised her was that it was all easy to eat with one hand. Had that been Micah's instruction? Or was his housekeeper that attentive?

"You're not eating?" she asked.

"I ate earlier." He sipped what looked like a Bloody Mary and sat with his introspective profile aimed at the lake.

She wasn't allowed alcohol while she was on the prescription-strength painkillers, but she sure would love some, especially now when she was so disconcerted. Any other time she had been in one of his homes, she'd been more Eden's guest than his and her friend had provided a buffer between them. Even when they'd been sneaking around, having sex, Eden had been a convenient excuse to maintain some boundaries.

She reached for her friend again, purely because she didn't know what else to say.

"I'm glad you and Eden are speaking again."

"Me, too." His tone dripped sarcasm, probably because he was still coming to terms with the Yasmine news. He snapped his head around, pinning her with one of his most penetrating stares. "Do you think that's why she married him? Because of—"

"No. Wipe that from your mind. Eden loves Remy." A little schism in her chest felt offset by that fact, but it didn't change the veracity of it. "I know it seems fast and very… Eden. She sees the world through rose-colored glasses, absolutely. But she was eating her heart out for five years after meeting Remy in Paris. It's the same for him."

"That's lust. You and I had that, but we didn't make any hot runs to Gibraltar."

*Had.*

Quinn subtly breathed past the hard lump that lodged in her throat. She looked at her plate, but her appetite was gone.

"We only wanted to share our bodies, not our lives,"

she pointed out quietly. "What they have is different. It was love at first sight."

After a pause while he seemed to absorb what she'd said, he dismissed it. "Please don't start sipping whatever it is Eden's drunk on. I expect more from you. You don't believe in love any more than I do."

"I don't believe in marriage," she contradicted. "Love is real."

"How can you not believe in marriage? Marriage is real. Marriage is something Eden is now stuck in. Love is an illusion. It's pheromones. It's something a woman tells herself has happened to her when she finds herself pregnant and is scared out of her wits to tell her parents. I'm talking about my mother," he clarified shortly.

"You don't think your mother loves you?"

"We're not talking about that kind of caring, are we? My mother said she loved me, but I still had to leave with my father, so it's not some all-powerful force. Love is just a word, one that looks pretty on greeting cards. It has about as much substance as a piece of painted cardboard."

"Wow. I knew you were cynical, but okay." At least she knew where she stood—in the opening of an icy, bottomless cavern.

He only sipped his drink.

"Regardless of what you believe about the true nature of their feelings, they're married. You'll have to accept that, same as I have," she said stonily.

His eyes narrowed. "If you believed she was in love with him all that time, why didn't you put a stop to her trying to marry Hunter?"

"First of all, she was pretty adamant about marrying Hunter. And honestly? I didn't see a path for her and

Remy. Not given how you felt about him. Plus, I knew if she married Hunter…" She bit her lip, but she wanted it off her conscience. "This doesn't make me look very good," she acknowledged glumly. "I knew if she was married to Hunter, she would still need me. Which I know is selfish," she hurried to add. "But she's kind of all I've got. I'm happy for her, though. I genuinely am."

She chewed on a cheese ball, feeling small as she awaited his judgment of her petty, needy heart.

"I have the same sense that he's trying to take things that are mine," he admitted, lip curled in self-deprecation.

"Hmph." There was no real humor in her snort. "I sometimes think you and I have all the wrong things in common. We're possessive. Pigheaded."

"Broken."

"What?" She took that like a knife to the stomach and sat back to absorb it.

"You said it first," he muttered, working his thumb in the dew on the glass he loosely clutched.

*"When?"*

"When they brought you back to your room last night."

"You said I didn't say anything stupid!"

"It wasn't stupid. It was correct."

"I'm so embarrassed." She set down her fork and tried to hide behind her one hand.

"I know you were stoned off your face, Quinn. I didn't take it to heart."

"What exactly did I say?"

He sighed. "Nothing incriminating. You were glad that I was still there and wanted to hug me, but you were upset that your arm wouldn't work. You thought it was broken and said, 'Why are we both so broken?' I had just ended my call with Eden and was wondering the same thing."

What she'd said was awful enough, but she made herself ask, "Did I say anything else?"

"Why? What are you afraid you said?"

"Nothing." She picked up her fork and shoved another tortellini in her mouth.

"Eden is right," he muttered, looking out to the water. "You should expect more from me. We should expect more from each other."

"Like what?" A panicked sensation fluttered into her chest.

"I don't know." Only the tic in his cheek suggested this was a more uncomfortable conversation than he was letting on. "But I was serious when I left Toronto, that we need to make a decision."

"You did." She was unable to keep the crack from her voice. "I revealed we were having an affair and you walked away cold turkey." That still hurt. So much. Not a word. *Over.*

He turned another inscrutable expression on her. "Yet here I am, not gone anymore. Am I?"

"Don't." She scowled at her plate. "I don't want to fall into a trap where we're both feeling a sense of loss over Eden's marriage to Remy so we glom onto each other, convincing ourselves there's more between us than there is. I was never going to upend my life for you, Micah. I have plans. And what could you possibly want from me besides sex?"

"I don't know. *You?*" he suggested.

Her heart turned itself upside down and inside out.

Did he not realize this wasn't anything anyone had ever wanted? Not really? Look at her.

She swallowed and said sincerely, "What we had was very good, Micah. We made some very nice memories and I'm glad we're ending on good terms. That's all anyone can expect from life, don't you think?"

She made herself look at him, but her eyes were hot, her facial muscles tight beneath the blank expression she was trying to hold.

He was staring at her so hard, she felt it as a laser that penetrated to the pit of her stomach. It made her shift uncomfortably, giving her the most awful feeling that he was disappointed in her.

But didn't that prove her point?

A firm, feminine voice sounded in the house, speaking Italian. The words grew in volume as they approached the open doors to the terrace.

Micah swore under his breath and rose. He took a step toward the doors, but a woman was already striding out and across the stone pavers, designer heels clipping in a way that meant business.

She was a stunning woman of sixty-odd years with coiffed silver-blond hair and a complexion like creamed honey. She wore a pastel green sheath with a matching green blazer trimmed in black.

"Aunt Zara," Micah said, polite, but frosty. "I wasn't expecting you."

Oh, snap. Quinn rose and pushed her company smile onto her face, certain this would be awful, but she wouldn't have missed it for the world. Micah had never, ever let Eden meet any of his Gould relatives. Quinn was highly curious.

"You should have." Zara offered her cheek for the buss

of his, then sent a distinctly appalled look at Quinn's taste in fashion. "And you have a houseguest. Micah should have included you in my invitation last night. Zara Von Strauss." She held out her hand in a way that forced Quinn to come to her.

"Quinn Harper." She shook the proffered hand, recognizing this particular air of passive-aggressive superiority. Recognizing that it was a blatant lie that she would invite a penniless orphan dressed like this to sit at her table with her family and friends. "Micah was helping me last night. I was in hospital."

"How kind of him." Her smile was a stretch of painted lips. Nothing more.

"Quinn is a close friend of my sister's," Micah said, sideswiping Quinn's heart with that designation that distanced him from anything more personal between them.

She couldn't really blame him, given all they'd been through lately, but it was hard to keep an unaffected look on her face.

Strangely, Zara seemed to stiffen in an effort to hold her own aloof expression as she turned back to Micah. "Here I thought you were evading your responsibilities to family."

"When have I ever?" Micah asked mildly. "Would you like to sit? I'll order coffee."

"Another time, thank you. I won't interrupt your lunch." Another disparaging look was thrown at Quinn. "But we need to discuss a few things while you're in town."

"I'll be tied up with Quinn, then I'm due in Berlin for the Innovation and Design Awards. I've sent tickets to your grandson. I'll introduce him to our executive team.

I'm sure more than one will be eager to coax him into their department."

The boss's grand-nephew? No doubt.

Zara struck Quinn as the type who liked to micro-manage, though. She wasn't entirely pleased that Micah was leaving her grandson to sink or swim, but she had to accept Micah's action with a satisfied nod and a cool, "Thank you."

"I've also told my property agent to touch base with yours, to review the assessment of the property you've recommended. You've never steered us wrong. I'm sure things will proceed in due course. Was there anything else?"

This was like a tennis match between greats, the undercurrents thick, statements served and volleyed with powerful returns.

"Someone I wanted you to meet." Aunt Zara was not cowed by the flash of warning in Micah's gaze. "You'll need an escort for the award ceremony."

"I never have before. Quinn will accompany me if she's up to it."

"Oh? How nice." It was not nice. She was livid at the thought. "I won't take up any more of your time. It was lovely to meet you, Ms. Harper."

"And you, Mrs. Von Strauss," Quinn lied.

"Will you walk me out?"

"Of course," Micah said, ever the gentleman.

"Your sister recently married," Aunt Zara said as they strode through the lounge toward the foyer. "We haven't had a chance to discuss that."

"There's nothing to discuss. As you said, she's married."

Aunt Zara's mouth pinched, but she knew the rules where Eden was concerned. That's why Micah had invoked her outside, to warn her against insulting Quinn to her face or behind her back. He had made clear a long time ago that he would not stand for any criticism of his mother or sister.

It hit him that, at some point, he would have to reveal to Zara and the rest of his father's family that Yasmine existed. They were going to have a collective stroke.

"It's charitable of you to help your sister's friend." She never used Eden's name. "I can't fault your loyalty to family." Her smile was chilly. "But you have responsibilities to *all* your family, Micah. Everything you do affects us. It reflects on us. Kindly remember that."

"How could I forget when you're so diligent about reminding me?"

"A young man may enjoy his amusements. A man your age needs to secure his dynasty," she asserted. "You need an heir, Micah. And a wife who is an asset to the entire family."

Oof. He wanted to take her arm and walk her out to hear what Quinn would say about a woman being an "asset."

"Is she really accompanying you to the award ceremony? Like that? Please let me send my stylist, if so."

"'She' has a name. I'll take care of everything Quinn needs," he assured her stiffly.

"Hmph." She offered her cheek and said her farewell.

He stood there a moment after closing the door, recognizing that he'd always known he would have to marry and produce an heir one day. It had been made clear to him thousands of times, especially in the last few years, but he hadn't seriously contemplated marriage because…

Truthfully? Because he'd been keeping himself available for Quinn. It hadn't been a conscious decision. He simply hadn't been interested in anyone else. Aside from setups like being seated next to someone eligible at his aunt's table, he hadn't even dated.

He couldn't imagine spending his life with one of those socialites she pushed at him. They were always attractive and well-educated and eager to do "good work" for a charity, but he'd never met any who possessed a spark of real personality. None lit a fire in him the way Quinn did.

He'd never considered Quinn for the role of his wife because she'd always made it clear she wasn't interested in marriage and babies.

*What could you want from me besides sex?*

*That*, he realized. Marriage. The babies were negotiable, but in terms of sharing his bed, waking next to her and bickering over breakfast, she was already his preferred partner.

He pondered that as he walked back outside, briefly alarmed that she wasn't at the table, but she'd only wandered to the water's edge where she was crouched, feeling the temperature.

She glanced up when he joined her.

"I wish I could swim, if only to wash my hair."

"I'll wash it." For better or worse, he thought with irony. Was he really going down this road?

"Don't be silly." She tipped slightly, trying to stand.

He caught her good arm and steadied her under her elbow, helping her rise.

"I'm very serious." He was talking about more than a hair wash, but marriage was a conversation that would have to be handled with care. She was in no shape to hear it now, still half-drugged with painkillers.

"What would Aunt Zara say to you playing ladies' maid?" She widened her eyes in mock scandal.

"Aunt Zara is a snob. She drove my mother away, but she understands now what a mistake it is to attack people I care about. If she or any member of my family treats you in a way that is offside, you'll tell me immediately."

Quinn tucked her chin, smirking in a way that suggested he was overreacting, but her expression shifted as she realized he was not joking.

That seemed to disconcert her, being lumped in with "people I care about." She rolled her lips together and looked to the water.

"I feel privileged to have met her."

He choked slightly.

"Not like that." Her grin flashed. "No, I asked Eden once what your relatives were like and she said she'd never met any of them. Now I have."

"It's true. For my mother's sake, I've always kept a firewall around Eden, not letting any of my Gould relatives play their mind games on her. Zara just tried to bait me into criticizing Eden's marriage. She still believes the story that Remy's father stole from mine."

"Oh." Her brow pleated with empathy. "That's going to be complicated, isn't it?"

"Tell me about it," he muttered, realizing he wanted this, too—her immediate comprehension of his problem. He liked that she understood his complex family dynamic without him having to show her all the skeletons and label them.

"I shouldn't have said you were broken." She looped

her good arm around his and briefly hugged it. "You're split in half. It's different."

"Torn and frayed." Definitely losing his concentration. He could feel the soft give of her breast against his elbow. Impure thoughts bled through him.

He gave in to temptation and let his arm curve around her lower back, mostly because he'd been moved when she'd been so upset last night, so filled with despair that she couldn't hug him. It was one of the reasons he'd wanted to sleep next to her, so she'd be comforted.

So he would.

His hand thought about wandering down to her ass, but he only aligned her a little closer, very gently, under his arm.

Marriage to her could work. He knew it could. He only had to make her see that.

She looked up at him, wary of this casual affection. Uncertain what it meant.

He wanted to kick himself for ever going along with keeping their affair a secret. For only coming together with her in passion, not basic companionship.

"This is good, you know. This injury of yours." He nodded at her sling.

She choked. "Oh, yeah. That's what I've been thinking this whole time. It's great."

"I mean that it's good we can't fall back on having sex to avoid talking about things that are hard." He closed one eye in a wince. "I heard it as I said it."

She chuckled, but stepped away. She always stepped away.

"Do you *want* sex?" She was looking at the water, not letting him see her eyes as she spoke with breezy but vague interest.

"With you? Always. I would think that was obvious." A waver of uncertainty tipped into his chest. Everything he'd been thinking in the last few minutes slid down into a jumbled pile. Maybe he'd killed whatever she'd felt toward him when he'd quit on her so summarily in Gibraltar. "You?" he asked.

She drew a deep sigh and let it go, like a balloon deflating. "Yes."

"You're so good for my ego," he muttered, but she was very grounding, never letting him take himself too seriously. "What I'm saying is, titillating as the clandestine hookups were, it's good that it's not an option right now. We'll have to use our words."

"Ew. No, thank you." She cast him a grimace.

"Coward."

"It's my deepest, darkest secret. Now you know."

She wasn't a coward. That he knew. But she was afraid. Afraid of being alone, afraid of having no say over herself or her future, afraid of revealing her heart.

Looking at her was like looking at a cracked, distorted reflection of himself.

"Come." He jerked his head. "Let's go wash your hair. It will be fun. Like a team-building exercise." Maybe they couldn't make love, but he would still get to touch her.

"Are you saying hair washing is something you do with your executives at retreats?"

"Before the pillow fight and s'mores, yes. Let's go."

It took them longer to figure out the "how" than it would take to actually wash her hair, but eventually Quinn found herself propped on a padded bench pushed up against the edge of a claw-foot tub.

Rolled towels softened the curved lip of the cast iron so she was as comfortable as it was possible to be with her head hanging back into the tub and a shirtless Micah leaning over her, hairy chest inches from her face.

"Is that too hot?" He used the handheld spray nozzle to wet her hairline.

"It's fine." She closed her eyes, but she could smell traces of aftershave emanating from his jaw and discerned the heat of his skin radiating toward her.

He took his time dampening her hair, picking up the length and squeezing the water through it before he squirted some lime-and-sea-breeze-scented shampoo onto his palm.

What on earth was he doing? He smoothed the shampoo across her wet hair in little dabs, then gently began rubbing it into the tresses before piling it all together while he slowly worked up a lather. She was never this fussy. Soak, scrub, go. She used whatever was on sale when it was time to buy shampoo, combed it out and let it air-dry.

"Oh," she murmured as he began a swirling massage with his fingertips against her scalp.

"Did that hurt? *Did* you bump your head yesterday?"

"No, it feels really good," she murmured. "How do you know how to do this?"

"It's what they do when I get my hair cut." His thumbs worked against her temples.

"Your barber does this?"

"I've started seeing a woman in Berlin."

She snapped her eyes open.

"She gets in here…" His strong fingers dug into the tension at the base of her skull while she stared at his Adam's apple.

As tension released, she groaned, "Oh my God," and let her eyes flutter closed again.

"You're a train wreck, aren't you?" He tenderly attacked the muscles in the back of her neck, using the soap like oil to lubricate the long strokes of his fingers against the tendons before he edged back toward her scalp and turned her whole body into melted wax.

She wallowed blissfully, finally compelled to tell him, "This is better than sex."

"You're making the same sounds."

"Don't make this weird."

"You started it."

She kept her eyes closed, but smiled. She liked when they were like this, when his hands were on her and their jabs at each other were playful and teasing.

When he began to rinse out the shampoo, he asked quietly, "Will you tell me something?"

She opened her eye, suspicious. "Is this still a pajama party? You're supposed to say 'truth or dare' first."

"I dare you to tell me the truth."

"Cheater. What?"

"How many homes were you in?"

She clamped her eyes closed. "Why do you want to know?"

"I don't know." He began to work a tingling, brightly scented conditioner into her hair. "I've been thinking about how angry I was with Remy. I did blame him when I thought I was finally going to live with my mother and sister only to wind up back at boarding school, but the reality is, I didn't hate boarding school. At least I wasn't living with my father or my grandparents. I was in the same boat as the rest of the boys. They were mostly the same boys, year after year, so I knew what I was going back to. I imagine it's harder to walk into someone's home and be the only new person, to have to figure out what the rules and dynamics are. I've been wondering how many times you were put through that."

"It's not that hard once you're used to it. Use your manners, do your chores, finish your homework. Probably all the same rules you had to abide by." She kept her eyes firmly closed to hide that it had been a hellscape of anxiety, every single time.

"So you don't want to tell me?"

"Eleven." *It's just a number*, she told herself, but it felt very damning, as though it marked her in some way. If someone had truly wanted her, she would have had a home for more than a year and two hundred and fourteen days, which was her record for her longest stay anywhere.

If she could have, she would have sat up, but she was stuck in this position, tied by his hands buried in her hair, unable to get away from his tender touch or relentless curiosity.

"From the time you were how old?"

"Four."

His fingers stopped, then restarted.

"At least my mother lived with me until I was six. I still saw her a couple of times a year and talked to her often. What happened to your parents?"

"Boating accident. My grandmother was babysitting me when it happened." She rushed through the details. "She couldn't raise me. She was really old. I saw her sometimes, at first. Then she died."

"There was no other family?"

"None that wanted me."

He swore under his breath. "I'm sorry, Quinn. That's really rough."

"It is what it is." She had had to accept that. "Sometimes my birthday wish was to stay in the house I was in, sometimes it was to leave. Eventually, I realized it didn't matter what I wanted. Things happened the way they happened regardless."

That's why she was so obsessed with having her own say over her life. That's why she wanted to fix systems that continued to push children around like objects rather than people.

Micah didn't say anything as he rinsed her hair squeaky-clean. He dabbed the droplets of water from her cheeks and forehead, then wrapped her hair in a towel before he helped her sit up.

"Stay there," he said when she started to stand. "I'll comb it out."

"You don't have to." She was feeling very weak and shaky despite only lying there, passive.

"I want to."

She would struggle to do it herself, but she was feeling very exposed. No one had ever wanted her. That was her real, deep dark painful secret.

She made a joke to deflect from how raw she was. "You really do have fantasies about being at a girls' pajama party, don't you?"

"Every heterosexual male does, I assure you," he drawled, settling behind her on the bench, splayed knees bracketing her hips.

As he set the comb against her hairline, she said, "Pro tip, start at the bottom. Otherwise, I'll have a rat's nest here." She chopped into the back of her neck.

He did and she watched him in the mirror. His expression was intent as he carefully picked the tangles from the tails of her hair.

"Do you know what I keep thinking about?" he asked as the comb climbed higher.

"I think we've established it's pajama parties."

"Besides that." His expression was very solemn. "I keep thinking about when you said yesterday that I was so rich I could afford to throw away one sister and get another." His gaze crashed into hers in their reflection. "How much do you hate me for having two when you don't have any?"

"I don't." She dropped her lashes, throat cinching tight. "I'm just jealous."

"Don't be." He squeezed her good shoulder and set his forehead against the back of her damp hair, as though hiding from his own reflection. From his conscience. "I still don't know what to think of it. Her. I think about you, wishing you had even one sister, and I know I should welcome this news, but I'm deeply ambivalent. And embarrassed that I feel this way."

"Oh, Micah." She cupped his jaw, urging him to lift his face as she turned her head to look at him over her shoulder. "You're allowed to have feelings. And they don't all have to be neatly organized and pretty."

His mouth twisted. "Are you sure? I thought it was our thing that we didn't allow those messy, unpleasant things."

"It's *my* thing to refuse to do that. You can."

"Mmm." His mouth pulled to one side in dark humor. It was such a nice mouth. Vaguely wicked in the way the corners were so sharp while his bottom lip was full and carnal.

She licked her own lips, inviting…

"We're not supposed to do that, either," he chided softly.

His attention was on her mouth, though, she saw when she glanced into his black-coffee irises.

"It's just a kiss." She twisted a little more.

He met her halfway.

And yes, this was what they did so they didn't have to suffer the agony of existence, but the agony was always right here, buzzing in her lips, filling her with yearning. It was in the groan that rumbled deep in his chest as he slanted his head and captured her lips more fully.

It was in her shoulder, when she instinctually started to twist and reach for him. Lightning shot through her left side. She jolted and sat straight, breath zinging in her lungs.

"Okay?" His hand splayed on her waist, ready to catch her if she tipped.

"No more spin the bottle," she said in a strained voice. "I think it's time for popcorn and a movie."

A pause of surprise, then, "What do you want to watch?"

"Something where teenagers beat the system by dancing."

"I'll assume that's a dare," he drawled. "I'll go along because I'm a good sport. Also, you're due for another painkiller so I assume you'll fall asleep ten minutes in."

It was twenty, but he watched to the end because she was leaned against him and he didn't want to wake her.

# CHAPTER NINE

THE NEXT FEW days passed in a blur, probably because Quinn napped more often than a newborn.

When she wasn't sleeping, she was arguing with Micah—and losing.

"Set up this phone for yourself," Micah said, handing her the latest model, still in its box. She'd started shopping for a refurbished one, but he said, "You and Eden text too much for me to be the middleman."

Her mistake was in acquiescing to that, not wanting to be a nuisance. He seemed to take that as a green light because more goods quickly arrived.

"Your laptop is too old for the latest dictation software," he said when a young man turned up with a new one and wanted to configure it for her. There was also a headset and an adorable little dictation recorder that Quinn secretly fell in love with, especially after the tech showed her how easy it was to speak her notes into it, then set it to auto-type into a document while she walked away.

She would have stopped there, but Micah ordered clothes.

"You need things that are easy to manage," he said, as if she was the unreasonable one when he had hired a stylist who brought a selection of original pieces from *Milan*. "You're in no shape to sift through boutiques, trying things on. When you're feeling better you can buy your own things. Let Antoinette outfit you for now."

Quinn did tire very quickly, and her best clothes had been donated to the hospital incinerator. Aside from pajamas, she had a pair of holey jeans that she couldn't fasten and a T-shirt that claimed feminism was her second favorite F-word. The new clothes *were* easy and comfortable, so she gave in.

Then the private nurse arrived.

"Are you kidding me? I don't need a private nurse," she marched into his den to inform him, leaving the middle-aged woman blinking in confusion behind her. "Sorry," she added over her shoulder. The woman seemed perfectly nice and must think Quinn was extremely ungrateful. "He didn't tell me he had hired you," she explained, then turned back to Micah. "*Why* did you ask her to come?"

"You said you were tired of the sponge baths. I would be happy to help you bathe, if that's what you prefer." His steady look promised to soap all nooks and crannies very thoroughly.

She didn't bother calling his bluff because she knew it wasn't one. Instead, she blushed to the ends of her hair and thanked the woman for her patience when she helped her in and out of the tub.

By the time Dr. Fabrizio pronounced her "healing nicely," Quinn was feeling a lot better. Her shoulder was tender and still needed to remain immobile, but the worst of her bruises and scrapes were fading. She switched to an over-the-counter painkiller, which meant she was more alert and she was permitted one short glass of wine with dinner.

Thus, she felt confident saying, "I can take a train to Vienna," when Micah's housekeeper was dispatched to pack her new clothes into her new luggage. Granted, that would all be tricky to manage on her own, but Micah was flying to Berlin. "Berlin is completely out of my way." And would keep her in his.

"We have the awards banquet." He glanced up from sliding his laptop into his leather bag. "If you think you're up for traveling alone to Vienna, you should be able to sit through a dinner and a handful of speeches— which will sap my strength, I'll grant you."

He was looking ridiculously gorgeous as usual. His crisp bone-colored trousers held a break over his Italian loafers. The sleeves of a matching pullover were draped over his pale blue shirt and tied beneath his open collar. The front spikes of his hair were bent under the weight of his sunglasses and his jaw was smooth from recently shaving.

"We'll stay the night in Berlin, then carry on to Vienna tomorrow afternoon. Which reminds me, I'll want this hard drive if I'm working from there." He used his thumbprint to open a safe behind his desk.

"You're coming to Vienna? I thought you spent all your time in Berlin these days."

"We're building a new head office there so I've been on hand, but it's a quick flight if I'm needed. Why?" He paused to take in her reaction. "Would you prefer to be alone in Vienna?"

"It's your house, Micah. I'm not going to say when you can or can't stay in it. I just presumed we'd go our separate ways once I left here." She examined a hangnail.

He came to the front of his desk and leaned his hips there, arms folded as he regarded her. "I presumed we'd spend the next few weeks seeing where this relationship takes us."

Alarm leaped through her blood.

"We don't have a relationship. We can't. You live here, I live seven thousand kilometers that way." She thumbed over her shoulder without any sense of whether it was west or not.

"Let me say it differently," he said with flinty equanimity. "I would like to spend the next few weeks coming to a shared understanding of what this relationship is. For instance, this has been like old times, having you under my roof in the summer. Is that how you'd like it to remain?"

"With me freeloading off of you? I mean, sure, if that's what floats your boat."

"Don't do that, Quinn," he said very chillingly. "I give you what I'm comfortable giving. I wouldn't do it if I didn't want to. There's no obligation on your side, no catch, and no judgment on you for accepting."

"It's not a cup of coffee, Micah. These things are expensive." Even the laptop bag he'd given her, which he'd told her was pre-owned, was vintage Chanel. It was quilted denim with gold stitching and had a number of practical pockets within. She'd coveted it too much to refuse.

"They're just things," he dismissed.

"And that's all you're comfortable giving me?" She thought she was being very clever with that lofty remark, but as her gaze clashed with his, his eyes narrowed.

"Along with my time, yes, which I assure you I never waste. Are you prepared to give me yours?"

Her heart quivered in her chest. She did want more time with him. She had been dreading saying goodbye, thinking at least when he'd walked away from her in anger, she hadn't had to fight to keep her composure in front of him. It had been the proverbial bandage torn off without ceremony.

Spending weeks with him in Vienna would be a slow, painful peeling that would take some skin, she knew it would.

"Why does it bother you when I give you things?" he asked quietly. "I still remember all those clothes going back, you know. Why did you do that? Because I had the temerity to point out you were too young for an affair with me?"

"No. Because—" He'd been furious over the nightclub debacle with Remy. She'd thought he blamed her for it. But yes, she had also been furious over his calling her a child.

It went even deeper than that, though.

"Because you don't have to take care of me." It was really hard to say that, given that he'd been taking really good care of her this week. She genuinely didn't know how she would have managed if he hadn't, but, "You're not the first to want to rescue me from my hard luck story, you know. That's why I don't tell it. I don't want to get used to this, Micah." Did he even realize the level of wealth and privilege he possessed? What a seduction it was for someone like her?

"My entire childhood was a parade of being given things that I started to care about only for them to get left behind as I was moved around. I can't let myself want things or care about them." The same went for people. "Everything disappears eventually. Nothing is permanent." No one was. Not Eden. Not him. "It's better when I end things on my own terms."

She would have crossed her arms if the one wasn't trapped in her padded sling. She used the other to press against the ache in her stomach.

"Use them while you're here, then. If you don't want to take them when you leave, then don't." He turned to zip his laptop bag, giving her the impression he would be deeply insulted if she returned everything again. Maybe even hurt.

When he turned back, his expression was bland. "But I'd like you to come to Berlin and the ceremony. Will you?"

Her mouth was too unsteady to form words. She nodded once, jerkily.

Because she wasn't ready to say goodbye yet.

Quinn had stayed in Micah's Greek villa, his château in Switzerland, his mansion in Paris and recently his lakeside villa in Bellagio. Flying in his private jet was also something she'd done, although this one was new.

"Smaller, faster and greener," he dismissed with a shrug.

It was still very sumptuous with its ivory-and-chrome decor. A curved sofa was tucked into a corner that otherwise hid the galley. A dining table between two comfortable chairs had the pattern of a chessboard inlaid upon its top. Abstract art and soft pillows added splashes of color and the crew was as courteous as ever.

All of that should have prepared her for his apartment in Berlin, but it was simply too modern and space-aged for her to keep her gasp of astonishment to herself.

Two walls of windows were slanted upward to a peak

on the upper floor. A winding staircase made of chrome and glass slithered like quicksilver down to the main floor where the open concept was situated around a central fireplace. All the furnishings were sleek and contemporary and inviting. Outside on the terrace, an infinity pool glowed blue while the fading day turned the Berlin skyline mauve.

"I have some appointments. Ask Olga for anything you need." He had already introduced her to the housekeeper. "Your stylist will be here in two hours to help you get ready."

"My stylist? I thought this thing was for engineers and computer programmers. How formal is it? I only have what you've bought me so far." Terror was creeping in on her. She had thought the pleated skirt with a light jacket would be business-casual enough for the event.

"It's become quite splashy in recent years," he said with a fatalistic shrug. "The organizers began recognizing music video and cinema technologies alongside the architecture and automations so it garners more interest from the press. There will be a handful of celebrities presenting and accepting awards so there's a red carpet."

"And I have to walk it? With this?" She waved at the sling.

"Your stylist is bringing a selection of gowns. She knows your taste and your situation. I'm sure you'll find something that works. I have to run. I'll see you in a couple of hours." He touched a kiss to her slack lips and disappeared.

She panic-texted Eden, who called and did a poor job of relieving the sense of pressure.

"I think it's nice you two are going on a date."

"It's not a *date*," Quinn cried. "Why would you say

that? Have you been talking to him about me?" She narrowed her eyes in suspicion.

"No. We texted about Mama's birthday the other day, but otherwise I've only been texting with you. What do you think tonight is, if not a date?"

"Bring Your Houseguest to Work Day," she cried, but her stylist arrived so they switched to Eden helping her choose a gown. They signed off when it was time for Quinn to have her hair and makeup done.

Quinn was not a girlie girl in the sense that Eden was, enjoying high fashion and cosmetics and complex hairstyles. Thankfully, her stylist did have a good sense of her tastes. She kept her makeup subtle and only set her hair so her wild curls fell in orderly ringlets. After that was done, she helped her into a strapless silk gown with a flattering princess cut that flared around her feet. A matching plum stole was a genius touch that allowed her to drape it around her upper arms and across her sling.

Nervously, she put on her shoes—pretty slingbacks that she was able to slip on easily—and carefully walked down the stairs, holding the rail and watching her step.

When she finally glanced up, she realized Micah had been standing below the whole time, watching her descend like a little fawn on its newborn legs.

She paused and clutched the rail tighter, feeling even weaker under the impact of his attention. It was such an intense blast, it nearly blew back her hair. It definitely left her heart tripping unsteadily. *He* did.

"I thought you were still in your room, changing." He was already in a tuxedo, freshly shaved and so flawless and casually sexy, she had to ask helplessly, "Why do you always look so good?"

His head went back slightly, as if the question didn't register.

"Probably because I wasn't allowed to leave my room unless I passed muster," he finally answered.

That took her aback. "What do you mean?"

"My grandmother was very fastidious about appearance. If she noticed one hair out of place, I was sent back upstairs. Sometimes that worked to my advantage. If I didn't want to go to a particular dinner or opera, I dripped some toothpaste on my shirt. Sometimes I missed something I wanted to attend, though. I learned to keep it tight."

"What kinds of things?" she asked with concern, recalling asking him if his father had been abusive. Apparently, the whole family was pretty heartless. "Birthday parties?"

"Science exhibits."

"Well, that's the cutest thing I've ever heard." She bit the inside of her lip to hide her amusement. "I often forget you're nothing but algorithms and load-span calculations under those bespoke suits."

"And spreadsheets. I do love detailed analysis." The way his gaze drifted over her told her exactly what kind of sheets he was referring to.

She blushed and chuckled, making herself finish descending the stairs, but her knees were not quite steady.

"You look beautiful," he said, gaze still drinking her in. "I mean, you're always beautiful, but—" He paused as she made a noise of skepticism. His brows rose imperiously. He came closer and tilted up her chin, forcing her to look him in the eye. "Strawberries and cream is my favorite dessert." His thumb caressed her cheek. "It doesn't have to be served in fine china for me to want to eat it, but when it is, I certainly appreciate the presentation."

She was trying to work up a snappy retort, but the housekeeper was bringing someone in from the foyer.

"Ah. This is Hans Gunter and he has something else I hope you'll wear. It's for a good cause," he assured her as Hans offered a large flat purple velvet box. "This necklace will be auctioned off in a few weeks to benefit an organization that helps children displaced by natural and man-made disasters."

The pendant was a cushion-cut purple amethyst surrounded by white-gold filigree with diamond accents. It came with a script about the auction. Apparently, Hans would shadow her throughout the evening to ensure its safety, but what was she going to do? Say no to helping children?

She turned and let Micah clasp the weighty stones around her neck.

A short while later, she was on Micah's arm, walking the red carpet, overwhelmed by all the shouting and camera flashes.

A microphone was shoved in her face and a vaguely familiar celebrity asked her, "Who are you wearing tonight?"

"The gown is from House of Lakshmi, the necklace is from the Barsi group. The sling is by prescription," she deadpanned.

That caused a ripple of laughter in the gallery and another flurry of flashes, but she and Micah were finally allowed to enter the building. The rest of the evening was sedate by comparison. Micah had ensured that everyone at their table spoke English and one was the wife of his project manager who worked at the Canadian embassy here in Berlin, which was a thoughtful touch on his part.

They ate and awards were presented, then the lights changed and the orchestra switched to ballroom tunes.

"Shall we?" Micah held out a hand. "We missed our chance at Eden's wedding to Hunter."

Quinn was so shocked by his saying that, as if he'd been looking forward to dancing with her, she let him lead her into the growing crowd. Once there, she had to admit, "I don't really know how to do this." She felt awkward with her one arm fixed in the sling and his searching for her waist beneath it.

"Let me lead." He shifted them slightly so one side of her body was pressed closer to his, then he easily guided her through the steps.

With him, anything physical was easy. Natural. As though they were made to move together in coordination.

"Thank you for coming tonight," he said. "Everyone is completely charmed by you."

Charmed? That was laying it on thick, but a short while later, one of his executives subtly prodded for details of their relationship.

"I don't think I've ever seen him bring a date to one of these things. Usually it's his assistant or a VIP from elsewhere."

Quinn started to brush that off and insist she was "just a friend of his sister," but stopped herself. It felt demeaning toward him and maybe herself to pretend they meant nothing to each other. What *did* they mean to each other, though?

She couldn't speak for his feelings. Passion, obviously, but she was always throwing herself at him. The fact that he didn't take other lovers, or seem to date anyone else, was heartening, but he was a busy man. It didn't follow that he preferred her in some way.

He was decent enough not to lead anyone on, though. And kind enough to spend a night in hospital with her. He was generous, but possessed enough acuity to know she would rather use the cost of a necklace to help children than own such an extravagant piece herself. Not that he would buy it for her in the first place. They weren't *that* tight.

But they were close enough he knew how to make her laugh. He made her feel a lot of things.

Oh, dear. As she struggled to close her clutch over the pearlescent pink lipstick she had just refreshed, she blinked hot eyes, fearful she was falling in love with him. No. She had always loved him, of course, in the way of an adolescent crush and "my best friend's brother" way. She had always trusted him and admired him and found him deeply attractive.

Somewhere along the line, she had managed to convince herself that she could feel all those things and keep those feelings in safe little boxes that wouldn't swish and leak into each other and flood her up with other more dangerous emotions like yearning and insatiable hunger for his attention. Like an attachment that needed to see him and hear his voice and touch him every single day.

*No, Quinn. No. Everything ends.* Everything.

Disturbed, she returned to the ballroom where he asked if she wanted to dance again.

"Do you mind if we leave? I'm ready to give up custody of this necklace."

The bodyguard signed for it the moment they returned to Micah's apartment, then left them alone.

"Nightcap?"

"No." She was still shaken at how her emotions were running away with her. She was at war with herself, wanting to self-protect, but also thinking that if things were going to end between them sooner rather than later, she wanted to make the most of the time they had.

"Tired?"

"No. I— Will you come to my room?" she asked in a request that left her standing out on a narrow plank.

He went still, not playing dumb, only saying solemnly, "I thought we weren't going to do that."

"I don't want to find words." There weren't any, not for all the emotions swirling in her. They were too vast and disarming. "I just want you."

Even saying that much left her walking a tightrope suspended between skyscrapers.

He ambled closer, exuding intensity and sexual tension. Gravity. His light touch on her jaw was almost electric, making her want to jolt away from a sting that wasn't there. At the same time, she wanted to fold in closer to him. She wanted his arms around her, sheltering her.

"Do I need a condom?"

"Not on my…" She cleared her throat, staring at the ruffles of his shirt. "I haven't been with anyone else."

"That means something, you know." His hand cupped the side of her neck, hot and heavy. He waited for her gaze to slowly climb to his. "We've seen each other nine times in four years and never slept with anyone else."

"You keep count?" He could probably feel her carotid artery pounding with her elevated pulse against the heel of his palm.

"You don't?"

Of course she did.

His thumb grazed her jaw. "I keep count of what counts, Quinn."

*It's just sex*, she wanted to argue, but she wasn't capable of just sex. She was realizing that as he dipped his head and brushed a soft kiss across her lips, once.

"Come to my room," he said in a low rumble.

"Why?"

"Because I want you in my bed." He took her hand and drew her up the stairs.

Her eyes were stinging. So was her throat. This was silly. They'd done this before. She wanted to make love with him. There was no reason to feel nervous, but she was suddenly clinging tightly to his hand so she wouldn't slip on the stairs. So she wouldn't slip up and let her heart show.

His room was the top of the spaceship, the walls and ceiling made of angled windows. The space was enormous, accommodating a massive bed and full sitting area. Toward the back, the shower was a huge cubicle in the middle of the room. One side was tiled and plumbed, the other open to the sunlight that would soak down from the windows. A freestanding tub stood nearby, close to the doors to the private terrace. The double doors to a walk-in closet were open; the single closed door likely led to the toilet.

He touched something on the wall and panels inside all of the glass panes began to lower, enclosing them in privacy.

*It's an intriguing place to visit, but this is not your world*, she reminded herself wistfully as she began to draw her stole free from its tuck against her sling.

Micah made a noise of protest. "Let me. I've been mentally undressing you all night."

She gave him an admonishing look as he carefully tugged the silk, slithering it across her bare shoulders in a way that caused her skin to roughen with goose bumps and her nipples to rise against the cups of her strapless bra.

"Don't worry. I admired other things about you." He sent the swatch of silk drifting toward a chair and moved behind her.

"Such as?" she prompted, cringing slightly that she was reduced to fishing for compliments.

"How easily you make people laugh." His fingers tickled her spine and her gown began to release. "I've always been envious of that."

Envious? It was a defense mechanism she had developed to avoid being picked on. He didn't need tricks like that because he had all of this.

He also had wide hands that slid into her open gown and caressed her waist and hips, making her stomach muscles quiver while her brain blanked.

Cool silk brushed her thighs as it fell, but he didn't let her step out of it. He stayed behind her, roaming his light touch across her skin, finding the lace of her silver bra and matching cheekies. His touch seemed a random map until she realized each pause of his touch was extra sensitive because he was trying to erase her bruises with the brush of his fingertip.

"Are you sure you're up for this?" he murmured.

"Yes." She was already shaking with anticipation. Surely he could see that.

"I'll be careful with you," he promised in a voice that rasped across her senses. He set his mouth against her nape, hot enough to brand her skin.

She lifted her hand, wanting to touch him, but she

could only sift her fingertips through his hair as he placed more of those tender kisses across her shoulders and spine.

She had missed him, missed touching him. Being naked and close and awash in the kind of pleasure that erased all the pain of living.

His mouth opened and he scraped his teeth on the taut tendon in her neck, making her gasp.

"I like that," he said, wrapping his arm around her stomach to draw her back into the rough-soft textures of his tuxedo. "I live for the way we react to each other."

"Be careful of the gown," she said, aware of it piled around their shoes, but he slid his hand into the front of her underpants and she lost her voice.

She held still, afraid of trampling the gown, erotically trapped in the cage of his arms. Trapped between the wall of his clothed body and the blatant caress of his fingertip teasing her lips apart, seeking moisture and spreading it. As he lazily tantalized the knot of nerves, she shivered and turned her head, searching for his mouth.

He only teased her with a kiss on her cheek and the corner of her lips. "Tell me what you want," he said in that wicked grate of a voice. "Tell me when you're close."

"I am," she moaned, lifting her hips into his touch, then rocking back to grind into the erection prodding through his trousers at her backside. "Harder. Don't stop," she pleaded.

His arm around her shifted. He avoided her sling and slid his touch to cup her breast. While his thumb pressed her nipple through her bra, his other hand continued to circle and delicately torture her until she lost her ability to breathe. Lovely shudders washed over her, weakening her knees.

He held her in strong arms, mouth pinned to her neck where he left a sting and a rueful curse a moment later.

"I've just added to your bruises." He kissed the damp spot. "I thought I was going over with you."

She was dizzy and blinking herself back to reality, barely tracking as he released her bra and dropped her underwear, then guided her to the bed where he sat her on the edge to remove her shoes.

He stayed there on his knees while he kissed her a long time, until she was clinging her good arm around his shoulders and nearly off the bed and into his lap, she was so eager to be close to him. She wanted the hair of his chest on her breasts, the hot shape of his sex against her mound. She wanted their mouths sealed and their legs intertwined.

She couldn't touch enough of him, couldn't get close enough, darn this wretched sling!

"Don't do that," he admonished, misconstruing her noise of anguish. "I said I'd be careful with you and I will." He nuzzled against the strap of her sling where it sat above her breast, then flashed her a look of lusty amusement. "I kind of like this bondage situation that forces you to be still while I have my way with you."

"It turns you on?" She tried to sound disparaging, but wicked excitement tightened her nipples and sent a fresh wash of heat into the juncture of her thighs.

"It really does." He reached for a couple of pillows and stacked them behind her, urging her to recline on them while he stayed on the floor and ran his free hand over her stomach and thighs, then up to her breast. He cupped one and leaned to give her nipple a lascivious lick. "I'm going to kiss every inch of you and you're going to lie there and take it."

For some reason, that scared the hell out of her. Not that she felt genuinely helpless. She knew he would stop if she told him to, but the way he picked up her hand and set his lips on the inside of her wrist, then trailed kisses to her elbow made her shake. It was too tender. Too sweet. It made her feel special and cherished and she *wasn't*.

But she wanted to be. She wanted this shower of care and attention. She drank it in like a desert cactus soaked up rain after a hundred years' drought.

"Micah." She tried to caress his erection and tease him into the same blind lust that was gripping her, but he shifted, leaving her breasts and collarbone for the tremulous territory of her navel. "I really want you inside me."

"I want that, too." He nipped the point of her hip. "I can't wait to feel you gripping and shattering around me. But look how pretty you are." His one hand plumped her breast and he rose to suck her nipple again.

Lightning shot between her legs. She tried to press her thighs together, but he was in the way. There was no relief.

He sent her a knowing look and dipped a little lower, touching his mouth to her loosely curled hand where it stuck out of the sling. His tongue prodded at the seam of her fingers, right below her knuckle, and another wave of heat washed through her.

"You're being…" She couldn't think words.

"Thorough?" He moved to touch kisses all across her quivering abdomen, then rubbed one side of his face and the other like a giant cat who seemed to be affectionate, but was actually leaving his scent on her skin. Such a possessive male.

With casual strength, he lifted her knee, tipping her more fully into the pillows behind her as he parted her legs so he could kiss the inside of one thigh.

She had never felt so much his. *Claimed.* Her loins pulsed with longing, but he teased his attention all the way down her calf before kissing and caressing his way up her other leg, driving her mad with want.

Only when her legs were shaking and she thought she would die if he didn't penetrate her did he hiss in a breath of tested control. He left her weak and sprawled on the pillows while he rose to shed his own clothes without ceremony, revealing his muscled chest and the hair bisecting his tense abdomen. The pale skin behind his boxer briefs appeared along with the steely thrust of his erection.

"I could—"

"I would kill for that, I really would, but I need to be inside you, Quinn." He slid onto the bed and drew a pillow close, inviting her to spoon in front of him so her injured shoulder could sit on the pillow, elevated and protected.

"I want to touch you," she sobbed even as she maneuvered into a position that should have felt awkward, but was actually really comfortable.

"Poor you," he crooned without any mercy whatsoever. "I get to touch you however I want." He slid his splayed hand across her hip and down her thigh, adjusting her leg as he settled closer in behind her. Then he guided his tip between her thighs, searching out her aching core. "This is how I want you to hold me. When you're tight around me, I think I'm going to die from how good it feels."

"Yes." Her voice throbbed. "Do it."

A rough noise escaped him and he shifted slightly, gaining leverage to press inside her.

She tried to hold herself still for him, but she was shaking with arousal. Utterly boneless and weak with wanting.

Rising on his elbow behind her, he surged his hips against her backside. She arched, trying to accept more of his thick, hot presence within her. She wanted it fast and hard, but this position left all the power up to him.

"Softly," he whispered against her cheek. "You know I'll wait for you. Relax and let me make it good for you."

He was talking about an orgasm, but his words went straight into her heart, past all her firmest defenses. Tears of yearning sprang to the backs of her eyes so she had to close them tight. It was her only way to hide, but there was no hiding from the exquisite sensation of his flesh dragging and resurging into her. He moved with gentle, lazy power, sending wave after wave of joy through her. He was generous and patient and determined to draw out their pleasure as much as possible.

"Micah!" She clenched her hand in the blanket, feeling as though he was breaking her apart, it was so unbearably good.

"You're so perfect, Quinn," he was crooning, hand playing across her stomach and thighs like a violin with a bow. "How do we ever walk away from this?"

She couldn't answer. She was submerged in a sea of pleasure, rocked by his easy thrusts. His whole body was tense and shaking with the control he was exerting, but he held himself from crushing her as he held himself back from the wild tempo they usually sought.

He held them on the precipice of absolute perfection.

With no other way to express her tortured joy, she groaned out her pleasure.

"I need you," she moaned. "I need you so much." It hurt to say it. To know it was true. To *feel* it. If she wasn't careful, she would give him every last shred of herself.

"I've got you," he murmured, and his touch moved to where she was clamping her slick flesh upon him. He caressed her and suddenly the climax that had been soaring and circling out of reach plunged down like a raptor, swooping and pulling a sharp cry from her lips.

As she tumbled off the cliff, awash in powerful contractions, he pinned his hips to her backside, set his teeth on her earlobe, and released the longest, sexiest groan in history.

# CHAPTER TEN

MICAH HAD ALREADY made up his mind to ask Quinn to marry him before they arrived in Berlin. Waking beside her every day for a week had only reinforced his decision, but he waited for the rings to be sized and catch up to them in Vienna.

This apartment was one of his smaller properties, but also one of his favorites. Built in the 1860s for an industrialist, the exterior melded with Vienna's rich history. The handful of units within were spacious and updated for modern life while Old World touches remained, like parquet flooring and a wine-making operation beneath street level.

When his housekeeper pointed out the courier parcel that had been brought up first thing, he ordered bubbly from his private reserves in the cellar. It went into a bucket next to the breakfast table.

He could have waited until dinner, but twice this week, Quinn had been so caught up in research, she had stayed late. Other times, he heard her through the door between their offices, dictating notes and stumbling into the occasional trouble with them.

"Scratch that. Scratch that. Don't type *scratch that*

you idiotic—stop! End! Quit document you absolute—ahh! *Stop*."

After a late night, however, they'd agreed to have a lazy start today. He was sipping his coffee, reading headlines on his tablet, when she came down the stairs.

She had managed to knot a scarf around the loose corkscrews of her hair and had dressed in wide-legged pants with one of the sleeveless wrap tops she seemed to find so convenient to put on and take off.

"Hungry?" he asked.

"Don't be smug." She was still yawning and blinking, but gave him a smug smile of her own. She was feeling much better these days and last night had been a taste of their previous energetic and adventurous encounters.

"I damned well will be. For once, I left you sleeping. Come here."

She wrinkled her nose at him, but bypassed her own chair to come give him a kiss that tasted of toothpaste.

He resisted the urge to pull her into his lap. Barely. Especially when his gaze found her modest cleavage before she straightened. Those freckles sprinkled across the upper swells of her breasts never ceased to mesmerize him.

"Where are we going today?" she asked as she moved to her chair.

"I thought we decided to walk in the park." He deliberately didn't rise to help her. She was already sinking into it and he was waiting for her to notice what was on her plate.

"Maybe we could visit the—" She cut herself off and stared at the green velvet box. It was open, showing a set of three rings. The two wedding bands were almost identical. His was a wider band of gold, but they both held a stripe of flush-mounted diamonds across the top. The engagement ring was similar, but it held a break where a large square-cut diamond floated, also flush with the rest of the setting so it wouldn't catch easily.

It was clever and understated in its artistry, both beautiful and complex, if one took the time to notice. Like her.

"Before you make a crack about getting your minerals..." Had she gone pale? An uncharacteristic jab of self-doubt shot through him. "I propose we marry."

She closed the box with a snap and set it aside, hand shaking. "Would you pour me a coffee, please?"

Wow. He genuinely felt like he'd been kicked in the face.

He poured, brain going numb. He nodded as the housekeeper peeked in. Seconds later, she brought in the serving dishes filled with a ham and potato hash, eggs in mustard sauce, and an oven-baked pancake sprinkled with powdered sugar and fresh fruit.

"Is that your answer?" he asked when his housekeeper had retreated.

"You already know my answer, Micah. I don't believe in marriage."

"Marriage isn't like Santa Claus. It's not something made up by—"

"The church?" she cut in crisply.

"It's a commitment, not a human rights violation. I won't keep you from having a career, if that's what you're afraid of. Finish your doctorate. I'll support you in every way I can."

"Then what? You'll move to Canada so I can work there?"

He had never seen her as a naive person. "Brace your-

self for a hard truth, Quinn. As admirable as it is that
you want to bring about change in government policy,
that's not where true power lies. Use me. Use my wealth
and position to get the results you want."

Dismay and conflict flexed through her expression.
"Become part of what's most wrong in this world? Is that
why you want to marry me? To keep me from challenging the order that benefits you so much?"

"No," he said flatly, biting back a curse. "It's not that
complicated. I want to marry you so I can wake up next
to you every morning." Most mornings it was a very
pleasant start to his day.

"That is not what you want," she returned hotly, voice
turning strident with anxiety. "I know that your aunt is
after you to marry and secure the family legacy. Eden
told me that ages ago. I'm not going to give you babies,
Micah. *Ever.*"

"I didn't ask you to." He tried not to shorten his tone,
but rejection was not something he suffered often. It
stung, especially from her. Like this. She wasn't even
considering it. "Although I am compelled to point out
there are arrangements like surrogacy."

"It's not just about carrying a pregnancy."

"What then? Because I would love to understand your
aversion. I would think someone without family would
want to make one of her own."

She flashed him a look, one brimming with umbrage
at not being understood before her brow flinched. She
looked past him, mouth briefly working to find words.

"I do think about children sometimes, but I can't get
past…" She stabbed a bite of egg, but left it on her fork,
staring at it sickly. "What if I die? Then I've left a child
to navigate this world alone, the same as I've had to."

His heart flipped over. "Don't say that. You're healthy."

"I was hit by a bicycle. It could have been a car. Life is tenuous."

"Nevertheless, Eden would—"

"I would never ask her to raise my child," she cut in with aversion. "She wants to start her own family with Remy."

"Exactly. She's not afraid of what *might* happen. She's getting on with the business of living."

"And good for her! But they have a wide network of people who would race in to take their baby if something happened to them. I don't have that, Micah. Even if I adopted a child, I would still be running a risk of leaving them with nothing and no one."

"What about me? I have family."

"The family who persecuted your mother into abandoning you? The people who already think I'm not good enough for you? The ones who ostracized you when you misbuttoned your shirt? Those are the people you want raising your child?"

He pressed his lips together, not answering, but she was right. He wouldn't want his child raised by anyone with the last name Gould. Maybe not even himself. Micah viewed his role in this family as a gatekeeper who stopped them from spiraling back into the avarice that had been his father's trademark, but he was always on guard against selfish behaviors of his own.

As for his mother, as much as she would want to raise his child, the stark truth was that she was aging and still grieving the loss of Eden's father. Micah wasn't inclined to write off Eden as quickly as Quinn did, but his sister *would* be having her own children soon. And, as much as Eden's father had welcomed Micah as if he was his own son, the knowledge that Micah wasn't really part of his mother's second family had always been blindingly obvious to him.

"I'm sorry if staying here with you has led you to think I would want this," Quinn said shakily. "I'll—"

"Do not say you are going back to Canada. You are not running away. You want to know why I want to marry you? So you'll have to sit there and work things out with me for a change."

"There's nothing to work out," Quinn insisted, and did walk away.

Quinn's heart was knocked sideways by his proposal. On the one hand, it suggested he had deeper feelings for her than he'd ever let on, but it also felt threatening.

She had promised herself for years that she would never marry. Partly because, as a feminist, she did think marriage was an outdated institution, but, more importantly, as someone who had been dependent on people who didn't really care about her, she couldn't stomach anything but complete self-sufficiency.

That was why she had made such a point of keeping an ocean and every other type of boundary between herself and Micah. At least, she had managed to until this last week when she had become almost completely reliant on him.

Even on an emotional level, she was sliding down a slippery slope.

She further panicked when she arrived in the room they shared. The bed was still mussed from their active night, reminding her of all she would be giving up if she ran away, but she genuinely felt herself in peril.

If she stayed, she would finish falling in love with him. Her heartbreak would be even greater when everything fell apart later so why not leave now, when it was on her terms?

Amid her agitated flitting, trying to work out what to do, her phone pinged with a text.

Yasmine.

Can you call me when you have a minute? Any time is fine.

Worried it had something to do with Remy and therefore Eden, Quinn jabbed the button for a video chat.

"That was fast. Hi! How *are* you?" Yasmine greeted brightly. She wore a colorful scarf over her locks, shimmery gold eyeshadow and violet lipstick. "Remy told me about your shoulder. I thought if you're in a sling, you wouldn't want to type."

"Calling is easier. Thanks." Her heart warmed that Yasmine was so understanding. "So this is a social call? I was worried something was wrong."

"No, I'm fine. Definitely social." A pause, then, "Mostly."

"Oh? Do you need something?"

"No," she insisted. "No, I actually saw your photo on the red carpet in Berlin and I guess I was surprised you were still, um…" Her gaze seemed to search Quinn's through the screen. "Seeing Micah."

"I'm not." Her own voice sounded so high she thought it ought to crack the screen on her phone. "I've been staying with him, but I was thinking about checking flights to Canada today—"

She realized Micah had come to the bedroom door.

She swallowed as she met his grim expression.

"I heard my name. Is that Eden?"

"Yasmine." Her throat dried to a rasp.

His cheek ticked once before he drew the door shut and, presumably, walked back downstairs. Maybe left the apartment and the building and the country.

Oh God.

"Is it bad that we're talking? I didn't mean to start anything between you," Yasmine moaned.

"You didn't. I promise. We're going through our own thing."

"Oh?" That was concern, not lurid curiosity, but Quinn didn't want to get into her own baggage about marriage and family and how very deeply she was hung up on Micah.

"It's nothing. Honestly," Quinn lied.

"How, um… How is he?" Yasmine asked apprehensively. "Remy told me he knows about me. Is that why he walked away? Believe me, I get that he needs time. I wasn't trying to impose myself on him. Oh, maybe I was trying to get his temperature," she acknowledged with a small cringe.

"It's understandable that you're curious," Quinn said faintly.

"I am, but…" She blew out a breath. "Eden mentioned introducing us when he comes to Canada for their mother's birthday. I don't want to put him on the spot like that. And with Remy there, weighing everything we might say to each other? That would be way too much tension for everyone involved. I guess I called you hoping you would tell him I don't expect him to meet me if he doesn't want to."

"I can do that," Quinn promised.

"But if he does want to meet, I would like that," she hurried to say, brow crinkled with distress. "I shouldn't put this on you. Honestly, when I realized you were still in Europe, my first thought was to ask if you want to get coffee sometime. I'm in Paris for a few weeks. Now I feel like I've dumped all over you. I'm sorry."

"Don't apologize! I want to help if I can." Quinn lowered onto the edge of the bed, never wanting to be the one in need, but always a sucker for being needed. "I don't want to speak for Micah or how he feels, but I'll definitely tell him what you've told me. And I would love to get coffee. With or without him."

"Thank you. I would love that."

"I'll get in touch once I've figured some things out."

*"Thank you."*

She was going to check flights?

Micah didn't know who he was angrier with, Quinn or himself. He should have broached marriage as a discussion, not presented her with the rings. He knew she didn't like people making decisions for her. He had thought it would be a romantic surprise, but now he wanted to throw the damned things out the window.

And she was up there talking to Yasmine? About him? He would never tell her who she could be friends with, but that was a slap in the face, it really was.

Not that he could avoid the reality of his secret half sister forever. He had shoved her into a file labeled "later" because it was too hard to look at. Micah's father had been a master of dirty deals, building his fortune on exploited workers and intimidation tactics. He had deliberately taunted Lucille with her access to Micah, using him to punish her for leaving.

Then he'd lost his memory to all of that, succumbing to early onset dementia just as Micah was growing into a full awareness of his father's character flaws.

Only nineteen and not even finished school, his father's allies had thought they could turn Micah into their puppet and pressed him to step into his father's shoes.

Micah hadn't wanted to assume such a soiled heritage, but it was the only way to clean it. The moment he'd been given the seat at the head of the table, he'd begun what was now referred to as the Great Purge. He'd fired back-stabbing cronies and put people like his aunt on notice. He had made clear they could follow him into the new way of doing things—with ethics and transparency—or strike out on their own.

Once everyone understood that he wielded power rather than being seduced by it, they began coming onto his side.

He probably would have fallen in with the old, corrupt ways if he hadn't had his mother's influence and—even more so—his sister's. Lucille refused to come to Europe, but Eden had been Micah's semiannual reward for wading through the muck. He would send for her on school holidays and her spritely energy would remind him there was good in the world. And that it was up to people like him to make sure people like her didn't become cynical and disillusioned.

Then there was Quinn. Had she influenced him? Absolutely. Some of Eden's friends had been the sort of opportunists he was all too familiar with. He'd vetted them and discouraged her from pursuing those friendships, but Quinn had been so ethically solid, she was almost annoying with it. Did she put him on notice every single time he slipped toward patriarchal attitudes? Hell, yes.

She had pushed him to be better. To walk the walk. Slowly, Micah had evolved into a man who was still jaded and cautious, but one who was honest and fair. He might have gone so far as to call himself honorable.

He had believed he had made up for his father's worst transgressions.

Then he learned of Yasmine. She was proof that his father had sunk even lower than Micah could have imagined. How could he not feel the rot of it all over him?

How could he expect Quinn to attach herself to that? Was that the real source of her refusal to marry him?

"Micah?"

He stiffened and tried to curl his hand into a fist in his pocket, but the ring box prevented it. He turned.

She chewed the corner of her lip.

"Yes?" he prompted. If she was leaving, he wanted her to say it, not stand there blinking at him like she had a grim medical diagnosis to impart.

"Yasmine is in Paris. She asked me if I wanted to meet up with her. The invitation includes you."

He snapped his head back, not expecting that.

"There's no obligation," she assured him.

"But you'll meet with her regardless." His sternum turned to rusty iron. He looked to the window again.

"Not necessarily. I wanted to see where your thoughts were." She edged closer, brow pulled with consternation. "She said Eden mentioned introducing you two when you go for Lucille's birthday."

Micah choked out a curse, not ready to participate in *that* family dinner. He loved Eden, he really did, but she was such a glass half-full. If he didn't run through a meadow and catch his long-lost sister in his arms, Eden would be devastated.

"Yasmine thought that was a lot to put on both of you." Quinn's voice was rueful. She knew exactly where Eden's best qualities tipped toward impossible to live up to. She touched his sleeve. "It's completely up to you, but I have to wonder if the prospect of meeting her will hang over both your heads until it's done. I could go with you," she offered gently.

"To Paris?"

"Or somewhere else. What's halfway between Vienna and— Oh. Switzerland." She lifted her brows in discovery. "The great bastion of neutrality."

He twisted his mouth, but he didn't hate the idea. At least it would give him something different to brood about that wasn't Quinn.

"Yes." Even as he nodded, his mind skipped ahead to all the arrangements he'd been contemplating where Yasmine was concerned. "Set it up."

# CHAPTER ELEVEN

QUINN FEARED SHE was prodding Micah onto a plank of some kind.

He became very remote as she and Yasmine took a few days to firm things up. He left for meetings and accepted calls at odd hours and, even though they continued to sleep together, he came to bed late and rose before she woke. He asked about her museum research a couple of times, but she could tell he was only half listening.

Desperate to reach him in some small way, she joined him in the shower the morning they were heading to Zurich. She was allowed to remove her sling for bathing now and had begun some rehabilitation exercises, mostly to ensure the rest of her arm didn't atrophy while her shoulder finished healing.

His whole body went tense as he raked his gaze down her naked form, but he waited until she touched him, pressing her cool body up against his hot, wet one. Then he fell on her like a starving wolf, consuming her lips and pressing her to the tiled wall before he dropped to his knees and pleasured her with his mouth.

She was still weak and dazed from a powerful climax when she realized he was using his fist to take care of his own orgasm, groaning into the spray as he did so.

"Micah." She tried to catch at his shoulder.

"Thank you for that, but—" He cupped her cheek and pressed one hard, wet kiss across her mouth. His eyes didn't meet hers. He looked to be in pain of some sort, but he only said, "We should get on the road. Traffic might be heavy this morning."

With a huff of disbelief, she finished showering alone.

Doubts were firmly entrenched in her by the time they landed in Zurich. Yasmine had suggested a picturesque village not far from the city. It only had cable cars, no real ones. One would carry them up the mountain to a restaurant built into the cliffs.

It had sounded like a pleasant setting that would give them something to talk about so they wouldn't feel pressured to dig through difficult emotions, but Micah had become the most aloof, impossible-to-read version of himself.

Quinn feared Yasmine would take that as dislike or rebuff. Her own palms were sweating, but as the cable car gently swayed on its way up the mountainside, she reached to hold his hand.

For a moment, he didn't react to her touch on the back of his. Then he turned his head to ask distantly, "Why did you come?"

"What do you mean? I said I would."

"But why? To see Yasmine?"

A small sob of helplessness left her. "Why did you come to the hospital even though we'd had a huge fight?"

He grumbled out a noise, but his hand turned to grasp hers. He didn't let go as they took the short walk from the cable car terminus to the restaurant.

Yasmine was seated under a big red patio umbrella

on the terrace. She waved and stood, smiling nervously. Her outfit was vaguely safari inspired, but turquoise with bright yellow palm fronds painted across the fabric. Her makeup was toned down from her usual, but still shimmery and colorful.

"This place is amazing," Quinn said as they briefly embraced. "I'm so glad you recommended it."

"I didn't know how to dress. Am I going for lunch? Are we hiking?" Yasmine turned her heavy boot, then thrust out her hand to Micah. It was visibly trembling. Her dark brown eyes were wary, yet seeking. "Hi. I'm Yasmine."

Quinn held her breath.

"Micah." He took her hand and shook it. Gently. His voice wasn't quite steady and some of his frost melted away so fast, he seemed to flinch at the sting. "It's good to meet you."

In that moment, Quinn knew she was in love with him. Completely, utterly, "tumble all the way to the bottom of the valley" in love.

Micah couldn't have done this without Quinn here.

She made Yasmine laugh and kept the conversation moving. Occasionally, Yasmine asked him a direct question, mostly innocuous things about travel and whether his company did this or that. Twice she uncannily did exactly as he did, once by ordering the same sandwich without cheese—sacrilege in this corner of the world, but like him, she didn't care for it. Then, after lunch, she chose the same hiking trail he preferred.

Granted, there were only three to choose from, but Quinn wanted to go down to the alpine lake.

"Then we have to walk back up," Micah and Yasmine said at the same time.

"I'll go as far as that lookout and take a photo. You two go ahead. I'll catch up."

"Subtle," Micah said as Quinn darted down the path. He resisted the urge to call out that she should hold the rail. She wasn't a child, but he'd be damned if he would let her put herself back in hospital.

"I like her a lot," Yasmine said as they began to stroll along the trail.

"I don't know anyone who doesn't." Except herself, Micah realized with a jolt. Not that Quinn hated herself. She wasn't that twisted, but he didn't think she appreciated how special she was.

"Thank you for coming," Yasmine said with an earnest flash in her gaze. "I know it must have been hard news to hear."

"That my father was a monster? It wasn't news to me that he was one, only the full extent." He paused at a rail that allowed him to see Quinn below, taking photos of the sharp peaks across the valley. "I'm sorry, Yasmine. I'm truly sorry for what he put your mother through. Your whole family. And for how I've behaved at different times, believing my father's version of the past."

"There was no one to tell you differently. My parents hid the truth even from me." Her smile flickered and faltered. "To be fair, my father did actually double-cross yours."

In retaliation for the crime against his wife. Micah didn't blame him for that, especially when Kelvin Gould had made every effort to punish them. Her parents had had to move to Canada to get away from his father's attempts to destroy them financially.

"I want you to know that I've spent the last few days asking my legal and accounting teams for a market value assessment of all that I inherited from my father."

"Oh my God. Micah, no. That's not why I wanted to meet you." She was horrified.

He wasn't surprised by her refusal, but ignored it.

"I know it won't make things right, but it's important to me to try. Your parents might be gone, but your family deserves compensation for what my father put them through. They would have had a different life if my father hadn't made it impossible for them to stay in Paris. And you have certain claims that are rightfully yours. A board seat. We can find a way to appoint someone to vote your share if you don't want to identify yourself to the rest of my family. I completely understand if you would rather not. At some point I'll have to tell them that my father was responsible for another child. They'll want a paternity test, but we can redact your name and all of that can wait until you and I have negotiated the settlement."

"Micah, *please*." Her eyes were boggled. "All of my needs are met. I don't need anything from you."

"It's not from me, Yasmine. It's what he should have done. Don't let him get away with what he did. Don't let the rest of his family blindly continue to benefit from his lack of consequence."

She frowned with consternation, absorbing that.

Quinn finally caught up to them. She was clutching her chest, huffing and puffing. "I forgot about the elevation. That climb nearly killed me."

"We didn't want to be right," Yasmine said, following as Micah steered Quinn toward a nearby bench.

"It just comes naturally?" Quinn suggested pithily, looking between them.

Micah shared a smirk with his sister.

Micah seemed both relaxed yet still keyed up as they returned to Vienna late the next day.

By then, they had sent a group selfie to Eden who had soon replied.

This makes me so happy! It's my new lock screen.

Privately, Eden had messaged Quinn.

When are you going to tell me what's going on between you and Micah?

"Why am I here and not on my yacht?" Micah asked as they started to take a glass of wine onto the terrace only to be chased back inside by the dry city heat.

"Don't let me hold you back." Now that the visit with Yasmine was out of the way, the argument they'd had the morning over the rings seemed to flood back in and fill the room.

"You need to know something." Micah eyed her over the rim of his glass as he took a healthy gulp.

"What?" She froze part way to seating herself on the sofa.

"I've made a decision." He moved to top up his glass. "I'm not going to make children, either."

"What—? That's a pretty big decision, especially for a man in your position. And there's no danger for you, physically. Unless you're concerned something of your father would be replicated in your child? You and Yasmine both turned out to be kind, upstanding human beings. I think his behavior was more nurture than nature. Don't feel like you have to nip off your branch. I don't think it's diseased."

"I'm not suggesting that. Yasmine can have all the kids she wants and they can inherit an appropriate share of the company. That's fair and right. But I told her she shouldn't let my family benefit from the fact that my father never suffered the consequences of his actions. I meant it. If my aunt wants so badly to see her brother's bloodline continue, she can ask Yasmine very nicely if she's willing to do so, but I won't produce children for the sole purpose of ensuring his DNA maintains possession of all he acquired. That's wrong."

"You could have children because you want them," she pointed out. "And they just happen to inherit all this. You feel one way now, but you don't know how you'll feel in the future."

"Excuse me, Quinn," he said with heavy irony. "But are you trying to say I'm not capable of knowing my own mind and making my own decisions around reproduction?"

She bit her lip, chastised, but amused. "You know I hate it when you throw my own words back at me."

"That's why I do it." He took another generous swallow from his frosted glass. "It's not as impulsive as it sounds. The pressure from my aunt has always bothered me, probably because you've drilled into me what an archaic system progeniture is. My own father didn't want to be a father. He accidentally got my mother pregnant and married her because his mother said she might be carrying his potential heir. *Potential*. If I'd been a girl, there would have been a quiet divorce and she would have been raised in Canada with a lot less baggage to carry around and none of the responsibility I shoulder. Then, because I was his heir, my father used that fact to push my mother out of my life. She wasn't deemed good enough to 'prepare' me for this life. Can you imagine what sort of sociopath I would be if I hadn't had her and Eden? So no. I refuse to make children knowing they would have to bear the weight of these same expectations."

She watched him pace a few steps, not knowing what to say.

"Having said that…" He paused and looked straight at her. "If you wanted to foster or adopt, I'd be open to it. I think you'd make an incredible mother. I don't know what kind of father I'd make, though. Better than my own, I would hope." His brow furrowed in contemplation.

Her heart melted into a puddle inside her chest. She opened her mouth, but still couldn't find words. Her eyes were blurring.

A week ago, he had proposed and she had thrown up a wall of defensiveness, terrified at the prospect. Now she knew herself deeply in love with him. If she hadn't been, this little speech of his would have done it.

"Micah, why did you offer me those rings?"

She didn't expect him to say he loved her, but maybe she hoped he would. Maybe that's why she was holding her breath.

His expression grew somber. He sat down and set aside his glass, letting his hands hang loosely between his knees as he leaned forward with his elbows on his thighs.

"We're good together, Quinn. You know we are." He

held her gaze with magnetic force. "I want to be together, every day. Otherwise, I'll be worried you're being run down by some other idiot who isn't paying attention. Is there some other man you're anxious to be with? Because I'm the one you keep coming back to. I want to make it official. That's all."

No words of love, then, but according to him, love was just something that looked pretty on a greeting card anyway.

She wanted to tell him that love was actually something that licked inside you like flames. It was a hungry fire that she knew would only smolder and make her feel acrid if she didn't see him every day to keep it bright and warm.

She couldn't say the words, though. She didn't want to see his pitiful look at her deluding herself that it existed.

She left her seat and let her knees touch the floor between his feet.

As he blinked in surprise, she cupped the side of his face. "Micah, will you marry me?"

His nostrils pinched as he drew in a sharp breath. His cheekbones seemed to stand out tautly. A dozen emotions flickered across his face, each gone faster than she was able to interpret, but the hot satisfaction at the end lingered. The tenderness that shone from his eyes bathed her in the sweetest, softest, warmest light.

"That scream you just heard was my sister starting to plan our wedding. C'mere." He gathered her into his lap and kissed her.

They spent two weeks on his yacht where Quinn diligently did her exercises and rehabilitated her arm with some lazy swimming. When they detoured through Bellagio on their way to Lucille's birthday in Canada, Quinn was pronounced by Dr. Fabrizio "better than new."

Micah breathed a sigh of relief, but he then had his mother's dinner to endure.

It began with an ecstatic Eden running out to embrace both of them, over the moon about their engagement.

Yasmine had been invited and waited on the porch with Remy and his mother. Lucille was equally teary and welcoming. Yasmine beamed widely and hugged them both.

Remy was far more circumspect. He nodded at Micah and greeted Quinn with what looked like genuine warmth. They all trailed inside where the women were soon chattering bridal showers, engagement parties and wedding plans.

"Just a wedding," Quinn insisted. She explained that she had decided to put her PhD on hold. "There's an interesting opportunity at the Canadian embassy in Berlin that I've put in for. Even if I don't get that one, now that I see what might be available if I look, I'd rather work for a few years, then go back for my doctorate."

"Before the babies start coming," Lucille said brightly.

Micah stepped in before Quinn had to respond to that.

"Mom, would you consider coming to Germany for the wedding? It's a big ask, considering who will be there." He meant his family. "But the hotel renovations in Wildenfels are nearly complete. We could book it out before the official opening in October." The project was ahead of schedule and he and Quinn were planning to spend the next weeks in Berlin so the residency requirement would be easy to meet. "It's convenient for the business associates I'm expected to invite."

"It won't be a huge wedding anyway," Quinn interjected. "This is friends of the bride right here." She drew a circle to indicate their little party. "And you're all related to Micah."

"That's not true," Eden scoffed, and began rattling off mutual friends from school who absolutely *had* to be invited.

Quinn had floated the idea of an elopement, but since German marriages were typically conducted in private civil ceremonies at a registrar's office, and the pomp was actually the reception, she had agreed to Micah's desire for something bigger. He didn't want any rumors it was a shotgun wedding. A splashy celebration would set the appropriate tone, especially with his father's side of the family.

"I would go anywhere to see you two marry," Lucille assured them. "When were you thinking?"

"The hotel is scheduled to open in a month, so three weeks from today."

"That's not enough time!" Eden cried.

It was too long, in Micah's opinion.

"If I'm designing your gown, that starts today. Let me get my tablet," Yasmine said, searching for her bag.

"Mama, do you still have those bridal magazines from when I was planning my wedding to Hunter? They always have checklists in them." Eden turned on Micah. "I know what you're doing. You're making this happen fast so I don't have time to go over-the-top with the arrangements. You are underestimating me, my friend," Eden warned playfully.

Quinn, the devil, took advantage of the mild chaos to bring Micah two open longneck bottles of beer. She tilted her head toward Remy. He was pretending an interest in a romance novel Lucille had left on an end table.

"Take him outside and tell him about your dream wedding. Or discuss women's rights. Or socket wrenches. Dealer's choice."

He knew damned well what she wanted him to talk to Remy about. He walked over to offer one of the bottles. "Shall we get this over with?"

Remy accepted the beer and nodded for Micah to precede him out to Lucille's extremely well-tended garden. She opened it for a week every summer to walking tours as part of a cancer research fundraiser so it was an immaculate network of paths among water features, a freestanding swing, and a "pollinator's paradise" of fragrant blooms that attracted butterflies and other insects.

"Congratulations on your engagement," Remy said, helping himself to a raspberry off a cane.

"Congratulations on your recent marriage," Micah said with equal parts sincerity and irony.

For a moment there was only the chorus of crickets in the long grass beyond the fence.

"It was a nice offer you made to Yasmine, but she doesn't need anything, so…" Remy's tone suggested Micah get very lost.

"I'll wait for her to tell me that herself. As I've been informed many times, women are allowed to make their own decisions, so…" *Bite me.*

They both took a long pull on their beer.

"Eden has low blood pressure," Micah thought to inform him. "If she gets dehydrated, she faints. On a day like today, put some pretzels or salted nuts in front of her."

"Aware," Remy said starkly. "She passed out on the beach and scared the hell out of me. It won't happen again." He jerked his chin toward the house. "If Yasmine gives you something to wear, wear it. It hurts her feelings if you refuse. She's always right anyway. And you could afford to loosen up a notch." His side-eye hit Micah's tie.

It was his mother's birthday dinner. He had dressed appropriately. Although Remy did look comfortable yet smart in his raw linen shirt over striped trousers.

A burst of female laughter came from inside the house. They both glanced that direction.

"Never get between Eden and Quinn," Micah said gravely. He was doubly invested in that one.

Remy snorted. "I pity the fool who would think to try."

"Good answer."

They clinked their bottles and finished their beer in companionable silence.

# CHAPTER TWELVE

LIKE ANY BRIDE, Quinn became so caught up in planning her wedding, dispensing with the vestiges of her life in Canada and securing a job, she overlooked the fact that she was completely changing her life. For a man. A man who didn't love her.

A man who was very, very different from her.

Reality began to crash back in around her when they arrived at the hotel in Wildenfels. It had actually been built as a Prussian palace and had housed eighteenth-century royalty. Part of it, a tower overlooking the court-yard, had been built in the 1200s. During Soviet times, the buildings and land had been used for collective farming. Later, it was renovated into apartment living, but as those units fell into disrepair, Micah's aunt had targeted it for purchase and redevelopment.

Over the last two years, marble floors had been un-covered, murals were cleaned, and plaster was restored. It was completely modernized, then decorated with crystal chandeliers, rococo-style furniture and sumptuous bedding. The staff were suitably intimidated by the owner's arrival and eager to please.

Aside from a handful of intimate social engagements, Quinn hadn't been out with Micah much. They stayed in a lot, made love a *lot*, and it had somehow slipped her mind that he was actually a very well-known, wealthy and powerful man. When it was just the two of them across a breakfast table, she felt like equals.

They were not equals.

"It's not like this is our home," he dismissed when she remarked on the opulence that surrounded them. "It's an upscale hotel. It's supposed to impress."

"But you own it. And it's one property of many." Hundreds?

He shrugged off her concern, saying that he wanted to meet with the management team to ensure there would be no hiccups on their big day.

Quinn was left to change for greeting guests as they arrived, but that was another mental wallop.

Much of her trousseau had been designed by Yasmine, but the list of items to include had been recommended by Eden. How had it become so many outfits? She had a tea gown for their welcome reception, a little black dress for the cocktail mixer later, then a dinner gown for the "intimate" family dinner they would host tonight in a private dining room.

She had a negligee for tonight and a peignoir for breakfast. In between, she had silk pajamas to wear while getting ready and a "going away" outfit for the end of the night. For the wedding, she had two different gowns! One was a simple satin crepe with organza-covered buttons down her back that she would wear for the civil ceremony. The other was a more elaborate A-line cut with a sweetheart neckline covered in appliqué lace that she would wear when they entered the reception. None of that included the two suitcases that were packed for their honeymoon.

Quinn had been happy with every single outfit because each felt like "her." They were simple and pretty and none were particularly ostentatious, but taken together the cost made her light-headed.

It was the vertigo of climbing far beyond her station in life. The fall from here would be catastrophic, and what was stopping her from falling?

The door opened and Micah startled her into hugging the beaded dress she was holding to her front.

"It occurred to me that we won't have a minute alone again until our honeymoon." He secured the lock and padded toward her like a jungle cat. "Would you like to enjoy one more hour of sin before we make this legal?"

She was so shaken by how swiftly she'd lost control of her life, her fingers went limp as he tugged the dress free of her grip. His mouth covered hers and she clasped onto what felt solid. Him.

Their tongues brushed and their groans of pleasure intermingled. He released a satisfied noise at her near-nakedness and cupped under her bottom, inviting her to leap onto him. She did, hugging him with her legs as he carried her to the bed.

It was like old times—almost frantic. As though time was limited. As though each time was the last time. *This* time felt like their last time.

"Quinn." He lifted his head once to look down at her, nostrils flared and cheeks flushed with lust. "What's wrong?"

"Nothing. I want this. I want you." She practically tore his buttons trying to open his shirt.

He popped them himself as he swept his hand down and yanked it free of his trousers. He tore the delicate French lace of her underwear rather than slide the silk down her thighs. His hand cupped her, hot and possessive.

"I love knowing this is all mine. Forever."

Her heart took a swerve at what she thought he almost said, I love... But he was kissing her again. Caressing her in a way he knew emptied her mind. They tangled tongues and she sucked on his bottom lip and scrambled to open his fly to take him in hand.

She was rushing both of them, she knew she was, but she needed to feel him *there*.

As she guided him, he rolled atop her, clothing in disarray, but still on. With a ragged noise, he gathered her beneath him and pressed.

She arched as she took him, savoring the slight sting as an echo of her distraught emotions.

"What's going on?" he asked gruffly as he smoothed her hair off her temple. "What do you need?"

"You. Just you." She swept her touch over every inch of bare skin she could access, inciting him to begin thrusting.

He kissed her again, deep and hot. His hips began a slow, powerful rhythm that made her groan. She felt his smile against the edge of her jaw.

"Shall we play our old game? How many times can I make you shatter before you destroy my control?"

Back then, their lovemaking had been a game. They'd been equal players locked in a sensual power struggle, playfully taunting each other with sensual caresses and teasing licks.

Today, he had the upper hand. She had given up her old life for him. She verged on taking his name and he even held her heart.

Recognizing that, she might have tried to hold something

back, but she couldn't. She loved him too much. She clung to him and met his thrusts and let her cries of pleasure release with abandon. When he rolled onto his back, she rode him with fervor, grasping at his hands on her breasts and touching where they were joined. She met his narrowed gaze even though he must see into her soul. He must.

Time blurred and she lost track of how many times she shattered. When they were both stripped naked and lost to passion, all pretense at control completely lost, she let the truth spill from her lips.

"I love you."

He shouted with his release.

She joined him one last time.

Micah woke alone, which ticked him off. It was too much like their old pattern, him falling asleep after explosive sex, her slipping away while he snored off his orgasm.

Today had been different, though. Quinn had told him she loved him.

His heart lurched as the frantic edge on their lovemaking came back to him. When he'd returned to their suite, he'd expected a playful tumble, not such a torrid hour or this disturbing grit it had left in his breastbone.

Perhaps it had been the throes of passion, the same way he said things like *I love the way you taste*? She didn't expect him to say he believed in that emotion, now that she had agreed to marry him, did she?

His chest tightened at the thought. He valued honesty too much to lie to her, but that word was so ephemeral, yet loaded. *Love* wouldn't magically keep them together. Commitment would. He cared about her. She had to know that. Wasn't it enough?

She came out of the bathroom in a robe, bringing the

humid fragrance of bodywash with her, but her hair was dry as she yanked the towel from her head. When she saw him, she halted abruptly, making him realize she'd been hurrying.

She had been trying to leave before he woke up!

Wordlessly, she veered to the mirrored dresser and picked up her hairbrush, wincing as she began running it through her hair. Her shoulder wasn't quite up to the task, but she did it as a sort of therapy.

"About what you said—" he began reluctantly.

"Ignore it. It didn't mean anything."

That landed like a mule kick in the chest. "Then why did you say it?"

"Let me rephrase," she turned to say hotly. "I meant it, but I know it didn't mean anything to you so forget I said it."

For three pulsebeats, he stared into the abyss that was her challenging expression. He saw the shadows of doubt and hurt flickering behind her eyes.

"I know you care about me, Quinn. We care about each other. That's as it should be."

The tendons in her neck flexed as though she was absorbing a blow. She looked away and slipped a mask over her face that he hadn't seen in a long time. It made a tremor start behind his heart, the first cracks of a long fracture.

"What does that word even do? It doesn't change anything. Do you think a man saying it would mean he's bringing more to the table than I am? Is he going to be more faithful than I am? Take better care of you when you're sick? We're a good match, Quinn."

"We absolutely are not." Her voice cut a low swath across the room. "Look around. Nothing in this room is mine."

As she looked around, vaguely frantic like someone

waking from a dream and not fully comprehending reality, he realized they stood on very shaky ground.

"This is cold feet." He threw himself from the bed and stepped into his boxers. "These last weeks with you have been some of the happiest of my life." Not just because of the steady diet of sex—although he really enjoyed that. "I like having you in my life, Quinn. I like seeing you thrive."

She widened appalled eyes at him. "You like taking care of me."

"I do," he said without shame. "Because the opposite scenario, where you don't have what you need, makes me sick to think about." It wasn't like she was completely dependent on him. She'd just landed that job in Berlin and had blossomed with shy excitement at how much regard they had for her. He'd nearly died of pride.

Her cheeks were carved out so her cheekbones stood out starkly. Her eyes were bright.

"It does mean something to me that you would say those words. I know you wouldn't lie about something like that." He picked up her hand to kiss her fingers. They were cold and trembling.

He frowned and tried to warm them, but there was a knock at the door in the main room.

"Did you order room service?" he asked her.

"It's me," Eden called from behind the door.

Micah opened his mouth to say they were busy, but Quinn was already pulling her hand from his grip, hurrying to let her in.

With a light curse, he quickly found a robe in the bathroom and came back to the bedroom to see Eden pulling a dress from the closet.

"Oh, this is gorgeous. Quinn is coming to my room

to get ready. Remy had to go to the airport to get Yasmine so we won't see them until the cocktail party. Vienna is on the same flight. Two fer one. But now that I've got you both..." Eden hugged Quinn's dress to her middle. "It's still early, but Remy said I could tell you since you'll be leaving for your honeymoon after tomorrow and I can't wait until—"

"Oh, Eden." Quinn rushed her, crushing the dress as she weepily embraced Eden.

"I know. I'm so happy!" Eden was teary as she held on to Quinn. Eden waved Micah to come into their hug.

"I'm happy for you," he said sincerely as he moved her hand from possibly putting too much pressure on Quinn's shoulder, then gently wrapped his arms around both of them. "For you and Remy," he assured her.

"Thank you. He's really happy, too." They all broke apart, but Eden poked him in the chest. "*Now* will you believe he's always been in love with me? And me with him?"

His head briefly swam, as though the rug had been pulled from beneath his feet. "I believe you believe you're in love. I believe you both want what's best for each other." As the words came out of his mouth, he could hear them striking Quinn at an angle, causing her to stiffen.

Quinn turned away to gather underthings and a pair of shoes.

"Quinn," he said.

"I'll see you downstairs." She threw a meaningless smile over her shoulder and left with Eden.

Quinn tried, she honestly tried not to cry, but as Eden was busy chattering about due dates and which room would be turned into a nursery, the pressure inside her just sputtered up and out.

"Quinn!"

"I'm sorry," she sobbed. "I want to be happy for you and I am. I swear I am."

"What happened? Just tell me what happened." Eden dropped everything to come sit beside her on the sofa.

"I love him. I told him I love him and he doesn't *care*. And now I've changed my whole life for him. Now I'm going to be a perpetual houseguest who brings nothing to his life and I can't walk away because he'll hate me and so will you!"

"I will never hate you. I will always love you," she soothed, gathering her into a hug. "You will always have me. Always, always. I should have come when you were in hospital. I knew that I should have, but I wanted to give you and Micah time. I thought... Well, I'm not going to make excuses for him. If he's broken your heart, he has to live with the consequences. Which includes the fact that he is dead to me."

"Don't say that, Eden." Quinn drew back and accepted the tissue Eden offered. "I was really mean to him when he didn't call you. I don't want to be the reason you two aren't getting along."

"But you are the reason. He's being an idiot."

"He's being honest! And I'm being selfish. He's a good person. I thought it was enough if I loved him. At least when it was in my head, I could convince myself we were both in love and not admitting it, but I *said* it. And now I know he doesn't love me and it hurts so much, Eden. So much more than I can stand. I don't know what to do."

"What do you want to do?"

"I just want to go home and..." She didn't even have a home. Fresh tears welled against her lashes. "But I can't walk away from my own wedding."

"Actually, you can. It's something people do now. Or so I've heard," Eden said with self-deprecation.

"I can't do that to him. I can't do it to you and your mom."

"Quinn." Eden took her hands. "You deserve to be loved. If he doesn't love you, then he doesn't deserve you."

Their first appearance was a tea reception on the terrace overlooking the pond, very casual. Summer was waning so it was a pleasant temperature with a hint of crispness on the air and an intense blue sky.

Micah and Quinn were supposed to be greeting guests with refreshments and conversation while staff hurried to register guests and take up their luggage.

She wasn't here. The longer he didn't see her, the more acutely his insides twisted with guilt and shame.

He'd hurt her. He had known he was hurting her as he was doing it and why? Why would he do that to someone he cared about?

Because to say he loved her would be to give her the power to hurt him. Devastating power.

His gaze drifted to where his mother spoke with an old friend, one he had deliberately invited so she would have some friendly faces here. That woman was highly influential. Even Aunt Zara would hesitate to get on her wrong side. His mother was smiling, but he recognized the tension in her. She was braced for having to face his father's family.

Nevertheless, she had come here for him. Because she loved him.

And he loved her. It had always been a very painful love, though. One filled with brief, happy reunions and too-soon goodbyes. It was the same with Eden. Love was always there, but it was rarely *here*.

Love was absence and pain. He was trying to spare Quinn. Didn't she see that?

But the pain had arrived regardless. If she wasn't with him, that's all he would ever feel. Pain.

Quinn finally found it. She'd gone through all the suitcases, but she'd finally found her hoodie.

She sank to the floor, still in the bathrobe she'd worn to Eden's room, and hugged the soft jersey to her chest. She hadn't wanted to leave without it, but now that she had it in her arms, she didn't know what to do.

That's how Micah found her.

The door into the suite opened and he called urgently, "Quinn."

He halted as he entered the bedroom, taking in the tossed suitcases.

He wore the shirt Yasmine had designed for him. Privately, he had told Quinn he wasn't sure about the burgundy pinstripes with the white tab collar, thinking it too casual for today, especially without a jacket, but matched with the merlot-colored tie and tie clip, he looked as polished as usual, with a bit more flair.

He crouched before her, brows pulled in anguish. "What are you doing?"

"I'm really tired of leaving without the things I love." Her eyes were dry, but stinging from all the tears she had shed. Her voice was hoarse. "Look. This has my name on it." She turned it over. "It's from my third year at university. My shoulder was bothering me so I asked the rowing team if I could dry-land-train with them. I knew my shoulder wasn't strong enough to row and compete, but they asked me to be their coxswain. We won a regatta, then everyone went their own ways, but

I had this to prove that for that little while I belonged to something. I was wanted. Needed even."

"You're always wanted, Quinn." He shifted to sit, one knee bent, the other cocked. "I want you. Always. I'm not talking about sex. I'm talking about you. I want *you*. I need you. Do you understand that?"

She balled the hoodie in her lap, stomach churning with chagrin.

"Micah, I think I agreed to marry you because I wanted to be part of your family. I wanted to be Eden's sister-in-law and Lucille's daughter-in-law and finally be part of that."

"You *are* part of our family. I don't understand how you don't know how important you are to us. To *me*. Quinn, listen to me."

He shifted closer so he could take her hand. That's when he noticed her engagement ring was gone. He sucked in a breath and cradled her fist as though it was broken.

"If you don't want to marry me, Quinn, that's fine. It's fine. We can get past that, but don't leave me, Quinn. You can't…" An agonized flinch flexed across his expression. "I can't keep saying goodbye to the people I love."

She gasped and tried to take back her hand, but he held on.

"I tried not to love you because I knew that if you ever walked away—and you always walk away, Quinn…" His voice shook with accusation while his brows crashed down. His hand closed over hers, not hard, but squeezing enough to transmit his agony. "I knew if you left me for good, it would be more than I could take. So I tried not to love you. I tried to let it be what you seemed to want because at least I understood that kind of relationship. But I *do* love you, Quinn. It scares the hell out of me how much I love you."

"You don't have to keep saying it if—"

"Don't you dare throw it back on me. You wanted this, Quinn. Now you take it, same as I have to. We love each other. We have to watch the other person hold our heart and it's going to hurt. Loving hurts. It makes you vulnerable and when they hurt, you hurt. When they're lying in a hospital bed, you wonder if you'll have any reason to live tomorrow. But when they're happy…" He lifted his gaze from where he was abrading the back of her hand with the restless rub of his thumb. "When you are happy, Quinn, I don't need air or water. I want you with me and I want to see you smile. Is that too much to ask?"

She wasn't smiling right now. Tears were running down her cheeks as she reached toward something she wanted so badly, she didn't know if she would topple or finally touch it.

"I'm really scared, Micah. I love you *so much*. I wanted to leave, but I wanted my sweater. Then when I found it…" She looked down at it in her lap. "It's not enough anymore, to only have a memory of belonging once. I want to really belong. Forever. I want to belong with you." It shook her very foundations to ask for that.

"You do," he promised solemnly. "We belong together whether we marry or not. I think that's been true for a very long time."

"Yeah," she agreed, sagging with relief. She let the last of her defenses fall and tried to find a smile, but her lips were still quivery. "I just didn't know what it looked like to belong with someone, so I didn't recognize it when it happened."

"Same." He gathered her closer and touched his unsteady smile to hers. "But now I know it looks like red hair and freckles."

"And sounds like sarcasm," she tacked on.

"I'm not being sarcastic." He drew back from his almost-kiss and gave her a disgruntled frown.

"No, I was saying that I'm sarcastic and I belong with—oh, never mind. If it takes too long to explain, it's not a clever joke. Will you kiss me? Please? You promised that no matter how badly we fought, I could always ask you for what I need."

"Yes, but you have to come all the way into my lap because that's what *I* need right now. And promise me that if you ever do leave, I'll be the thing you wreck a bedroom looking for, so you can take me with you."

"Or I could stay and wreck a bedroom with you," she suggested as she nestled close, one arm behind his back and the other twining around his neck.

"Wrecking a bedroom together will always be my preference. Now stop talking. I have a kiss to deliver."

"I really do love you, though. You know that, don't you?" she asked anxiously.

"I do know that. Now tell me you know I love you. That the knowledge and belief is all the way in here where it can never be doubted or get misplaced." He touched the middle of her chest.

His touch seemed to light a glow inside her, one that grew hot and bright under the fierce light in his eyes. It dispelled old shadows of doubts and warmed all her cold corners of loneliness. There was no hesitation in her as she accepted it. She deserved this, deserved him. She deserved love.

And she had *his* love, which was extra special for its rarity and strength.

"I do," she vowed.

# EPILOGUE

THEY MARRIED AN hour later at the registrar's office.

Micah left the decision to Quinn whether they would go through with it or simply live together for the rest of their lives.

Quinn chose to marry him. She wanted the commitment, not because she doubted either of their steadfastness, but because it cemented where they belonged—with each other. Also, she really, really didn't want to put Lucille through watching another of her children cancel a wedding.

Micah assured her that his mother would understand, but he also leaped on calling the registrar's office to ask if they had an opening today.

"We have that many dinners and socials to get through, you might change your mind again," he joked, holding the phone to his chest. "What do you say?"

"I say 'yes.'" She rose from the bed and put on her engagement ring from the dish where she'd left it. "But I won't have time to do that dress justice."

She wore her blue hoodie. Micah left off his tie and didn't bother shaving so he had a hint of shadow around his jaw.

It was short and sweet and when they were pronounced husband and wife, he kissed her reverently. Then he held on to her for a long time. His heart crashed against hers and his mouth rested against her hair.

"This is genuinely the happiest day of my life," he told her in a quiet rasp.

When they finally drew back, she smiled her biggest smile at him. He cupped her face, and his eyes were wet with happy tears.

They spent the evening making appearances with their guests, the only hiccup when Quinn had to head off Eden as she bore down on her brother, ready to take a strip off him.

"Look. Shh… We have a secret of our own." Quinn showed her the second ring she wore.

Eden cried, of course, and hugged her hard.

The rest of the celebrations went ahead as scheduled. It was like a fairy tale, one that Quinn would look back on and marvel at, partly because it was so movie-perfect, but more because her husband made her feel so loved. He didn't make any grand gestures. No, it was in the quiet touch on her back and the meeting of her gaze that told her she was precious. It was the way he looked for her when she returned to a room and the way he absently centered her rings when he held her hand. It was in the way they made love that night, with their whole hearts open, sealing their love for all time.

It was frightening to believe she was wanted and needed and loved this much, but hour by hour and day by day, her trust in what they had grew. Month by month, she turned each of their houses into a home. They were building a lift together that was solid and secure, everything she had ever needed.

Then, one day, shortly after their second anniversary, Quinn came home to tell him with soft solemnity, "I think I met our daughter today."

Micah pushed away from his desk. "Tell me."

They had already begun the process of becoming foster parents. Quinn had dropped some certified documents at the agency and had glimpsed a five-year-old girl holding a brand-new teddy bear. There'd been a half-stuffed garbage bag at her feet.

"Her foster mother had a family emergency. It was Abigail's third house in two years."

Abigail came into their home a few weeks later. She was shy and polite and didn't mention that her shoes were too tight. Micah noticed when he was helping her struggle to get them on. He immediately took her to buy new ones, which made her cry, because she didn't want to give up her old ones. She loved them too much.

A special trunk was procured for items that meant a lot to her. She flourished, and soon Abigail was offering her items from the trunk to other children, secure that she had all she needed in the vast, enduring love of her parents.

\* \* \* \* \*

# THE BOSS'S
# STOLEN BRIDE

NATALIE ANDERSON

MILLS & BOON

For Soraya—again and always!
I'll always be grateful for your whip-cracking and cheer!

# CHAPTER ONE

ELIAS GREYSON HADN'T just mastered the art of avoiding inconvenient emotion, he'd perfected it—effortlessly ignoring not just his own, but that of all others. To be unmoved in the presence of histrionics made all decisions—be they business or personal related—clinical and easy. Rage, recriminations, pleas or guilt trips didn't penetrate his armour. No matter the provocation, Elias Greyson didn't overreact, didn't get riled, and definitely didn't make snap decisions in the heat of the moment because he always ensured any heat was eliminated from important negotiations. Emotional reactions led to poor outcomes, he found. A measured, rational, controlled response was right. And if he were occasionally accused of being a cold-blooded, ruthless bastard, so be it.

But today Elias was having a rare, *imperfect* day. Irritation burned up his spine—an irritation that had been building for the last two weeks. He checked the clock on his computer and said irritation roiled higher. He gritted his teeth. Of all the days for his ultra-efficient assistant to finally fail him. He was flying from London to the US in a few hours and he wanted everything organised ahead of take-off. His latest acquisition target, a venture capital firm based in San Francisco, was proving a dif-

ficult fish to hook. While the company would be useful
for Elias to push further into the North American market,
its chief exec, Vince Williams, considered 'values' to be
important. The old man's diligence searches went beyond
company balance sheets all the way to any prospective
raiding CEO's silk ones. Apparently perfect Vince had
been married to his childhood sweetheart Cora for over
fifty years and was known to disapprove of a party lifestyle. Elias wasn't quite the playboy he'd been a couple
of years ago but apparently the fact he was still single
was enough to cause 'concern'. It was ridiculous and
Elias would be informing Vince of the fact face-to-face
at their meeting tomorrow.

He would also be taking over the firm regardless.
But he'd prefer the acquisition not to be hostile, which
is why he'd wanted everything squared away in an impeccably prepared offer that would be impossible to refuse regardless of anyone's 'values'. So the last thing he
needed was to be let down by his primary assistant a few
hours before departure.

Darcie Milne had never been late. Not once in the two
and a half years she'd worked for him. Usually she was
seated at the desk just outside his office before he even
arrived, and he arrived early. But that chair was still
empty. He snatched up his mobile. The text messages
he'd already sent her remained unanswered so now he
actually phoned her. It went straight to voicemail.

'I need you in the office. *Now.*' He stabbed the screen
to end the call.

Five more minutes crawled by. His supposedly superior ability to ignore inconvenient emotion slipped as a
sliver of worry crept in and splintered his concentration.

Had something happened to her? Every muscle tensed. Where the *hell* was she?

At that exact moment his office door was flung open. Darcie Milne stalked in and slammed the door behind her.

Elias stared, rooted to his seat, jaw hanging. Because Darcie Milne was not wearing her customary office attire of loose-fitting white shirt, even looser grey trousers and boring brown brogues. In the dreary uniform's place was a knee-length cream-coloured skirt and matching jacket. Both of which were a little too large on her frame, but that skirt offered a very rare glimpse of her ankles and calves and creamy skin. The room temperature shot up at least ten degrees.

He forced himself to shut his mouth and lift his gaze, but she wasn't looking at him anyway; her focus was on his wide wooden desk between them. She'd not looked him square in the eyes once in the last fortnight. *That* had irritated him, too. He'd gone for so long without being bothered by her. Frankly he'd been proud of the degree to which he'd remained impassive to her presence. Until two weeks ago, that is. Because two weeks ago she'd—

'What the hell time do you call this?' he growled, refusing to think of that night. But the effort cost him his customary cool.

'You don't remember anything outside of the current deal, do you?'

Shocked by the uncharacteristic bite in her tone, that unfamiliar irritation almost overwhelmed him. Darcie had never given him moody attitude. She—like he— was usually calm. She was diligent. Dutiful. Sure, she sometimes challenged him but only when required, only ever about business and always very coolly. She was

quite often correct, too. Not that she was some docile
doormat, more an efficient, aloof automaton. One he
refused to look at for too long. Only today—now—he
stared at her. *Hard.*

'What's going on?' he clipped.

She put a file on the desk before him. He could see
the familiar neon sticky tags she preferred and the neat
notes in her clear print.

'I've narrowed it down to five. That ought not to be
too taxing for you to have to interview,' she said.

'Interview?'

'The applicants for your executive assistant.'

'*You're* my executive assistant.'

She stiffened and her expression was different again.
'Have you really forgotten the resignation letter I emailed
you a fortnight ago? I left a paper copy on your desk, but
I know you read the email. I got the receipt.'

Oh, he'd not forgotten. He just knew his rights. He
glared at her grimly. 'Your contract requires *three* weeks'
notice. As you sent your letter only a fortnight ago,
there's one week left.'

'But as I have so much accrued annual leave owing
I'm taking the last week of my notice period as a holiday. You're paying the remainder of my accrued holidays out.' She shrugged. 'It's a lot.'

Something rippled beneath his skin at the unashamed
defiance—sass—in her reply. She'd never crossed that
line. Not until that night in Edinburgh.

'So you're going on holiday now?' he asked. Where
was she going in that ill-fitting cream suit—a nunnery?

'Correct.'

Elias had lost many employees in the past and initially
he'd been determined not to give a damn about Darcie's

unexpected decision to depart. Then he'd decided to get her to change her mind. But he'd not addressed it with her directly yet. Truthfully it had taken more assimilating than he'd expected, especially after that other issue.

But while he refused to beg, he couldn't stop himself from testing her loyalty. 'You realise it's a terrible time.'

'It's *always* a terrible time,' she said, her voice clipped. 'There is always some massive deal on the table that you need everyone all over. It wouldn't matter when I handed in my notice. It was always going to be an inconvenience to you.'

'It's far more than an inconvenience.' The admission growled out.

'You're being dramatic,' she said crisply. 'You'll be fine. You always are.'

His jaw dropped. Dramatic? 'Not fine.' He scrambled to keep on track. 'You know this deal is—'

'Imperative? Vital? Does the company's future hang in the balance because this is the biggest deal you've ever done?' She cocked her head and actually rolled her eyes at him. 'They always are, Elias. But admit it, this one is all but sealed. The meeting tomorrow is a mere formality. You don't need me there. You don't need anyone. Besides, I bet you've already lined up the next deal and doubtless it's even bigger than this one. Am I right?'

He stared at her. Who was this woman? Where had calm, capable Darcie gone?

Her mouth twisted. 'I knew it. There's no *final* deal for you. You're always on the hunt for the next passion project before you've finished with the one right on the table in front of you.'

His skin tightened. Passion project? Was she talking business mergers or personal ones? Elias made no apology for his voracious appetite. At least he was honest about it. Which was more than she was. There was passion and hunger within Darcie, too. He'd known that from the moment he'd met her. He'd just been pretending not to remember ever since.

'I'll double your salary.' Somehow the offer slipped out.

But it didn't have the desired effect.

Storm clouds swept into her eyes, enhancing the blue, and he couldn't have moved if he'd tried. Because then Darcie put both palms down on his desk and leaned across it to vent. 'I have given you almost every hour of every day for nearly three years. I've never before denied you. But enough is *enough*.'

He blinked, shocked by her sudden vitriol. Darcie was never emotional at work. Not even when she'd worked thirty-one hours straight and was paler than tracing paper with smudges beneath her eyes. Not even then had she lost her cool with him. She was always professional. Or she had been. Until that one very strange, very unforgettable night. Then she'd been anything but.

'It's *just* like you to have forgotten.' Lightning fury flashed from her. 'Do you know I don't have to be in this office at all today? I'm only here because of misplaced loyalty.' She dragged in a breath and twisted the knife. 'To my colleagues.'

'*Misplaced* loyalty?' The comment had him in a car racing towards a cliff edge. To the ravine he'd avoided at all costs. Until now. Because now he was pissed off, and the emotion was all-consuming. 'To your *colleagues*, Darcie? Not to me?'

'No.' She lifted her chin. But she still didn't quite meet his gaze. '*Not* you.'

'But—'

'I can't stay to argue, Elias,' she snapped. 'I don't actually have time.'

Why not? But he couldn't seem to ask. He couldn't seem to think. He could only stare at her as now she finally stared right back at him and her captivating eyes were full of things he couldn't stand to see—resentment, anger, *hurt*.

'Don't you even want to know why?' she breathed.

His obliging executive assistant, always anticipating, a step ahead of everyone except him, had turned on him. The quietly efficient woman who didn't fawn but who got everything done was gone. In her place, radiant with energy, was a beautiful, furious firestorm.

'Today is my *wedding* day and yet I've *still* come running at your damned summons. But this is it. I'm done.'

*Wedding?* The shock ripped through him like a tornado, turning up—

Her *wedding* day?

Before his heart could beat she stormed out, slamming the door behind her and leaving Elias struck still in the suddenly cavernous room. Bile burned his mouth as his body launched its own violent response. He brutally swallowed it back, but bitter rage gripped him regardless as her words reverberated.

*Wedding day.*

He hadn't been spoken to like that—hadn't been excoriated by someone's scorn—in so very long. Who the hell was she marrying? She didn't have time to date anyone. And how *dare* she after—?

He vaulted out of his seat and strode to the door, flinging it open to glare across the office. Naturally Darcie was nowhere to be seen. She must have sprinted. Was she that desperate to escape him or was her speed to get to her groom? His fury mounted.

Without exception his remaining staff had their gazes glued to screens; apparently all were suspended in eerie still silence. Of course, Darcie was the one who'd usually stare back him and ask what he wanted. Or she had been. Until these last two weeks.

*Can you please pretend this never happened...?*

To say nothing. To do nothing wasn't Elias's usual style. He didn't know why he'd said yes to the *second* of her breathy requests that night. But he'd been saying nothing and doing nothing regarding Darcie Milne for months. He was practiced. Besides which, it had been the right thing to do.

'*Where* did she say she was going?' he demanded, too furious to bother pretending they hadn't heard every word of that argument. 'Is it *really* her wedding day?'

One of the assistants attempted a smile. 'It's so romantic, don't you think?'

No, he did not. It was *not* romantic. It was a sham.

'What do you know about it?' He turned towards the woman. And how come he didn't? Because he spent more time with Darcie than anyone.

'Not much.' The woman swallowed, her smile fading. 'It only came out at her farewell party last night.'

A party that he'd known nothing about and certainly hadn't been invited to. Insult to injury, much? A rosy cloud of rage misted in front of him. Never mind that he never socialised with his staff. Had Darcie sipped champagne the way she had a fortnight ago? When she never, ever drank. In all the nights she'd travelled alongside him, not once had he seen her touch alcohol. Until then.

*Come upstairs with me?*

Had she invited some other guy to her room the way she'd invited him?

'Where's the wedding?' he rasped.

'The register office in the city.' A wary response.

She was getting married in a register office on a weekday morning? Something was off. Darcie was off—just now she'd most definitely not been herself. This wasn't—couldn't be—real. It certainly wasn't right. He nodded, his feet moving fast. Because as far as Elias Greyson was concerned, Darcie Milne wasn't getting married anywhere today.

Not to anyone.

# CHAPTER TWO

DARCIE PACED THE CORRIDOR, keeping her gaze on the main entrance. It was only ten minutes until the allotted time for the ceremony, but all she could see was Elias's expression as she'd fled his office fifteen minutes ago. He'd gone white—piqued because she'd snapped and not jumped to his summons. There was nothing more to his annoyance. No deeper emotion. There was never any real emotion with him. He was just too used to getting his own way. And right now she needed to forget the long-standing infatuation that had led to her making a colossal fool of herself a fortnight ago. She sucked in a breath and slammed the door on that mortifying memory once more.

It. Was. Over.

She wouldn't see Elias Greyson ever again. She was about to marry someone else. As long as her groom actually arrived.

Her whole body suddenly ached like she'd come down with insta-flu. She checked the time again and her nerves exploded. Why *wasn't* Shaun here already? She knew he'd been reluctant but she'd thought she'd convinced him. Darcie would do anything for her best friend and Shaun had loved Zara, too. And Lily was the one—the *only*—part of Zara that lived on. That little girl needed them. There was no way Darcie was letting Lily remain in the foster system any longer than necessary.

Shaun had eventually agreed when Darcie assured him she had enough money saved to give him what he needed to build his business. She'd have agreed to anything to secure Lily's future. And she'd have just enough left over to stop work for a little while.

In a few months Lily would start school and Darcie could return to work while also helping Shaun. Now that she had the experience of working for Elias Greyson on her résumé, she'd get any number of jobs through an agency. Unless Elias didn't give her a good reference. Which, given she'd just yelled at him, was a possibility. Nobody raised their voice at Elias and he certainly never raised his. But it would be too unfair if he held that one lapse this morning over her. For more than two years she'd worked all hours for him and yes, she'd been paid well. But for that last moment this morning she'd always remained in control of herself. Never once biting back the way she'd sometimes wanted. Never once saying anything inappropriate. Because she'd needed the job and he was her boss.

Okay, aside from today there was just that one time she'd said something she shouldn't. But he'd agreed to forget it.

But she still couldn't forget his face just now. He'd truly expected her in the office today. He'd not even noticed that she and most of the others had gone for pizza last night for her to say goodbye. Of course she'd not included Elias on the email invite, knowing he wouldn't come, but it shocked her that he hadn't even known about it when ordinarily nothing in the office passed him by.

He'd looked stunned. Part of her would've laughed if her stupid heart hadn't been breaking. Because her stupid heart had been his from the first moment she'd clapped eyes on his ridiculously handsome form. She had to work so hard not to look at him too much in these last two years…

But he'd not even cared about her resignation. Only that she hadn't been at her desk first thing this morning to see through this latest deal. Too hurt to admit, she stared at the floor and willed Shaun to arrive.

'Darcie? Sorry I'm late.'

She looked up, startled her wish had come true. Shaun hurried over, dressed in faded jeans and tee. She swallowed and forced a smile. It wasn't as if she'd gone to all that much effort either. She didn't even have a posy of flowers. But her treacherous mind reverted to Elias. What would he wear to his wedding? Doubtless it would be a glamorous affair. He'd stun in a bespoke tuxedo and he'd have literally a model bride…

'It's okay,' she reassured Shaun as cold sweat slicked her back. 'Thanks. It's almost time.'

Shaun shoved his hands in his pockets. 'Haven't you sent the money over yet?'

'I haven't had a chance. I got called in to—'

'If I don't pay that deposit I'll lose the deal. You know I need it now, Darcie.'

She refocused and studied Shaun more closely. Sweat beaded on his upper lip and he fidgeted, moving from foot to foot as if he didn't want to remain in place.

'Come on, you know we're going to need this,' Shaun added impatiently. 'Transfer it now and I'll forward it right away.'

Darcie's inner alarm inside sounded.

*You can't ever trust anyone.*

She'd known Shaun for years. She knew his weaknesses. But she also knew he was fighting them just as she was hers including the doubt—that alarm—she was feeling right now. The assumption that she would be let down yet again by someone she'd thought she could trust was an automatic reflex she constantly had to combat.

'Can't it wait an hour?' she asked.

'I promised him the money yesterday, you *know* that.'

Shaun's frustration was increasingly obvious. The last thing she wanted was him walking out. This marriage would secure Lily's future and she *had* to trust Shaun to follow through. He'd been through the same system so he knew how important this was. But neither of them looked like they were about to marry. Neither exactly happy and blushing.

'Okay.' She nodded. 'I'll do it now.'

At least the task would stop her from dwelling on Elias. She leaned against the wall and pulled up her banking app, telling herself it was going to be okay. Yes, Shaun had faced hard times and, yes, he'd made mistakes, but he was pushing to do his best. And they'd be leaving here as husband and wife. What was hers was his and vice versa. She'd be doing the accounts for his new business and thanks to her time working for Elias, she actually understood all that stuff. It only took a few taps to transfer the money.

'All done.' She nodded at Shaun. 'It should be there now.'

'Great.' He pulled out his phone and walked farther along the corridor from her. 'I'll let him know the money's on its way.'

'We only have a few minutes,' Darcie called after him.

He nodded distractedly and turned away, already holding the phone to his ear.

'Darcie?'

Her heart stopped. Was she hearing things?

'Darcie!'

She turned towards the entrance. Elias Greyson was all imposing height and anger, striding in her direction in the manner of some vengeful warlord from medieval times who was coming to…to…grab her wrist?

Darcie was so shocked she froze. Never, in the almost three years she'd known him, had they touched. Not even to shake hands at her initial employment interview. And now he had her wrist firmly in his hand and it didn't seem as if he was about to let go.

'What the hell is this about a wedding?' he whispered furiously as he lifted her arm and inspected her fingers. 'No engagement ring,' he added accusingly. 'You've *never* worn one. Not ever.' His blue eyes sparked at her.

Her heart pounded. He'd noticed that?

'Not everyone is hung up on accumulating material possessions,' she muttered, horribly breathless.

'He's too cheap?'

Her jaw dropped.

'You cannot be serious.' His grip tightened and sparks shot up Darcie's arm. 'You're really getting married?'

'Yes.'

'Here?' He shot a cursory, dismissive glance at the faded paintwork in the stale institutional building.

Darcie took the chance to glance down the corridor at Shaun. He was still on his call but had turned and was watching them with wide eyes. As she looked back she saw other people in the waiting room were staring at them, too. But then everyone stared at Elias. He was taller than most, impeccably dressed in that crisply tailored suit that cost more than most people's monthly wages, and had that air about him that commanded attention—efficiency, capability, authority. Naturally he didn't notice they were watching, and if he had he wouldn't care. He was so used to it he was apparently immune to any kind of self-consciousness.

'Yes.' She drew a breath.

'Wearing that?' He looked incensed.

She flinched at the horribly judgemental tone. Elias had never once commented on what she wore and the first time he did it was slung as an insult? She glared right into his beautiful, arrogant eyes, too angry to hold anything back. 'What does it matter to you what I'm wearing? Why are you even here?'

'Why do you think?'

'Because I'm taking my last week as leave?' She furiously goaded him. 'Didn't you like that? Was it a surprise? Can you really not cope with my not dancing to your tune for *one* day?'

'It has *nothing* to do with that.'

Suddenly he was too close—towering over her and still holding her wrist and near enough for her to feel not just his heat or his strength but his fury. Elias didn't get furious. Elias, as far as Darcie knew, didn't feel anything particularly strongly. Other than the unquenchable desire to build his business. But now she was unaware of anyone or anything else other than the intense link suddenly forming between them—not the feel of his fingers on her skin, but the searing pulse of raw emotion. It was as if the veneer of civilisation she'd cemented her soul in for so long had been shredded and the danger buried in there was exposed. The danger she'd almost successfully avoided for so long—bar that one lapse. But now, with his touch, with his taunt, her control was torn.

'What I'm doing today is really *none* of your business,' she whispered.

'Not my business?' he challenged silkily.

She froze as she saw a strange glint in his eye. Her heart kicked. 'Elias—'

Another electrical pulse shot from his hand to her wrist, charging her blood.

'Who are you?' Shaun roughly interrupted them.

Elias's hold on Darcie's wrist tightened. 'You can't marry him.' His intense gaze didn't waver from her. 'You're not in love with him.'

Her heart stopped.

'I *know* you're not in love with him.'

She was so shocked, so horrified, she couldn't respond.

'I know,' Elias repeated softly. 'Because—'

'*Don't…*' Mortified, she finally whispered.

His jaw clamped and he glared at her, waiting for her to say more.

But she shook her head. He couldn't be here. Not now. Not putting everything at risk. It was too precarious as it was. 'Don't say it. Don't you *dare*.'

A white ring formed about his tightly held mouth while furious energy leapt in his eyes.

'Of course she's not in love with me,' Shaun said testily. 'And I'm not in love with her.'

A muscle in Elias's jaw ticked. Darcie wanted the earth to crater and consume her.

'You're the groom?' His question was so softly asked it was seemingly emotionless.

But Darcie knew different. Because *Elias* was different. Her spine prickled in warning because she knew Shaun would hear condescension and arrogance. Elias was the epitome of everything Shaun despised. Successful, wealthy, powerful, privileged. Like the man who'd got Zara pregnant with Lily five years ago. She turned and saw the expression in Shaun's eyes. Worse than sneering distaste, it was resentful defeat. 'Shaun—'

'This is nothing but drama, Darcie.' He shook his head. 'Maybe you're better off dealing with it with your rich jerk here.'

'Shaun!'

But as he backed away she didn't move. She couldn't, because there was still that hard grip on her arm holding her in place. And in less than two breaths, Shaun was gone.

'Darcie Milne and Shaun Casey?' a clerk called.

Darcie remained silent as she struggled to process the fact that her groom had just abandoned her. She'd known, hadn't she, that Shaun had been unsure. It was why she'd delayed making that payment until he was here, and if they hadn't been interrupted they would be getting married now.

'Darcie Milne and Shaun Casey,' the clerk repeated. 'Darcie and Shaun?'

She turned and stared up at Elias with savage bitterness. 'Now look at what you've done.'

'Better now than after the vows.' His tone was impassive but there was more than watchfulness in his eyes. There was wildness—a stormy emotion that she read as satisfaction and it destroyed her. Every last shred of self-control was obliterated in a tsunami of anger.

'How dare you,' she breathed. 'You swan in here,

swaggering around as if you somehow know it all. That you have the right to assume and to judge and to change everything?'

'It's just a wedding,' he retorted. 'It's not like it's a matter of life and death.'

'And that's where you're wrong,' she flung at him. 'I *needed* to get married today.'

'Well, your groom is pretty weak if he fled just because I showed up.' Elias snapped back. 'He wasn't in love with you,' he added obstinately. 'He even said so to your face.'

'Of course he wasn't in love with me.' She nodded, bitterly, awkwardly hurt. 'Who would want me, right?'

A frown flashed in Elias's eyes, but she was too far gone to give a damn.

'Marriages aren't always some ideal romantic fantasy, Elias,' she said harshly. 'Sometimes marriage is a practical solution to a real problem. But you don't have any clue about real problems in your high-flying, billionaire party world.'

Elias stiffened. 'What's the problem?'

As if she was going to tell *him*?

He leaned closer, his fingers tightening. 'What's the problem, Darcie?'

She glared back, angrily marvelling at the arrogance and ignorance of him. He was literally blocking her path to where she wanted to go.

'I hate you,' she muttered. 'This is all your fault.'

She was furious with him for appearing—unannounced, uninvited, ruining everything she'd worked so hard for, for so long. His timing could not have been worse. And she was even more furious because part of her had leapt to life at the sight of him. The stupid hormone-driven sexual part that she'd almost managed to completely ignore. And it was firing up again.

'What gives you the right to turn up where you were never invited? All because I dared to walk out on you?' She rose on tiptoe to slam her truth right into his face. 'There was never going to be a good time to leave you. There is always some imperative deal you're working on—you're always pushing for more.' Part of her admired him for that. She'd learned from him. 'But you know what, Elias? This was *my* deal. My *one* deal. It was the only one I've *ever* wanted and it was my only shot to get it and you've *wrecked* it.' Her breathing quickened and her heart was racing and racing and she was terrified of bursting into tears.

'He's a jerk,' Elias shot back savagely. 'It was obviously never going to last.'

'That wasn't the point!' Darcie completely lost control, her voice rising. 'That didn't matter! It would have lasted long *enough*!'

Defeat swelled within her. Overwhelming, horrific defeat that brought forth bitter blame as the implications sank in. Her application to care for Lily would have to be delayed. Lily who was so little, so lost, so lonely—Lily, who mattered more than anything. As for the *money* she'd just transferred to Shaun—would she get that back from him? Or would he disappear for months like he had before? And she wreaked all that anger, all that futility, on Elias. The literal roadblock in her way.

'You can't think about anyone beyond *yourself*,' she berated him. 'It is always about everything you want and need and it always has to be right now. Well, I have wants and needs, too, and I needed to get married. *Today*.'

'If that's the case then let me fix the problem I've created.' He seethed wildly. 'You *need* to get married today? Then fine. You can marry me.'

# CHAPTER THREE

FOR ONE CRAZY moment Darcie actually believed him and her raw reaction was extreme. Excitement soared so high her senses spun out. She heard nothing but her heart beating a refrain—*Marry. Elias. Greyson.*

Impossible hope filled her lungs so swiftly, so completely, she shot past the point of pain. But when she was finally forced to release it, cold reality hit and she laughed—a bitter burst that sprang from the deepest despair. 'Don't be *ridiculous*.'

His expression was rigid but his pupils had blown. 'I'm not.'

But Darcie didn't believe him. He was being snide and she was so *hurt*. She looked down and saw his big hand still wrapped firmly around her wrist. The sizzle of skin on skin would surely leave a mark. But as if it were possible to be branded by his one touch? She shook her head. She was so *pathetic*. He didn't want her. She knew that already.

'It wasn't a joke,' he insisted curtly. 'It just needs some organisation.'

His blithely unrealistic understatement refuelled the remnants of her anger. He was beyond arrogant.

'As if it's that easy?' She'd worked for *months* to get

to this position and he'd decimated it in seconds. 'We're not in Las Vegas, Elias.' She sarcastically informed him of the banalities that made his supposedly simple solution impossible. 'We're in England. There are forms that have to be filed days ahead of time.'

'Isn't there somewhere north…' He frowned, then his eyebrows lifted. 'Gretna Green?'

'Gretna Green?' This time her brief laugh was more of a squawk. 'What do you this is, some Regency romance in which we elope because I'm underage?' She shook her head. 'It's the twenty-first century and even there we *still* have to file paperwork weeks in advance.'

'Speed really is of the essence?'

Darcie couldn't wait any longer because *Lily* couldn't wait. Lily, who was about to be shunted into yet another foster home that would never be good enough and Darcie would lose her last opportunity to provide for her. Darcie, who'd been so single-minded, so determined that she'd put up with every one of Elias's endless and outrageous demands. The guy was an inexhaustible tyrant—ruthless and relentless in his requirements—and she'd borne it all in biddable silence because she'd needed to, but now futility swamped her. 'It was. Yes.'

'And it really doesn't matter who the groom is?' he asked, puzzled and searching.

But Darcie saw no need to explain anything to him. Elias Greyson was unlikely to ever marry anyone and most certainly not her. When she'd first begun working for him, she'd soon learned he was a playboy who dated an endless array of socialites and models and influencers—all of whom tended to be slender or beautiful or well-connected or successful or more commonly, *all* of the above. Darcie wasn't *any* of those things. Definitely not slender, nor beautiful enough to wear slinky dresses, and she definitely didn't come from the right side of the tracks. She didn't dance at the right clubs, in fact long ago she'd danced at the absolute opposite of the right clubs, not that she could ever tell him that. She didn't have an elite education or spring from some society family. And unsurprisingly Elias had paid no attention to her as anything other than his dutiful assistant. She wasn't and would never be his type nor an appropriate match. And she knew that fact *intimately*. As all her anger flooded back she finally twisted her hand and jerked her wrist free of his hold.

'Just forget it and *leave*, Elias. You've done enough damage already.'

She turned her back on him. But just as suddenly her energy slumped. Her legs felt empty. So did her soul. Depleted, she was left bereft of everything.

Elias stared as Darcie literally sank into the nearest chair. This wasn't the flounce of a pouting creature denied her own way, it was the collapse of someone whose whole world had just shattered. Paler than he'd ever seen her, she gazed unseeingly at the floor and the trembling of her limbs was visible even from five feet away. His formerly impeccably calm assistant was in pieces and apparently it was all his fault. She'd never spoken to him the way she had. No one had spoken to him that way in *years*.

He winced. His limbs didn't feel all that steady either as he struggled to recover from her elated expression the split second after he'd said he'd marry her. But a breath later she'd broken and laughed in his face. That bitter, blameful laugh had then excoriated him, decimating his own surge of excitement. Now shame slithered

through his cells, sweating out through his skin. He'd
never screwed up like this. He'd vowed never to interfere with another person's personal life—never to be so
arrogant, so controlling, the way his father was. The realisation that he'd just done exactly that was unbearable.

But honesty mattered, too. Intentions mattered. And
Darcie intending to marry someone else… He'd thought
she was a liar and that had infuriated him because betrayal did. He'd not been able to stop himself from chas-
ing her here to find out what and who and now *why* was
it so imperative she get married at all. Why so quickly?
Was this some kind of residency issue? A work visa?
But Darcie was English so that didn't make sense. *None*
of this made sense. The only thing that was completely
obvious was her distress and inwardly he still rebelled
at the accusation that it was *his* fault.

*I'm not in love with her.*

That slimy coward had walked out on her the second
he'd had the slimmest of opportunities.

*Sometimes marriage is a practical solution to a real
problem.*

Elias glanced about and saw another couple glaring
at him disapprovingly. Yeah, apparently he *was* the vil-
lain here, which was outrageous. Hadn't he just saved
her from marrying a fool who clearly didn't want to be
there? He looked back at Darcie. The despair in her posture made his discomfort snowball. He didn't have the
desire nor the ability to deal with emotional problems.
Ever. His parents hadn't exactly given him the skills with
their toxic, unbalanced mess of a marriage. It was why
he kept so firmly, so calmly, to business. But this was
Darcie and she was alone and it was unbearable to watch.

He moved to hunch beside her chair. 'Where are your witnesses?'

She kept staring at the floor. 'We were just going to use the city administrators.'

'You don't have any family here?' he pressed. Why was that? Why hide this from those closest to her? Shouldn't a wedding be a big celebration? It made him more suspicious. 'Not even any friends?'

She didn't answer. He'd worked alongside Darcie for a long time and he'd never seen her like this. Was she really in love with that jerk even though she'd denied it?

*No.*

Every instinct rejected the idea and for more than one reason. She'd been more focused on venting her anger at him rather than running after the guy who'd just jilted her. Her devastation wasn't the guy, but the wedding itself. Whatever the reason was, he knew her marrying was imperative. He recalled again that momentary leap in her blue eyes, that unguarded response when he'd said he'd do it…and something hot churned in his gut. But then she'd not believed him. Her dismissal stung. *No one* dismissed him.

His steely resolve returned. Elias Greyson did not fail. He did not allow it. And he hadn't built his business from the ground up without accumulating some organisational skills. Furthermore he could delegate. Just not to Darcie. Not this time.

'Come on,' he ordered briskly. 'We need to leave.'

Darcie didn't move. She couldn't.

'You need to get married, right?' Elias pressed.

She was too heartbroken to bother trying to explain to him about Lily. Elias Greyson was a playboy with zero intention of settling down and having a family. He would never understand.

'You have your go bag with you?'

At that she looked up into his eyes. 'No,' she said scornfully. 'I resigned, remember?

'We'll swing by and pick it up from your place on the way to the airport.' He ignored her sarcasm and went straight for solution.

Her place? The airport? What?

'You're wasting time. Let's go.' He literally hauled her out of the chair and wrapped his arm around her waist.

Being pressed this close to Elias was overpowering. She was tall but he was taller and so much stronger, and frankly she wasn't sure if she was walking or if he were half carrying her. Feeling the lean strength of him made her all the more weak and just as she realised how mortifying that was they got outside and his car was right there and Olly his driver was studiously not staring at her.

'You know Darcie's home address, right?' Elias checked.

'Of course.'

Darcie folded herself into the farthest corner of the back seat and stared at her phone. Shaun hadn't messaged her. She sent him a quick text asking if he was okay. She didn't dwell on the money she'd transferred only ten minutes ago. There was no point. Her plans were ruined. Elias said nothing; he was busy tapping some thesis on his phone. Back to the deal, no doubt.

When Olly pulled over she immediately opened the door.

'Thanks for dropping me home,' she muttered stiffly. 'You don't need to come in.'

'No?' Too bad. Elias wasn't letting her walk in there

alone. He got out of the car and matched her steps. With every one his disapproval grew. Why did she live in such a run-down, unsafe area? That Olly had never told him where she lived made him inexplicably angry. He'd have done something about it. He stood beside her, clamping his jaw to stop his annoyance unleashing as he followed her up the stairs and watched her unlock the door. He moved inside before she could stop him. And then he stared and all the anger that he'd thought he'd got back under his control emerged again.

'Do I not pay you enough, Darcie?' he asked softly.

It wasn't even a flat. It was a sparse and uncomfortable bedsit with a narrow bed, no sofa, no oven, just two hobs that didn't look like they'd been used recently. Her clothing hung neatly on a wooden stand. The grey trousers and white blouses that were so familiar to him and somehow made him even more annoyed.

'What do you wear to relax?' he muttered beneath his breath.

Of course the room was so small that she heard. She shot him a look. Right. She *didn't* relax. She worked all the hours for him. She was always willing to accept an extra project. He didn't even ask anymore; he just handed them to her because he knew she'd get it done. And he'd paid her more than enough, of course. But this was such a small place in a hellish part of town so what was she doing with the pay cheque? Was there debt? Yet he couldn't see how she'd accrued any because she'd not got tertiary qualifications until she'd started working for him. So then what? Why?

Far too late he realised he didn't know anywhere near enough about her. And he didn't like it. So that was going to change.

He caught sight of her travel bag tucked under the small fold-up table and grabbed it.

'What are you doing?' Darcie asked.

'What you want,' he replied coolly, hefting the bag in his hand and opening the door for her. 'We're getting married in Vegas, Darcie. And we're going there now.'

# CHAPTER FOUR

DARCIE DIDN'T KNOW WHERE—or how—to start. They'd been on this plane for half a day already and Elias hadn't asked her again if she was serious or why she needed to get married. He'd simply acted on her demand and remained silent ever since. She'd been angry and shocked but now she was too scared to say anything in case he changed his mind. In case she woke up—because this had to be a dream, right? Because every so often she glanced across the aisle and caught him watching her and he had the oddest expression in his eyes. Ordinarily Elias was cool and focused and seemingly devoid of emotion. But right now? It looked strangely like *amusement*. But that just couldn't be right.

As usual they sat on opposite sides of his luxurious private jet, diagonally facing each other in the roomy reclining chairs. His legs were stretched out and apparently he was reading, as was his custom, but she was aware he hadn't turned the page in nearly twenty minutes.

She stared at the cover of the book. She'd found one like it on one of the first flights she'd taken in his private jet and had thought it belonged to the pilot. But it had been Elias's reading material for the flight. Not a report, or business journal, but science fiction. The guy read stories of survival in extreme, hostile, other planetary environments. Escaping from this world right here. She didn't understand why he had to. Because Elias's world was perfect, wasn't it?

He had a level of excellence everyone around him was expected to meet and he didn't ever let emotions get in the way. He didn't respond to emotional outbursts, either. Unmoved and impervious, he didn't flare with anger but simply turned away as if he had some inner force field repelling emotional manipulation. If an employee disappointed, they were dismissed. Initially from the room. Ultimately—if the disappointments were repeated— from the firm. There was no volatility or raging; he just had barriers. Though she'd never thought he was cold, nor careless, just *controlled*. He didn't have the time for hysterics or anger. Or even—she sometimes thought— enjoyment. The only outward satisfaction she'd ever seen upon the successful signing of a deal was little more than a nod. He'd put a tab on a bar for his employees to splurge, occasionally he bothered to show, but if he did he'd barely have one drink and then leave. His mind was always already on the next deal.

*Or the date no doubt waiting for him.*

Yeah, there were the women. Or there had been. But they never lasted and there'd not been many in recent months. Okay, any. And yes, she was tragic for knowing that.

But what he was, was a workaholic. She really didn't understand why because surely he was wealthy enough. Yet no one worked harder than he did. Not even her. And every one of his employees was stupid keen to impress him. Herself included. She didn't know why it mattered so much, only that it did. And it was daft because she deeply knew how impossible it was to please people. It didn't matter what else you did, you only had to make one mistake and it was all over. And today Darcie Milne had made a massive mistake. One she had to address. Soon. Absently she rubbed her wrist. She still felt the warmth and weight of his hand on her skin.

She shivered at the memory and muttered her thoughts before thinking better of it. 'Are we really going to Las Vegas?'

'I was flying to the States anyway,' he drawled. 'This is simply a sidebar on that journey.'

She stiffened at his uncharacteristically sardonic tone. 'So glad it's not an inconvenience.'

Elias actually chuckled.

Darcie had to grit her teeth to stop her jaw falling open. This really was *amusing* to him? When was Elias *ever* amused by anything she said? As she stared at him, she saw challenge build in his eyes. He was waiting for her to say something more.

But she didn't. She couldn't. Because *this* time she thought first. She remembered what was most important. Lily. She had to focus on Lily. Because if there was the slightest chance Elias would follow through on his mad proposal, she had to take it.

Elias sprawled back in his seat, disappointed that Darcie hadn't said anything more and wondering what on earth had happened to get her to this level of desperate. Anyone else and he'd be confident about getting to the bottom of whatever the problem was in minutes—and equally certain it wouldn't be anything requiring a remedy as drastic as marriage. He could find other solutions to all kind of problems without breaking a sweat. But this was Darcie and he knew her attention to detail. If

Darcie felt it was imperative to get married, then it was imperative. So *why* did she need to be wed so swiftly? When was a marriage ever a 'life and death' situation? His imagination ran riot. Was there some stalker she was hiding from? Was it a shotgun wedding—was she *pregnant*? He almost growled. Not to that guy, she wasn't, so if she was pregnant, then to who?

*Come upstairs with me?*

Something in his veins simmered at the echo of a hesitantly whispered question. Was *that* why she'd flirted with him so abominably the other week? Was she desperate to find a father for her unplanned pregnancy? He had to count to ten before he could breathe again. Now his curiosity wasn't just eating him up—his conjecture was growing wilder by the second.

But as much as he wanted to, he refused to ask her right now. She'd never spoken to him like that before. But before, she was his employee. Now he was no longer her boss and he couldn't order her about. He would wait until she was ready to speak to him. He wanted her to *want* to speak to him. And right now she clearly didn't.

During a flight like this Darcie would usually work through her checklist, making sure all the deal preparations were in place while Elias read because he was usually ready. But he wasn't ready today. He was astonished to realise that not only had he not thought about the Williams deal in hours, he had zero concentration to give it now and even more shockingly didn't give a damn. Because his curiosity ran unabated. He flicked through his files on his phone, accessing the résumé the temp agency had originally sent when they'd put Darcie forward for a position at his firm. But it didn't tell him anything he didn't already know. He wanted to *understand* Darcie, and it was a shock to realise he knew nothing of actual substance about her. Nothing personal.

*Fancy cheese.* Yeah, that was about it. He knew she liked fancy cheese. Because at one event early on in her employment he'd watched from a distance as she'd surreptitiously sneaked a piece of soft brie from the buffet table at the back of the room. Her reaction had been both gorgeous and gauche. He'd kept watching, wryly amused as she'd tried so hard—and failed—to resist sneaking another. Then another. And then he remembered that working late one night a few weeks later he'd noticed her growing pallor and it dawned on him—belatedly—that she'd not eaten. He'd been on an adrenaline rush and forgotten about food, plus he was supposed to have a late dinner date. But Darcie had had nothing. He'd gone to the office fridge and found some cheese and watched the colour return to her cheeks. Her deep inhalation, her sigh of contentment, her appetite *satisfied*...he'd got inexplicably angry.

'Why didn't you tell me you hadn't eaten?' he'd challenged her. 'Why didn't you complain?'

She'd offered the faintest of smiles. 'It's not in my job description to complain.'

'It's your job to ensure *all* details are met. You can't do that if you're not properly fuelled.'

'Well, if we're considering blame, then perhaps it's your job—as my employer—to factor in proper breaks for your workforce. It's late and we've been going nonstop for hours.'

It was one of the rare times she'd challenged him—with a hint of insolence that had barely surfaced since.

That night Elias had planned to celebrate prepping the deal with his date of the day. But he'd cancelled. He'd never stopped to truly consider why before. But he'd got sidetracked watching Darcie Milne eat cheese. And from then, he now acknowledged, he'd ensured such snacks were always available in the office. Over time he'd discovered it wasn't just cheese she was partial to but dried fruit—apricots, mango, apple—and nuts—walnuts, cashews, macadamias. She was like a little mouse who needed frequent feeding because she point-blank refused to attend business dinners with him. If they were abroad she retreated to her hotel room to work. He'd not argued with her decision. In fact he'd appreciated the barrier it kept between them. They were professional, never personal. But he'd always ensured there was a platter available for her. But she'd touched none of the supply he insisted was kept on the plane today. He pointedly gestured to the plate the flight crew had put on the table.

'You're not hungry?' he prompted her.

She shook her head.

He didn't like her silence. He didn't like the bruised look returning to her eyes. And he certainly didn't like the hot feeling tightening his gut.

His rule was to reject responsibility for how someone else *felt*. He always, always maintained emotional distance. After the hellish years with his father's coercion and his mother's misery, he'd rejected such a future for himself. Yet he hadn't been able to stop himself not just reacting to Darcie now, but provoking her in turn. And his reaction wasn't only irritation any more.

At the register office she'd been so compelling he'd been unable to release his hold on her. But she'd barely spoken since lambasting him then. He knew she was striving to regain her self-control and it was taking quite some doing—just like the day he'd met her. He'd never forgotten the emotion she'd tried and failed to hide during the interview. Fear had widened her eyes. He'd almost dismissed her as too nervy to cope with the relentless hours he frequently required in the office. But that same thing had made him take a chance on her. She'd not only wanted work, he'd sensed she'd desperately *needed* it.

Frankly he hadn't been afraid to use that need—hungry workers were driven and focused. Turned out none more so than Darcie Milne. She'd not allowed any distractions to interfere with her performance. She'd been available almost any and every time he'd asked. The one exception she'd stipulated was a two-hour stretch on Sunday afternoons. She'd made it clear nothing could interfere with that and given how accommodating she was the rest of the time, he'd respected it. Though he'd long wondered what the appointment she kept so religiously was. Even when they'd been abroad she'd locked herself in the hotel room for those two hours for a phone or video call. But he'd never asked.

He'd known from the first that she was smart, that she could grow into someone indispensable. And she had. Two weeks from when the agency had sent her he'd offered her a permanent position at four times her agency rate. Then when he'd found out she was working towards some qualifications online late in the evening when she wasn't working for him, he'd insisted on paying the tuition fees. He was reaping the reward of her diligence anyway. But even with that extra workload, she'd never broken down, never lost it with him for asking too much—not even after they'd pulled all-nighters to get deals ready. It was a miracle in his experience. Prior to Darcie he'd burned through executive assistants.

He wasn't volatile but he knew his expectations and demands on their skill and time were extreme. For those who could hack it, it was great. Those who couldn't left. Many had left. And because of his father's infidelity with his secretary Elias never mixed business with pleasure. The moment he'd offered Darcie Milne a job was the moment he filed her in the *do not touch* category.

*Do not* think about her beyond the professional. *Do not* wonder about what she did at night when she wasn't working, and certainly *do not* dwell on who she may or may not do that stuff with. Yet shockingly Darcie Milne sometimes slid into his dreams. He couldn't control those. So for a time he'd been determined to prove she wasn't his type. He'd dated other women the absolute opposite to her. He'd refused to get hung up on one individual he barely knew and who was utterly out of bounds. Only his dating had become more sporadic in these past few months. It was because he'd dived even deeper into work.

But he'd battled an inappropriate arousal from the second she'd stormed into his office this morning. That mood had been brewing these last two weeks and now it exploded. *Want*. Such bone-aching, endless want. Painful and intense, it was building into an unfettered firestorm of craving that was almost, *almost* uncontrollable.

Sex was a physical release. But the emotion and expectation of relationships—the burden of someone else's feelings beyond immediate gratification—he'd mastered the art of avoiding those. He didn't allow strong feelings of his own. Lust was recreational and love didn't exist. He liked his life straightforward, and his interactions with women were *very* straightforward. He always made it clear he wasn't looking for a wife. Some were fine with that while some had pretended to accept it, but thought they might change his mind. They never had. Never would. As for children? No. People screwed up their kids. But he wasn't going to because he wasn't having any.

But Darcie was different to him. She had more emotional intelligence. One time she'd shot him a shockingly disapproving look when an analyst had turned in sub-par research and Elias had let him know. He'd caught her soothing the guy after, which was irritating because it wasn't as if Elias had yelled at the guy. He never yelled at anyone. He'd never allow himself to lose that level of control. She'd told him he could be very 'dismissive', which had irked him more than it should. But the fact was her people skills made the office run more smoothly and he didn't want to lose her. She was a key asset in much of his success, and Elias liked success. He liked the challenge of taking on a competitor and beating them. He enjoyed researching—coolly, rationally assessing the qualities of each investment or acquisition. He picked winners. He was good at it.

He spread his fingers, still feeling her warm, fragile wrist, as he considered what she'd said she needed now. To be married. Darcie *herself*, he realised, was a prospective acquisition for him personally. If he were to list the attributes of an ideal partner, she would fit most. Calm—usually. Not demanding—usually. She had a similar work ethic plus she already understood his needs and not only accepted them, she worked well alongside him. At least in the business sense. She could give him the 'values' he was lacking. She would, he decided, make a *perfect* wife. She wouldn't ask too much of him emotionally. And the fact that they had undeniably shocking chemistry was quite the juicy cherry on top.

'Are we landing already?' She suddenly sat up.

'Yeah.' He stretched the tension from his spine. 'And we're all booked in at a chapel. We'll go there right away.'

Her eyes widened but her chin lifted and he felt that anticipation ripple through him again. Was he actually enjoying himself? He'd not done something this rash in, well, ever. This was spontaneous, quite possibly insane, and while it would be easy as anything to stop, he really didn't want to. He wanted to see just how far Darcie Milne would go with this.

Her luscious lips parted, but she said nothing as she stared at him.

'Isn't that what you wanted?' he asked blandly.

That spark flared in her eyes. The one he'd not seen enough from her—*challenge*.

At the sight of it he almost purred inside. Yeah, to his amazement he was enjoying himself. Immensely.

'Because whatever it is you want, Darcie,' he added, 'I'm here to deliver it for you.'

# CHAPTER FIVE

DARCIE STILL WASN'T sure her voice was going to work and certainly wasn't sure of what she was going to say. They'd quickly cleared customs and the waiting chauffeur had driven them straight to a chapel in an outrageously large limousine that had given her plenty of space from the man formerly known as her boss. Now she hovered just inside the doorway while he conversed in smooth undertones with a gloriously neon-clad receptionist.

Sick with nerves, she checked her phone again but there was still no message from Shaun. Taking a breath, she put it in her pocket and finally let herself look at Elias properly. She'd struggled not to stare at him for the entire flight. Correction, she'd struggled not to stare at him for *years*. Tall, dark, devastatingly gorgeous with his lean, muscular frame and hair that needed rumpling and shoulders that deserved to be clung on to…the guy was a long, lush glass of impossible.

'It's a veritable mix-and-match platter,' he said with a sardonic lift of his eyebrows on his return. 'We can choose any number of things, including variants of our vows depending how flowery you want to get.'

She couldn't appreciate his looks now. This was all

too real and impending panic made her stomach churn. 'Elias—'

'Would you like to freshen up after the flight?' He grasped her arm and steered her along the corridor and into a private room. 'This is our dressing room. I'd assumed I'd wear a suit but perhaps you'd prefer me in denim?'

'*Elias.*'

He was on a rampage of sarcasm-edged activity—determined to prove that he could arrange this. Even when it was ridiculous. But he wasn't going to stop until she told him to. Until she told him *why*. 'I can't let you do this.'

'*Let* me do this?' It was a coolly spoken challenge, but his hot gaze tilted her world on its axis all over again. Elias didn't talk to anyone like this. He didn't act like this. Ever. Swift yes, but not rash. Not impulsively.

She swallowed. 'Try to help me.'

His focus narrowed. 'You said you had to get married. Today.'

'Yes,' she agreed. 'But the reasons are complicated and they're really not your problem.'

'Are they not?' he queried silkily. 'I thought this was all my fault. I thought I'm the ogre who ruined everything.'

'You are,' she ground out, trying to rein in her flaring temper all over again. She dragged in a calming breath but with him being so in her space it was hard to think. The combination of shattering disappointment and frustration and futility meant she was losing her already slim grip on herself. 'But while I appreciate all your effort to try to fix things…' She shook her head and mumbled. 'I should have said all this hours ago.'

'Why didn't you?'

'I got *so* mad…' She closed her eyes. She'd got so *hurt*. So frustrated—she'd wanted to make him feel something, to expose *any* kind of emotion. She'd wanted to lash out and make him pay for stunning her with that hit of hope and of sheer *want*. But like she could tell him *that*? She'd not been able to tell him what she really thought for years but as for admitting such mortifying and unrequited emotion?

'Did you want to see how far I'd go, Darcie?' he asked softly as he stepped towards her.

She didn't know how to answer that. He lightly put his hands on her waist. So lightly. But she stilled, completely.

'Testing me is a little dangerous, isn't it?' he asked.

'No. Because I don't think you're dangerous.' Only he was. Dangerous for her heart. Right now it was skipping every third beat.

'No?'

They'd never stood this close. Any time they'd inadvertently brushed too closely—getting into a lift or passing in a narrow corridor—one or other of them had always quickly moved off. But not today. Today his grip on her tightened and she didn't step back like she should.

'I'm sorry,' she mumbled, dropping her gaze, desperate to hide the swarm of emotions his touch was unleashing. That mad desire to provoke him resurged. What was with her inner rebel coming to the fore?

'No. You don't get to say sorry and expect me to just forget about it.' His voice was husky. 'You don't get to walk away without a real explanation. Not this time.'

She didn't mistake the softness of his voice. 'Elias…'

'Why don't you just tell me what the problem is?' he

suggested too coolly. 'And maybe we can work it out together. We're quite the capable team, you and I.'

*Team?* She actually quivered at being bracketed with him. So *stupid.* Of course she owed him the entire explanation. He'd just flown her to Vegas on her ill-tempered whim and she had to pull herself together. 'There's someone else involved.'

His grip hardened. '*Another* man? A different one from that other guy?'

She shook her head. 'Someone young and innocent. Someone who's lost enough already.'

'Meaning?'

She swallowed again because her throat was awfully tight. Just speaking about Lily upset Darcie. 'Her name is Lily. She's four years old and I'm going to foster her.'

'A child?' His eyes widened.

'My best friend's daughter.' She sighed. 'Zara died a few years ago and Lily's been in the system ever since.'

'She has no father around?'

'Not from the start.' Her words tumbled out. 'Lily's already been removed from one home. I can't let her face a future of constant upheaval…' It meant so much, touched nerves so raw she struggled to articulate it.

Elias's expression eased ever so slightly. 'You don't think there'll be other good foster parents?'

'There's no guarantee she'll get someone good and frankly there's no one as good as me.' Desperation shuddered through her and released in a volley of raw truth. '*I'm* here. *I* know her. *I* love her. And I can care for her better than *anyone* else ever could because I *know* what it's like!'

It took her a second to realise that not only had Elias

stepped closer, but somehow she was basically leaning against him.

'You have a relationship with her.' The softest query.

'From the first.' Darcie couldn't bear to think of those years when she and Zara and lived together in their cramped, cold flat. 'Now I see her every Sunday unless I'm away, but even then I talk to her by phone. I refuse to disappear from her life and I will *never* stop fighting for her.' She drew breath and pushed back, pulling her wallet from her pocket she flipped it open so he could see the photo of Zara holding Lily. She needed to show him, to see his reaction.

He released her and remained still, the slightest of frowns knitting his brow as he studied the picture. Then he looked back up at her. She knew he was processing. *This* was the Elias she understood. Quick at comprehending. Quietly assessing all angles at lightning speed. Evaluating and deciding.

'But you've not been able to foster her until now,' he clarified.

Yeah, straight to the problem.

'They won't let me.' She dragged in another breath. 'At least they haven't until now. Apparently I was too young to apply to care full-time for a foster child when Zara died.'

There was a little more to it than that, but some things were too personal. Too mortifying.

'How long ago was that?'

'Just over three years,' she explained. 'Now I'm older but her latest social worker implied that being married will make me appear even more mature and capable of caring for her. That they'll think I'm less likely to ditch her and go clubbing.'

Bitterly she remembered the judgement of the case worker who'd come to see her the day Zara had died. The assumptions the woman had made when she'd seen where Zara and Darcie had lived. She'd instantly decided she'd never allow Darcie to keep caring for Lily. Darcie had had to fight hard to even stay in touch with the child.

'Clubbing? You?' Elias's gaze intensified. 'Have you ever gone clubbing?'

'Not in recent times,' she muttered, a cinder of embarrassment curling up from someplace buried deep.

'What else does this social worker suggest you need?'

'To be financially stable.'

'That's why you live in that place,' he muttered. 'You were saving all your money.'

'Yes.'

'But you can't raise a child in that tiny room.' He leapt to the next point. 'Where were you and whatshisname going to live? Does he have more of an apartment than you?'

'His flat is perfectly adequate.'

'Is it?' His mouth compressed into a flat line.

His scepticism made her defensiveness flare. 'We don't all need to live in a glass penthouse a stone's throw from Michelin restaurants and celebrity haunts. Some of us have more simple requirements.'

'Living within a stone's throw of Michelin restaurants isn't a necessity for a child,' he agreed. 'I'd have thought parks and peace would be more of a priority.'

'His flat was near a park.'

The muscle in his jaw flicked. 'So you need financial security, a good place to live and the appearance of stability in your personal life to enhance your application, do I have that correct?'

'It's the start, yes.' There would be interviews and assessment and monitoring but she would have the chance at least to prove that she could provide a loving home for Lily.

'I assume you'd need to present a happily married facade and demonstrate you're decent caregivers for the girl.'

'I would be the primary caregiver.'

'Of course.' He nodded. 'How long?'

'How long what?'

'For how long were you planning on being married to him?'

'Long enough for my foster care application to get approved. Possibly even made permanent.'

'That could take years.'

'We hadn't really nailed down a finish date. It was going to depend on how things worked out with the initial application.' She licked her lips. 'Of course there were going to be hoops.'

'The first of which was him sticking around for the wedding ceremony,' Elias said dryly.

The dart hit home. 'Shaun hasn't had it easy,' Darcie said defensively. 'I knew it was a big ask of him. But he would have gone through with it if you hadn't stormed in there like you owned—' She broke off and glared at him. 'Like you had any right to...'

'To what?'

'To follow me. To question me.' She flung her head back. 'To interfere with my life in *any* way.'

He was closer again now. 'He doesn't love you.'

So what? No one did. Almost no one ever had. Except for Zara. And Darcie loved Zara's daughter Lily like she was her own. She *was* family. The only one she had. 'And

I already told you, marriage isn't always about love. And since when were you such a *romantic*? You don't care about anything other than your work. You'd never consider marriage. You're so cynical and controlled you—'

She broke off, realising how far over the mark she'd trod.

'Don't stop now, Darcie. Tell me how you really feel.'

How she *really* felt? About the hope she'd felt when he'd proposed—that it had been so selfishly centred? She shook her head and reminded herself of the basics. 'This isn't about that anymore. This is about Lily.'

Darcie ached to spare Lily the life both she and Zara had experienced.

He stared down at her. 'And you would do anything for her.'

'Yes.'

'Then why haven't you married me already? We could've been done five minutes ago.'

'Because you didn't know the whole story.'

'And now I do.'

'Yes, but—'

'Why the hesitation?' He suddenly frowned. 'Oh, I see, they've met Shaun. You turn up with a new groom now, you're going to look sketchy.'

'Actually, I hadn't told them yet.' She bit her lip. 'I wanted to make sure it was going to happen first.'

'You thought he might not come through for you?'

'I just wanted to be sure.'

'Can you be sure with me?'

She didn't know how to answer that.

His eyebrows shot up. 'You've been working for me for years. Do you not know me well enough to know you can count on me?' A sharp intake of breath. 'I've even brought you all the way here, Darcie. Now I'm really offended.'

'I didn't mean to offend you,' she mumbled. 'But it's not personal. I'm never sure about anyone.'

'No?' His gaze on her narrowed. 'Then be sure about this. I believe you've investigated all your options. You're highly intelligent and capable. If this is what you think you need, then my offer stands,' he said bluntly. 'You don't just need secure accommodation. You need a family home.' He listed off the requirements. 'You need financial security, space. If you would prefer not to work while you go through the system to get Lily, that's not a problem. I can provide all of these things for you.'

'But Lily needs more.' Darcie drew breath and faced reality—knowing it would make him change his mind. 'If you do this, then you'd be in her life. You'd have to have a relationship with her.'

'I wouldn't really be in her life.'

'You couldn't avoid her. Children pick up on—'

'I'm at work all day and I travel a lot. I'll be on the fringes. Her primary relationship is already with you. I would only pop in here and there.'

Something made her doggedly deny this would be that easy. 'If you didn't really want her, she would know. She would feel it. '

His mouth thinned. 'I would want her to be happy and secure. She would understand that. Did you have concerns about this with your previous groom?'

'Shaun loved Zara and I knew he would love Lily because of that.' She lifted her chin. 'But you don't believe in love. And apparently you don't believe in marriage without love. Ergo, you don't believe in marriage.' She questioned him. 'So *why* would you do this? Why would you even *want* to?'

He gazed beyond her for a moment and then looked back. His blue eyes cooler, sharper somehow. 'Because there are advantages to my getting married. Especially to someone like you.'

'Like *me*?' She stiffened. What did he mean by that?

'We have much in common,' he said. 'Neither of us is ruled by excessive emotion. At least—' a rueful smile curved his mouth '—not usually. We're able to recognise a good deal and we both understand the sacrifices needed to make sure it happens. We can coolly work through the benefits and the costs of any kind of arrangement.'

The benefits and the costs? Darcie shivered at his clinical assessment of their commonalities, and in reality he was wrong.

She'd had no real choice other than to keep her cool in the office. And if she had a real choice now she'd stomp out of here in a heartbeat. Only the thought of Lily kept her back. And okay, *he* kept her back. Her desire for them *both*.

'You're able to suppress your appetite and emotions in the business environment. You have extraordinary control, Darcie. It's admirable.'

'It's not some admirable strength, Elias,' she said harshly. 'It was a necessity.'

'Because you needed the job. You needed the money.'

'Yes.'

'Even so, plenty of people couldn't cope the way you did. They'd get another job. You didn't. You stayed. You were determined to, I think.'

She lifted her chin. Yes, there was that. She hadn't wanted to be bettered by him. He was the challenge and she'd revelled in rising to his requirements and never letting him know how close to the edge she really was. But long term it was unsustainable because of how she really felt.

Something gleamed in his eyes. 'You're a match for me, Darcie. And I won't deny the appearance of stability in my personal life would be advantageous for me at this time.'

Elias Greyson liked to win and he was very used to it. But this particular challenge was one he now wanted with a need that sliced bone deep. But she'd been dependent upon him for her job and only now did he understand why she'd so desperately needed that income. That power imbalance had prevented her from being completely honest—perhaps even completely herself— with him. And here he was setting himself up for more of the same, was he not? Because her *gratitude* to this marriage could constrain her behaviour. He was going to have to be careful, ensure they fully communicated. He was going to have to keep this controlled. But recapturing his usual cool clarity was challenging because there was one last piece of the Darcie puzzle he'd yet to properly solve. While there were still shadows and secrets in her eyes, some things she couldn't hide, and that included the very basic, very strong, chemistry sparking between them. And suddenly all that mattered—the urge overriding reason—was that she did not walk out the way she'd walked out this morning. The next time she left him it would be on his terms and at a time of his choosing.

'You said not all marriages are for romance or based in love. They're a solution to a problem,' he said harshly.

She didn't move. 'Yes, but I still don't understand

what problem you face. This would be a huge imposition—an awfully big sacrifice for you to make.'

That this all *was* about a child had made him feel both better and worse. He didn't want to think of Darcie pregnant by some other man. Yeah, it was an appalling gut reaction—he'd no right to feel possessive or jealous. Yet he had.

'You don't think I'm capable of making a sacrifice for someone?'

Colour flooded her face. 'No, that's not what I meant.'

'Sure it was,' he said softly. Offended all over again.

Surely he was a better bet than the jerk who'd walked out on her only moments before their wedding?

'But you're still not grasping the advantage for me,' he said more calmly than he was feeling. 'This would be convenient.'

'Convenient?'

The flight had bought him time to consider the pros and cons of joining forces with Darcie on a more permanent basis and the more he'd thought about it, the more sense it had made. She'd been right in that he didn't believe in marriage, but marriage could be viewed as simply another merger. Political alliances dating back hundreds of years, across all cultures had succeeded. Without confusion or complications, they worked. And although he certainly didn't believe a couple should stay together for a child, the point here was he and Darcie *wouldn't* stay together. It was only until Lily's guardianship was awarded to Darcie that the arrangement needed to last.

The thought of that child being lonely and scared in an unsafe place was untenable. It hadn't been often for Elias, but he had felt unsafe at times. And while Elias had never wanted to be a father—he knew he didn't have the skills—he didn't hate children. And the thought of this one orphaned and alone made his gut ache. A child needed and deserved to be wanted. And Lily was. By Darcie. But it was more than the thought of Lily driving him now. It was the expression in Darcie's eyes when she'd described the little girl's situation, and her desire to be there, that compelled him. *Her* heartbreak.

He ached to ease it for her. More than that, there was a fierce, irrational drive to keep her close.

*Not irrational.* It was pure basic instinct. He'd not acknowledged to himself before how much he wanted her because he'd had to push it away. It had been inappropriate and out of bounds. But now?

'I don't do love, Darcie, but it seems you understand that already,' he suddenly snapped. 'You're not in love with me, correct?'

'Correct,' Darcie instinctively snapped back.

'Then this is nothing more than another deal. After a year we'll understand the likelihood of success in your application to care for the child. We'll review the arrangement then.'

She blinked. He'd give her one whole year to try for Lily. 'Why would you want a wife for a year?'

'Why wouldn't I?' he countered. 'Especially a wife who understands the pressures of my work upon my time. A woman who understands my lifestyle. A wife will give me the air of humanity I'm often accused of lacking and a beautiful wife is the one thing I currently don't have as a societal measure of success.'

A *beautiful* wife? She shook her head as she realised how out of her depth she was. 'I'm not the sort of wife you should have.'

To her amazement he actually smiled. 'In what way could you possibly be deficient?'

She rolled her eyes. 'I'm not well-educated. I didn't go to the right schools and know all the right people. I don't have the required etiquette. I'm not a clothes model. I'll embarrass you.' There. A matter-of-fact assessment of her shortcomings. Not *quite* all of them, but the only ones she was prepared to articulate now.

'I don't want a model wife,' he said bluntly. 'I want someone who understands what I do and how much it matters to me. Someone who can fit in with minimal disruption. And, yes, I'm aware you're bringing a child with you but your demands upon me won't be those of a normal wife because we already understand that this is going to be a business relationship. My benefit is knowing I'll no longer be judged for dating or for my lifestyle.'

'But you don't care what anyone says about you,' she pointed out, equally bluntly.

'I care when it impacts on my deals.' He lifted his chin. 'And Vince Williams doesn't like my lifestyle.'

So it really was only for business.

'After the end of our brief marriage, I will, naturally, be devastated and vow never to marry again. Perhaps people will finally consider I have a valid reason to remain single.'

'That's preposterous.'

'Yet enchantingly believable.' He actually smiled again. 'People will think it serves me right. You'll have to be the villainess who breaks my formerly impenetrable heart, Darcie. Can you cope with the momentary vilification or shall you not care?'

'No one will ever believe I broke your heart. People will perceive it to be the other way round.'

'And will you cope with that?'

She straightened. 'Of course, because I'll have Lily and I really don't care what anyone says about me. And this is just a pretence.'

'Exactly. A pretence that serves an admirably worthy goal.'

Yet she still couldn't quite say yes. There was still one thing they had to address. 'What would you expect of me personally?' She braced when she saw a flicker of amusement around his mouth. 'Do you expect we'll be intimate?'

He shot her a coolly devastating look. 'You weren't averse to the idea of being intimate with me a couple of weeks ago, Darcie.'

Yeah, it had been inevitable that he would point that mortifying fact out.

'Why did you do it?' He finally asked the question that had been hanging between them for days. 'Why did you proposition me that night in Edinburgh?'

Darcie swallowed, buying time even when she'd had days to dream up some flippant reply. But she had none. She had to be honest, because apparently the man was seriously still willing to give her the chance to get almost everything she wanted.

'You were planning to marry someone else,' he added when she didn't immediately reply. 'I assume you were engaged at the time you asked me back to your room?'

'Yes.'

'You would have cheated on him.'

She shook her head. 'It wasn't a real engagement and it wasn't going to be a real wedding. We weren't going to...' She huffed the tightness from her chest. 'I wasn't going to sleep with Shaun. We don't have that kind of relationship.'

'Really?' Elias's eyes narrowed. 'You're what, *friends*?'

She didn't know why he sounded so sceptical. 'Is that so hard to believe? We were in the same group home for a while.'

'Group home?'

'Foster homes,' she explained.

'Why was Shaun doing it then?'

Darcie hesitated. She was unsure of what Elias's reaction would be to the fact that she'd given Shaun money. So she opted for partial truth. 'I told you he loved Lily's mother, my friend Zara. He was doing it for her.'

'Not because he wanted you?'

'No.' She braced again. 'Aside from the fact that he told you, isn't it obvious given how quickly he abandoned me when you showed up and started raging?'

Elias's frown only deepened. 'So you weren't going to sleep with him at all through the marriage?'

'I wasn't going to sleep with *anyone*.'

'But that night you decided the engagement didn't count and you thought you'd try me? Did you want one last romp before you sacrificed your sex life so you could foster your friend's daughter?'

She felt a blush burning its way up her entire body. She'd thought it her one chance for *any* kind of sex life. 'I guess you could put it that way.'

'How else would you put it?' He leaned closer. 'Explain it to me, Darcie. Why, when you've worked for me for years, did you suddenly decide to proposition me out of the blue?'

'I knew I was leaving and you weren't going to be my

boss anymore, and I got a little drunk and I was…' She rolled her shoulders. She'd hoped he'd forgotten those five minutes of pure mortification, but she couldn't explain the last part. It was *too* personal. 'It doesn't matter anyway. You didn't want me. Nothing happened aside from me making a massive fool of myself.'

'I didn't want you?'

'Obviously not.'

'Obviously?' He was like a statue again. 'You knew I couldn't possibly say yes.'

She stared at him sceptically. He never said no to other women. He had short flings all the time. Sometimes it had felt like he'd sleep with anyone *but* her.

'You were tipsy,' he gritted. 'I'd watched you. You'd had three glasses of champagne when you never normally drink a drop.'

Well, yes. She'd been drowning her sorrows and crazy courage had surged in their place.

'Moreover, and more importantly,' he rasped, 'I was your boss. There was a power imbalance—one that had been there from the moment we met.'

'But I was leaving.'

'I didn't know that then,' he shot back.

But it wouldn't have made any difference. She'd humiliated herself. 'I'm sorry I put you in an awkward position.'

'An awkward position?' He echoed in disbelief. 'You have no idea what position you put me in that night.'

Heat scorched her face.

'Darcie Milne. Assistant extraordinaire.'

Bitterness rose. 'You didn't want to lose me as an assistant.' She wasn't a *woman* to him. She didn't think he'd ever seen her as one.

'No. I was never going to risk losing my best assistant.'

'But then I resigned.' Could she sound any more desperate?

'Until this morning I was confident I could get you to change your mind and stay.'

She blinked. She thought he'd forgotten or simply didn't care that she'd resigned. But how had he planned to change her mind? 'Because you're good at convincing women to do whatever you want them to?'

'I've never treated you in that way.'

Yes. Didn't she know it.

'And I certainly wasn't going to take advantage of you at the time,' he said.

'Because I was tipsy and you were my boss.'

'Yes,' he growled impatiently.

'Is there any situation in which you would take advantage of me?'

Somehow the shocking question slid out. There was a silence. And mortification. All over again.

'I *never* want to take advantage of you,' he said.

Of course it was the right answer. So why did that teeny tiny part of her feel crushed?

'I would far prefer to have you as my equal, Darcie. Where one of us doesn't take advantage of the other.'

'We're *never* going to be equals, Elias.' He had too much power. 'We're too different—our backgrounds, education, everything.'

'I disagree. I think we could be equal in curiosity, integrity and loyalty and we could even be equal in this marriage. If it goes ahead, I wouldn't want you breaking your vows to me and I won't break mine to you.'

'You'll survive a sexless life?'

Something flickered in his face. 'It's only one year, is it not?' He stepped closer. 'If this happens then this lingering power imbalance between us has to be gone. As my wife, you're not *required* to do anything. Certainly not sleep with me. Though—' Laughter suddenly flashed in his eyes. 'You might actually have to dine with me on occasion. And engage with my clients in a capacity that straddles the business and the personal.'

She gazed up at him, knowing she should say yes, yet something still held her back. 'You don't really need me for any of that. It's still not much of a win for you.'

'Perhaps it's the most simple win of all. The intangible, altruistic satisfaction of doing something for someone else.'

Her heart thudded hard then. 'For Lily.'

'Right,' he nodded. 'For Lily.'

That's when she got lost in his eyes, trying to understand the man she'd thought she knew.

His lips compressed and he glanced at the clock on the wall. 'We don't have much longer, Darcie. You need to decide.'

But her brain was oddly sluggish. She'd seen Zara try the 'love' route and it had ended in disaster. Playing on old loyalties and emotions—like what she'd tried with Shaun—hadn't worked either. A cool businesslike contract? Maybe that was the answer.

She'd known all her life that people couldn't be trusted. Ultimately—always—they left. Both her parents had left her. Zara had left her. Shaun had just left her. Elias would, too, eventually. But he wasn't promising forever. He wasn't promising any kind of frills. He was being up-front about the facts. This wasn't just a fake marriage; it was a short-term one. And she knew Elias.

He was ruthless but he was also fair. She *had* seen him follow through on deal after deal. She'd seen him have high expectations of people's performance but he'd also rewarded those who deserved it. Including her. Maybe she could trust him to maintain his side of this bargain.

She understood that he would be absent a lot. But if she were successful at getting her placement, Darcie would be Lily's primary caregiver, and one person could make all the difference in another's life. You could have a big family and feel nothing but lonely and isolated. Or worse. Sometimes you needed just *one* person. Lily needed her.

She searched Elias's face. She had no idea what kind of family he'd come from or even whether he was in touch with any of them. Did he have siblings? Where were his parents? In almost three years there'd been no reference to them at all. What would they think of this? But if he wasn't concerned, then she shouldn't be either, right?

And if there was no emotion between them, maybe there'd be no real expectations that neither of them could live up to.

'Well?' he prompted, his customary curtness restored.

It was enough to solidify her thinking. This was her last chance. He wasn't going to repeat it, or wait for her to think about it long. She knew how he operated. Once he made an offer, the clock started ticking. Accept quickly or miss out forever.

'Okay.' Courage slammed into her veins. 'Let's get married. Right now.'

# CHAPTER SIX

ELIAS'S SUDDEN SMILE was a dazzling flash of pure triumph that Darcie hadn't expected. But he turned away so abruptly she could hardly absorb let alone enjoy it. She dragged in a breath as he went out of the room and called something to the receptionist. The man was even more incredible when he smiled, and that wasn't often enough.

'Would you prefer gold or platinum for your wedding ring?' he asked when he returned. 'You can choose a fine or a heavier set band.'

Darcie blinked at the small collection of gleaming silver and gold rings in the sleek box he'd pulled from his pocket. 'Did you bring this from your collection?'

She knew he kept a supply of jewellery. The first time he'd cancelled a date early on in her employment she'd assumed he'd ask her to arrange a flower delivery or some such, but when she'd offered to do just that—in an attempt to demonstrate her ability to anticipate his needs—he'd looked miffed and coolly informed her that he dealt with his own personal messes, particularly 'clean-up' operations. He'd bluntly added that she wasn't paid to be some kind of emotional nanny. That's when she'd seen the stash in his office safe. 'Clean-up' clearly meant 'pay-off'. He had to have a subscription service to a top jewellery house so he'd always have something appropriate to give a date on any occasion—from the first date to final farewell. At the time she'd almost admired his cold-blooded, richer-than-rich efficiency. But today his practical, clinical planning annoyed her.

'No,' he said blandly. 'The driver collected them from a jeweller on his way to pick us up. Choose one, and if it doesn't fit properly we'll have it adjusted back in London.'

Darcie just pointed to the first one.

'Do you wish to vary the vows or use their standard template?' he asked, his smile audible.

'Standard template is fine,' she muttered mechanically.

'And we'll just stay as we are clothing-wise.' He glanced at the clock on the wall. 'Two minutes and it's our turn. Are my organisational efforts almost at Darcie Milne standards?'

'Almost,' she said stiffly.

Three minutes later it was almost over.

*To have and hold... For better. Worse. Richer. Poorer. Sickness. Health. To love...always.*

The words on the small tablet the marriage celebrant held seemed to float in space in front of her. That she was audible was a shock. More shocking was that faint smile seemingly glued to Elias's face. That he was doing this at all astounded her, but that he was amused by it?

Her heart galloped as anticipation burgeoned. They were going to kiss. Actually kiss. Because now they were husband and wife and the celebrant was looking at them expectantly and there was a skinny teenager holding up a camera.

She froze, breathless, as expectation built to unbearable levels. Elias leaned close. So close. Her eyes drifted shut. The brush of his lips on hers was gossamer light. So light and cool and yet there was an infinitesimal hit of—

He lifted away. He was gone and it had lasted less than a second.

Darcie's eyes flashed open. She stared—shocked and dismayed—because her disappointment was catastrophic. And for a far longer moment than that paltry 'kiss' he looked right at her with an intense, but inscrutable, expression.

'Right,' he suddenly snapped. 'Let's go.'

Darcie nodded, unable to answer.

She was so *stupid*. He hadn't wanted her two weeks ago and he hadn't wanted her now, either—not the way *she* wanted. That 'kiss' had merely been the symbolic, societally required confirmation of their *deal*, not a demonstration of undeniable lust.

Mortified, she wondered what hell she'd just thrown herself into. Because she ached for the man who was now her husband in name only and she had the horrible feeling he'd just seen that. She *had* to pull herself together.

'Do we go straight back to the airport?' she asked desperately.

'We do.' He walked with her to the waiting limousine.

'Good. I need to get back to London as soon as possible.'

There wasn't going to be a honeymoon. That five-minute marriage ceremony meant nothing more than a means to an end. She shouldn't feel this crushed.

'*After* the meeting for the Williams acquisition,' he said.

Oh, right. She'd forgotten that. She scrunched into the far corner of the back seat and pulled out her phone to distract herself. He'd done the same, was firing off message after message. Keeping the company running, no doubt.

'You're worried about Lily?' Elias asked after a few moments, his face still focused on his screen. 'Don't be. I'll get the legal team on it right away.'

The awful thing was she'd hadn't thought about Lily at all in the last few minutes. She'd been thinking only about *herself*. Now she focused. Lily needed her. And then she remembered Shaun.

'Darcie?' Elias's query was soft yet commanding. 'Is everything okay?'

She'd been so fixated on wanting him to touch her she'd forgotten everything that was far more important. Now she willed a message to ping on her phone. But there was nothing. *Hell*. She had to face the reality that the bulk of the independent funds she'd accumulated for herself was all but gone. It wasn't as if she'd never been let down before. But it was embarrassing to have it all happen in front of Elias, who was always so together and who simply wouldn't stand for such treatment. She didn't want to tell him. She didn't want his pity, or his anger, she wanted another kind of attention altogether. She wanted his—

'Is there something more I ought to know?' Elias pressed. 'You look…'

She didn't want him to look at her. She didn't want him to see anything she was truly thinking. Maybe it was better to admit one embarrassment over a far more brutally personal one. 'It's Shaun,' she said baldly.

'What about him?' Elias almost bristled.

Yes. It was a good distraction. 'I need to get in touch with him.'

'Because?'

'Because I gave him money to set up his business and I need to make sure the deal has gone through.'

'You gave him money? When?' Elias's eyes widened. 'Darcie, did you *pay* him to marry you?'

'It was a business arrangement, not so different to this one, really.'

'But he's taken the money and run without delivering his end of the deal,' he said curtly. 'How *much*, Darcie?'

What did it matter? 'As I said, he needed money to invest in his business. I wanted to help and I was going to oversee the accounting once it was underway. If he'd made it a success it would've been good for us.' She saw Elias's expression turn thunderous. 'It's my fault, not his.'

But she'd really thought Shaun had it together. Bitter embarrassment surged. 'I bet you're wishing you'd pushed for more from me now, huh. Knowing I was desperate enough to pay someone almost everything I have.'

'Almost everything?' Elias couldn't believe what he was hearing. 'How much did you transfer to him? When?'

She couldn't look at him as she told him and he couldn't look away from her. He'd scarcely been able to look away from her since that moment in front of the celebrant—when he'd very determinedly not kissed her again; when he'd seen her reaction; when he'd felt terrible.

Now he felt worse. Because now he registered how pale she'd grown. There were smudges beneath her eyes and her mouth drooped. She was exhausted—not just physically, but emotionally, and for the first time since that first job interview she looked fragile.

'That's a lot of money.' Elias battled the urge to pull her

close and make her lean on him. Instead he forced himself to look away and focus on the scenery out the window. The afternoon was closing. It would be late by the time they finally arrived in San Francisco. Too late to talk through what they'd just done. And he had a million things to organise. 'You saved all that from working with me?'

'I didn't have a lot to spend it on.'

'Not that you chose to,' he countered.

But maybe it wasn't that material things didn't interest her…she'd just had to make choices. Plus, she'd had little time to spend money on experiences because she was always working for him. So yeah, no wonder she'd been able to save so much.

'My goal has always been Lily. To do everything I can for her,' she confirmed his thinking. 'If I couldn't become her caregiver then I planned to pay for her to go a good school. I hoped they'd agree. I thought that would have given her stability in that way at least.'

He couldn't resist trying to slake just some of his curiosity. 'Did you go to a good school?'

She shot him a startled look. 'What? No.'

But she was very bright. He knew she could have aced any scholarship exams but he suspected she'd never been given the chance. Why was that? How long had she been in the foster system? Because she had been. She knew 'what it was like'. The injustice of it burned. Her focus was fully fixed on giving her friend's daughter a better life than either she or her friend had had. But what about her own life—her dreams for *herself*? What had those been? What were they now?

His curiosity burned hotter—and most intensely— about her personal desires. Because he'd seen the awareness in her eyes as he'd approached in that sparse, speedy ceremony. He'd felt the receptive softness of her lips. He'd instinctively pulled away. *Immediately.* He'd had to end it—making it the most minimal of kisses. But he couldn't have the first time he kissed her properly be in front of costumed strangers complete with camera in hand. He'd ached for privacy and space.

But then he'd seen her face. He'd seen the yearning and the disappointment. That's when he'd truly understood the depth of her desire. And he was yet to get his heart back to its normal rhythm.

*Want,* right? Pure, physical want. Still now, even as they were driven back to the plane, he fought the irresistible urge to press her luscious body to his. He wanted to plunder. He wanted everything here and now and it had never been as impossible. Because she was exhausted. So exhausted.

So he had to ignore that unbearable, hungry ache running the length of him. He couldn't quite believe the events of the day—couldn't yet figure why he'd reacted to such an extreme. He'd *married* her. Yet what he was discovering today challenged everything he'd thought he knew. Emotionless Darcie? That couldn't be further from the truth. And she was nowhere near as immune to him as she'd been acting for these last two years. He'd known that—but not the degree of her interest.

He battled the urge to reach for her hand. If they were to kiss again, it had to happen in privacy. It had to happen when there was the time and space to do *everything.* Because if it happened again there would be no stopping. But it couldn't happen at all until she was ready.

Until she *said.* And that was never going to be tonight.

Darcie followed Elias back into the waiting jet.

'The flight to San Francisco isn't long,' he said almost

bracingly. 'It'll be better to get there tonight so we'll be fresh for tomorrow.'

'Do you really need me to attend the dinner?'

'You know Vince Williams has strong views. If he hears I've got married—and doubtless he will—then he'll deeply disapprove of my not bringing you.'

'I really don't know that I can project the image you're going for,' she muttered.

'You don't think you can look happy to be married to me?' He shuddered. 'Darcie, you devastate me.'

She rolled her eyes as she fastened her seatbelt. 'I just don't see how it's going to be believable.'

'Why not?' he asked.

There was chemistry that was obvious between a couple, wasn't there? And there clearly wasn't any on his side. She was still smarting from that no-nonsense, barely happened kiss. She gripped the armrests and braced through the take-off and kept her mouth firmly shut.

'We can say we kept our affair under wraps for a long time,' he said when the plane finally levelled out. 'What with the sticky issue of you being my employee until today.'

'What about the fact that your other employees all knew I was getting married and that it *wasn't* to you,' she couldn't resist pointing out. 'It's going to cause a huge gossipy scandal.'

'At your job interview with me you told me you weren't there to make friends, but to get the job done,' he said. 'But it wasn't true. You were friends with them. You told them about your wedding.'

'I hadn't intended to. It slipped out the night before.'

'At the dinner you didn't invite me to.'

'You wouldn't have attended even if I'd asked you. It's not what you do.'

'Dinner isn't what you do either,' he pointed out. 'But it was only pizza, right?'

She stared at him, startled. Because yes, it had been exactly that. Pizza when they were all standing at a bar, not even at a table.

Then his smile suddenly appeared. 'Given that I stormed out of the office after you this morning, I think they'll spin it as some great romantic story—'

'You what?'

'I was too shocked to think.'

'Shocked that I was getting married?' she asked, stung.

'No. Because I thought you were…' He frowned. 'Cheating or something.'

Oh. 'That really pushed your buttons,' she said softly.

'I was so angry I couldn't tell you what I was thinking.'

It had been strong emotional response. Though she knew it wasn't *her* he'd responded to, but the situation. The fact he thought she was cheating. He'd felt for her *groom*, right? Plus, he'd been annoyed that she'd walked out on him. Elias was used to getting what he wanted. But maybe he hadn't always in the past.

They were married. Surely they now needed to learn some personal things about each other—at least to project the illusion of being happily married. 'Have you… had experience with how horrible it is to go through that? To be betrayed by someone?'

His expression shuttered. 'I've seen the fallout from an affair—I know how bad it can be.' He cleared his throat. 'But anyway, all my employees are paid extremely well. Their contract includes discretion. They won't sell us out. Not if they want to keep their jobs.'

He was probably right. And he hadn't wanted to explain anything more about whatever—whoever—that affair was. She got it. She didn't like considering her past much either. And that thought made her realise another danger.

'Shaun might,' she said.

'Shaun might,' he agreed. 'But then he's not going to look very good in it, is he? Especially when he still has the money you transferred to him.'

Yeah. She'd tried to buy a husband. She'd tried to play on Shaun's feelings for Zara. It wasn't that he and she were that close. And she hadn't had anyone else to call on. No family—she'd never had that. No friends—because she'd lost Zara. And since that terrible moment, she'd been working—striving towards getting Lily. It cut deep to realise yet again how alone she was. She didn't want Lily to be alone the way she was. She wanted to build a better life for them both.

She tried not to pay attention when Elias unfastened his seatbelt and moved to the rear of the compartment. She had to get back to not looking at him too much again. But then he appeared right back in front of her. He'd rolled up his sleeves and she couldn't help drinking in the sight of his strong forearms. She knew he went to the gym to work out, but those muscles and that tan suggested outdoor activity as well. He was long, lean and strong and bending towards her and she wanted him to—

'Oh.' She bit her lip.

'I don't believe you're not hungry, Darcie.'

'This looks amazing.' She hurriedly gestured towards the fresh platter he was holding. 'There's always cheese in the office,' she added inanely, desperately trying to cover that embarrassing moment. 'Actually, there are all kinds of snacks in there.'

'Yes.'

She narrowed her gaze suspiciously because that purring answer didn't sound benign. An odd thought occurred. There hadn't always been snacks. Not at the beginning. The other assistants had commented on it when they started appearing. Her heat began to rise.

'Did you...' She trailed off and shook her head. That was a *stupid* thought. All of a sudden she was reading everything into nothing.

'Did I what?' He retook his seat and then gazed across at her with that amusement glinting more visibly in his eyes. 'Did I order all those snacks that are in the office especially for you? Why yes, Darcie, I did.'

Especially for her? She gaped. 'Why would you do that?'

No one had done that—not thought of her tastes, not done something solely for her—in ages. Not since Zara. They'd have done anything for each other, and Darcie would do just that for Zara's daughter. Literally anything. Even marry a man she didn't love.

'Why wouldn't I?' Elias asked casually. 'You function best when you're not starving.'

She bristled. 'I have *never* not functioned well.'

Nor had she starved. Well, not really.

His amused expression deepened. 'That's not what I said. I meant that your performance is *optimal* when you're properly fuelled. Though how you can never seem to manage an actual meal is beyond me. But you like to snack on small plates interspersed throughout the day and that's fine. It is in the company's best interests to supply you with them.'

'The *company's* best interests?'

'Fine. Mine. As I basically am the company. So I guess I really mean me.'

'I guess you do,' she said huskily.

She was astounded he'd even noticed her habits, let alone surreptitiously *supplied* her preferences. But he'd not told her. Not until now. Why? Didn't he want her to think he was actually kind? Too bad. She already knew he was. She'd seen him do things in an annoyingly abrupt way for others—he was thoughtful, yet sandpaperish at the same time. It was those barriers of his, she realised.

'Thank you,' she said softly. Her flush built. It wasn't something she was used to saying because people didn't often do things for her.

He was watching her too closely. 'It was my pleasure.'

Her pulse pounded. It was a courteous reply. He didn't mean it in an *intimate* way. Except his voice was gravelly and the heat in the cabin had increased even more.

'Now will you please enjoy it?' He gestured to the platter.

But she nibbled only a little because strangely her appetite still hadn't made an appearance. It wasn't anxiety; it was hotter than that. 'What about you?'

'I'm enjoying watching you.'

Again there was that thread of something that shouldn't be there. That she couldn't really have heard. She was tired, right? Hearing things he wasn't intending. Except she wasn't all that tired anymore. When she ought to be exhausted, she was growing more alert by the second. But Elias turned to his computer, apparently content to work on the journey for once. That was on her; she'd stolen his time.

They finally landed and were driven to the hotel in the heart of San Francisco. Darcie's breath got shorter, her awareness more intense.

'We have the penthouse suite,' Elias muttered to her as the concierge deferentially stepped forward to greet him.

Darcie lost her stomach in the lift as it whisked them to the top of the building. She heard the beep as the door unlocked and she stepped forward into the suite. There was a large lounge with stunning views across the sky-line and several doors leading from the vestibule. Elias walked to the nearest and opened it. Darcie stilled.

He glanced back from the threshold. 'Good night, Darcie. Sleep well.'

Stunned, she watched him close the door behind him.

He'd left her alone. On automatic pilot, she walked to another door. The bedroom was stunning—luxuri-ous and peaceful—but it didn't soothe the resentment that had suddenly soared. It was her wedding night and she was lying alone in an enormous bed. An unclaimed virgin bride. She'd married a man she knew to have a 'healthy' appetite towards sex. A billionaire playboy no less.

But even he didn't want her.

# CHAPTER SEVEN

DARCIE HAD DECIDED the easiest thing would be to work. To pretend they weren't actually husband and wife. Elias, however, had other ideas.

'What do you mean you don't want me to help you prepare for the meeting?' She glared at him across the dining table in their suite. It was littered with toast, fruit, pastries and a coffeepot, all of which they were both ignoring.

She'd taken so long to get to sleep that by the time she finally had, she was so exhausted she'd entered deep sleep mode and then actually slept in far later than usual. Now it was almost ten thirty and Elias was due for the first of his meetings at Williams VC headquarters.

But apparently he wasn't in a hurry to leave. He shook his head. 'Everything is done. The last report I needed has come in from London. You can relax here and take your time getting ready for tonight.'

Take her time getting ready? What was he expecting?

She bit her lip. The *last* thing she wanted was several hours in which to grow even more nervous. She'd basically been working all the hours of all her adult life and frankly didn't have much socialising experience. Faking it behind a clipboard was one thing. Having to front up and engage not just with other people, but with *him*, was a challenge.

'I'll re-read the report on Williams and his wife in readiness,' she said.

'You wrote the report, didn't you?' He eyed her with amusement.

She had. And she knew its contents. So obviously there were other ways in which to 'get ready'. 'What should I wear then?'

A wary look entered his eyes. 'Should you wear?'

She drummed her fingers on the table between them. 'I don't normally attend business dinners with you.'

'Because you never wanted to. You always said you had paperwork to attend to.'

'Right. But this time I'm required and you'll be introducing me as your wife.' She gestured towards her white blouse and grey trousers. 'So is my usual outfit suitable or do I need to dress more like…' She shifted uncomfortably. 'More like one of your dates.'

'What do you think my dates normally wear?' His mouth twitched.

Not much, from what she'd seen in the photos that splashed across social media and 'celebrity spy' sites. Because they often were celebrities. Socialites. Models. Actresses. Savvy influencer entrepreneurs. He'd dated a bunch of gorgeous women who weren't afraid of being seen. And judged. *Not* something Darcie was confident with.

'Glamorous strappy dresses,' she said.

'You'd prefer not to wear one of those?'

She wouldn't know where to buy one, plus now she couldn't really afford one and yes, she had major doubts as to how good she'd look in one. 'What would people expect your wife to wear?'

She just had to make it to passable; perfection was obviously out of the question.

'I don't know about other people, but *I'd* expect my wife to wear whatever makes *her* feel comfortable. Don't wear something you don't like because you think you have to. Wear whatever you want.' He glanced at her speculatively. 'Just as you are is more than adequate, Darcie.'

More than adequate? Her irritation mushroomed.

'Of course, given you had little time to pack anything else yesterday, you might choose to shop for something new,' he then added thoughtfully. 'And if you did want to do that, then I'd expect you to use my account. After all, this dinner is effectively a work meeting. But you don't have to if you don't want. It's your choice.' He held her gaze captive. 'Everything is your choice, Darcie.'

There was a seductive edge to his voice that made her shiver. She tensed. She couldn't embarrass herself all over again. She'd literally offered herself to him once already and he wasn't interested. What he'd said yesterday—about not being able to take up her offer because he was her boss—that was just a line. He couldn't have made it more clear that even though he was now her husband, he wasn't interested. He'd bestowed a micro-kiss on her at the altar before bundling her out of that wedding chapel and got them back on his plane as fast as was humanly possible. Then he'd all but broken his neck to get himself into a separate bedroom from her. While she was exhausted because she'd not been able to sleep at all, he, drat him, looked well rested and more gorgeous than ever.

Didn't he have *any* concerns about what they'd done? Didn't he have anyone else he even ought to tell? But she'd worked alongside him for years and, while there was much she knew because of that, there were so many things she didn't. Important things.

'Won't your family wonder about you getting married in such a rush?' she asked recklessly. 'Won't your parents think it's random?'

He poured himself a coffee. 'I'm not close to my parents.'

'You're not going to tell them?' She stilled.

'I'm sure they'll find out. But not from me.'

'Won't they wonder if—'

'I don't care about other people's speculation.'

But they weren't talking about other people. They were talking about his *parents*. She watched as he pulled some papers closer. Back to work? *Really?*

'You don't care about anything much as long as it doesn't impact on the business,' she said slowly.

'That's right.' He glanced up, his tone unapologetic. 'And my taking on a wife and a foster child certainly isn't going to look bad for the business.'

'But if you don't care, then you really don't need us to rehabilitate your image so people think you're actually human.'

He suddenly laughed. 'Am I all cold-blooded capitalist, Darcie? Maybe you're right. I must admit I spent most of last night trying to figure out just how I ended up here.'

'Temporary insanity?' she suggested.

'I think partly it was because it was the *last* thing you expected of me. I enjoyed confounding you.'

She stiffened, a little annoyed. Because yeah. She'd

seen that. 'You've landed yourself with a whole lot of trouble just for the momentary thrill of one-upping me.'

His smile turned wolfish. 'Who says the thrill is momentary?'

Awareness prickled, followed by a lurching desire to provoke something more from him again. She looked down and fiddled with the coffee cup. 'Fortunately for you, our marriage isn't consummated. It's not too late to get an annulment.'

The silence stretched. Ultimately Darcie couldn't resist it. She had to look back up at him.

Elias was simply staring at her and Darcie found that not only could she not move, she couldn't breathe. She gazed back, amazed at the swirling depth of emotion in his eyes. He usually kept that masked. Kept it contained. But there had to be an outlet for it sometime, right?

*Beautiful women in strappy dresses.*

'Darcie, you know me well enough to understand that I'm not someone who quits,' he said softly. 'Not ever. We're in this together until we win.'

Were they? She wasn't sure what the prize was anymore.

'Actually, I do have something I'd like you to wear tonight if you're so inclined.' He reached into his pocket and put a box on the table. 'A little material possession for you.'

Another jewellery box. Was it another item from his collection of emergency pacifiers for problematic dates he wanted to detach himself of? 'Trophy of *your* possession, you mean?' she asked acidly.

'You were concerned about believability.' His eyes glittered as he opened the box. 'And people will never believe that a man as wealthy I wouldn't bestow a trinket upon my bride.'

'A *trinket*...that's what you call this?'

'What would you call it?'

'Ostentatious.'

She refused to appreciate the stunning piece. This meant nothing to him. This was money he didn't know what else to do with.

He took her hand and she battled the instinctive tremble.

'I like that it can be seen from a hundred feet. It makes it fit for purpose.' He slowly slid the sparkling diamond solitaire down her finger. 'You're the one who wanted this.'

'Not *this*.'

'Not all the finer points?' he queried. 'You hadn't thought everything through?' He shook his head. 'That doesn't seem like you, Darcie. You're a details person. But in this it seems you were just going to wing it.'

And he was teasing her for that by going full out with everything she'd basically forgotten. Or chosen not to consider. A brief kiss at the altar. An engagement ring. Things she hadn't been going to have at all. But that now she discovered that she wanted. Desperately.

But not a wedding night.

'Isn't it fortunate you always have jewellery on hand,' she said tartly.

'I've never needed an engagement ring before.' That smile in his eyes deepened. 'I had to go to a jeweller first thing this morning and choose it myself with only you in mind.'

She gritted her teeth.

'So there's no need to be jealous, Darcie,' he added

lightly. 'You're my wife, and as such you're the *only* woman I'll give jewels to henceforth.'

'I'm not—'

'Hard as you might find it to believe,' he continued, smoothly ignoring her strangled outburst. 'While it's some time since I last dated anyone, I've no intention of breaking the vows I made yesterday.'

Something hard lodged in her stomach. He met her gaze steadily, yet that unspoken emotion swirled and still she couldn't decipher it.

'I'm sure I can cope,' he added.

Darcie, poor fool that she was, would have told him he didn't have to 'cope' at all. He could have *her* as a lover here and now. But it turned out her supposedly philandering ex-boss had developed a chivalrous streak.

'What about you, Darcie?' He leaned back. 'How long since you last went on a date?'

She stared at him wordlessly. There was literally nothing she could say to that.

'You've an insight into my life, yet I've none into yours,' he added. 'You're quite the closed book.'

'Not at all. You know my life is spent working for you. All the hours.'

'Not the very small ones in the middle of the night,' he countered.

'It's not going to be a problem,' she mumbled.

'You're going to be able to cope?' His voice was light but there was an intensity she didn't understand in his gaze.

'Of course.' She wasn't going to miss something she'd never had.

Except she was starting to *crave* that very thing and it made her butterfingered and clumsy. She ached for his touch. She was thinking about it all the time, worse she was reading interest—*intimacy*—into details she knew he didn't even mean: his occasional hesitation, that teasing smile, the way he watched her…like the way he was watching her *now*.

His smile suddenly deepened, turning him even more impossibly handsome. And he knew it, didn't he? Darcie glared at him. Was he *provoking* her?

Well, maybe she'd do the last thing *he* expected of *her*. Maybe she'd confound him. Maybe she *would* spend his money today.

'It seems you're all over everything today,' she said. 'I'm going to go make my preparations for tonight,' she said huskily. 'I'll be sure to charge it to your account.'

And she was going to enjoy every second of it.

Elias showered and dressed in a fresh shirt and suit. The meetings had been interminable but successful and more pleasingly, he'd had significant success in his plans for their return to London. Darcie wanted to put forward the best application for Lily and he would ensure that happened.

Now all he had to do was get through the damned dinner party he'd agreed to celebrate with Vince and his wife. But Darcie hadn't been in the suite when he'd got back. For a moment he wondered if she'd left. But then the concierge had phoned to tell him she'd been slightly delayed.

She'd never been delayed before.

He walked to the window, not really seeing the city skyline at sunset. He'd barely slept—firstly he'd made all those arrangements, then his mind had been too busy replaying the day's events, incredulous at the decisions he'd made and the action he'd taken. Yet he didn't regret it. More astoundingly he'd scarcely been able to wait for her to wake to see how she'd handle him today.

'I'm sorry I'm late,' she called from behind him. 'I didn't appreciate how long a full beauty treatment takes.'

'Was it your first?' He turned to face her.

'Actually, yes, it was.'

But Elias couldn't reply. Couldn't tease any more. Couldn't think.

'Did the meeting go well?' she asked.

'Hmm?'

'With Vince.'

Oh. 'Yeah.'

'Elias?'

He just stared.

She walked forward and waved her hand in front of his face. 'Are you okay?'

'Yes.' He blinked, but it didn't matter. He was still transfixed.

'Really?' A caustic note sounded in her voice even as the colour in her cheeks steadily deepened. 'You're going speechless on me? Just because of a dress?'

It wasn't the dress. Although that was a stunning silky confection that enhanced her height and shape. And he'd never seen her with her hair loose either; she always had it tied back—either in a ponytail or a plait, or coiled into a bun. Tonight it wasn't pinned back at all. It was longer than he'd realised and it shone in the light and he wanted to run his fingers through it. But it wasn't her hair rendering him brainless, either. It was the shimmer in her eyes and the sparkle in her teasing smile, and they were not created by cosmetics. That was spirit. Vitality. Darcie herself. All Darcie. The part of Darcie she'd kept hidden from him for such a long time.

'Uh…' He cleared his throat. 'You're glowing.'

'Oh. That must have been the full body massage.' She suddenly smiled. 'I've never had one of those before, either.'

'Haven't you?' He almost choked as he blinked away the images that sprang to mind. 'And you're usually in grey.'

Until yesterday he'd only ever seen her in those trouser suits. With minimal make-up, it had been a simple, perfectly acceptable style that she'd never switched up despite the steady increases to her pay packets. But now that silky blue wrap-style dress showed skin. Smooth, satiny skin that screamed warmth and softness. He'd known those curves were there—the usual uniform of loose blouses and wide-legged pants couldn't hide everything. They'd hinted, tantalised. And maybe because he'd not looked for so long, now he couldn't stop staring.

'Yes. It was my intention to be as unobtrusive as possible.'

Unobtrusive? He stared at her for another second before an involuntary laugh shook him. She looked shocked, then insecure. Instant regret swamped him. Darcie was *vulnerable*. And he'd been such a fool to ever think she were as emotionless as he.

'The grey accentuates your eyes. They're the palest blue…' But now this dress brought out a different shade. It brought warmth. He stepped forward and took her hand. 'You could never, *ever* be unobtrusive, Darcie.'

For a second she looked stricken again. And he understood she'd *wanted* to be. She'd wanted to hide. She'd never wanted to draw attention to herself.

'Why would you want to be?' Why, when she was so beautiful, so capable, so fierce? Because she was fierce now.

'Unobtrusive is safe.' She bit her lip but kept her head lifted. That blue of her eyes was now the narrowest of rings around pupils that were dark and dilated and drew him closer still.

'Safe?'

'If you're not seen, you're less likely to be sent away. Old habits, I guess.' She lifted her chin. 'Is this okay or should I change?'

Okay? The silk hugged some curves, skimmed others, and the tips of his fingers screamed with the desire to slide the material away altogether.

'What do you want to do?' he asked huskily.

Heat surged. Not just the stirrings of attraction that he ought to suppress. This was a tsunami.

'We should go,' Darcie breathed. 'They'll be waiting.'

Yet neither of them moved.

Elias didn't give a damn about the deal anymore. He wanted to pull her close and explore every one of those generous curves. She was a voluptuous, sensual goddess and he wanted to stay right here and learn so many more of her secrets.

'Elias.' She swallowed. 'This is what you wanted.'

Two hours later and Elias couldn't recall a single reason why he'd ever wanted to attend this celebratory dinner. Watching Darcie attempt to tackle a full four courses was a sensorial nightmare. He wasn't surprised at all to see her skip dessert in favour of a cheese selection.

He'd tried to keep the conversation on business as much as possible. Tried not to stare at Darcie too much.

But, given she was seated opposite him, it had been impossible. He was ready to abandon the attempt altogether.

'You're very patient to put up with business meetings only the day after your wedding.' Vince Williams smiled at Darcie.

'To be honest I understand more about hedge funds than I do about being a bride,' said Darcie.

'You've plenty of time to figure the marriage bit out.' Cora lifted her glass. 'Are your parents excited?'

Elias braced, realising too late he'd not considered the fact they might impose into Darcie's past. But she answered before he could divert them.

'I don't have much family,' she said. 'I grew up in the foster system.'

'Oh.' Vince instinctively leaned forward. 'That can be very challenging. Years ago Cora and I fostered a number of young people.'

'Oh?' Darcie was noncommittal.

Elias got the sense not all foster experiences were equal. Not in Darcie's world.

'Teens mostly,' Cora added. 'The ones who were considered too old for long-term placement but who didn't thrive in group homes. We tried to offer them a couple of years of stability and offer some skills.'

Darcie carefully sliced a piece of cheese but didn't eat it. 'Are you still in contact with any?'

'Some. Not all.'

'A lot had had it rough,' Cora elaborated on Vince's answer. 'They'd been isolated a long time.'

'Yes.' Darcie smiled. 'I was lucky to find some close friends in the system. We made our own family.'

She meant Zara. Maybe even that guy Shaun. Lonely kids banding together, trying to forge themselves a better

future. He hadn't any real idea about her past before now.
At work she was more than businesslike, she was reticent. A fact he'd appreciated on an unconscious, instinctive level. Because knowing more about Darcie would
have been intriguing—fascinating in fact. But now she
wasn't his assistant, she was his wife, and he *ought* to
know everything because he ought to be able to ease the
edge of distress he knew she was near. But he couldn't.

'And now you have Elias.'

Darcie nodded.

'Perhaps you'll be able to build a bigger family together.'

'Perhaps,' Darcie murmured. 'If we're lucky.'

He couldn't take his gaze off her then, seeing that
yearning so close to the surface. Apparently his self-control over his own mind was obliterated. All he wanted
was to cart her upstairs and discover for himself every
tiny detail.

He lifted the water glass and knocked back a deep sip.
Having to battle rampant sexual thoughts in the middle
of a business dinner was unacceptable. But he kept replaying that pathetic kiss in his head. Why hadn't he
taken advantage of that opportunity? Why hadn't he
pulled her close and explored the chemistry he knew
they had? The electricity from the simplest, tamest of
touches had him on edge. His warning system sent chills
down his spine. Their situation was volatile, their new
status wasn't stable, this could blow up in his face. Yet
he couldn't resist leaning nearer.

Because now, as the conversation moved on, Darcie
relaxed—she even laughed. And Elias discovered that
relaxed, laughing Darcie was pure torture. The change
within—the inability to put these thoughts out of his head?

'You're even cleverer than I thought, Elias,' Vince said shrewdly. 'Your sublime assistant is now yours forever.'

'Sublime assistant?' Darcie overheard the words and echoed them, a full octave higher.

Vince smiled at her. 'That's how he referred to you more than once.'

Darcie turned to Elias with a stunned expression. *'Sublime?'*

Vince and Cora both laughed. But Elias saw how genuine her shock was. And then the flash of hurt she fast hid. Did she really not know?

'It's true.' Elias desperately reached for the water glass again and pretended to direct his comment to Vince. 'I wanted Darcie from the first moment I saw her.' He watched the sweep of colour surge beneath her skin and she looked to the table. 'But she worked for me.'

So he couldn't touch. He'd told her that, hadn't he? But hadn't she believed him?

'You're not working for Elias now, Darcie?' Cora asked.

'No,' Darcie said. 'I'm taking a little time off and then I'll find something different.'

'I'd offer you a job anytime, Darcie,' Vince said.

A flare of anger smoked the last of Elias's brain cells. Fortunately Darcie spoke before he could.

'I'm not in the market for a new job right now, but in the future if that changes, I might call.'

Elias ground his teeth. That wouldn't be changing in the future. He'd keep her occupied. With something. Anything. Maybe something very basic—such as himself.

He'd seen little of the passionate, emotional side of Darcie prior to yesterday. And the more he saw of it, the more he wanted, the *nearer* he wanted. He wanted her to talk to him. To tell him. To ask him again. But she was too good at masking her emotions. In the office he'd relied on that ability to keep her head cool. And her ability to keep up to his speed. She'd often explained things to others that second or third time that he didn't have the time or patience for. He only needed tell her something once and she had it locked in.

Now he realised what he'd done. And what he'd not done.

He'd told her *no*, once. He'd not kissed her properly at their wedding. He'd left her alone on what was their wedding night.

So what had she learned from him doing—and not doing—all that? Did she really think him seeing her as sublime was *shocking*?

He needed to get behind the wall she was trying to rebuild. He wanted more of challenging, confrontational, bold and brave Darcie. The one who spontaneously laughed and who not-so-secretly adored soft French cheeses. Who'd once invited him to—

'Where are you going on your honeymoon?' Cora looked at them from one to the other in the following pause that neither of them filled. 'You are going on a honeymoon?'

Elias was too focused on Darcie to answer. Her pillowy lips had just parted in surprise. He'd tasted and she'd softened—far too briefly. Now he wanted her to soften against him again. Now he wanted to pull her into his lap and kiss her until she was hot and sighing and asking him to take her to bed.

'Eventually,' Darcie smoothed over the moment as

Elias entirely failed to answer. 'We're just finalising some work first.'

'All work and no play isn't healthy for anyone, and certainly not a newly married couple.' He didn't know if it was Vince or Cora who answered her.

'We're aligned in our desires.' Huskiness entered Darcie's voice.

Elias couldn't resist playing up to the frisson she'd lit—even it was unintentionally. 'We very much like the same things.'

It was true.

'A power couple.' Vince chuckled. 'There's certainly an energy between you.' He leaned back at winked at Darcie. 'But I do wonder which of you is really the boss?'

No one was the boss of Darcie.

'We take turns,' she deflected lightly.

He was unbearably aroused by the ideas that innocuous statement set off in his head. All he wanted to do was to have her aloof focus fully, exclusively on him. He wanted bold Darcie of two weeks ago back. The one who hadn't hid her desire. Who couldn't. Because now *he* couldn't.

'You look like someone who's found long-lost buried treasure and can't actually believe it,' Vince said to him quietly when Cora and Darcie were engaged in conversation.

Yeah, and he wasn't about to let some raider come and steal it. She was his. She always had been. He'd just been blind to the fact. But he'd woken up now. 'You won't mind if we wrap this up?'

Vince laughed. 'Not at all.'

He never skimped on time with clients and certainly not prospective acquisitions. But he didn't care about

business tonight. Tonight he needed to be with Darcie.
Properly. He less than smoothly said goodbye on behalf
of them both and Vince and Cora, bless them, headed
off. Which left him alone with her at last.

Just before pushing the button to summon the lift,
he turned to her and made his play. 'Come upstairs
with me?'

# CHAPTER EIGHT

DARCIE DESPERATELY NEEDED to get out of the lift. He'd
echoed that mortifying invitation she'd made to him.
But he'd meant it as merely a teasing reference and it
was only infuriating because she was too frustrated to
see the funny side.

'It was a very successful evening.' He followed up as
the doors finally slid open.

'Do you think?' Darcie ground her teeth as she walked
into the glittering lounge of the hotel's penthouse suite.
They were finally alone and she could get away from
him. Sitting opposite a tuxedoed Elias Greyson had stolen one appetite while stoking another and it had been
almost impossible to concentrate on even the lightest of
social conversation.

Tomorrow they would return to London. Not soon
enough. They'd get on with the application for Lily. Everything was going to plan yet she felt unbearably edgy.
Jumpy. Yeah, *frustrated*.

'I didn't know about their involvement with foster
children,' she said, trying to divert her thoughts. That
hadn't just startled her, it had raised her suspicions.

'Nor did I.' He followed her progress into the lounge,

his intensity building when she shot him a sceptical look. 'You don't believe me?'

'It's just a little convenient that you take your former foster child bride to meet the man you want to impress and it turns out *he's* been a foster parent.'

'I didn't know you were ever in the foster system till yesterday, Darcie, and I'd already offered to marry you by then.'

She knew her angry reaction was illogical, but she was still cross with him.

'Besides which—' he rubbed his jaw thoughtfully '—I had no real need to impress him.'

She turned jerkily. 'I know. But it makes me nervous to see how easily you can lie.'

'I can lie?' he echoed idly, and smoothly slipped his jacket off. 'When did I lie?'

'Tonight. With Vince.'

'Oh.' He tossed his jacket onto the nearby armchair and slowly advanced on her. 'What do you think I lied about?' He untied his tie and undid the top button of his shirt.

'When you said…' She was distracted by his slow undressing and increasingly awkward that she'd said anything at all. She should have made like him last night and gone straight to her bedroom.

'I didn't lie to Vince, Darcie. I never lie,' he said softly. 'For the record, every word I spoke tonight was true.'

No, it wasn't. She instinctively took a step backwards.

His mouth quirked. 'Can you explain which bit bothered you?'

Well, she wasn't about to repeat it now.

'Don't hold back, Darcie.' His voice dropped to a whisper. 'I want to know what you're really thinking. I know you've not always felt in a position to do that before. But now is different, isn't it?'

It was appalling the way she melted when he said that. She swallowed.

'I never thought you'd be a coward,' he jeered lightly as he kept walking towards her with the feline grace of some dancer. Or predator. 'But I thought we pulled off the image of happy newlyweds without needing to lie at all.'

That assessment annoyed her even more. She didn't want to be beholden to him. 'The whole thing is stupid,' she muttered as she kept backing away from him. 'I shouldn't have had to do all this.'

She wanted to be there for Lily. She knew she could take care of Lily without needing—

She hit the wall. Literally. She huffed and put her hands on her hips and glared at him. 'The last thing I wanted to do was actually get married to anyone. *Ever.*'

'No?' His eyes widened but he still kept walking. 'Ditto. Yet inexplicably, here we are.'

He stopped, right in front of her. For a charged moment she glared up at him only then, to her shock, Elias smiled at her. And she suddenly giggled. A pop of laughter just bubbled up and burst out.

'You never wanted to marry?' He asked when she sobered—almost instantly. 'Not ever?'

'Of course not,' she mumbled. 'I know I can take care of Lily all by myself. I don't need some guy rescuing us. But they just won't accept that I'm good enough on my own.'

'Good enough?' He regarded her solemnly. 'Darcie—'

'Don't. I know it's not true.' She had to believe that.

It was why she was fighting to do everything she could. 'But it's the way of the world, right?'

'Maybe.' A glimmer of a tease resurfaced. 'What of love, Darcie? Don't you believe in that either?'

Her heart puckered. She held little hope that *she* would ever find it. 'Truthfully I haven't seen many examples of long-term happily married couples.' She swallowed. 'Except maybe Cora and Vince.'

'Yeah, they seem pretty together,' Elias murmured. 'Are you going to tell me what it is you think I lied to him about?'

He was too near now. Too near, too big, too stunning. She couldn't say anything.

'Darcie…' He gazed down at her and his voice roughened. 'Ask me again.'

She knew he wasn't talking about tonight any more.

He leaned closer. 'That night you asked me to come upstairs with you, you meant to come to bed.'

*Yes.* His nearness sent her brain into meltdown. She was so tempted to breathe the truth. Too tempted. And it paralysed her.

'What if I promised the answer would be different this time?' He gently brushed her hair back from her flushed face. 'Where has my confident, capable, calm Darcie gone?'

*My* Darcie?

She closed her eyes. 'Confident, capable calm Darcie was all a fake.'

'No. I don't believe that,' he countered. 'Not for all that time.'

Not for work maybe. But when it came to this—to intimacy—there was no confidence, no capability and certainly no calm. She couldn't hold back the raw reality any more. 'You want the truth, Elias?'

'*Yes.*' A heartfelt whisper she couldn't ignore. 'Always.'

She opened her eyes and stared straight into his. 'I've never slept with anyone.'

He stilled. She saw him mentally repeating her statement. Saw the widening of his eyes as her words registered and felt the withdrawal of the warmth.

'*That's* what I was asking from you,' she added before he could say anything that would only mortify her more. 'It's *why* I asked you that night. Because I thought I was getting married and even though it wasn't going to be real...' She shrugged her shoulders. 'I wouldn't have the chance again, not for...'

'Because you'd be loyal even though it was going to be a paper marriage.'

'Yes,' she admitted softly. 'So I wanted...'

'Something for yourself first.' He gazed down into her eyes. 'Your first. Me. For one night.'

'Right.'

Elias couldn't breathe as the oddest sensations unfolded within him. Anger. Hunger. Protectiveness. Possessiveness. All at the same time. He was unravelling and the terrible, terrible urge to take her was taking precedence.

But he froze. Because discovering this now meant that this marriage—this supposed elegant solution to her problem—was suddenly a whole problem within itself. He'd thought they'd overcome their former status as employer and employee. He'd thought she was now his *equal*. But she wasn't. She was inexperienced not just with men, but in other relationships. too. She hadn't had a family. She'd felt so vulnerable it was her default status to try to stay beneath the radar in her suits.

And he *had* to walk away. He couldn't take the responsibility of doing this. 'You must be tired. It's been an intense thirty-six hours.'

Her eyes widened. 'Tired?'

He didn't sleep with virgins. He had flings with women as worldly as he was. Women who enjoyed the expensive restaurants to which he took them. Who enjoyed the jet and nice jewels and who didn't expect anything much more than great food and even better sex. An evening's pleasure was very straightforward and very finite and there was no emotional burden.

He rubbed his chest, surprised by the sudden ache there. Darcie was effectively bound to him, but she was more forbidden than ever. When he'd spent the evening—hell, many other evenings, too, if he were being honest—fantasising about taking her to bed and imagining her response. But knowing now that it would be her first time? Logically it shouldn't matter, yet it did. He remembered her unexpected behaviour that night in Edinburgh. She'd had to *drink* to gain courage to ask him something other women offered all the time with a literal bat of their eyelids.

Yeah, while Darcie was worldly and was wise in so many other ways, he also now knew she'd experienced things no one should have to endure—abandonment, isolation, fear for her security. And in this she was unbelievably inexperienced. In relationships.

And honestly, so was he. He didn't do them. He didn't do emotional support. He was rubbish at it. He'd inherited the lack from *both* parents. He'd failed his mother and he wasn't letting anyone else down ever. So he couldn't take her on in this. Because she'd need more than just *sex*, wouldn't she? And she should have it. She should have much more than the little he could ever offer.

'It really makes that much difference?' Reproach bruised the blue of her eyes.

Oh, she was pissed off with him. And it made everything ten times worse.

'Yeah. It does.'

'Because now you think I'm somehow deficient? Or incompetent in my decision-making?'

'No.' His frustration swirled. 'I just… I don't want you to feel obligated towards me.'

Because he'd married her, to help her. And everything was all muddied in his head.

'And *I* don't want you to feel any kind of obligation towards me, either. I don't want your *pity* kisses, Elias, just because you now know I'm inexperienced. I knew I shouldn't have told you. Do you really think I can't separate feelings of gratitude from lust?'

'So you do feel gratitude.' That was the last thing he wanted.

'*And* lust. Or does the latter not count?' She tilted her chin at him. 'Do you really think I'm attracted to you because I see you as some kind of rescuer to me? Do you think my feelings aren't fully formed?'

He stared at her. 'Feelings?'

'I have a number towards you right now, Elias. Anger being one. And yes, lust is another. You don't seem to mind other women wanting you. Is it just me who's not allowed to appreciate your form because I've never done this before?'

'My form?'

'You're physically compelling, yes. You always have been.'

'You have a lot going on,' he said stubbornly.

'Most people do,' she said. 'Even you. But you bury it deep and use work to block it off. And maybe, when there's a lot going on, there's something to be said for a blow-out. You do that. Just not with me. That's fine. You don't have to. So you can stop making excuses because I'm beyond embarrassed, I don't care anymore. You don't have to want me. But you didn't need to lie about it tonight.'

He gritted his teeth. 'I *didn't* lie.' He stepped forward, right into her space. 'Darcie—'

'Don't come near me now,' she snapped. She was so angry with him.

But he didn't back off. He stayed still.

He was the only man she'd *ever* considered asking. And he was only one she'd thought might actually agree. She knew he liked sex. She'd seen him date an array of women over the time she'd worked for him. So she'd thought that maybe…maybe he'd have said yes to one night even as a novelty or something. Because she'd also known—courtesy of the hours they spent working—that he'd not dated a woman in a while *recently*. She'd half hoped he'd have been feeling base-level sexual frustration that he'd have been happy to act on. But he hadn't. He'd rejected her. Immediately. Coolly. And he'd done it again now. She should have known he was always going to deny her. Everyone did. So she was going to remain a virgin wife. Unclaimed. Unwanted. She was always unwanted. As a child she'd sought a family for so long and never got one. Even now as an adult she didn't get the things other people got. And she was furious about it.

'You're upset.' Elias remained like a statue.

'Yes. So I might say something I regret. I might—' She broke off and blinked back angry tears. 'Just leave me alone, Elias.'

'I'm not leaving you while you're upset.'

'Even if your presence makes me all the more upset?'

His hands fisted by his side. 'I've tried do what you want, Darcie.'

'What I want?'

Not everything. Not *nearly* everything. But she was selfish and impetuous and greedy, and it hadn't worked, and she wasn't going to ask anymore. She wasn't going to risk rejection all over again. It hurt too badly because she wanted it too much.

'You look at me with those big blue eyes. Did you know they shimmer, Darcie?' He growled. 'And there are secrets in there. Tell me your secrets.'

'I just did.' Her voice croaked. 'And still you said no.'

'Because hedonism doesn't seem like your style, Darcie. You're more serious than that.'

'Well, I've never really had the chance to find out, have I? There've always been other considerations.'

'Aren't there other considerations still?'

'They're not going to change.' She waved an irritated hand. 'Our sleeping together wouldn't have changed anything, either. It was one night.'

'Naive Darcie. It would change things. And one night would never be enough.' He dragged in a breath. 'Did you ask anyone else after I turned you down?'

'Obviously not.' She was so shocked by the question she snapped the answer instantly.

'Because you'd thought about me.' His voice was low

and that husky edge signalled danger. 'Because you only wanted *me*.'

'Really, Elias?' Her rebellion flared. 'You want a complete ego trip?'

'We have chemistry, Darcie, and chemistry is something I can do. But this marriage isn't forever. *That's* not going to change. So if we sleep together, even though it's going to be good, it won't change the fundamentals. It won't change our future.'

'Do you think I *want* it to?' She was even more furious with him. 'You really are arrogant. I just told you I never *wanted* to get married and I certainly don't want to stay that way!'

'Good.' He stepped in closer still. 'Then ask me to kiss you.'

'*What?*'

Oh, he really wanted the full ego trip. But he was so close now. So hot he was crowding her with his scent and his intensity, and her thinking ability was sliding.

'Ask me.'

Her heart pounded in her ears and that heat had exploded, scorching her from the inside out.

'I won't do it until you ask me again.' His breath brushed hers. His lips were so close. And she was so confused.

'You want me to ask you for…?' Her furious drawl was a bare mumble. 'A kiss?'

'Good enough.' His lips covered hers.

The brush of his mouth was gentle, too gentle. It made her ache worse and she gasped, a breathy moan.

He lifted fractionally away. 'Ask me again.'

That deep ache overcame her anger. She wanted more. 'Kiss—'

He did. Stronger than before, yet impossibly even more tender. Her heart pounded as he slid his fingers through her hair. He tilted her head so he could deepen the kiss and she arched closer to meet him. His tongue lashed hers, giving her a desperately needed taste of deeper intimacy. But when he pulled away again her brain kicked back online.

'Ask—'

'What are you doing?' she interrupted reproachfully.

'Training you,' he said softly.

'*Training* me?' She glared into his face. 'Like some performing animal?'

His pupils were so blown she couldn't see the blue for the black.

'I want you to understand that when you ask me for something, I'll deliver.' The intensity of his answer literally shook her.

But she was lost to emotional intensity, too, and her most deep-seated yearning was torn out.

'What if I don't want to have to always *ask* for everything?' She growled. 'Why can't I just be gifted it? Why do *I* always have to fight so hard to get a few things that others seem to get so easily?'

Fiercely devastated, she shoved him away. Hard.

But he didn't move and she was suddenly *so* exposed. She lifted her hands to hide but he grabbed her wrists and pulled them to her sides. She closed her eyes so she wouldn't have to see his pity. So he couldn't see the stupid yearning in her.

'Darcie,' he muttered. '*Darcie.*'

'*Don't* pity me.'

His grip on her wrists tightened and he suddenly

leaned in, pressing the full weight of his body against her. Pinning her to the wall with every inch of him.

'Feel me,' he muttered. '*Feel* me, Darcie.'

She did. She felt the coiled steel of tense muscles and the rapid thud of his heart. She felt the swerving emotions—frustration, anger, *arousal*. It was there—his huge, hard shaft pressing deep against her belly. She quivered uncontrollably and he pushed closer still. Her breath hitched, shortening as sensation—yearning—tumbled inside.

'*This* is how I've wanted you,' he growled. 'Here like this. With me. So close that...' He dragged in a difficult breath. 'From the moment we met. But from that moment you were my employee.'

Her throat was so dry she couldn't swallow. She couldn't move—and yet she was, secretly her insides were shifting. Her blood was heating, muscles softening—priming. Not just her insides. Goosebumps lifted on her skin as she shivered and her breasts tightened—her nipples peaking, pushing back against him. Welcoming him.

For a long moment they remained sealed together. So still. But their breathing shifted—hot and shallow, faster and faster as desire surged to the point of detonation.

'My father had an affair with his secretary,' he said harshly. 'It was a mess. For her. For my mother. For my whole family.' His tension built and stiffened his muscles, and he instinctively tightened his grip on her wrists. 'So you'll understand it was a line I could never, *ever* cross.'

She also understood that it had cost him something to tell her that.

'But you're not my employee now.' His mouth was by her ear. A hot, husky, *hungry* whisper.

She couldn't see his eyes but she could breathe in his scent, his heat, his intensity, and she understood she was about to get everything he could share of himself. Everything she wanted.

'I want to kiss you again, Darcie. And if I do, I won't want to stop. Is that okay with you?'

She felt him, believed him, and all the need she'd locked away for so long surged. 'Yes.'

# CHAPTER NINE

SHE DIDN'T KNOW what she'd expected but for some reason his total tenderness was a shock. The kisses he dropped on her cheek and jaw and then her neck were soft and light, and he was so unbearably careful her eyes stung. She closed them and released her caught breath on a sigh of blurred delight and despair. She wanted this. Him. *So much.* His thumbs swirled over the fragile skin on the inside of her wrists and the simple caresses swept her further and faster along the tide of arousal—of *emotion.* Thank goodness for the wall at her back; she was literally melting. He crowded closer, sensing she needed support, and slid his leg between hers. It only made her heat and soften even more. 'Elias…'

'I'm not going anywhere.' A husky promise that made her quiver.

His grip on her wrists tightened and he lifted them, placing her hands on his shoulders. Finally she was free to cling and she did. Shamelessly.

'Please.' She *needed* his kiss.

He lifted his head and gazed into her eyes as he glided his hands back down her arms, torching skin that was already ablaze for him before dropping them to her waist. He nudged his leg closer and tightened his hold on her.

She couldn't resist rocking her hips ever so slightly as the hard heat of him pressed right where she ached most and she heard the answering hitch in his breathing. His eyes gleamed as he leaned in.

'Darcie.'

Her response was effervescent and uncontrollable. She met him, her tongue swirling—dancing—with his. She needed the kisses deeper, to be everywhere. She needed him like this—his whole body flush hot and hard against hers—and she needed to touch *him* everywhere. Yet her fingers could only curl into his shoulders and cling. Desperate, she shook—unable to stand any more. But Elias had her. With an exultant growl he scooped her into his arms, effortlessly tossing her lightly to adjust his hold. Pressed close to his chest, she threaded her fingers through his hair as he carried her to the bedroom he'd taken last night. He smiled at her—a laughing, lustful smile the likes of which she'd never seen—as he placed her smack in the centre of the big bed.

Darcie then stared, slack-jawed, as he took charge. He'd never looked as handsome. Her innards liquefied as he pulled something from his pocket and tossed it up so it landed near the pillow. She glanced, realised it was protection. And he'd had it on him already? He'd considered this might happen? Her heart raced as she turned back to watch him toe off his shoes while also unbuttoning his shirt. Two seconds later he'd shucked his trousers in record time. She sank deeper into the mattress as he advanced on her clad only in black boxers.

'You're far too well-dressed for this,' he muttered.

He toyed with the slippery satin fabric of her dress, seeking the hidden fastenings, the zip, and releasing them with practiced ease. She shifted as he worked, helping him slide the material from her.

A pause, an intake of breath from them both as her skin was bared. Spread before him in only lacy bra and panties, Darcie couldn't believe this was happening. But the expression in his eyes grounded her in searing reality. The intensity, the concentration, the evident desire in his body all combined to set her every sense alight. But this wasn't only superficially hot. This burned on the inside, too. With every kiss, every caress, he heated her *heart*—melting it, re-forming it, making it his.

'Elias…' she gasped.

She was completely naked in moments. And he was kissing parts of her no other person had ever seen, let alone touched. Her breathing quickened even more and she stretched out her hands seeking purchase but finding only the soft silken sheets. Her fingers curled into fists as he touched her, teased her, *tasted* her. With every lush swirl of his tongue he showed her how searingly hot such an intimacy could be and just how responsive her own body was. And how much her body hungered for *his*. She strained upwards, locking her hips as he drove her swiftly towards the brink of ecstasy. One arm holding her in place, he growled, a guttural husk of approval, before deepening his attentions—sliding a skilled fingertip inside while sealing his mouth to her highly sensitive bud and repeatedly lashing her there with his tongue. Darcie screamed as the sensations tumbled, her body convulsing in pleasure as wave upon wave hit and he held her tighter still, helping her ride it through.

She breathed hard in recovery but even through the aftershocks, arousal resurged. Because his hand was still cupping her intimately, his finger locked inside her.

But he'd moved higher up the bed so he could look into her eyes.

'Do you want the rest of me?' he asked bluntly, raggedly.

The ferocity of arousal in his expression made her breathless all over again. She couldn't yet speak. Couldn't yet comprehend the power of what she'd just experienced. And that there was more to come?

'Darcie?' Strain tightened his face.

He began to slide free of her but she clamped down, desperate to keep him deep inside her. His gaze bored into hers.

'I have many talents, but mind-reading isn't one of them, sweetheart,' he muttered roughly. 'I understand that you don't want to ask for everything all of the time, but you're still going to have to communicate with me on some things.'

'Like you do with me?' she challenged softly, feeling a foreign power flood through her now. Feeling confidence in her sensuality for the first time ever. Feeling as if she knew what she wanted and she knew how she might get it. 'It works both ways, Elias. And I don't know that either of us is too good at communicating when it comes to personal things.'

He took a couple of deep breaths of his own. As if he, too, were seeking recovery. And control. 'I wanted to hear you ask me again,' he admitted huskily. 'Last time I couldn't answer the way I wanted, and I wanted a do-over. I wanted to feel that burst of…'

She fell a little harder for him, burned a little hotter. 'Are you saying I made your day with my offer?'

'You made my decade.'

Arousal flooded her and she knew he knew. Because

he felt it—the slickening of her channel. His eyes smouldered and she felt his muscles bunch.

'Yet you denied me.' Her reproach was husky.

'You know I had to. But I've thought about you for so long.'

She couldn't resist rocking harder into his hand, seeking more from the fingers that had resumed their soft, skilled torment. 'Elias—'

'I watched you when I thought it was safe. When you were focused on your screen or had your back to me, and I wondered if you ever looked at me when I wasn't looking at you, too.' He pressed closer, quickly kissing her nearest straining nipple as he then confessed, 'Like a teen with a crush. I wondered and wished and was so uncertain because you were always so aloof you didn't even deign to dine with me. And then one night you appeared, and you looked me directly in the eyes and asked me to come upstairs with you.'

She was shallowly panting now.

'Part of me wanted to shout in celebration but I had to say no. And then you didn't look at me at all. I've still not forgiven you for that, Darcie.'

'It's scary how well you hid it,' she breathed. 'You seemed so cold.'

'I was *controlled*. There's a difference.'

She never would have guessed. She'd read his reaction as emotionless and she'd thought she could read him well—after all, it had been almost three years in which she'd seen that poker face in boardrooms and high-level meetings. She knew displeasure. She knew precision. Attack. But that most primal of emotions—lust. *That* she'd not seen in him. He could mask up frighteningly well. Could he hide other emotions, too? Other real, deep feelings? That possibility was something she filed away. Yet she had seen more in these last couple of days. She'd seen anger. *Amusement.* She even thought she'd seen the flash of jealousy.

'I never want to initiate something you don't want. I always want to know you're on board with me. It matters. I'm a powerful person. People say yes to me even when they might not want to. I never want that cloudiness so I always clarify consent. I always ask.' His gaze skittered down her body, taking in the stiffness of her needy nipples, the sheen of her heated skin, the rhythmic rock of her hips as she met his teasing fingers.

'That's a good thing.' She swallowed and licked her lips. 'But I think…with this…maybe you don't have to always ask. Maybe you can trust that if you start something, I'll tell you if I don't want it at that time…'

'And now?'

'You know I want it all. All of you.'

He closed his eyes briefly. Then moved.

Darcie was bereft at the sudden loss of intimacy, of any contact. But he was fast, reaching for the foil package he'd tossed down by the pillow. Her body went lax as she watched him discard his boxers and she saw him naked before her for the first time. She swallowed, nerves rising, as he rolled the condom down his broad, engorged length. He glanced over and smiled as he read her face.

'Don't worry, I'll help you,' he promised.

She nodded. She was going to need it, because she had no idea how—

He straddled her and began again—kisses, deep, lush kisses that made her brain evaporate, leaving her able to do nothing but feel. And that worry ebbed as his hands swept over her, reheating skin that had barely cooled, pushing her to an even higher state of need. She parted her legs instinctively, the empty ache at her core driving her.

He muttered something indecipherable and dropped his body onto hers. The weight of him was heavenly, offering both security and challenge. Looking into her eyes, he slid his hand between them, stroking her nub till she twisted, then he teased her apart. He nipped her lips and slid his tongue into her mouth, possessing her there as he retook her intimate space with not one finger, but two this time, gently teasing so she grew more supple and pliant with every caress. She moaned, drowning in desire. She knew he was preparing her, but she was more than ready now.

'Please,' she begged on a breathless groan. 'Please.'

He nudged her legs a little farther apart and slipped his hand from her only to grip himself, guiding the tip of his length to her slick, heated space.

Darcie stilled. The pressure was intense as he slowly breached her entrance. She couldn't breathe, couldn't move. All senses burned. She went tight and soft, hot and shivery all at the same time and moaned helplessly in the power of it. With a guttural growl Elias thrust hard and took total possession of her body. She gasped, both shocked and sated in that very second. He was there. *Hers.* And the sharp, stabbing pain disappeared as quickly as it had hit.

'Okay?' A strained plea from Elias.

She panted as she nodded. He kissed her—long and sensuous and still with that generous tenderness and time. Finally he eased from her only to press back deeper. Then harder. Then again. And Darcie looped

her arms around his strong, slick back and held on. Held
him close.

'Elias…'

'More?'

'Yes.' Her eyes watered—not from pain, but from the
pure pleasure and the deep, deep emotion of this moment. 'Yes. *Yes.*'

It was glorious. *So* glorious as he showed her—shifting their angle, alternating the pace, teasing her. *Pleasing*
her. She was breathless in seconds, instinctively rising
to meet him with her hips, with hands, mouth. With everything she had. Her nipples were so tight and she loved
the rub of his chest against them. Pleasure shot along
every nerve ending and as he choked and changed up
his hold to clutch her even more tightly to him and she
began to shake.

'That's it. Oh, Darcie—'

Her name was lost in his throaty growl of pleasure
while she could only shudder as the ecstasy hurtled her
into oblivion.

She didn't know how long it was until he moved. But
she kept her eyes closed, not wanting to return to reality.
She wanted to remain floating in this bliss. Only then she
felt him walking two fingers up her belly. They moved
slow but firm, gently bypassing her navel before reaching
her sternum. She quivered, passion and energy trickling
back. Those two fingertips moved an inch or two higher.
Her nipples tightened in anticipation.

'Do I go left or right?' A deep, murmuring tease.

The giggle just bubbled up. She opened her eyes, looking to see him on his side facing her, his head propped
on one hand. He looked flushed and dishevelled and yet

still impossibly debonair. And the gleam in his eyes was pure satisfaction.

'You must be pretty pleased with yourself,' she murmured. 'I didn't know it was like that. I didn't know...' What she'd been missing out on for so long. 'Is it always...'

'So wonderful?' he said gently. 'No. I've never had it that wonderful.'

'You don't have to say that. Don't ruin it by—'

'Telling the truth?' One eyebrow rose. 'The truth is you're gorgeous, Darcie. Just gorgeous. And honestly I can't stop wanting to touch you.'

He stole her breath. Her words. Her mouth was his... her whole body was his all over again.

'For the record, you can touch me anytime you like.' He shot her a smile a whole lot later.

'Anytime, anyhow?' She couldn't resist teasing.

'Basically.'

She laughed.

His smile widened. 'You're going to take advantage of that permission, aren't you?'

'Possibly.' She shrugged, as if not that bothered. In truth she was going to do that any chance she had.

'I'm so glad.' He pulled her to rest against his chest.

Warm, sleepy, yet still intrigued, she traced the parts of him accessible to her with light fingertips—sating her curiosity, savouring the freedom she now had to touch him all she wanted. She glanced up and caught him gazing at her with an odd expression.

'What?' She paused her explorations.

But he covered her hand with his and pressed it back on his skin, encouraging her to continue. 'I'm struggling to understand how it's possible you've never had a sexual relationship before now.'

'You know working for you has taken up almost every waking moment for the last three years,' she muttered.

'But before that? You're twenty-three, Darcie. Was there no first love in your late teens?'

'Not for me.' She wrinkled her nose, because this totally wasn't a topic she wanted to consider right now. But at the same time she appreciated his interest and she couldn't resist opening up to him a little more. 'I wasn't…' She shook her head awkwardly. 'Zara always had a boyfriend. She was stunning and confident. I was the nerdy sidekick, third-wheel best friend who wasn't good at any of that stuff.'

'Darcie, trust me,' he said. 'You're good at everything.'

'*No one* is good at everything,' she countered realistically. 'Not even you.'

'What? You wound me!' He chuckled and rolled, pinning her beneath him as he laughingly interrogated her. 'At what do I fail?'

For a moment she stared up at him, basically seduced into brainlessness again already. But then she thought of something.

His gaze narrowed and she felt him brace as she started to laugh. 'You're worse than I am at taking holidays.'

# CHAPTER TEN

'HOLIDAYS?' ELIAS ECHOED, assuming a perplexed air. 'What are these "holidays" you speak of?'

She giggled again and he couldn't resist kissing her. But when he lifted his head and gazed down at her he realised she was right. He couldn't remember the last time he'd bothered to take a sustained break from work. But why would he? Work was energy and excitement. He liked moving from one project to the next without time to take a breath—it *was* breath to him. But Darcie thought that he was *worse* than she was, which meant she'd take a break if she *could*. He'd been so very blind when it came to her. And in so many ways.

'In all this time working for me you've not taken any time off,' he mused. 'I probably should have been sued by an employee's federation or something. I'm pretty sure it's been illegal.'

'It was a privately negotiated contract,' she said valiantly. 'I wanted to work.'

Wanted to or *had* to? Because there was a difference. And he didn't like thinking of her *having* to. Nor did he like her trying to make him feel better about it. 'Doesn't make it okay, though. When did you last have a holiday?'

She dropped her gaze. 'School holidays.'

Well, that was a while ago. And also not true. 'You worked all of them,' he said. 'From your mid-teens you took whatever job you could—fast-food outlets, then data entry. Once you got your first job you never had a break. I rechecked your agency CV on the flight to Vegas.'

Her gaze shot back to his. 'You did? Why?'

'Because I realised that despite working alongside you for almost three years, I barely know anything substantial about you.'

She swallowed. 'You could've just asked me.'

'And you'd answer properly?' He watched her with wry amusement, feeling an odd ache in his chest at the same time. 'You're reticent about anything personal.' And now he just wondered all the more about her background. He had the horrible feeling she'd been very lonely. 'That was understandable in our working relationship, but now we're married...'

Her blue eyes turned intense. 'Well, you don't exactly offer up much personal, either.'

True. 'Perhaps it's a "work on" for us both. Let's trade.' He leaned back. 'You go first. Tell me, have you ever really travelled?'

'Frequently.' She shot him an impish grin. 'I'm very used to your private jet and still appreciate it, every time. Thanks to you I've seen the Eiffel Tower, the Colosseum in Rome, even the Hollywood sign in LA.'

'Those were literally fly-bys and not for recreational purposes.' He fiddled with the edge of the sheet, wary about asking too much too soon and uncertain as to why he suddenly wanted to know so badly. 'You never went on holiday with your foster family?'

Her expression instantly shuttered. 'It wasn't something many of them could afford.'

How many foster families had she been placed with?

'But you *can* afford it, yet you don't go on holiday either.' She deflected the focus back to him.

And yes, she had him there. 'I take long weekends.'

'Not often.' She looked back up at him. 'And not recently.'

Also true, and it was because he usually only took a long weekend on the request of a lover and there hadn't been one those in a while. His exes liked yachts, clubs, glamorous events—easily achieved in the short time format. Brief flings that didn't go emotionally deep. But Elias's expansion plans had kept him busy recently, and every weekend for the last four months he'd been working alongside Darcie. They were together once more, but this weekend could be very different.

'We could stay here an extra day,' he suggested huskily.

'Wow.' Dry amusement sparked in her eyes. 'A whole extra day?'

'Yeah.' He refused to let her soft snark slay him, because something was better than nothing. 'It's a good offer, Darcie.'

'You think?' Her eyebrows arched but she shook her head. 'No. We should get back to London and get the application under way.'

'My lawyers are already gathering advice and information to prep us both. And it's the weekend—we could stay until tomorrow night and still be back in time for that meeting first thing Monday morning.'

For a second, temptation turned her eyes smoky, then she blinked. 'I meet Lily on Sunday afternoons.'

Of course. He'd forgotten. As had she, and he knew she felt guilty for that small lapse. But she needn't. It

was okay to have been distracted. He smiled at her reassuringly. 'Then we'll stay today and return to London early tomorrow so you're home in time to meet her
face-to-face.'

Her expression softened but there was wariness still
there. 'Are you sure?'

Was she worried about disappointing him? He really didn't want that. 'Absolutely.' He wanted to please
her and he'd take what he could get. 'We can laze by
the hotel pool, eat luscious food, literally do nothing
for the day.'

That sly amusement sprang back into her eyes. 'It's
not within your capability to do *nothing*.'

'That's very true.' He grinned at her. 'I guess I'll have
to entertain myself with *you*.'

Twenty-four hours later Elias strode through the airport distracted by the memory of his adorably dishevelled wife struggling to fasten her safety belt in time
for landing back in London. He'd quite deliberately
stunned her with his attentions as they'd flown over
the Atlantic, feeding that edgy need within him. The
need that was determinedly refusing to abate in any
way. But now the sultry, flushed smile she'd rewarded
him with was stuck in his mind and all he wanted was
to do it all over again.

'I'll drop you to your visit with Lily and pick you up
after,' he said absently. It would give him just enough
time to ensure everything was as he'd requested and,
yeah, he was a little wary of how she was going to react
to what he'd done.

'You're driving? Where's Olly?'

'I thought we might deal with the rest of the world

tomorrow.' He didn't want to have to share her yet. One more night of this sensual bliss and then reality would return.

Darcie struggled to rein in her excitement as she played with the building bricks Lily favoured. It was only an hour, but the first face-to-face visit they'd had in a while.

'I'll see you next week?' Lily asked.

Darcie nodded. 'Of course.'

She couldn't promise the little girl anything more even though she desperately wanted to. But she would never promise Lily something she couldn't come through with because she knew all too well how it felt to have those promises broken. Repeated disappointments slowly destroyed a person.

But now the precious hour was up and she found Elias double-parked outside the building. She couldn't hold back her smile as she walked to the car. The man had so much more to him than she'd imagined. He wasn't only a workaholic billionaire, he was a playful *tease*. The way he'd sparked stunned her. As for his physical skills…sensations still tumbled inside her from the way he'd toyed with her on the jet. Appallingly, there was apparently no end to the neediness that surely should be eased after a weekend in which they'd barely left that big bed…all she wanted was for him to kiss her again. Now.

He was watching her as she struggled to fasten her seatbelt. Amusement curved his mouth, and heat shone in his eyes. 'You okay?'

She nodded jerkily.

'It was a good visit?'

'Yep.' She stared out the window trying to find a better distraction for her inappropriate brain. Then she realised their direction. 'This isn't the way to your penthouse.' They were moving out from the central city, not towards it.

'I know.' His hands tightened on the steering wheel. 'We're going to our new home.'

'Our what?'

'Home.' He cleared his throat. 'I thought it would be better for our chances with Lily if we had a house that's secure and warm and has everything she could want.'

'I didn't know you had an actual house.'

'I didn't.' He pulled into a quiet street in London. He got out his phone and tapped something on the screen. The large gates of a big property at the end of the street opened automatically. He turned into the driveway and the gates smoothly closed behind them.

Darcie gazed at the beautiful brick building. It was big, private, in a sheltered quiet street in a leafy, wealthy suburb. 'So you're renting this, just for now?' She swivelled in her seat face him.

He shook his head. 'Bought it.'

'*How?*' She gaped. 'Even for you, that's a fast deal.'

His grin flashed. 'It's been a busy few days. Come on, let's go exploring.'

But for a second Darcie could only stare after him as she struggled to compute what he'd just said. Did that mean that while she'd spent the weekend out of her mind with bliss in his arms, he'd been organising a house purchase on the side? How had he managed to do that? Because he'd have supervised all this even from the distance, no way would he have delegated it completely. Slowly she followed him. It wasn't that she didn't appreciate it, she was just stunned that he'd thought of so much while that whole time she'd barely been able to think at *all*. Clearly he hadn't been as swept away as she. And *that* was a reality check.

She drew breath as she glimpsed more of the property. 'There's a lawn.'

'A place for her to play, yes.' He unlocked the door with a security code and stood aside for her to enter. 'I believe it's a little sparsely furnished, it's been empty, but we can work on that.'

Darcie couldn't believe her eyes. The house was *four* stories high, spacious, stunning and doubtlessly eye-wateringly expensive. She walked through the two living spaces into the gorgeous open-plan kitchen and family living area.

'It's not a stone's throw from a Michelin restaurant but I got them to deliver us a few meals,' Elias drawled softly.

But Darcie was too blown away to be able to answer. The living area opened out to that lawn—a private little park already complete with a small swing and slide set. There was even a luxurious yet cosy cinema room farther down the corridor. Darcie could so easily see herself curled up on that big plush sofa watching the latest cartoon musical movies with Lily. Or snuggled next to Elias late at night…only Elias didn't watch movies, did he?

'You don't like it?'

'*Like* it?' She shook her head at him. 'It's incredible, Elias.'

He was incredible. She was stunned that he'd thought of all this, done all this in those few days.

His eyes narrowed on her. 'You can redecorate anything, of course, I won't be offended. It wasn't as if I chose anything in here.'

'You hired an interior designer.'

He nodded. 'A team have been working round the clock since Thursday.'

'And they've done a fantastic job. It's beautiful, Elias.'

'There are a couple of rooms for home offices. And a gym. An indoor pool. But the bedrooms are up here.' He led the way. 'I thought maybe this could be Lily's room.'

And there was the giveaway—he must have done a virtual tour of the place, planned out what he'd wanted, considered *everything*. She stopped just inside the door-way and stared at the framed photograph on the wall. It was the one photograph she had of Zara and Lily.

'I took a photo of the one in your wallet and a studio did a digital touch-up.' He looked awkwardly at her. 'I hope you don't mind.'

'*Mind?*' She blinked rapidly. Because Lily remembering Zara meant everything to Darcie and that photo was a personal touch that *he'd* thought of. 'It's a really nice thing to do.' Yet her nerves rose. 'How many bedrooms are there?'

'Seven. Even more bathrooms.'

Darcie's mind whirred. There was more than room for Lily. There was room for a whole *bunch* of kids. And was her lower belly aching all of a sudden? She pressed a hand to her stomach as for the first time in her life she realised she craved a child. She yearned to give Lily a sister. A brother, too. She would love to centre Lily in a huge, whole family. And *she* longed to be part of a huge, whole family, too. Something lurched inside as for the first time such a prospect didn't seem quite so impossible. But this was such a secret dream—something she'd always longed for but never let herself acknowledge… because it *was* impossible. Wasn't it?

'This is the main bedroom.' Elias had moved up to the next level.

Darcie stood in the doorway and absorbed the stunning room. There were wide windows opening onto a balcony with a view of the trees. There was a the massive bed made up with luxurious-looking linen. On the other side of the room an open door revealed a large dressing room. A selection of his clothes already hung there and the glimpse of the bathroom made her bones melt. She knew they'd both fit in that massive bath easily.

'I'll send someone to get your clothes from your flat,' he muttered.

Darcie's heart thudded. On one level this was so very real. They were going to live together and share that big bed and all of this most gorgeous *home*. The thought literally shook her. She had to turn her back. She had to walk away. She couldn't look at him just this second because she couldn't let him see how much this meant to her. He wouldn't have intended for her to take this as seriously, or as emotionally, as she was. This was nothing to him. He'd whipped up in a couple of days. But for her? This was like having her most secret wish granted.

*A beautiful big home in which she'd live with the ones she loved.*

It was everything she'd ever wanted. But it wasn't *real*—the intention was for *Lily*. Not for her. She had to remember that she and Elias weren't going to last. There weren't going to be siblings for Lily and there would be no forever for them. This was just for now. One year. Maximum. That was the deal.

Darcie was so silent Elias grew increasingly concerned. He followed her back downstairs to the living areas. 'I should have checked with you first.'

He'd stupidly thought it would be a good surprise but maybe she didn't like this part of London. Or the size of the house. Or the fact that she'd had no say in any of this whatsoever. He should have *asked* her. Should have given her choices.

Was it that big main bedroom that had freaked her out? Did she not want to sleep with him in there? But he'd deliberately chosen a large house so there would be plenty of room for them to have their own space. She could have her own bedroom if she preferred. Because they'd not discussed the duration of their affair at all. Perhaps she wanted it to end now they were back in Britain? He didn't know. And he hated not knowing. Hated thinking he'd somehow screwed up.

And still she didn't say anything.

Elias gritted his teeth. Turned out he *was* like his father—controlling everything, assuming that he knew everything and doing what he thought best without consultation. He felt increasingly awful. Chilled, he strove to regain his self-control. He couldn't let his emotion get the better of him here. He had to apologise. 'I should have—'

'Can we see the pool?'

He turned towards her. Darcie's eyes were shadowed but her cheeks were a little flushed. 'Of course.'

He followed her. The indoor pool was large and benefitted from clever lighting, calming decor. He watched Darcie walk the length of it. She opened the sleek cupboard at the end and stilled.

'There's everything in here.' She showed him a selection of child-sized inflatables stowed inside. 'You thought of everything.'

Her gratitude was too much and too unwarranted because really that had been the interiors team, not him.

He'd only told them to prep it for a five-year-old's entertainment. And he'd not asked Darcie's opinion at all. 'You know you've not married a hero, right?' he said huskily. 'You've married a hunter.'

'That's what you think you are?' She actually giggled. 'You don't?'

For a moment their eyes met and he checked, reading her need. Anticipation rippled through him—blasting out the chill he'd felt before. Rendering him beyond control again.

'How deep is the water?' She suddenly seemed oddly breathless.

'I'm not sure,' he muttered. 'Did you want to find out?'

A smile flashed. Spontaneity sparked. He watched, utterly in thrall as Darcie unleashed and her vibrancy bubbled free. Her skin glowed and her blue eyes sparkled and her soft laughter bounced against the marble walls. He couldn't speak. It wasn't just the rush of sexual attraction but another sort underpinning him. It was new and solid and he wanted to hold on to the sensation. *Joy*, he realised. Unfettered, holistic joy. Because Darcie, now clad in just her underwear, dived into the water and stretched out like a gorgeous nymph.

'Zara loved the water,' she said. 'She'd jump in fountains on a hot day like this.'

Elias stood at the edge of the pool, unable to tear his gaze from her. 'She was a free spirit?'

'Absolutely.'

The lights beneath the water illuminated Darcie's face, making her glow even more brightly and as far as Elias was concerned, Darcie was the sprite. The nymph. The goddess.

'We'd escape to the park any time we could. Any park, but preferably one with a decent pond. Zara adored water lilies. Which is why Lily is named Lily, of course. She was such a romantic. Lily's a water baby, too.' Darcie floated on her back and smiled up at him. 'She's going to love this.'

Yeah? Elias was loving this, too. Because it was Darcie he was learning about and she was more free-spirited than he'd ever realised. More than she'd allowed him to see before now. Her circumstances had limited her ability to do as she desired. But now she was literally in a space in which she could do as she pleased. At least, he hoped she felt that way. Right now she seemed to and he wanted her to stay like this—purely, unashamedly her vibrant, sensual, playful self.

*Sharing* wasn't something he had much experience with. His dates had been more transactional—he provided entertainment, interesting destinations, a diamond bracelet or earrings to sparkle at the restaurant and to remember the night by. Very simple and straightforward. But this was different. Pool toys meant more and Darcie's obvious delight in all this was the best reward he could ever ask for.

Oh, who was he kidding? He wanted so much more. And now. He toed off his shoes and shrugged out of his shirt, glancing up to see Darcie treading water in the middle of the pool, watching him, with a different, smaller smile on her face. One that snared him completely. *Yes.*

Darcie was more siren than mermaid and right now she was summoning him to his fate. All he could do was dive in and surrender—to drown in her embrace.

# CHAPTER ELEVEN

'THERE ARE SO many forms.'

Darcie spread paperwork across the table, baulking at the level of detail required. Elias's lawyers had visited first thing and they'd been full of confidence and assurance. They'd sat here at the large family table in the living area and talked them through the process. They suggested Elias and Darcie apply to permanently foster Lily first, with a view to eventual adoption. The lawyers believed they had a strong chance given Darcie's existing relationship with her. But looking at all the requirements again now, Darcie was far from reassured.

'I had no idea there were so many things we had to do.'

Security clearances. Full medicals. Training.

Her nerves tightened as she flicked page after page, listing every instruction, every requirement. They'd have to complete two foster parenting courses over a couple of months, meet with other prospective parents, do a paediatric first-aid course…

All the hoops meant it would take a minimum of four months before they could even go before the frankly intimidating interview panel that would decide whether or not they'd be approved as foster parents. It would be the biggest test of her life. She'd be quizzed by a bunch of strangers who would determine something so incredibly important and while she knew it was right that they have to do all the training, it felt like it was going to take forever. All she wanted was Lily—to be safe, to be with her so she could give her everything she'd missed out on.

'You haven't seen all these before?' Elias asked her curiously. 'Didn't you apply in the past?'

That lump in her throat grew and it hurt when she shook her head.

'Darcie?' He cocked his head. 'Why not?'

Because she'd known they'd decline her. The social worker had told her at the time that she had no chance.

But Elias looked astounded. 'You're ridiculously efficient and always prepared, Darcie. How have you not looked at this in much detail before now?'

She rubbed her forehead. He was so confident and such an over-achiever it would seem incomprehensibly stupid to him. 'Because some things are *so* important it becomes too hard to really try, do you know what I mean?' She glanced at him but of course he probably didn't get it. Her incompetence was embarrassing. 'If I didn't know the details—the harsh reality—then I could still believe it might be possible. I could keep dreaming.'

He sat back, still frowning as he slowly nodded. 'So you avoided finding out for sure.'

Embarrassed, she nodded. 'Deluded myself with ignorance.'

He was silent, then spoke more softly. 'You didn't delude yourself, Darcie. You were scared because it means that much to you.'

'Means everything. Yes.' Her eyes filled because he did get it. 'But it might not work. It still mightn't.'

'Why would you think that?' he asked.

'After what had happened when she was taken…'

She'd been so scared off by the social worker that she hadn't even taken the forms to fill in. She'd been young and burned by the system herself so many times she just knew she'd never win back then. Truthfully she still didn't.

'What did happen?' He leaned closer, his gaze filled with concern as she remained silent. 'You know you can tell me anything, Darcie.'

Darcie wanted to believe him. She wanted to trust him. He'd sat there so calmly, looking so devastating in his jeans and tee. But she didn't talk about her past. People could never understand, and it made them uncomfortable. But she also knew she owed Elias some explanation because he'd been beyond supportive, and if they were to have any chance of succeeding then he needed to understand *Zara's* story more than her own.

'I met Zara when she came to the group home I was in. She was crazy, beautiful and kind, and we just hit it off. Other kids came and went but we stuck together. As soon as we were old enough we shared a tiny bedsit. I'd done well at school with computers, so I started in junior office jobs. Zara worked in clubs.' She paused. 'I'm sure you know the kind.'

'Clubs? Going clubbing…' he echoed the social worker.

'She was a dancer.'

'You mean an exotic dancer.'

Darcie lifted her chin. 'She was beautiful and fierce and she worked hard to look after Lily.'

'So did you.'

She saw the question in his eyes and knew exactly

what he was wondering. 'She made good money whereas my entry-level office admin jobs initially were minimal pay. So yes, I tried dancing once. I hated every second and I was rubbish and I earned almost nothing. So I stayed in the offices working because I was quick at picking it up, good on computers, and I progressed. But then Zara got pregnant. She thought Lily's father was going to save her.'

'He didn't.'

'Of course he didn't. I'd tried to tell her, tried to warn her. But she trusted so easily.'

'While you don't trust at all.' He regarded her sombrely.

'Once people have had what they want, they leave,' she said.

It had happened to her mother. It had happened to Zara. Darcie had been determined not to let it happen to her. But both Zara and her mother had left Darcie, too.

'I worked during the day and Zara looked after Lily and then I was there for Lily at night while Zara went back to working the clubs,' she said before Elias could ask her anything awkward. 'I didn't want her to but she was determined. She'd had her heart smashed so many times but she was such a dreamer.'

'You didn't have dreams, Darcie?'

'I was the realist. One of us had to be. But she thought she'd meet someone else…' She looked at him. 'Zara was hurt. We were all damaged in different ways but she'd suffered the worst. Don't judge her.'

'I'm not. You did what you had to do,' he said simply. 'And you did nothing wrong.'

'That's not what the social worker implied.' She'd

made her feel cheap and worthless and that she wasn't good enough to care for Lily.

'Everyone has things in their past that they're embarrassed about, or not proud of,' Elias said. 'If they don't let people have a few mistakes, then they wouldn't have *any* prospective foster parents.'

'I'm embarrassed about some things, but I'm not *ashamed*.' She blinked and looked him in the eyes. 'I'm proud of Zara and I'm proud of me. I'm proud of what I did and who I am and where I've come from. What I've overcome.' She smiled at him a little sadly. 'Maybe it wasn't ideal, but it worked. We survived and it was pretty okay. I was working my way up and we were saving for a new flat. But Zara got the flu. I didn't want her to go to work because she finished late and it was winter and cold but she insisted that she couldn't miss her shift or they'd replace her. She collapsed in the street on her way home.'

'Darcie—'

'It had got into her lungs,' she said hurriedly, needing to finish this last or she'd never be able to say it. 'It was so quick. Everything was *so* quick. They took Lily away that same day.'

'Oh, Darcie, I'm so sorry.'

It had been the absolute worst. In hours she'd lost everything. The social worker had been so condescending. They'd disregarded her arguments. She'd had to fight to find out where Lily even was and getting permission to visit—simply to stay in touch—had taken weeks. But she'd been determined to keep Zara's memory alive for Lily and determined to ensure Lily was as safe as she could be. She'd showered all the love she had to give on the girl each week. It was the highlight of her life.

She bit her lip. 'I thought I was so smart with the marriage plan. I thought it would make it easy—like be a magic wand or something. But I didn't appreciate how unrealistic it still really is.' Her eyes suddenly filled.

Elias took her hand in his and pressed it to his chest. She felt not just the warmth, but the firmness of his grip, the strength of muscle. It wasn't a sensual touch but supportive. He was literally solid and dependable and it was kind. It should have made her feel better. One tiny part did. But she was spiralling inside.

'You keep visiting Lily. I'll come, too. It'll strengthen your case.'

Wanly, she teased, 'You coming with me is going to make all the difference?'

'Absolutely.' He flashed a smile.

But she still couldn't smile back yet. 'This is too much to ask of you.'

'Because it's going to take longer than you hoped?'

'Because it's going to take more of everything. And even then there are no guarantees. We might fail.'

'That doesn't mean we quit before we've really begun. Not this time. No avoiding it anymore, Darcie. Because this does really matter. This is for Lily and we do this together. I want her to have a good home, too.'

'But I should be able to care for her without you having to do all this.'

Elias bit back the frustration roaring inside. His gut instinct was to fight—he wanted to help her and he didn't want her declaring that she didn't need him. For Darcie to have been so scared of failing that she couldn't draw on her usual capability shocked him. This wasn't the Darcie he knew—the capable woman who seemed unable to be broken. But of course she wasn't invincible. She'd just learned to mask her fears and work didn't matter to her anywhere near as much as this little girl did.

She was almost paralysed when facing the things she wanted most.

Now he understood her bond with Lily. Zara and Lily were her family and she'd have done anything to help them and she felt like she'd failed. He knew how that felt, too. He'd failed in his attempts to free his mother from his father's control. It all just made him want to help Darcie more.

'That's why you worked as hard as you did,' he said. 'Why you saved all your money.'

But he wondered about her early childhood. Why had she already been in the group home? Why hadn't her foster family placement worked out? What had happened to her birth parents? But he shelved the questions for now. He didn't want to push her—that she'd opened up as much as she had already this morning was something.

'I was good at spreadsheets. I could write reports. I learned I could earn more when I asked for it. It was how I could save for my freedom. And then for Lily.'

And she was right; that should be enough. Maybe it would have been—she'd not applied so she didn't know. She'd thought she needed a partner to project stability.

'And then you contacted Shaun.'

'I know you think I shouldn't have trusted him.' She looked at him. 'But don't judge him, either.'

He hadn't had much luck tracking that jerk down yet and hell, yes, he was judging him. He was also—horribly and unjustifiably—jealous. Even though he knew it was Zara who Shaun had loved. Even though he knew Darcie hadn't been intimate with any man other than himself.

Releasing a tight breath, Elias attempted to lighten the moment for them both. 'You know what you need?'

She gazed back at him blankly.

'Lunch. It's been a long, stressful morning and you need refuelling.'

It took him less than two minutes to empty packets onto a platter.

She chuckled as he placed it on the table. 'That looks amazing.'

The cheese and nut selection looked like little more than bar snacks to him, but he did know this about her. 'You like salty things, rich things.'

'Salty and rich?' She suddenly giggled as she snaffled some tamari almonds. 'You just described yourself.'

He was glad to see her wit slide back. 'And you like *me* very much.'

She rolled her eyes. 'Arrogance.'

'Truth,' he countered, and hit her with some more. 'And you need more than just a snack. Why don't you like actually dining with people, Darcie?' He watched her closely. 'What is it that scares you about that?'

She put the almond down and he saw that rebelliousness enter her eyes. 'Do you have to be so pointedly clever?'

It seemed calm Darcie had entirely disappeared.

'Don't feel sorry for me,' she muttered.

'I wouldn't be much of a human if I didn't feel for you, Darcie.'

'But I don't want your pity,' she breathed, her tone changing completely. 'You know that's not what I want from you.'

Oh, he knew. A sudden wave of anger swept through him, too. And rebellion turned to fire.

# CHAPTER TWELVE

DARCIE HAD GOT LAZY. There was no denying it. In the week since they'd returned to London she'd spent more time relaxing than she ever had in all the rest of her life. Yes, she'd filled in all the foster application forms, arranged appointments for the checks required that she could so far, and she'd tried to track down Shaun—though she'd failed that latter. But she'd also slept in that large bed. Well, she'd not slept that much. She and Elias had other things to do in that bed. And she'd swum, lots. And now, yet again, she was having a hard time reining in the inappropriate direction of her thoughts. Never had she imagined she'd spend most of her mornings lying beside a luxurious heated pool watching a hunk of a man swim several lengths. Today, as it had every other day, her mouth dried while another part of her softened in readiness for his possession. She ached for it more and more. She didn't think she was ever going to tire of that delight.

'What are you thinking about?' Elias called to her from the water, teasing and husky and so, so hot.

He'd caught her staring—which hadn't exactly been hard seeing she couldn't seem to stop herself.

'Got an ache somewhere?' He pushed out of the water.

She nodded.

'Let me ease it for you.'

Thank goodness he seemed to share this rampant need right now. It was insatiable and the attempts to assuage it were so much fun. She'd never known physical pleasure could be like this. And she'd never known this kind of almost constant touch—never known how much she would adore it. Afterwards they lay on the day bed by the pool. His leg was pressed against hers, his hand holding hers. Their arms brushed and his breath warmed her shoulder. She'd never been the recipient of as much physical connection in all her life either. She'd thought herself quite insular before now. But maybe that was why now she had it she couldn't get enough. She *really* needed something else to occupy her mind—something other than Elias himself and other than her worry about Lily.

'This is bad,' she groaned. 'If I don't so something soon I'm never going to get my mojo back and I'll be this greedy sloth for ever.'

He looked down into her eyes. 'Would that be so bad?'

She chuckled. 'A little, yes. Maybe I should come back to work.'

He froze.

'What?' She laughed because she couldn't think what else to do in the face of that reaction. 'Would *that* be so bad?'

He smiled but it was forced. 'You can't want to come back to work, you *definitely* haven't had enough of a holiday.'

Because *work* was too bad? 'You know I liked working for you.'

'I don't want to be your boss again, Darcie.'

A finite tone. One she chose to ignore.

'You really think you had all power over me?' She shook her head. 'You know I could have got another job that paid as well, Elias.'

He sat back, his eyes widening. 'then why didn't you?'

'Because you thought you were so capable.' She suddenly chuckled. 'But you weren't completely. You know you never would have closed that Clarkson deal without me.'

'I *what*?'

'You know it's true. Who was it who came up with that killer concept?' She tilted her chin at him. 'Me. It was me.'

His mouth opened. She closed it with a nudge of her fingers to his chin.

'I liked working for you, Elias. You weren't all that awful. You just had high expectations. Truthfully your worst failing was that you needed help and couldn't admit it.'

'I needed what?' He looked astounded. *'Help?'*

'You couldn't do it all on your own anymore,' she said, amused again by the strangled way in which he'd spoken. 'I enjoyed meeting the challenges you set. I liked it. You didn't abuse your power, Elias. You paid all of us well. You were never a bully. Honestly, working with you was stimulating.' She chuckled and waggled her brows at him because she didn't mean it in *that* way. Well, not entirely. 'I didn't resign because I didn't want to work with you anymore. It was only because I needed to support Shaun and I hoped I'd have the time to settle Lily in before she started school. But I was good at my job. So good you barely realised how much you'd come to rely on me.'

Elias watched the animation in her face and felt an

easing of an uncomfortable load inside. Because maybe she was right? He hadn't talked through the deals with anyone the way he did with Darcie. And yes, he'd given her more and more responsibility because he'd known he could rely on her. She'd anticipated his requirements because she'd understood exactly what he was trying to achieve. Sometimes she saw things he hadn't thought of. She was more than smart and she did hold her own with him…but she'd still not been completely honest. She'd not been able to be.

'I thought we worked pretty well together,' she said when he didn't say anything.

'I thought that, too. Which was why I was never going to risk jeopardising that with—'

'I know. But it's different now, isn't it?'

He stiffened. It was. But she didn't know the whole truth about his parents and why he couldn't be her boss now they were in a relationship. Because it was too messy, too easily abused. He wanted her to be free to say anything she wanted to him. That honesty meant more to him than anything. And he never wanted to take advantage of her. Never control her.

'You can't do it all on your own, Elias.' She lifted her chin. 'I bet you're missing me in there.'

He simply couldn't answer that honestly. 'What about a career of *your* own, Darcie?'

Her eyes flashed. 'I have a career. I'm good at what I do.'

'But you could do *anything*,' he countered. 'You didn't have the chance when you were younger, but you could study now if you wanted. Anything you like.'

'But I *liked* working with you.' She leaned closer. 'Is

this because of your dad cheating on your mum with his secretary?'

This was because of so much more than that. So much that he'd never said. The abusive coercion his father had wielded over them all—his secretary, his wife, his son.

'Because this wouldn't be like that, Elias. I know you wouldn't cheat—'

'No.' Of course he wouldn't.

This was about controlling. Not cheating.

He stood up from the day bed and ran his hand through his hair because he couldn't stand to remember it. 'Let's think about it some more.' He turned from the disappointment shadowing her eyes. 'We need to get ready for the visit with Lily.'

Truthfully, he was ambivalent about meeting Lily. Primarily he was going because he didn't want Darcie to go alone. Not again. She'd been alone a lot in her life and he understood isolation. Darcie had been alone through so much, for so long. He wanted her to get what she wanted—which meant he wanted Lily not to be alone, too.

It turned out Lily was a brown-eyed poppet with co-coa-coloured hair. From first glance he saw she was strikingly pretty. She was also shy. But the second the little girl spotted Darcie, she lit up. It was the one area in which he could totally relate to the child.

Then he saw Darcie light up too. Watching her with the girl made something in his bones ache. He'd never spent much time with kids. Never wanted to. Now he didn't have much choice and he needed to at least try. But it didn't come easily to him. He felt awkward and not even the encouraging approval shining in Darcie's eyes could make him feel completely good about it.

But the second visit he had his first genuine, easy interaction with Lily. He made her laugh by inadvertently acquiring an ice-cream moustache when they all had a cone from the truck at the park. Darcie had laughed, too, and the hit of pleasure within him had been insane. Making them both laugh had then become his mission. It had been surprisingly easy to achieve, simply by unleashing his inner idiot.

But after the fourth visit Darcie was uncharacteristically quiet on the drive home. As he followed her into the kitchen he thought through the afternoon. He'd thought it had gone well. They'd had a nice walk through the park; he'd spent some time pushing Lily's swing while Darcie spoke with the supervising social worker.

Now he watched her pour a glass of ice-water. 'What happened to make you upset? Did the social worker say something?'

She actually trembled and had to set the glass down before drinking any. She leaned against the bench, her head bowed, and his whole body ached with tension.

'It's going to take too long,' she said. 'The social worker said they might have to move Lily again.'

'Move her again?'

'To another foster home. She's in short-term placements.' She sighed deeply. 'I didn't want her to have to change places so often.'

Elias read the stiffness in her body. The agony she was suppressing. And he knew it ran deep. 'Is that what happened to you?'

He felt like he'd been stabbed when she didn't answer. But he didn't blame her. What right had he to pry into her painful past when he couldn't share his own? When he could hardly say anything of how he felt? Because talking about feelings—about history—had always led to hurt. But he needed to do better for Darcie. Now.

'My parents have an abusive relationship,' he blurted huskily. He ducked his head, unable to meet her eyes as she turned to him. 'I've never actually said that out loud before.'

Certainly he'd never told anyone.

'Elias—'

'My father is coercive,' he said quickly. Needing to just get it said. So she would know and possibly understand why he was the way he was. Why he found situations like this so difficult. 'He controls my mother. He always has. He tried to control me and for a while when I was a kid he succeeded.'

Darcie stepped towards him, but she didn't touch him. She just stood nearer. Elias turned his head slightly so he couldn't see the compassion blooming in her eyes. He couldn't stand to see that.

'He doesn't hit her,' he said with a rasp. 'But he's mean. He yells, berates, rages. So you're always on edge, you know? But then he's clever. He manipulates her— twists the facts and makes her think it's all her fault, that she caused the crisis. He's put her down for so long, he's been so entitled and so demanding and...' He rubbed his forehead and closed his eyes. 'I can't get her to leave him. I *want* her to leave him.'

He wanted that more than anything.

'But she won't,' he said. 'I don't think she ever will.'

He felt Darcie's hand on his arm. 'Elias...'

He shook his head jerkily. 'He did it to his secretary, too, you know? Controlled her. Used her. In the end she finally left but it took her more than a decade to gather the strength. He's a master of it.'

'And your mother?'

'He allowed her one child and wasn't it fortunate she gave him a son? Apparently I owed it to him to do everything he wanted. She was "lucky" he chose her and I was "lucky" to have him as my guide. Don't you know I'm just like him—smart and successful. I'm a natural leader and I should *always* insist on getting everything I want because it's my right, you know?' He spoke harshly, echoing the brash orders of his father who'd flared up at him time and time again. 'My birthright—my *duty*— was to be his heir in everything. I was to do exactly as he told me. Because mother and I would have nothing, and be nothing, without him.'

'But you left.'

'I had to.' And he'd left early, vowing never to be like that man. Never to lose control in the way that he did on the daily.

'And your mother? Do you see her at all?'

His heart shrank. 'A few times a year. I'm too successful for him to stop her from seeing me now. He needs to be able to brag. So he lets us meet. For her birthday, then mine. We have lunch together a week out from Christmas. Without him. Always without him.' He paused. Because he couldn't stand to be in the same room as that man. He couldn't—not without deteriorating into a raging mess of vitriol—because then he would be that man's equal and he couldn't ever allow that. So he remained distant and in control. Always. 'I ask her to come home with me. I tell her that if she wants to go somewhere— anywhere, anytime—I can make it happen. But she never says yes. I don't think she ever will. She's too broken.'

'I'm so sorry, Elias.'

He pressed his hands to his forehead, unable to look

at her. Afraid, horribly afraid that he would fall apart if he did.

'She might yet.' Darcie's whisper was too sweet. 'It can take someone a long time to believe they can... But she knows you're there. You'll always be there for when, if, she's ever ready, right?'

He nodded jerkily. He knew all he could do was be there.

'And maybe...' Darcie sighed. 'Maybe seeing you is enough? Maybe there are other things in her life—while he's at work? I don't know much, Elias, other than that things are often so complicated. Sometimes so hard to understand.'

'Yeah.' And coercion was horrifyingly scary and difficult to escape. The only person Elias wanted to control was himself. Yet he was losing it, wasn't he? Even here. Now. 'I don't want to...'

He couldn't say it aloud—that worst fear of his. But he didn't want to be like that man. But he might.

Because he liked touching Darcie too much. He tried to tell himself that need wasn't a symptom of possessiveness but simply the need for connection—to touch her somewhere, anywhere—even just the light pressure of her knee against his thigh as they sat beside each other. But *needing* a physical link wasn't something he'd experienced before and to find it irresistible—to feel the silkiness of her skin, her warmth, the softness and the strength. He savoured every time he sank into the deliciousness of her body.

But the need was now more than sexual. When she was gone from the room he chilled and ached with emptiness. He'd become like a damned pack animal that always needed to lie in contact with its mate—seeking solace, and comfort in the knowledge he only had to move a mere millimetre to feel her. It was a comfort he'd never known he liked. And he liked to *hear* her admit she wanted him. He liked to hear that over and over. Since when was he so *needy*? Wasn't that controlling, too? He couldn't allow this to turn into an obsession. He didn't want to turn into his father. So somehow he needed to ensure Darcie kept her freedom—even from him. *Always*.

Darcie didn't know what else to say, how else to help him. The trembling of his fingers gave away the deep well of emotion he'd exposed. Of course he was upset. He was *human*. He couldn't deny that. But she understood now how he tried—why it was that he rarely opened up, rarely expressed emotion. No wonder he never raised his voice, never showed strong feelings. No wonder he tried to remain at a distance and never let relationships last more than a few weeks at most. He'd been scarred by his parents. And was scared of becoming something else.

The day they'd married had been the one time she'd seen him visibly lose control of his emotions—when it wasn't cool disapproval but white-hot fury that had rolled off him. His reactions had been driven by that rage. She still didn't understand why he'd felt it so strongly. But he'd recovered himself quickly and worked through, deciding that their merger—marriage—was a good one. She wanted to help him now.

'This is why you're so focused on work,' she said.

He dropped his hands and a soft, weary chuckle emerged. 'You love work, why can't I?'

'You used it to get your independence.'

'Yeah. Sound familiar?' He lifted his head and looked at her. 'I wanted to earn enough to take her away and give her a damned palace, if that's what she wanted. But she didn't want it. She wouldn't leave him. I don't know if she ever will.'

Darcie's heart broke for him. 'Relationships are complicated,' she said. 'I've never really understood them all that well.'

'Ditto.' His lips twisted. 'Work is the outlet for my own controlling tendencies.'

She shook her head. 'You don't have controlling tendencies. You're not like him, Elias.'

'You don't know that,' he said painfully.

'I do,' she whispered.

But some of those things his father had tried to drill into him *were* true—Elias was smart, successful, a natural leader. And he did often get what he wanted. But because he *worked* for respect, not by bullying others into it.

'I've worked alongside you for *years*,' she added. 'More than long enough to know you're not manipulative. You're not coercive. You're not a bully. Not in any way. You never even yell at anyone.'

He inspired his employees. He didn't harangue them. Yes, he had high expectations—but the highest he saved for himself.

He sighed and bent his head again. 'Don't be kind, Darcie.'

'I'm being honest.' She brushed the backs of her fingers against his tense jaw. 'You should let yourself have more, Elias. *So* much more than just work.'

'Work is a good challenge. Safe.'

'There could be other challenges, too.'

'No. It's enough. It's all I need.'

No, he needed—and should have—so much more than that. Just as she should have more, too. Her heart ached for him because she knew what it was like not to have had a home that was a safe haven. Not to have had a loving family. And it couldn't be fixed. There was nothing she could say that could magically make this all better. It was what it was, and she knew that moving forward took slow processing, slow progress. So she stepped back.

'You know what you *need*?' She nudged his shoulder with her own.

He looked at her in query.

'Refuelling.'

He laughed briefly and shook his head. 'You know I'm bigger than you. I can't subsist on cashews and camembert…'

'Subsist?' she mock-screeched. 'Yeah, well, I mightn't be able to cook but I can reheat every bit as well as you do.'

They'd been heating assorted Michelin-starred meals all week. She figured it was her turn to use the microwave. It didn't take a moment to put one of the packs into the microwave and while the machine was humming she fossicked through the linen, silver and glassware the designers had stocked the cupboards with.

Elias watched her with mild bemusement. 'Are you actually setting the table?'

'Yeah, quick, do you want to take a photo?' she quipped tartly.

His smile flashed. She set the plates down on the placemats and they both picked up their forks. The food had been ordered in from another Michelin restaurant and melted in her mouth. She'd never had this kind of nourishment when growing up. She'd never had *any* of this before. And maybe Elias needed to understand that, too—to know why helping Lily was so important to her. And to let him know she understood something of the stress he'd felt in his own family.

'Dinnertime is such a happy family cliché,' she said softly. 'And I never fitted in to a happy family picture.' She inhaled. 'My father walked out before I was even born. My mother made it only a few months before handing me in to a refuge. I must have been…' She shrugged with the echo of hopelessness she'd long ago felt. 'I don't know what I was or why it was that I couldn't seem to last with one family for more than a year.' She swallowed. 'Some tried. Some were clearly just collecting the fee. One had their own daughter who was a similar age and when I did better at her in school, they decided I was too difficult and would be better off with a family that could give me the attention I needed.'

'But you didn't get it?'

She shook her head. She'd taken the thing that had made her stand out—her schooling—and pushed it as far as she could as long as she could alone. 'I was put into another couple of short placements that might possibly go permanent, but it was just more dinner table awkwardness. It's supposed to be intimate, right? The time when people—families, friends, couples—connect. When they talk and show they care about each other and they communicate.' It was when love was shown, was built, solidified. 'But when you're not really wanted, when you're sitting there but you're so out of place and uncomfortable and…'

'It became something you avoided.' He nodded. 'Because you were missing out on something seemingly simple, but that should have meant much.'

Yeah. It had been something she'd wanted for so long

and had never got. So she'd stopped trying to get close to anyone much. She avoided those social things and buried herself in work.

'I went into a group home. I got a part-time job after school and then I wasn't at the house for dinner. I was working.'

Elias put his hand over hers. 'I didn't love dinner at the table much, either. We got to listen to my father lecture me on how like him I was, how I was to follow in his footsteps. He berated my mother on the areas in which she needed to improve. Those were the good nights. Others were more volatile. Smashed plates and spilled wine.'

Darcie flipped her hand and locked her fingers with his. 'We could make dinnertimes for Lily very different. Very much better.'

'Yeah, one thing's for sure, we're going to need to employ a cook.' He grinned.

She chuckled back at him.

But Elias's expression turned sombre and he looked at her intently. 'You shouldn't have this burden.'

'Lily's not a burden.'

'I didn't just mean Lily.'

'Other people have far more to burden them.'

'Other people have far more support. You should've had people in your corner. People helping you get everything you should have had…you could have done anything.' He drew breath. 'But now you can. Now you have me.'

A flush heated her skin. She slipped her hand free and stood on the pretext of getting another glass of water. Because she didn't have him, really—not for long.

'Is it really so unfathomable that someone would want to go the extra mile for you, Darcie?'

She kept her back to him. She simply didn't know how to answer that.

Only then she sensed he was right behind her. He put his hands on her shoulders and his voice was quiet and gentle as he drew her back against him. 'I'm sorry you've been alone for so long.'

'Some things don't have easy fixes, I guess. Sometimes they don't have fixes at all.'

She closed her eyes and softened, allowing herself to rest on him. Because this sharing and this support… It worked both ways. Even if it was only for now. Because 'now' was all there ever really was.

'I'm sorry your dad's such a jerk,' she mumbled. 'And I'm sorry your mum can't leave him. Yet.'

'Are we cancelling each other out in the pity stakes?'

She chuckled weakly and turned to him. 'I think so.'

He framed her face in his hands. 'I guess that just leaves this.'

Emotion thundered through her as she gazed up at him. It left so much more than *this*, than lust. There was trust, there was care, there was *wonder*…and there was such sweet possibility. But he was pale and intense and so devastating, and he seemed to have frozen as he stared right into her eyes. She read confusion in his. Uncertainty even. He was, she realised, vulnerable. So she rose on tiptoe and pressed her lips to his.

'Darcie?' The huskiest whisper broke her apart.

'I'm here,' she breathed.

'Yes.' He melted, instantly. His hands spanned her waist, holding her to him.

But she pressed closer still, instinctively certain that he needed more. He, too, was lonely and right now he was unguarded—close to icing back up. She didn't want that. She wanted him to have it all. He, too, needed to be shown—to be gifted—love. And as she pushed, he stepped backwards until he rested his butt against the edge of the table. She pushed his chest and he let her— leaning right back, sliding onto the large wooden expanse. She breathed out at the sight of him there before her and then climbed astride him. She shifted clothes— unbuttoning his, shedding only what was required of hers to give them both access to those secret, heated, aching parts that could make them come together—whole.

'This is a much better use for the table.' He groaned. 'But I don't have anything—'

'I do.' She pulled the protection from where she'd put it in her pocket first thing this morning.

'Confident, capable Darcie,' he muttered with a strained half smile as he took it from her. 'Prepared.'

Yes, she was ready for him. She wanted him. Always. She kissed him deeply and felt the quake in his body as she poured everything into the caress. She needed to show him. To make him feel the way he made her feel— so content. And so complete.

'Let me help.' She pushed his hands to the side but hers were shaking almost as badly as his had. So she paused and let her mouth work him instead. The scent of him, the taste, the straining arousal made her own need surge. Having him like this—all steel, yet velvety and vulnerable—he was hers for the claiming. He was just hers. And she was his. For once she truly felt as if she had her person—the one to whom she truly belonged.

'Darcie!' A growl of warning, and of submission.

He put his hands on her hips and lifted her away only to reposition her so she was fully astride him before quickly finishing the job of protecting them both. And then, with her right there in place astride him, he let his fingers tease her until she was the one to growl again.

'My turn,' she snapped. Gazing down into his eyes, she swiftly sank and took him deep. 'Mine.' Moaning in pleasured relief, she smoothed her hands over his strong, broad chest and pinned him in place. 'Elias.'

'Darcie…' He released a shocked gasp as he shuddered. 'I can't hold back.'

'Good.' Because she didn't want him to. Besides, nor could she. She rocked, riding him harder and faster, feeling the power as he rippled beneath her. He was hers. To feast on. To pleasure. To take. The man she understood. The man she wanted.

The man she *loved*.

# CHAPTER THIRTEEN

THE NEXT MORNING Darcie woke later than usual. She took longer in the shower—distracted by the intensity and direction of her own thoughts. They were all on Elias, of course. On that profound moment they'd had last night. The moment that had extended when he'd carried her up to the bedroom and they'd silently, frantically, come together again. Then again. It was different than before—more physical, raw and uncontrolled. And it had been incredible. But on waking this morning, it was the first thing that entered her mind. The truth. She'd fallen utterly, irrevocably in love with him and now she longed for *everything*.

She pressed her hands to her chest, as if she could hold her poor heart together, as she considered all that had happened. All so quickly. He'd accompanied her on several visits with Lily now. They usually walked to the park not far from her current foster home. They played together on the swings and slide; ate an ice cream if the truck was there. It was the simplest of pleasures for both Darcie and Lily and she liked to hope Elias, too. His blossoming ease had taken her by surprise. He was gentle with Lily, interested, and he could make her giggle. Darcie, too. And he was just present—strong, supportive, with that half smile that always made her spirits lift. Unsurprisingly Lily was as bowled over by him as everyone else always was. Darcie recognised that eagerness to please him, to attract his attention. Elias was an impressive figure, but he was not intimidating to Lily. Not when he crouched down and greeted her each time with that charm and that increasing softening in his demeanour that she'd never seen in the office. He was a natural and he would be such a wonderful caregiver for Lily. For any other children, too. He was strong and successful, yes, but he was also deeply sensitive. He just hid it mostly and so very well. Because he, too, had been wounded. He, too, was wary of emotion.

As Darcie absently let the shower rain down, she ached for everything *impossible*. Because she knew that while he, like she, had never wanted to marry, his reasoning was different. Where she'd been afraid of being abandoned, he was afraid of being awful. Yet he couldn't be further from that. But he constrained his emotions and was clearly determined to keep distance from others. *All* others. Even lovers. And he *would* tire of her eventually. Because he was quick in mind and always hungry. To him this was just another project and once it was complete, he would grow restless. He would move on to the next. But after last night *her* stance had shifted. She wanted more. Sure, she'd felt him shaking in her arms. He'd swooped upon her and all but devoured her. He'd wanted her intensely and she suspected he *still* wanted her. Just not enough.

Darcie had never had anyone stay for her. Nor had she ever had a place where she'd been invited to stay for good. She'd never had her parents. She'd never had a permanent home. She'd found Zara, but lost her too soon. She'd lost Lily, too. Even Shaun and the others in that last home. She'd always had to move—*nothing* had ever lasted. She'd been rejected or abandoned repeatedly and all she knew for sure was that she was not having any of that happen to Lily. It would stop with her. So she had to be so very careful now. She couldn't ruin this. Not by asking for too much from Elias—for pushing too hard and expecting too much. Because it wasn't for her. It wouldn't be. But she could ensure Lily had it all.

'You're not going in to the office today?' she asked him as lightly as she could when she finally made it downstairs.

He'd not gone into the office much at all this week. He'd taken one of the rooms on the second floor and set up his computers, but even so he hadn't been in there often. Now he was seated at that large dining table—the one she couldn't look at without feeling a sensual quiver—taking his time over his coffee and toast.

'Apparently marriage is making me lazy, too,' he answered wryly.

'Don't forget this isn't a real marriage,' she muttered beneath her breath.

'But Darcie…' He shot her a look from the top of his mug. 'We have the certificate. We've consummated it. We live together…if it walks like a duck, quacks like a duck, then I think we can safely call it a duck.'

'Yes, but it's a *rubber* duck,' she said stoutly. 'As in not real. It only exists for Lily.'

'Right. It's vital for Lily that you and I share a bed and sleep very little while in there…'

This was one tease she couldn't quite handle. 'That's also a temporary thing. It's an education for me.'

'An education?' He half laughed, half choked on the coffee. 'And what do you think it is for me?'

She truly didn't know and she didn't really want to ask. She felt too unstable, so instead she tried to deflect with a joke of her own. 'An added extra? Bonus?'

'A perk of the job?' His smile faded.

Darcie awkwardly poured herself a mug of coffee. Not that she needed it. She already felt wired—wary. As if everything was going too well. Their set-up was now too lovely and too fragile to be true. And it wasn't true, of course. Which is why she'd just reminded herself. And she did again mentally—*it's not a real marriage.*

But that didn't stop her from wanting to keep it—not just to stay in his bed but to stay with *him* for good. Yes, she wanted this delight of a marriage to become real. But life didn't work like way. Things changed. Always. People left. She knew that and yet somehow still she'd fallen deeply, deeply in love with him. Desperately she took a large sip of the too-hot coffee. Because of course she loved him. How could she not? He was smart and challenging and considerate and bold and—

'I thought I'd go sort out some things from my flat this morning,' she mumbled. It was a weak excuse, but the only one she could think of.

'Need some help?'

She shook her head and left the room. She needed space to get her head back together and her careering emotions under control.

Forever only happened in fairytales. She knew there was only *now* and there was never, *ever* certainty. She knew that better than anyone. And yet again she made herself remember. Elias had been very clear—this wasn't going to last. It was an interlude. So as lovely as it was, she wasn't going to ruin it by professing her love for him. He'd be mortified and he'd pity her more than he already did and she really didn't want him to linger any more than he should if he felt some horrible responsibility for her emotionally as well as financially now. That would be terrible.

So she'd play it light and soon enough he'd give her one of those bracelets from the stock in that second drawer in his safe. His 'goodbye, lover' gift. Plus the house. Plus Lily… And she would hold her head high and stay calm. Stay silent.

Only part of her didn't want to stay silent anymore. She'd got used to speaking her mind with him. To demanding—if not simply taking—what she wanted. As she had last night. And she didn't want to stop. But to tell him this would wreck everything.

Her greediness was too much—yet hot anger bubbled, mixing with bitterness. Why did she always miss out? Why couldn't she get it all? After all, it wasn't so very much, was it? Merely an intangible.

The thing was, she knew he'd give her anything *material* that she asked for. But the unseen, ephemeral things—like trust and unconditional love—he wouldn't give her those. He wouldn't give *anyone* those. And she didn't blame him. So she'd keep her secret to herself. She'd make the most of each magic moment she had with him in this short time. She would keep her heart as safe as she could.

Elias couldn't stop thinking about Darcie. She'd been gone for a while and he missed her. Too much. It was *all* too much. He'd thought that the last week would have been enough to sate the desire between them. But it hadn't. Maybe the fact that he'd wanted her for so long, and suppressed it for so long, had made it stronger. Maybe it was because they were married. Maybe that super quick, flashy ceremony had somehow created something stronger than they'd intended. But that was impossible. In reality it was no more substantial than the thin paper that it was printed on and it could be easily burned away to little more than a few cinders. Yet still it felt like there was a bond building—like steel cord tethering them together. He wanted her to be happy. He wanted to help her with Lily. He wanted everything for her.

She'd been so serious, suppressing so much of her natural vitality, for the time she'd worked for him because she'd had to. She'd had burdens most people wouldn't cope with. Now she needed joy and laughter, fun and above all *freedom*. Not to have to work all the time. Not to have such responsibilities all the time. Not to be constantly afraid that everything was going to come crashing down. Because seeing these glimpses of her—laughing Darcie, natural and free and so beautiful, it meant everything.

*It's not a real marriage.*

She'd said that so softly, yet so intensely. As if, if she repeated it often enough it would remain true. As if she were reminding herself. And instead of agreeing like he ought to, there was a rebellious—okay, petulant—streak that had wanted to argue with her. For one mad moment he'd wished it really *were* real.

But *she* didn't want it to be real—hence those reminders. And perhaps it couldn't be real because they'd never been on the same plane. Never on an equal footing. They'd been out of balance the whole time they'd known each other.

She'd had no real choice but to do as he'd wished when she'd been his employee. She'd had to work because she'd been saving money to care for Lily. Even though, yes, she'd held her own with him and helped him more than he'd previously acknowledged, in the end he'd still been her boss. He'd still had far more power than her. And then—in their physical intimacy—he'd had the power then, too, right? He'd had the experience. Except for last night when she'd devastated him.

Since their wedding the floodgates had opened and he couldn't close them again. His emotions were at sea, the craving uncontrollable. He'd go away for a few hours and think he had himself back together but five minutes in her company and he was undone all over again, unable to stop all sorts of feelings, desires, memories assailing him. He wanted it all to stop.

His father had cheated. His father was controlling. His father had insisted on him following him into the family business. He'd told him again and again that he'd raised him to be just like him—a winner, all-powerful, in control of all. In the end Elias had fought hard to leave and he tried hard never to look back because he knew he'd failed his mother in being unable to help her escape. In convincing her that she even needed to—to recognise that what was going on was so damaging to them all.

But being with Darcie brought up feelings he'd forgotten. Feelings he'd not known before. But worst of all were the fears that things that had happened in the past might happen again. Yet he couldn't resist her. And he certainly couldn't leave her.

They'd married to secure Lily's future—it was meant

to have been little more than an arrangement. And while it had turned into more, she didn't *love* him. Yes, she felt desire. Gratitude. Amusement. But not love. And he knew that in their current situation, she didn't have the freedom to find out whether deeper feelings could blossom. For him they had. But everything was tangled and he couldn't trust what he thought was building between them and he certainly couldn't admit how he was feeling. Because it would make her feel all the more obligated towards him. She'd been denied support and caring and companionship for so long her response would bloom bigger because of that deficit.

So he needed to do the opposite. He needed to keep these burgeoning feelings to himself while somehow ensuring she achieved absolute autonomy. Because maybe if she knew she had complete independence—financially, emotionally—then that freedom would enable her to figure out the decisions *she* truly wanted to make. Maybe she could figure out how she really felt. Even about him. He had to gift her everything somehow. He decided to go in to the office—get a little space to see if that would help him think more clearly. Because he couldn't work out how he could do it for her. How could he set her free when it was the very last thing he wanted to do?

# CHAPTER FOURTEEN

LATE IN THE afternoon Elias found Darcie back at the table that he couldn't look at without remembering being flat on his back with her all but naked and astride him. Now she was clad in threadbare blue jeans and faded tee—some of the clothes she'd retrieved no doubt—nibbling on a wedge of brie cheese and just like that he couldn't think. But then he'd spent all afternoon thinking. Planning. Now he had to put it into action. But before he could speak she jumped from her seat.

'We're going to have Lily for an at-home visit!' She came close and slid her hands up his chest. 'The social worker phoned. She's really positive about how things are going and this is a *massive* step, Elias!'

'That's wonderful news.' Yet at the same time his heart sank beneath her touch. But she was so effervescent and kissed him with such enthusiasm he almost lost his head completely. He jerked away, trying to get his brain back.

Darcie blinked and froze but Elias barely noticed. He'd formulated a plan. A good one. He'd gone back to basics. To business. To the language they both understood. And he had to present the case now while he could still remember to.

'I have something for you,' he said.

'Oh?' She stared at the envelope he held tightly. 'What is it?'

His heart thumped as he handed it to her and she pulled the paperwork out.

'It's a postnuptial agreement,' he said, too impatient to give her the chance to read it for herself. 'Seeing we didn't have time to arrange things before we got married.'

It had been uncharacteristically reckless of him not to have all the details finalised before they'd married but all that had mattered at the time was making things right for her in that moment. He'd not considered the complexities, not realised the ramifications. Now he did. But it wasn't too late to straighten things out. He watched, his muscles tightening, as she scanned the document silently, quickly flicking through the pages, assimilating and understanding the text.

Finally she lifted her head and looked at him directly. 'Why are you doing this?'

Elias paused as he saw the coolness in her blue eyes.

'I'm not a charity case,' she added before he could answer.

That tone chilled him. Automaton Darcie was back. Only not quite—there was still emotion in her eyes. Except it wasn't an emotion he'd wanted to see.

He cleared his throat, suddenly wary. 'Lily is.'

She shook her head dismissively. 'But I don't need you to do this. I can take care of her myself if you don't want to be involved.'

He recoiled. 'If I don't…' He paused and drew a breath. He'd not made his thinking clear. 'Darcie. This is for *you*.' It was to free her completely. 'We should have arranged this before the wedding but we didn't have time. You know this makes sense.'

But her face whitened. 'How does it make sense?'

He took a couple of short breaths, increasingly on alert and suddenly unsure of how to proceed. But he'd not gone about this quite right. He'd sprung it on her and she wasn't comprehending why. 'Because this way you never have to worry about being able to care for Lily again. And *she'll* never have to worry. Lily's lost enough. Now she won't lose more. She won't lose *you*. You wanted to protect her from that, right?'

Darcie said nothing.

'You know I'm in a position to be able to do this,' he added. 'This is nothing to me.'

She shifted suddenly, turned away from him.

Uncertainty stabbed. But Darcie was the one person in the world who'd been Lily's constant and this was for Darcie, too. Because it wasn't Lily he saw in his mind. It was Darcie herself. Darcie as a child, desperately wishing—waiting—for a family, for a place to belong. Moving from one to another and it never working out. Trying to be unobtrusive. Trying to stay safe. Ending up avoiding getting too involved with any of those people because she didn't want to be hurt anymore. Hiding her true self and doing only what she thought she ought to. She wanted better for Lily. But he wanted better for *her*.

He wanted her to feel safe and secure and by ensuring Lily's financial future, she would be able to be honest with him. Able to explore whatever feelings were there...

'I don't want you to do this,' she said briskly, keeping her back to him. 'I'm not going to sign it.'

Were there feelings there? If there were, he'd just hurt

them. And he'd done it too easily. Too thoughtlessly. His own defences rose.

'Are you the only one who's allowed to help her? Isn't that a kind of arrogance of its own, Darcie?'

She whirled to face him. The emotion swirling in her eyes transfixed him. He stared, waiting, willing her to say what was on her mind. He *needed* that from her. He needed the truth—her free to tell him anything. Whatever was on her mind. Without fear. Without coercion. That was the whole point of this.

'In my experience,' she said, her tone brittle, 'people don't tend to follow through on their promises.'

'Right.' He breathed through the ache in his chest because he knew then that she didn't trust him. 'Which is why this is a legal and enforceable contract. It's why you're getting all the money you're going to need upfront. So you have full security.'

She shook her head and he finally understood the full gamut of emotion in her eyes. It was hurt. It was disappointment. And it was rejection.

'It's only money,' he said gruffly. 'You know I have more than I need.' But futility rose. He wasn't used to people not accepting the things he offered and this was the most important thing he could offer anyone, and he couldn't stop himself from trying to convince her again. 'This is your freedom, Darcie. You won't have to worry about money again. Work if you want, but you won't have to. You'll be able to care for Lily however you want. This is the one thing I can do with any certainty of success. It's nothing to me.'

She looked as if he'd just shot her.

'Nothing,' she echoed.

That bad feeling overwhelmed him. This had been a

mistake. She was taking this all wrong. He'd screwed up in such a stupid, obvious way. He never should have got the whole massive legal document drawn up, the funds assigned, everything—without even *talking* to her first. He'd not learned—and he should have learned that from buying the bloody house. Even though she'd loved it, he'd still done it without consulting her. And if he couldn't learn from something that basic, would he only regress the longer they were together? Would he eventually be everything his father was? Not just controlling—making every tiny decision with such autocratic arrogance, but manipulative and mean to boot.

He couldn't take the risk. He couldn't stand it if he did that to Darcie, to Lily.

'The *one* thing you can do?' she said, bitterness sharpening every word. 'Elias, you've *married* me. You've got a team of lawyers and advisers working round the clock and now you're offering me millions…that's all a little more than *one* thing.'

But it wasn't enough. It wasn't what she wanted. And he knew then that he could never, ever give her what she wanted. What she needed. What she deserved. She was better off without him. She and Lily both were. Because he would never get this right. It wasn't in his blood.

Darcie couldn't believe what she'd read in that paperwork. What he was offering. And the degree to which he was freezing on her now. But she knew *why* he was doing something so extreme. He'd had enough. He was finalising things so he could exit stage left and he was doing it on a grand scale because he felt *sorry* for her. This was her version of the jewellery he gave his dates—his parting gift. Only for her it was wads of cash. Did she get the extra big pay-off for giving him her virginity? Her bitterness washed over her in a vitriolic wave of acidity.

'Darcie,' he breathed out harshly. 'If you sign this then it doesn't matter what happens between us.'

Exactly. They could break up. He could leave and not have to worry—not have to think about her ever again.

'We fight? We fall out?' he said briskly. 'I can't withhold the money and Lily's security is assured. And you can be completely honest with me.'

Of course he thought they'd fight and fall out and he was prepping for the moment. Obviously he expected it to be soon. Well, it was going to be sooner than even he realised.

'You think I'm not completely honest with you now?' she asked.

She saw his hesitation and it appalled her. Did he know? Had he guessed that her feelings for him had changed—had deepened? How mortifying was that?

'I think you bit your tongue a million times in the last two years,' he said, his frustration audible. 'You "behaved" because you couldn't afford for me to fire you. I don't want you curbing your instincts because you're worried about me walking out on you. I want your honesty, Darcie. More than anything.'

Honesty was all he wanted. Not love. He didn't want that. Well, the truth would be excruciating for him to hear. She'd fallen in love with him and he was planning his escape from her—expecting her to happily agree to his over-the-top plan. As if she could *ever* be satisfied with this?

'You know I didn't have to handle you so very much,' she said. 'But I think you're almost as untrusting as I am if you think you have to *pay* for my honesty.' This felt so transactional. That if she didn't sign he wouldn't trust her to tell him the truth. That he was so wary spoke volumes. She'd thought they'd built a different, deeper relationship. But they hadn't. Or at least *he* didn't feel any such change. Whereas *she* couldn't curb any instincts or emotions around him anymore. That ability had disappeared in a flash. Which meant she needed to get out of here. *Now.* Before she revealed it all.

'I still want you to sign it,' he said doggedly. He stood, inflexible, his expression shut down—he was Elias of the boardroom and he didn't negotiate.

Too bad for him.

'That's not going to happen.' She met his gaze directly, summoning all her years of masking her feelings to hold herself together for just a little longer. 'Not ever.'

But she saw the flicker of emotion in his eyes. Then the cooling. The *steeling.* And she knew he'd gone.

'You want to do this on your own,' he said. Then he nodded. 'That's probably for the best.'

He was backing away from her but she needed to beat him to it. She needed to stop him from saying stupid platitudes and trying to be kind. *She* needed to avoid all that humiliation. She needed to *run.*

'You don't actually need me, Darcie,' he said. 'You don't need anyone.'

Maybe that was true. But she'd *wanted* him with her. She didn't want to lose what she thought they'd shared. And people did *need* other people. Humans weren't designed to be alone. They were social creatures who thrived better in groups. In *families.* She yearned for that fulfilment. For everything. She still wanted it all even when she'd never really believed she'd get it. And she wanted it for Lily. But Elias didn't—he didn't recognise that it even existed. She was never going to get it from him.

'I'm sorry I got you involved in all this.' She tossed the papers onto the table. 'It's a mess. But we both knew it was never going to last.'

His shoulders lifted but his gaze didn't leave hers. She watched the stiffness consume him. The suppression of emotion—or maybe that was still her wishful thinking. Because there was no emotion now. He was Elias of old—cold, clinical, controlled.

'You'll get Lily. I know you will,' he said. 'And I'll always do everything I can for you both. If you ever need anything, all you have to do is ask.'

She never would. She didn't want him to do anything else. Not now. She was just an unwanted obligation. A responsibility he'd never wanted. That realisation was her worst nightmare. She glanced about, seeking her escape, realising just how hollow and empty this house was.

'I can't stay here.' The admission leaked out. Not in this place she'd thought might finally be her home. The place where she'd hoped she might have a whole family. It was too huge. Too full of unrealised dreams.

'No, please stay. At least let me give you that.' He looked at her sombrely. 'At least for tonight. I'll leave. I'll go to the penthouse. Give you some space.'

His cool, oh-so-sensible decision struck like a sword to her heart. Giving her space? That was him being *kind*.

Too bad. She was leaving, too. She was *never* staying here even one more night. Because she couldn't stand it. Why was it always her? What was the defect within her that meant people left and she was unloved? Why would she never, ever be good enough?

Darcie did the only thing she could. She turned her back and left.

And Elias didn't even try to stop her.

# CHAPTER FIFTEEN

ELIAS SPENT THE best part of the next forty-eight hours convincing himself he'd done the right thing. Because he'd done what she'd asked—therefore that *had* to be the right thing. He wasn't standing in her way. He'd let her go—which was what she'd wanted. He wasn't trying to control her in any way. So why did he feel so damn terrible inside?

He'd always known that Lily and Darcie both deserved more than he could ever offer them—not just those material things, or even the emotional things. They deserved someone who actually wanted the *same* things they did. He'd never wanted a family—not some big home with a rambling garden, and a child's sports or dance practices tying up time every weekend. He certainly didn't want the burden of responsibility for someone's emotional growth and development. He wasn't ever going to be good at it and he loathed failure more than anything.

Except he'd enjoyed those too-few hours at the playground with Lily. He'd already been thinking about swimming lessons and seeing her enjoy that pool at the big home he'd bought before he'd even met her. The home that was now unbearably empty without the energy, laughter, vibrancy and sheer force of life that was Darcie. The home that mocked him with that big dining table. Not to mention the ostentatious diamond ring and solid gold band that she'd left behind on it. But he would only disappoint her even more the longer they remained involved. There'd be a slow decay as resentment built because he couldn't be all she needed. But it was at that point in his ruminations that Elias's inner arrogance emerged.

*You could be.*

He *didn't* want to be another person who'd abandoned her or who'd just disappeared from her life. He'd wanted to be better than that. He wanted to help her still—however he could. And so he would—by finishing the jobs he'd begun. While she'd *asked* for it to be over, he couldn't leave those things just yet. He still wanted her to have everything and he'd be there as backstop. He'd wanted her to know she had all the choices and that's what he'd strived to do. He'd tried to gift her everything—without her having to ask for it all.

But she'd made the choice she'd wanted. She'd chosen to leave him.

And why was that? Why didn't she want him? The horror of her rejection burned like acid and made anger rise. He'd been such a fool. Clumsy and bossy and uncommunicative. Why hadn't she understood his intention?

*Because you never truly told her.*

In truth, he realised, *she'd* run away before he could. And she was avoiding him now. She'd not responded to his message checking she was okay, making it clear it wasn't his business to know anymore.

But his heart begged to differ.

Darcie couldn't miss her visit with Lily. Even though she was heartbroken and struggling to hide it, she needed to show up for the little girl. She was never letting Lily experience that feeling of being let down, not ever from her. Fortunately the playground was busy and Lily was keen to race up and down the slide, needing little help from Darcie. It was enough for her just to be there.

'Elias is busy with work,' she'd explained briefly to both Lily and the social worker. She'd need to work on a better explanation when it came to revising the application forms, but she'd deal with that in a day or so. It was enough to get through today.

'Yes, he explained.' The social worker had smiled. 'But it's good he's able to do some of the modules online, though. So he won't fall behind.'

Darcie had stilled, then quickly nodded as if she'd known all along that had been his intention. But her lungs were still constricted and she was forced to take shorter breaths. Elias was still completing some of the foster parent training modules? Why would he want to? Was it simply because the man didn't like leaving things unfinished or did he still want to be involved in some way? It had been obvious he'd come to like Lily and that he'd wanted the best for her as Darcie did. But surely now they were no longer together he didn't need to do that? And had he actually gone away? Where to? For how long? For the first time in years Darcie didn't know his schedule and she hated it.

That night she couldn't sleep. Again. Her small bed seemed so empty, her room so silent. She missed the heat, the closeness, the soft laughter in the small hours when they teased each other. She missed *him*. Terribly. And as she lay, wakeful and her mind whirring, a shaft of uncertainty pierced through the fierce armour she'd been trying to knit back together. Why *was* he still doing the training if he'd been so determined to ensure Darcie had complete financial independence and thus could care for Lily alone?

What if she was somehow wrong about that? But how else could she take that horrible postnuptial contract? It had assumed an end to their marriage after all, hadn't it? Though what if he'd not meant to push them away quite so soon?

She struggled to remember his expression when he'd handed her the paperwork. Had he meant for it all to be over then and there? Or could she have had even just a little longer as his lover? But if she'd stayed, if she'd accepted less, then when he did finally pull away it would only hurt more because she would have fallen ever deeper in love with him during that time...

Yet Darcie didn't think anything could hurt as much as her heart did now. And now there was more than uncertainty, there was something more insidious, more dangerous. Now there was curiosity—and it brought along its even more dangerous cousin—the thinnest thread of *hope*. Because he'd shut down so quickly—hiding his emotions, his thinking. Because that's what he did when he was vulnerable. So did how he felt about her make him vulnerable in some way?

*Don't dream.* She tried to contain that unhelpful ache. In the morning she made herself a *plan*. Practical, achievable, realistic. She was a survivor and that's what survivors did. Firstly she needed a bigger flat if she were going to apply to foster Lily on her own. For that she needed work. But she had good skills and with a decent internet connection she should be able to get enough contract work she could complete from home until Lily was school age. Then she'd look for school hours. She signed up with her old agency and added another couple, finally in a place where she was no longer afraid to fully fight for this. She finally believed in herself enough to do this on her own.

The knock on her door startled her. For a second she froze, and then that hope—horrible, breath-stealing hope—skyrocketed. Hand pressed to her chest, she rose on tiptoe to check the security peephole. But while it was a familiar face, it was not the one she wanted. She opened the door and leaned against the edge as disappointment sucked the strength from her limbs.

'Hey, Shaun,' she muttered. 'You okay?'

He regarded her sombrely, guilt flickering as he nodded. 'Are you?'

She nodded and stepped back.

'I won't come in,' he said quickly. 'I just wanted to tell you I've reversed that payment. Your money should show in your account in a couple of hours.'

She blinked. That was so *not* what she'd expected. 'But what about your business? I really want you to have a crack at that…it's okay. Honestly.'

'It's not okay.' He sighed and looked skyward for a second. 'I'm sorry, Darcie. And so ashamed. You know I struggle…to commit to anything much. Anyone. And I avoid the…chances.'

For a moment Darcie couldn't speak. Those words— those issues—struck deep within her. 'I know. I get it.'

Because she was the same. It was the legacy of having chances offered, then stolen away too many times. Of having dreams flattened and unfulfilled. After a while one avoided reaching for them. One avoided the *risk*.

'I don't need the marriage thing to try to get Lily,' she said, trying to reassure him. 'That was just me being insecure about my own abilities, too.' She offered a wan smile. 'But I want you to have the money. You can pay me back once you're up and running and can afford to, but don't give up this chance.' She wanted *one* of them to succeed in *something* and she knew he could make a go of this if he let himself really try.

'I'm not,' Shaun said gruffly. 'I found another backer.'

'You did?' The wind was sucked from her lungs again. 'Oh.'

He didn't need her.

'Actually, he found me.' Shaun looked rueful. 'Turns out that guy's actually okay. I was the jerk. I should have been in touch so much sooner. But I…' He shrugged.

Darcie stared, stuck on what—who—he meant. "That guy?' Was he talking about *Elias*? 'Are you saying Elias has given you the funding?'

'He, uh, wanted to keep it quiet but I didn't want to hide it from you, Darcie.' He dragged in a breath. 'It's great you want to help Lily and I really hope it works out… I'm sorry…'

'It's okay.' She realised how much it hurt to be reminded of someone you loved and had lost. 'I shouldn't have asked you. It was me being afraid to fight on my own.'

'Yeah.' He shifted on his feet awkwardly. 'I'd better go.'

Darcie nodded, needing the space to think. 'Thanks. Stay in touch, okay?'

'Okay.'

She closed the door and leaned against it. Elias had tracked Shaun down. He'd ensured she had her savings back. He'd offered to give Shaun a chance instead of trying to make him pay. When had he done all that? Why?

Was he still trying to help her—still feeling sorry for her? Was it only because she'd refused to take his money that he'd made sure she got her own back?

The silence in the office was suffocating. The place was all but dead. His employees were all head down, hard-working, pushing to please him. It should have been great; instead, it sucked.

He missed seeing her there—*all* aspects of her. He missed efficient assistant Darcie, helping him in more ways than he'd let himself acknowledge. He missed hungry Darcie, surreptitiously snacking on cheese and nuts at the back of the boardroom, and he missed fiery Darcie. Demanding Darcie. Darcie who'd laughed—at him, with him. And breathless Darcie, he missed her, too.

And he didn't actually care enough anymore about any of the damn deals to be bothered working on them. Work just wasn't the same. Nothing was. It was suppos-edly the safe outlet for his demanding tendencies. The place where he could be in control, have the power. It was important and necessary and where he never lost emotional control. It was all paperwork—nothing per-sonal. Only now he saw the ghost of Darcie everywhere. And he thought once again back to that crazy day in his office when she'd been late and he'd been unbeliev-ably angry and then she'd declared she was leaving for her wedding.

He'd all but lost his mind. He'd not stopped to think. He'd just followed her and then there'd been no real rea-son for offering to step in as her groom other than that he couldn't stand to see her distressed. She'd been upset and angry and he'd just wanted to make everything better.

He'd wanted to please her. But there had been a reason for that. A much bigger, much deeper reason that he'd refused to admit. He'd wanted her for *himself.* Because he cared about her. That was why he'd been so angry. He'd had her there in the one way that he could—as his assistant. She was his—working with him, spending all her time with him. But really he'd wanted so much more. Stripped back raw, he just wanted Darcie. And the Darcie that he'd got to know in the week since she'd walked out? He wanted that Darcie most of all.

Unfettered, unafraid Darcie was vibrant and playful. But there had been a time when she'd had to get drunk to summon the confidence to ask what she wanted from him. She'd been hurt; she'd lost almost everyone important in her life. She'd learned to *avoid* the things she wanted *most.*

He sat very still, realising then just what a colossal idiot he was.

He'd been upset at her reaction to that postnup—but her reaction was *everything.*

Because she'd stood up to him. She'd called him out. She'd expressed her desires. And he'd listened, he'd acted on them. He'd respected them—as she said he always did. Which meant he *wasn't* trying to control her and if he ever tried to? She'd soon let him know. She'd soon put him in his place. Darcie was stronger than anyone he knew and he was not like his father. Not in this.

But he *had* still failed her. Because he hadn't told her *his* desires. He'd not explained what *he* really wanted and why he wanted it. And most importantly how *he* truly felt. And she deserved—in fact *needed*—to know that. Darcie needed not just to be shown but told. Darcie needed more evidence than anyone before she could believe. So he needed to fight for her. For them. *Now*.

Darcie couldn't stop her mind from going in circles. She'd done the right thing, hadn't she? She couldn't stay in an arrangement in which her emotional needs weren't being met. She couldn't let Lily have that as her relationship role model. It was better for them both for Darcie to be independent.

She wanted more for Elias, too. She wanted him to feel the same emotional freedom and security she wanted for Lily. For him to know that he could speak up. That he *could* lose control and know he wasn't ever going to become a monster. And that he would still be loved. Always.

She knew how to love like that. She'd loved her best friend Zara, she loved Lily. She'd fallen in love with Elias. And she loved him so hard. But she needed to be loved that way in return. That was what she was going to do for Lily. Lily would never again know what it was like to be unloved or unwanted or forgotten. She would never learn to be afraid of being honest—of being rejected for it. To be afraid of being out of control and wanting things. If she was lucky enough to succeed, she'd give Lily a home where it was safe to express her emotions. To say what she really felt and thought and not be judged for any of it. Not be rejected.

Darcie had *never* had that. So she'd kept her thoughts and her feelings to herself. But that wasn't to say she didn't have them. Of *course* she had them. And yes, she was sad and lonely now. But she'd recover. She still had Lily to focus on. She would rebuild her career, too. Her heart was broken but she would survive. That's what she always did. But being abandoned was the worst—feeling unwanted, knowing she was alone again—it sucked.

Her conscience pricked. Elias hadn't abandoned her. She'd all but asked him to leave. And she'd run away before he had the chance to because she'd thought it was inevitable what with that contract he'd wanted her to sign. But she'd not stopped to give him a chance to explain *why* it was so important to him. Instead she'd assumed the worst because she *always* assumed the worst.

But what if she was wrong? What if there was something more to it? He respected her boundaries. He always had—in fact he had a big thing about ensuring there was power balance between them. And given his parents' marriage she didn't blame him for being worried about the imbalance between them. He would never move to stop her if she'd made her wishes clear. And she had. Very quickly. Before he'd had a chance to say all that much.

But she hadn't made her *feelings* clear. She hadn't told him how she felt about him because she'd been scared and embarrassed. But maybe she needed to because she'd never felt like this before. And she wasn't sure he'd heard it before, either—from anyone. He meant so much to her surely she owed it to herself to speak up and give herself the chance?

Or at the very least to have the practice of opening up. And if he rejected her, it couldn't hurt worse than it already did, right? How could she not find the courage to do this when his actions subsequent to her leaving had given her the hope that perhaps he cared more than he'd let on? Perhaps he'd let her go precisely *because* he cared. Because he was trying to do what *she* wanted.

She had to give herself the chance to find out. She had to give *them* the chance. And she had to do it now.

# CHAPTER SIXTEEN

IT WAS JUST before lunchtime when Darcie walked into the plush vestibule of Greyson VC.

'Darcie?' Olly, Elias's driver, was just inside the doors and looked stunned, then concerned, to see her. 'I thought—'

'Where is he?' she interrupted. She didn't want to know what Olly thought. She didn't want to lose her confidence now she finally had it. She needed to maintain her momentum before fear forced her give up and run away. Again. This was too important. 'Can you take me to him?' she asked, awkwardly breathless.

'Of course.' Olly was moving before she'd even finished asking.

Twenty minutes later, in the rear of the sleek, discreet sedan, Darcie's heart pounded as she recognised the streets she'd bussed through only an hour ago. She leaned forward so Olly could hear her. 'Are we...?'

'I dropped him at your flat almost an hour ago.' Olly nodded.

Darcie flopped back as her pulse sprinted. Elias had come to see her? Why? What had he wanted to say? Would he be waiting for her or would he have given up already? A billion thoughts crowded in, almost over-whelming her. 'Is he still there?'

'I don't know.' Olly shrugged apologetically. 'But he hasn't called me to collect him yet. He said he wouldn't need me for the rest of the day.'

Her pulse went supersonic then. What did he want? The yearning to know was so severe she began to shake and suddenly she was terrified he'd have left already. If he had then she'd have to gather the strength to find him again and right now she didn't know if her central nervous system could cope.

The second Olly pulled over she escaped the car and hurried towards the stairwell, convincing herself that of course he'd have gone already. It was ages since Olly had left him. She stared down at each step as she raced up the two flights and got herself breathless and most definitely prepared for the worst. So when she almost tripped over the man sitting on the top step she was shocked all over again.

'Oh!' She halted on the landing just past him and spun back to face him.

He'd remained seated, half leaning against the cold concrete wall. He wasn't in a suit but jeans and tee and while he'd shaved there were shadows in his face—beneath his eyes, his cheekbones—making his classically perfect features more prominent. It had only been a couple of days yet he'd developed a stark edge that made her poor heart ache even more.

'Darcie?' He rose to his feet in a swift movement, and just as he was about to step towards her he suddenly froze.

'What are you doing here?' She didn't recognise her own voice.

'Waiting for you.'

*Yes, but why?*

She bit her lip. She needed to say her own thing first. She needed to explain why she'd pushed away the other day. She needed to tell him—

'I had to see you,' he said, filling the gap. 'I'm sorry.'

The last thing she ever wanted was for him to apologise for wanting to see her.

He looked down and ran his hand through his hair. 'I know you wanted space but—'

'I've just been to the office,' she blurted.

His gaze shot back to her.

'I went to see you.'

Elias's blood seemed to be rushing everywhere except where he needed it. His muscles were ready to work but his brain was AWOL. He tried to slow down. She'd gone to see him at the office? Why had she done that? He gazed into her beautiful eyes and what he saw within them made the most fragile tendrils of hope unfurl.

'Olly drove me back.' Her eyes filled as her voice weakened. 'I'm glad you're still here.'

Darcie had tried to find *him*. Something fierce and powerful flooded his system. *Right thing.* This was the right thing to have done. Seeing her—being near her—was so very right. But before he could touch her—and he wanted that more than his next breath—he had to tell her *why*. To explain, not assume. To be brave enough to be vulnerable.

'I wasn't leaving till I'd seen you.' He'd been willing to wait for as long as it took.

Her glance skittered away from him, then back. 'It's damp and hard in the stairwell.'

It was, but he didn't give a damn. The real problem

was now that all the words, all the things he'd thought he'd say, had evaporated in this searing emotion of seeing her again. Of knowing she'd sought him out. There was only one thing he wanted, one thing he could say.

'Darcie,' he breathed. 'Come home.'

She just stared at him—frozen—but at least not fleeing. He watched her remain locked so tightly wound, so very still. And then twin tears spilled from her eyes. It wrecked him completely.

'Please.' He stepped towards her; he couldn't not. 'I miss you. It's our home. You're my wife, Darcie. For real. And I love you.'

Her lips parted but still she didn't say anything.

'Darcie...' He huffed out a breath. 'I didn't know how to deal with everything I was feeling and I screwed up.'

'What did you say?'

'That I didn't know—'

'Before that.'

He paused and felt that kick in his heart. 'That I love you.'

She blinked rapidly. Swallowed. He knew she was battling to hold it together. He didn't want her to hold anything together and certainly hold nothing back. Not now. He'd put it on the line and ached to know everything she was thinking and feeling and wanting. But he also knew she wasn't quite able to yet.

'It's a first for me,' he said quietly. 'And I really don't know what I'm doing. I thought I could manage it but...' He shook his head. 'I got so tangled up in stressing about having too much power, that you were only with me because you'd had no real choice. That you needed work. That it was gratitude. That it was just lust. That you'd never really feel the same as what I do because there's *always* been another layer or ten in our relationship. And I've been so scared of turning into my father. You know when you're told something over and over you begin to believe it. Especially when you're told by someone important in your life.'

Darcie nodded. She understood. She'd been told she wasn't welcome, wasn't wanted, wasn't worthy—but not as often as his father had talked all that rubbish to him, yet it had been enough to sink in and stay lodged deep beneath the surface. Those lies were hard to dig out and let go of.

'But I'm not like him,' Elias said. 'In fact, in this, I've been more like my mother—not speaking up, *not* saying what needed to be said. Not saying how I really felt. I promised myself that I'd always do whatever you asked me to. That I wouldn't stop you from doing things you wanted. That I wouldn't ever try to control you. So the other day when you insisted on leaving, I couldn't stop you. But I should have told you things before you left. I should have explained *why* I really wanted you to sign that thing. Why I didn't want you to go. I wasn't honest with you, Darcie.'

He drew breath. 'To be honest I was too upset to even think. Like that day back at the office when you reminded me you resigned and then told me you were getting married. I just reacted. I was so angry. I've never been as angry and I sure didn't stop to consider why I was so blinded with emotion that I crashed into chairs on the way out. Why was I literally running to stop you? Why was I willing to do anything when I realised how badly I'd upset you? To try to fix things.' He shook his head. 'It's so bloody obvious, Darcie, but we've both been too blinkered—too scared—to see the whole picture. You weren't going to be in my life anymore and that wasn't just intolerable, that unlocked something in me that couldn't be forced back into the box it had been in forever. My heart, Darcie. You unlocked my heart. And not just the capacity to love but to feel everything—fear, jealousy, anger, resentment…*all* the things. And frankly on paper all those scary things outnumber love. They really do. They were all things I *never* wanted to feel. But then I realised love weighs more. It's *worth* more. And having you in my life is worth everything.'

She nodded—half crying, half laughing, unbearably relieved. Elias would never normally pour out his heart and she could see it was a strain for him to do it now. She could see the sheen on his skin, the uncharacteristic stumbling over words when he normally was efficiently eloquent.

'I used to think being left was the worst. Being alone. But it's not.' Her eyes burned and as she blinked more tears fell. 'It's having someone put up with you because they feel they *have* to, not because they *want* to. I couldn't stand it if I became a burden to you, Elias. I was so worried that would happen and then that you'd only resent me while I'd come to hate you because I want *so* much more than the passionless marriage we originally agreed to.'

'You want more?'

'I want *everything*,' she breathed. 'I want everything to be real. I want you and I want Lily and I want more children, too. With you.' And now Darcie's heart swelled to bursting because he wanted her to come *home*. 'You were worried about always having some kind of power over me, right?'

He nodded.

'You wanted me to be free—not to feel any obligation. That's why you brought that horrible contract home.'

He nodded again. 'I didn't realise you'd think it was horrible. I wanted you to be free to choose whatever you wanted. I wanted to give you everything.'

He'd tried to do it all—without her having to ask.

'So here's the thing,' she said huskily. 'I guess I've got pretty good at avoiding being hurt. But I've also got good at avoiding having to trust anyone. It's easier *not* to believe that someone will be there for me. Sometimes homes didn't want me but other times, I *chose* to escape before they could reject me.' She swallowed hard. 'Your rejection would destroy me,' she admitted. 'So when I saw that contract, I ran before you could do that. Because I didn't think you'd ever want me the way I wanted you to want me—'

'But you're wrong.'

'Maybe.' She caught the look in his eye and bit her lip. 'Okay, wrong,' she whispered. 'But I was so scared, Elias. And I'm sorry for that. But I realised I needed to be brave and tell you how I feel.' She rose on tiptoe and whispered to him. 'That's why I came to find you.'

She saw the flicker in his eyes. The shadow of vulnerability that she'd felt so deeply herself for so long. Her handsome, strong lover wasn't as invincible as he'd like his business opponents to believe. He was as human as she. As capable of being as hurt. And so, reaching for a kind of courage she'd never required more than now, she looked him straight in the eyes and told him the truth. 'I choose *you*, Elias,' she breathed, ignoring the tears still slowly tracking down her cheeks. This was too important to hold back or to be embarrassed about just how much emotion she was showing. 'I choose to be with you and I really hope you choose me back.'

'You know I already have,' he muttered roughly. 'But seeing you this upset is killing me, Darcie—'

'Then hold me together,' she begged. 'Just hold me.'

He shook his head but walked towards her at the same time. 'If I do that I'll never let you go.'

'Good.'

She saw the most gorgeous smile light up his face but then he was there, pulling her close and she closed her eyes in pure relief. His arms wrapped tightly around her and she heard his husky broken whisper into her hair.

'Don't ask me to let you go again, Darcie. I don't think I could stand it.'

'I don't want you to. Not ever. I love you.'

His arms tightened even more and it was heavenly. She lifted her chin and he met her lips. She was instantly transported, instantly warmed—from heartbreak to heaven in his kiss, his hold, his love.

'We, uh, need to get into your flat,' he muttered breathlessly.

'We do,' she gasped.

It took too long to fumble with the key but as soon as they were inside she was back in his arms. They stumbled together working through the swift, desperate dispatch of clothing and the feverish seeking of touch. Of connection. Of love. And when he finally, fiercely thrust home she cried out with utter joy. They moved together—fast and frantic, feverish and urgent—as if neither believed this was actually real and they were together again. Only then they were—moving as one, locked in sync with each other, driven to the sublime moment where the stars burst and bodies simply shook.

'Darcie!'

Absolute completion followed. And then, when heartbeats slowed and breath was caught, words returned.

'Feeling nothing—or nothing too deeply—was easy,' he murmured warmly. 'But it wasn't honest. Because I still felt everything. I just pretended I didn't. I just buried my emotions and made myself busy with other things. But they were still there until with you I couldn't bury it any more. Life is too good with you in it,' he groaned. 'We're *made* for each other.'

'We belong together.'

He cupped her face. 'I'm so sorry you've been denied this for so long. But no more being alone, okay? You have me now. Always.'

She'd never belonged to anyone before. Not like this. And he knew. Now she understood his intention the other day. She'd been too scared to believe it could be anything other than rejection when in fact it was the complete opposite and if she'd had just a little more confidence, a little more faith, she'd have known that then.

'I saw Shaun today.'

Elias looked at her astutely.

'You might lose your money.'

'That's less of a problem for me than it is for you.' Elias said gently. 'You worked so hard for your independence.'

'So did you.'

'And I'm a lot further along that path than you are.' He rolled his shoulders and shot her a half smile. 'I invest in all kinds of enterprises.'

'Not usually small owner-operated courier businesses.'

'He's an okay guy.' Elias sighed. 'He feels terrible.'

'I know,' she said softly. 'But you didn't want me to know.' She drew in a little breath. 'You didn't want me to be grateful for that, either?' She shook her head when he didn't answer. 'You don't want me to be grateful for anything? It's not going to work like that, Elias. I am always, *always* going to be grateful for *you*.'

He bowed his head and rested his forehead against hers. 'I finally realised we're even,' he murmured. 'You have power over me. Total power.' He cupped her hands in his. 'Because you hold my heart. I'm hoping you won't crush it and throw it away.'

'Never,' she promised, crowding closer still. 'You don't have to change for me, Elias. Not in anyway. I just need *you* with me.'

She'd strived for everything alone for so long and to have him—the one she wanted more than anything at her side—helping her and loving her and promising never to leave her…was utterly overwhelming. It wasn't that she didn't believe him but that she couldn't believe it was real at all. 'Just promise me I'm not dreaming?'

His gaze turned tender. 'I'm here. And I promise I'm not going anywhere.' He pulled her to him. 'I breathe deeper with you. Feel more. Do more. You're the energy in my life and I'm not going to lose you. We'll do it all, have it all, together.' He smiled at her with all the love in the world. 'I've got you, Darcie Milne. And I'll hold you. Always.'

# CHAPTER SEVENTEEN

*Two years later*

'COME BACK UPSTAIRS *to me...*'

Darcie's husky plea echoed in his head. She was still up in their bed and the last time he'd peeked he'd seen she'd fallen back to sleep. But he'd never ignore her request. He'd once said no to her. He'd never know how he actually did. And he never would again. Not when she'd been so wary of asking him for anything more. She'd been so afraid of rejection and abandonment, so untrusting, he was determined never to let her down again. He would be by her side any time and every time she asked. He'd slowed down on the mergers and acquisitions. He'd even sold off a couple of things. There wasn't the drive to accumulate as much anymore because he had other things to do. Like make breakfast in bed with his favourite little sidekick.

'She likes maple syrup,' Lily announced confidently.

'She does. Let's make sure we have plenty in the jug.' He winked at the little girl.

Lily had been with them for just over a year now—a permanent placement with adoption on the near horizon. And it was wonderful. Also wonderful were the more frequent lunch dates he had with his mother. Darcie came sometimes, too. And his mother had met Lily. It was one way in which he could enrich his mother's life—to just be there for her. Anytime she asked. And happily, she was asking more and more.

'She's having a really big sleep-in.' Lily said.

'Yeah.' Darcie had been tired lately and Elias had his suspicions as to why, but he was waiting for her to explain it to him.

'Will she be okay?'

'Of course.' Elias smiled reassuringly at Lily. 'Especially once she's had our amazing breakfast.'

When he opened the bedroom door for Lily, Darcie was sitting up in bed. Her smile widened as she watched Lily carefully carry the laden breakfast tray. 'That looks amazing, Lily. I love pancakes.'

But Elias noticed—with an inward smile—that it was the piece of plain toast Darcie picked up first.

'I've got swimming today,' Lily chirruped as she tore a piece of pancake from the plate. 'And then reader's club.'

'Yes.' Darcie smiled. 'Are you enjoying the book?'

Lily nodded. 'Elias and I finished it just before making you breakfast.'

'Time to go, Lily,' Elias said. 'Nanny's downstairs waiting to walk you to school.'

'You're not walking me today?'

Walking Lily to the school down the road was one of Elias's favourite ways to start the day. 'I can't this morning, sweetie.'

'Because you're looking after Darcie?'

'Yes,' he said seriously.

'Feel better soon.' Lily blew Darcie a kiss and then skipped out of the room calling for her nanny.

Elias turned back to Darcie and saw the emotion misting her eyes. 'Did you sleep okay?'

'I slept really well.' She bit her lip. 'But the silly thing is, I'm still really tired.'

He lifted the tray from her lap and put it on the table before returning to sit on the edge of the bed. 'Is that so very silly?'

'Maybe not,' she murmured. 'You know I have a secret…' She swallowed.

'Yeah… Good secret?' He asked huskily.

She nodded and a tear fell from her eye. 'The best.'

His heart swelled.

'But I think you've guessed already.' She gestured towards the breakfast tray she'd barely touched. 'Plain toast. Orange juice. Bottle of multivitamins?' Her giggle was watery and divine.

'But am I right?' Now his heart was about to burst. 'I really hope I'm right, Darcie.'

'Lily's going to be a big sister,' she whispered. 'We're going to have a baby.'

'Oh, Darcie.' He wrapped his arms around her and held her tightly. She was the centre of his world.

'Thank you.' Darcie pressed her face into his chest, her tears spilling. 'Thank you, thank you.'

'Darcie?' He framed her face in his hands.

She gazed up at him. 'You've given me everything. *Everything.*'

'Ditto.'

Darcie melted into the kiss and felt that familiar hunger kick. She would never, ever get enough of her handsome husband.

'I did the test this morning, while you were downstairs with Lily.' She'd been so nervous, so excited. 'So you're not going in to the office today?' She smiled.

'How can I?' he asked with mock innocence. 'You told me to come back to bed.'

She giggled.

'So I figure you're not going in to the office either,' he winked.

She wasn't. She'd taken on a job working for an organisation upskilling vulnerable women so they could take charge of their personal finances, re-enter the workforce if they'd been out a while, or escape unsafe situations. It was rewarding and invigorating. But while she loved it, she needed the break today to celebrate this moment with him.

'What are we going to do instead?' She felt that greediness open up inside her. Having Elias all to herself was such a treat.

'We're taking some leisure time. We're going to lunch at your favourite restaurant and later, when Lily gets home, we're taking the jet somewhere warm and sunny for our babymoon.'

Her jaw dropped. 'Babymoon?'

He looked smug. 'A little break before the baby arrives. I have plans for us to take a few, actually.'

'A few?' She giggled. 'You really did guess my secret.'

'Uh-huh.' He leaned closer. 'Are you okay with the idea?'

She nodded. She was very okay with it.

'But first I'm going to pamper you *personally*.'

'Oh?' she murmured. 'That sounds good.'

His wolfish smile flashed. 'I thought so.'

Making love to her husband was the most luscious thing in the world. How had she ever thought he was controlled and unemotional? When he breathed his vows to her she wrapped herself around him like a limpet. He choked, a little laugh, a cry of such relief in the ecstasy they shared, and the bliss that then flooded through her was enhanced all the more.

And later, when she was sleepy all over again, she laced her fingers through his and marvelled at all they'd built together.

'Lily has her place in the world. She's surrounded by people who love her,' she mumbled dreamily. Together they were like a net—holding her in security and love and with strength in their unity. It was everything she'd ever wanted for the girl. And for herself. She rolled to face him as her emotions wobbled out of control again. 'And so am I.'

'Yes.' He brushed back her hair and his smile was lopsided. 'We love you. So very much.'

She knew. She believed him. And she loved him right back.

'I didn't think I would ever be this lucky,' she breathed.

'I know. But it's not luck,' he said. 'You deserve it, Darcie. We all do.' His lips curved. 'Even me.'

She smiled tremulously, accepting it all and adoring the fact that he did, too.

Love had won.

* * * * *